BEYOND THE SUN

BEYOND THE SUN

Edited by
Bryan Thomas Schmidt

FAIRWOOD PRESS
Bonney Lake, WA

BEYOND THE SUN
A Fairwood Press Book
August 2013
Copyright © 2013 Bryan Thomas Schmidt
and in the names of the contributors

Fairwood Press
21528 104th Street Court East
Bonney Lake, WA 98391
www.fairwoodpress.com

Front cover image by
MITCHELL DAVIDSON BENTLEY

Book design by
Patrick Swenson

ISBN13: 978-1-933846-38-5
First Fairwood Press Edition: August 2013
Printed in the United States of America

For Bob, Mike, Nancy and Kris, whose stories have delighted me for years and who now additionally delight me with their friendship and support. I consider it an honor to call you friends. Thanks for being a part of this project.

CONTENTS

10   *Introduction* • Bryan Thomas Schmidt
13   *Migration* • Nancy Kress
30   *The Hanging Judge* • Kristine Kathryn Rusch
45   *Flipping the Switch* • Jamie Todd Rubin
61   *The Bricks of Eta Cassiopeiae* • Brad R. Torgersen
77   *The Far Side of the Wilderness* • Alex Shvartsman
85   *Respite* • Autumn Rachel Dryden
97   *Parker's Paradise* • Jean Johnson
111   *Rumspringa* • Jason Sanford
132   *Elsewhere, Within, Elsewhen* • Cat Rambo
146   *Inner Sphere Blues* • Simon C. Larter
161   *Dust Angels* • Jennifer Brozek
169   *Voice of the Martyrs* • Maurice Broaddus
185   *One Way Ticket* • Jaleta Clegg
200   *The Gambrels of the Sky* • Erin Hoffman
206   *Chasing Satellites* • Anthony R. Cardno
219   *A Soaring Pillar of Brightness* • Nancy Fulda
236   *The Dybbyk of Mazel Tov IV* • Robert Silverberg
253   *Observation Post* • Mike Resnick

INTRODUCTION

What lies beyond the sun? It's a question that's fascinated humankind for centuries.

I remember sitting on my Grandma's lap, reading together the scrapbooks she kept of every NASA mission in her lifetime. What might it be like to go to the stars, we wondered? What strange worlds and alien life forms might exist out there? She gave me a phonograph recording of the first moon landing, which also included President John F. Kennedy's famous "Land a man on the moon" speech. I listened to it over and over and dreamed.

And then they downsized NASA and, with it, possibilities but not my dreams. I still think going to the stars would be amazing. I still imagine all the discoveries awaiting us out there, so I thought it would be fun to take you with me. That's where the idea for this anthology, *Beyond The Sun*, came from.

Within these pages, you'll find stories of adventure, stories of action, stories of science, stories of exploration—some from the point of view of men, others the point of view of women, and a few from the point of view of aliens—which depending on who you are may seem synonymous with one of the genders I mentioned before. There's humor here, too. From a lot of fun friends I invited to take this adventure with me—legends like Grand Master Robert Silverberg, award winners like Nancy Kress, Mike Resnick, and Kristine Kathryn Rusch, newcomers like Anthony Cardno, and established writers like Cat Rambo, Jason Sanford and Jamie Todd Rubin, these stories explore the question: what lies beyond the sun? And what would it be like if we could go there?

From the pilots who transport colonists to the stars to the families and coworkers who go with them, from missionaries to inmates, outpost crews to scientists and even a judge, the stories cover a broad spectrum, including action, emotion, tragedy, humor, and yes, some science. Mike Resnick and Erin Hoffman offer stories from alien points of view, while others stories follow the colonizers. Each story posits possibilities of what we might expect or experience out there. Some have settled on colonies for religious freedom or to escape persecution, others seek wealth, resources, or adventure. Our tales involve both those who live in colonies, those who run them and those who travel around assisting colonists with various needs. Each author puts a unique spin on the concept, which is what I think makes them a fun read.

Maybe someday we'll go together to the stars. In a form beyond simply our imaginations, that is. For now, join me on an adventure of the imagination. You may be surprised where it takes you. I know I enjoyed finding out. And I hope you'll enjoy the journey as much as I did.

Bryan Thomas Schmidt
Ottawa, KS
Spring 2013

Welcome to Freedom, a Libertarian society, the only planet in the Coalition where genetic engineering is not only allowed but common. But that hasn't changed things for the pupcats, with their drive to migrate yearly back to the ice from which they came. Shipped off planet, captured, sold, many suffer and die each year from being kept away, so Lukas has come to put a stop to it. Only his own connection to them and their suffering is far more personal than anyone else could imagine . . . Philip K. Dick Award nominee and multiple Hugo and Nebula winner Nancy Kress launches our journey together with a surprising errand.

MIGRATION

NANCY KRESS

The night before the *Far Sun Princess* made orbit around Freedom, First Officer David Bridges knocked on the door of Lukas's cabin. Bridges, who had spent thirty years ferrying colonists and visitors to unimportant, hard-scrabble planets, had fantastically wrinkled skin, solitary habits, and kind eyes. Lukas puzzled him.

"May I come in?"

"Please, sir." The boy, quiet and polite, stood aside to let him enter. Even with the bed folded up against the wall, most of the small space was filled with a miniscule table, one chair, and Lukas's half-packed bag. He and Bridges filled the rest of it.

"Son, it may not be my place to say anything, but . . . you have family waiting for you on Freedom?"

"No, sir."

"Then you've picked an odd place to emigrate to."

The boy looked down at the deck and said nothing. Twenty or twenty-one, skinny, he had work-roughened hands and a sweet smile, which he was unaware of.

"I don't mean just the planet itself. Is there a job waiting for you?" Lukas looked an unlikely candidate for the types of jobs on a pioneer planet.

"No, sir."

"You understand that they don't take care of indigents down there? That the Three Settlements are completely Libertarian?"

"I understand."

"Is anyone going to meet you at the spaceport?"

"No, sir."

A note of impatience crept into Bridges's voice. "Well, do you even know where you're *going*?"

Lukas raised his eyes to the officer's. All at once he looked much older, and so much less sweet that Bridges was startled. "Yes, sir," Lukas said. "I know exactly where I'm going."

Only four people took the shuttle from the *Far Sun Princess* down to Freedom. The other three were immediately claimed by people awaiting them and whisked away in rovers. Lukas picked up his duffle and started walking. Just inside the door of the spaceport terminal, he stopped to stare at a cage of pupcats waiting export.

The animals, the largest native species on Freedom, were the size of Airedales and vaguely resembled a cross between the two Earth creatures for which they'd been named. Lukas studied their large heads, rounded bodies, huge dark eyes. It was an accident of evolution that their proportions echoed those of kittens even into adulthood. That large head held a specialized, though non-sentient brain. Those rounded bodies stored fat for life on the Ice. The big eyes evolved to see on Freedom's dim farside. Popular as pets on the nearest Coalition worlds, they looked so cute that humans inevitably broke into smiles around them.

Lukas did not smile.

He picked up his duffle, left the building, and started walking toward Deoxy. The gravity, slightly higher than one gee, did not slow him down. A warm wind from the desert blew through his hair.

Freedom lay close to its red-dwarf sun. Tidally locked, one face lay in perpetual, baking sunshine; the other was the Ice. Constant winds blew from the warmth to the Ice, and a permanent rainstorm raged at the equator. Along the northern-hemisphere terminator, with its comparatively milder weather, lay Freedom's three major settlements: Deoxy, Ribo, and Nucleic. Tourists thought the names were whimsical. They were not. Freedom, founded by serious Libertarians and so without government or laws, was the only planet in the Coalition where genetic engineering of humans, or the humans who resulted, was allowed. If you were born genemod on Freedom, you stayed on Freedom. There was no way to pass Purity Control at any spaceport on any other world.

Lukas trudged along the unpaved rover path, through scrub bushes of dull purple, and then among the foamcast buildings and bright holo signs of Deoxy. The glossy tourist hotels lay along the river; here was the frontier combination of crude structures and sophisticated technology. Without zoning laws, people built as they chose on land purchased from the Coalition charter company, which afterward left them alone. Capitalism on Freedom was a pure thing, even if genes were not.

An hour and a half later, Lukas pushed through the heavy door of Rosen's Bar on the western edge of town. Rosen's, whose door was supposed to keep out blowing grit and did not, was barely furnished with uncushioned foamcast chairs, plain tables, and unpainted concrete walls. The local color all came from the patrons.

"What'll you have?" growled the bartender. His skin, light purple, might have been a genetic mistake or the fanciful genemod wish of a parent. Either way, he had obscured most of it with inlaid metals. The result looked like a robot with leprosy.

"Local beer," Lukas said, and received a mug of some reddish liquid he didn't drink. His back to the bar—usually the safest stance in a place like this—he surveyed the room.

Two women at a table, both preternaturally beautiful, absorbed in each other under the furtive, envious gaze of several men. The blonde had four arms. The redhead's movements were so quick that she had to have augmented muscles and reflexes, which might be why they could drink here without being bothered.

The other people looked human standard, but of course most genemods didn't show. That man ordering another beer, that couple laughing together, could have any number of physical or mental alterations. Lukas had read all he could, before leaving New Europe and Aunt Carrie, huddled on their living room floor between tears and rage, her gray hair as tangled as the explanations that Lukas would not, could not, give her.

He didn't want to think about Aunt Carrie.

"Happen you going to actually drink that, boy?" said the big man beside him at the bar.

Lukas tensed. This was why he'd come. "Yes, sir." He took a tiny sip. "Buy you one?"

"Why?"

A mistake. The trapper's blue eyes—for of course he was a trapper, with that fat-storing genemod build designed for endurance and insulation on the Ice—stared at him suspiciously. Lukas had read that suspicion was built into Freedom culture. With no laws, the only protection was personal vigilance.

"I'd like to hear about the Ice," Lukas said.

It was evidently the right answer—direct, supplicatory, unthreatening—especially with Lukas's slight build. An even trade, in a Libertarian society built on unrestricted trade. The trapper relaxed.

"Buy me two," he said.

"All right."

"So what do you want to know?"

"How many trips have you made onto the Ice?"

"Eleven. Eight mating seasons in a row, skip two years, then three more."

"Did you capture many pupcats?"

"Happen thirty-eight in all."

"A trip lasts four months, right?"

"It do." The trapper drained his first beer and set the mug back on the counter. "You think you want to go onto the Ice."

"Yes. I can—"

"You can't do nothing. You think I'd take an untrained whelp? And you think the pupcat trade happen make you rich? Nobody don't get rich except the export company!"

"I know," Lukas said. "But I can do any grubby work you want. I'm stronger than I look, I can cook, I can haul, I have a lot of experience caring for baby pupcats."

"We don't like liars on Freedom, whelp."

"I'm not lying. I was raised on New Europe, with pupcats as pets. Ask me anything about their care." He did not say that, of course, both animals had died.

"Pets! And you think that fits you for the Ice?" The trapper threw back his head and gave a huge laugh, both artificial and sour. Then he gulped his second beer, shot Lukas a look of utter contempt, and walked off.

It was no more than Lukas had expected. So—back to the original plan.

He bartered with the bar owner to scrub the whole place in return for meals, for two nights sleeping on the floor, and for two hours' use of the owner's wife's Link. The next two days, he scrubbed. Everything was filthy, the bathrooms beyond disgusting. Lukas worked meticulously. In the evenings, ignoring aches in muscles unaccustomed to the postures of cleaning floors and toilets, he spent his last few coins in other bars, buying others beers, asking questions, and listening listening listening.

By the time the bar shone like silky white fur, he had his information.

Deoxy was full of tourists; the migration was due in a few days. Pupcats spent half of the year on the Ice. The other half, they migrated east to the terminator, feeding on fish and plants until their bodies grew round and waddley as the plush toys they so much resembled. Nourished, they migrated back onto the Ice to spawn. Trappers needed to take them as babies; the adults were impossible to domesticate, and the teeth in those adorable pink mouths were sharp and efficient. But if taken right after birth, the infants would imprint on humans.

Lukas passed a roverbus of tourists about to set out for the pupcats' feeding grounds. They were laughing and raucous, drinking redbeer, demanding from the driver to know if he was genemod—a seriously impolite question on Freedom but the other reason that tourists came at all. Lukas ignored them.

He found the clinic on Galt Street, among warehouses and motor depots. Small, shabby, the kind of place used by poorer people who'd saved hard to modify one embryo for the one child they could afford. From the stories Lukas had heard the last two days, Theobald Garner produced reliable results but invented a certain number of non-existent expenses along the way. His patrons, having started the genemod process, could not afford to switch clinics halfway through and so were stuck.

Lukas had heard other things, too. But, then, he'd already known them.

He lurked outside as, one by one, techs left the building. The staff, according to his Link research, numbered five. They all left. Lukas knew what Theobald Garner looked like. As the man, whistling, turned to e-lock his door, Lukas tackled him.

Garner was not genemod for strength, nor anything else. The attack bore him backwards into the clinic, and then Lukas straddled him, laser gun at his throat. "I want to talk to you. No, don't move so much as a tendon." The man might be able to summon private police, the only kind on Freedom.

Garner was still.

With his other hand, never taking his eyes from the man, Lukas undressed him down to his undershorts. If Garner had been braver, this would have been more difficult. He found the police call. "Does it activate if it's away from skin? No, don't wriggle—*does it?*"

"Y-yes."

Lukas tucked it into his own shirt. He'd been afraid Garner might have had a biological call: a tooth-tuck, for instance, activated by a touch from his tongue. In that case, the game would be over. But evidently Garner was as cheap as he was unscrupulous.

He gasped, "Who are you?"

"My name is Lukas Busch. Oh—I see you remember it. Why would that be?"

Garner began to babble. "It was an accident! I never intended—it was an accident, you must believe that!"

Now that the moment was actually here, Lukas marveled at himself. How many years had he dreamed, planned, worked and saved for this? Sometimes his anger had threatened to immolate him. Sometimes his despair had. Through all the sicknesses, one each year, with first his parents and then Aunt Carrie nursing him, sure each time he would die. Sometimes he'd wanted to. Yet here he was, and all he felt was an icy control. No—one more thing: contempt. If Garner had denied his act, there was no way Lukas could have proved it. But the man was that thing despised even more on a pioneer world than on a settled one: He was a coward.

Garner still babbled. "I was only experimenting, just to see if it could be done . . . DNA universal . . . scientists experiment, that's what we *do* . . . panspermia . . . the wrong embryo implanted in the client . . . an accident I swear by everything that—"

"Shut up," Lukas said. All at once, Garner sickened him. He stood up to remove himself from the man.

"How did you even get off-planet?" Garner said, still lying on the floor, not shutting up. "I mean you could get off Freedom, of course, nobody here checks anything, but to pass Purity Control anywhere else you—"

"I was still in my mother's belly. They're both dead now, those clients you 'accidentally' cheated."

Garner switched to bluster, the other stupid weapon of stupid men. "But you're alive! The genemod worked so nobody was cheated, and why are you complaining you're here and alive and—"

Lukas fired. He aimed at the floor next to Garner's head, but even so, his finger had seemed to move of its own volition, which scared him. Garner's eyes went so wide that the irises seemed to disappear.

He whispered, "Are you going to kill me?"

"No."

"Why are you here?"

"Because I had no choice. Because of you, I had no choice."

Garner's eyes did the impossible and went even wider. In them crept a sly satisfaction (*I did it!*) that proved the greatest test yet to Lukas's control. But he held both gun and voice steady.

"You're going to give me what I want. All of what I want."

"I can't . . . . You must know that a genemod done in vitro can't be undone in adulthood!"

"I do know that."

"Then what do you want?"

Lukas told him.

There was no way to hide the purchase of the three holo projectors on Garner's credit. They arrived mid-morning the next day, MoonDay, the staff's day off. Lukas waited all night with Garner until the truck delivered the projectors and Garner gave the trucker his thumbprint. She saw Lukas standing beside a nervous Garner, and there was no way to hide that either.

"The export company will come after me!"

"You know what to say," Lukas said. "I forced you at gunpoint. Damn it, it's the truth. For once in your miserable life, just tell the truth. But if you call them before tonight, I'll tell them everything.

They'll do a scan on me and then the Genemod Clinic Association will deal with you for scaring off prospective customers and wrecking trade. Is that what you want?"

Garner was too terrified to answer.

Lukas briefly tested all three projectors. When he glimpsed the recording, Garner actually began to howl. Lukas gagged and tied him, securely enough for everyone to believe he hadn't been able to get free till evening. After loading the three projectors onto a clinic dolly, Lukas threw a tarp over them and set off.

The wind had shifted, bringing rare cold blasts from the Ice, and rain threatened. Lukas cursed and pushed the dolly faster. The projectors were heavy. He'd brought the recordings with him on the *Far Princess*, but the shuttle weight allowance could never have covered projectors, even if there had been a remote chance of his affording them.

The poor, his mother had always said, *had to take what they could get.* She was a simple person, and Lukas had never pointed out to her the double meaning of "take."

He set up the first projector on the strut of a bridge over Deoxy's small river. There was a lot of foot traffic here and many people would see the holo. He was less happy with the location of the second projector, behind a trash can on Keynes Street. Here, too, foot traffic was heavy, but the location was exposed enough that the machinery might be stolen before it was activated. But he was running out of time. With the third projector, he had a stroke of luck—a construction site right beside a glossy genemod clinic. The projector was easy to hide in the rubble. Someone had even scrawled a graffito on a half-finished wall: STOP THE PUPCAT TRADE!

Perfect.

Late afternoon, and the clinic closed for the day. All over Deoxy, workers were leaving their jobs and heading home, picking up their children at daycare, heading for restaurants and bars. Tourists in their roverbuses drove in from the pupcat feeding grounds, heading for their hotels. The evening was cold but the rain held off.

Lukas pushed the buttons on the remotes, and all three projectors shot out high-quality holos ten feet high.

A pupcat wearing a pink bow, outside a house in Kali City on the planet Lennox. Night, and Freedom's red-dwarf star, only three light years away, hangs low on the horizon. The pupcat jumps toward the

*star, twisting and leaping, leaping and twisting, until it collapses in
exhaustion. Quick dissolve to the same animal, thinner, its fur falling
out in patches, still jumping toward the star. Another dissolve and the
pupcat, emaciated and covered with sores, makes a final futile jump
toward Freedom and dies.*

*A pupcat on the terrace of a high-rise somewhere in the Orion
Arm; the center of the galaxy arches overhead in a curve of stars.
The pupcat faces the other way, in the direction of the unseen planet
Freedom, and jumps toward the sky. Two more jumps and it hurls
over the edge of the terrace and disappears.*

*An exhausted, clearly dying pupcat, unable any longer to leap,
raises one paw to claw toward the night sky. A child, crying, tries to
comfort it. The pet bites the child. In the pupcat's huge, non-human
eyes is a very human despair.*

Two more vignettes and the holo began to recycle, silently
shouting its visceral message. The electromagnetic beam from
the remote was, of course, clearly detectable. At the far end of the
construction site, Lukas sat down on a pile of foamcast bricks and
waited for the Freedom Export Company thugs to arrive and kill
him.

They didn't. Or if they did, they were too late. A flyer swept down
from the sky; the door was flung open. A girl's voice shouted, "Are
you insane? Get in here, quick!"

Lukas hesitated only a moment. He climbed into the flyer, and it
raced off.

"What the hell did you think you were doing?" the girl said.

Her name, she'd said, was Marianne. Her mother, who'd been
piloting the flyer, was Eva. The three of them sat in the kitchen of a
small, expensive apartment overlooking the river, not far from the
strip of glossy tourist hotels. Three redbeers sat on the stone tabletop,
but only Eva was drinking. She gazed at Lukas steadily, an unblinking
assessment that he found unnerving. Both women were beautiful,
with masses of dark hair and golden skin. He had no idea what he
was doing there.

"I'm trying to stop the pupcat trade," he said. "If people know
what happens to the pupcats after they leave Freedom . . . You see,
the migratory instinct is so strong, stronger than anything found

genetically anywhere else in the galaxy, that the animals must obey it, and they die trying to get back to the Ice and—"

"We know," Marianne said. "Haven't you seen the graffiti? We've been trying for a year to stop it!"

"With *graffiti*? Are *you* insane? If you knew what happens to the pupcats off-world, why didn't you just broadcast the recordings?"

"You don't understand," Marianne said.

Eva removed her gaze from Lukas to her handheld. "All three projectors destroyed. Thirty seconds, one minute, twenty-nine seconds."

Lukas said, "So hardly anybody saw the holos?"

"No," Eva said.

He did reach for his redbeer then, groping over the table in blind fury, blind despair. To die for nothing at all . . . .

"You're not going to die," Eva said, and his startled eyes swung toward her. She said, "That is what you were thinking, wasn't it? Yes, I'm sure they can trace you. But I don't think anybody saw us snatch you up, and so nobody knows you're here. It may be possible to get you safely off planet."

He said flatly, "I can't go."

Marianne, who seemed much bossier than her mother, snapped, "Of course you can! But—what did you say your name was? Luke?"

"Lukas."

"Lukas—" she leaned forward, painful intensity on her face— "*are there copies*?"

"Of the recordings? Yes."

Eva let out a long, reverent breath. She looked at her daughter. "Then maybe we still have a chance."

Lukas said, "If you knew what happens to the pupcats, and if you think my recordings will help stop the trade, then why didn't you just use them yourselves? I collected them off the Link—do you think someone like me has actually *been* to all those worlds? You have money—" he waved a hand around the apartment—" so are you just cowards? Afraid to risk your lives for something you say you believe in?"

Marianne reached across the table and slapped him.

Shock spread through him—no woman had ever hit him before. He was too surprised to be angry. At the look on his face, Eva smiled and said gently, "You really don't understand, Lukas. Link transmission from off-world is tightly controlled by the Export Company. They own the equipment, so there's nothing to stop them from doing what they like with it. Their techs are so good that most people on Freedom don't even realize the Link is censored. The Company knows that pupcats all die trying to migrate back to the Ice, but practically no one else here knows. We few trying to stop it simply aren't believed. It's not a large group of people involved in the trade: a few hundred trappers and the Export company. If everyone else on Freedom knew, we might be able to sway public opinion to shut down the trade. In a Libertarian society, public opinion counts for a lot because it mobilizes strikes, boycotts, and maybe even violence. At least, it does if not too many people's livelihoods are involved. We're not cowards—we just had no proof. But if you have copies of the recordings—please tell me they're on your person right now!"

"Yes. But—"

Marianne said fiercely, "If people off-world know that the pupcats die, why hasn't the Coalition stopped the trade?"

Lukas said, "It's not that easy. The Company has sold only a few thousand pupcats, and they're scattered over cities, over continents, over *worlds*. You have a pet, and it gets sick, and you take it to a vet. She says, 'It's an alien animal and I don't know how to treat it.' She Links to Freedom, and the Company denies knowledge of what's wrong or how to cure the pupcat: 'Could be something environmental where you are, could be an anomalous genetic defect, could be some sickness picked up that their immune system hasn't evolved to handle.' That sounds plausible, and the pupcat dies, and the case is closed. Nobody connects the dots. And when I did, nobody was interested in a crackpot kid with no medical credentials."

After a moment, Eva nodded. Now it was Lukas who turned fierce. "*I* still don't understand. You could have gone off-world and collected the proof. You could—"

Eva stared at him steadily, and then he understood.

"You can't go to other worlds," he said slowly. "You're genemod."

Marianne said, "I am." She looked at her mother.

Eva's eyes filled with tears and she left the room.

Lukas hadn't eaten anything since yesterday. The redbeer muddled his head. He'd experienced too many emotions, in too rapid a succession. He put his hand in front of his eyes and mumbled something, not even he knew what.

Marianne's voice suddenly turned as gentle as her mother's. "Come with me, Lukas." She tugged him from his chair and he stumbled after her to a bedroom. "Sleep," she said, and he did.

He dreamed of Aunt Carrie, sobbing on the floor because he was leaving forever. Carrie, who had raised him after his parents died, who loved him. In his dream, she held a dying pupcat, who looked up at him and whispered in First Officer Bridges's voice: *"For nothing, nothing. All for nothing."*

When he woke in the morning, Eva sat beside his bed in the small guest room. Startled, Lukas sat up, clutching his blanket, under which he was naked. Eva didn't seem to notice. Her voice sounded thick. "She's ready."

"Who's ready? For what?"

"Marianne. Stay where you are." Eva left.

Bewildered and becoming angry—why the weird mystery?— Lukas reached down to the floor for his pants. A moment later, he stopped dead, one arm dripping fabric.

Something was happening in his mind.

Blurry at first, the intrusion abruptly sharpened. Moving images, strong and clear—*his images*. The pupcat with a pink bow, jumping toward Freedom in the night sky until, emaciated and covered with sores, the animal died. The pupcat on the terrace, falling to its death in the futile attempt to leap toward home. The pupcat unable to leap any longer, biting a child from its total despair at not being able to migrate, as every instinct of its genes forced it to do.

Lukas jumped out of bed, heedless of his pants, and hurtled himself from the room. Marianne slumped in a chair in the corner of the living room, breathing hard, pale as dawn. A small holo player, switched off, sat on the floor beside a glass of sludgy green liquid. He gasped, "How . . ."

Silently Eva removed his recording cube from the machine, handed it to him, and left the room. Her face looked like a hillside ravaged by storm.

Marianne tried to speak, couldn't, waited a few moments, and then got out, "Drink."

Lukas raised the glass to her mouth. Whatever was in it revived her, and more. Color raced back into her face, and her eyes grew too bright. She sat up straight and put a hand on his arm.

"Don't blame my mother."

"For what?" But he had already guessed. "You're genemod for telepathy."

"No. I can only send, only over short range, and at great cost. Lukas—you know what that means. Even on Freedom."

He did. Purity Control banned all genemods throughout the Coalition not because people with purple skin or augmented muscles represented a threat to society, but because genetic changes to the brain did. And among those changes possible, the most feared was anything that affected the electromagnetic field that both surrounded, and was, the human brain. Strengthen that field, extend it, manipulate it, and you created a tool to affect other fields, both machine and human. No one liked having their minds suddenly invaded with someone else's images. Even less did they like having images read from their own minds. Before he knew he was going to move, Lukas took a step back from Marianne, and his face distorted into a grimace.

She noticed. Her smile was bitter. "I can't read, only send, and that only for about twenty feet. No one knows. I would probably be killed."

"I thought Freedom was the sanctuary for genemods!"

"For most, yes. And probably some ad hoc vigilante group would avenge me. That's how it works here. But I'd still be dead, wouldn't I?"

"I—"

But whatever drug had revived Marianne kept her talking. "I said don't blame my mother, and I meant it. I blamed her when I was younger. Oh, how I blamed her! But not since the—Lukas, do you know who emigrates to Freedom? Do you?"

Her intensity was making him uncomfortable. He wasn't used to people more intense than he was. He shook his head.

"Three groups emigrate to a society without laws: criminals, idealists, and inventors. My parents were the last two. They had an idea that if the human race could be engineered to be more empathetic, more sensitive to each other's suffering, that might create a society that was just and good and caring. Eva is a scientist in fluid dynamics—she knew how one little alteration in direction in the right place, at the right time, can end up producing huge changes in the system overall. I was supposed to be that little alteration. But genes are funny things, and we don't really have control over their interaction, and it didn't quite work out that way. But, then, you already know that, don't you?"

Her eyes were very bright. Her whole body tensed toward him. Lukas, powerfully aware of her beauty, knew what she was asking. He knew, too, that she was his last chance. For many things. Could he trust her? No way to tell. But what other choice did he have?

Still, he hesitated; alone with his secret for so long, the idea of telling someone the truth seemed painful. But she didn't let him evade.

"What was done to you?" she said. "What genemod? Where?"

"Here," he said, and once he'd started, the rest came out more easily. "Here, on Freedom. I was an experiment, too, but not for an idealistic reason. I have pupcat genes in me."

Her eyes widened and her hand went to her mouth.

"Why not? After all, it's all just DNA, right? Only it wasn't supposed to actually work. But it did."

Marianne said, "You—"

"I'm compelled to migrate. Every year, to the Ice, like the pupcats. And since I couldn't, I got sick, every year, like the pupcats. Very sick. The only difference is that I didn't die."

"You came here, instead."

"I came here, instead," he agreed. "To stop it. And to go out on the Ice."

They stared at each other. Finally she whispered, "The migration starts in two days."

"I know," Lukas said.

"Can we—"

"I don't know."

There was a group of them, small and not rich, utterly dedicated to saving the pupcats. Did that crusade, Lukas wondered, take the place of the larger one that Eva had once envisioned, using genetics to free society from cruelty to and exploitation of humans? He didn't ask. The group, led by a middle-aged man named Paul with eyes like lasers and an incongruous paunch, was well organized. Within a few hours they gathered in Eva's apartment, and a few hours after that everything began.

They targeted the tourists first. Marianne walked through a

MIGRATION

roverbus terminal filled with tourists about to set out to the pupcats' feeding grounds. She projected as hard as she could, and in their startled minds unwound the terrible images of pupcats dying as they tried to migrate home. Some people screamed. Marianne was one of them, pretending to be as shocked as the others, collapsing to the ground to cover her eyes and sob.

She walked along Freedom's hotel strip at dinner time. People leaned into the wind, hurrying into restaurants and shops and bars. Into their minds came the same terrible images of instinct-driven migration ending in death for creatures helpless and appealing and loved.

She sent to a different batch of tourists, this time in a hotel dining room. Then one at the feeding grounds, with the adorable pupcats right in front of the minds into which she sent her terrible images.

"Is it true? Does this happen?"

"That's not the point, John! There's a sender here somewhere—ugh!"

"I'm leaving!"

"It shouldn't be allowed!"

"This is Freedom, remember? Everything is allowed."

"Well, I'm going to do something about it!"

"About the sender or the pupcats?"

"The pupcats, you idiot! Oh my God, those poor creatures . . ."

"Eleanor just bought one back home."

Silence.

Lukas, too, was silent. He couldn't help. The Export Company would have traced the holo projectors to Theobald Garner, and both Garner and the delivery driver could identify Lukas. He stayed in Eva's apartment with the windows opaqued and watched Marianne grow weaker after each sending. Eventually she would either give out or would be identified as the only person at each scene of telepathy. She stayed anonymous longer than he expected, disguised by the group's masterly efforts with clothes, make-up, prosthetics, wigs, and fortified after each sending by stimulants. But she was growing weaker.

The protests were growing stronger.

A small rally, held at the spaceport, was easily dispersed by The Export Company's crowd-control weapons. But the group had recordings—not, Lukas suspected, all of them true—of Company enforcers manhandling protestors. These found their way to the Link, before the Company techs could suppress them, as did the suppression attempts. All at once—and only then—did public opinion move violently in favor of the protestors. This was Freedom! How dare a corporation control any part of the Link that they did not own!

How dare they try to control rallies!

It wasn't such a large step from there to: How dare they try to exploit the pupcats that bring tourism to Freedom!

Eva said, "Economics trumps liberty. As always."

Paul, eyes glued to his handheld, said, "Well, not yet. There'll be more skirmishes. People unconvinced by the recordings, people more outraged by the telepathy than the animal cruelty, people who'll say that freedom to live however you want is more important than a bunch of dumb animals. The skeptics, the callous, and the fanatics. They are with you always, yea and verily."

Lukas said, "Marianne can't go out there anymore."

Eva said, "She won't have to. Look out the window."

A huge crowd surged along the river toward the spaceport. Paul sent out a robocam and Lukas, holding Marianne's hand, saw it all: the young people smashing the bars of pupcat cages, the older people talking to the press, Export Company security standing back, not interfering, under orders from managers who, true capitalists, could recognize a loss.

Eva, on the computer, said, "Company stock is plummeting. I think you're wrong, Paul—it is over. The exporters will fold in a week."

Marianne whispered, "The trappers . . ."

"Will hang on longer," Paul said. "They'll get furious, they'll bluster, and then their numbers will thin down to just a few who will bring back pupcats for locals who will let them migrate each year. Or—oh, I'll bet this is what happens!—the trappers who are left will organize tourist trips right out onto the Ice."

Marianne raised her eyes to Lukas's face. Too exhausted to speak again, she mouthed the single word, "When?"

He said, "Tomorrow."

They had outfitted him. Lukas knew that the group had all contributed more than they could afford to buy him first the necessary gear, and second, a trapper willing to take Lukas with him. Lukas tried to feel grateful, but there was no real room for emotion left in him. He had become a single tsunami-like urge: *Go. Go. Go now*. The sensation was familiar; he'd felt it every year of his life, and every year, it had sickened him as he kept desperate eyes fastened on a part of the sky not even strewn with many stars.

"Happen you don't keep up," the trapper growled at him, "I leave you behind. That's the deal I signed."

"I understand."

"You don't understand nothing, boy. These damn protestors . . ." He was off on a rant, full of obscenities and anatomical impossibilities, which Lukas ignored.

The migration had begun.

Thousands of pupcats began walking away from the Three Settlements and out toward the Ice. Bellies full from a month at the feeding grounds, some of the females already pregnant, they frisked and barked; the younger ones ran in jubilant circles. Light from Freedom's dim star played over their silky white coats. In a few more days, they would be deep enough into the farside that the star would have disappeared, and the only glow on the pupcats would be starlight. The pupcats would travel nearly 1,000 miles over the uneven and treacherous Ice, Ice riddled with crevasses and mountains and snow fields, and Lukas would be with them. Migration.

It filled his mind, his muscles, his vision, and would do so until the instinct engineered into him was satisfied. Even last night, saying goodbye to Marianne, it had been difficult to keep his mind off the Ice. But he had tried, pushing away both the exaltation and the deeper resentment that he must feel that exultation, without choice.

"It's not really Freedom, is it?" Lukas said. "Not here any more than anyplace else. We're still our biology. All of us, even the so-called human standards."

"Yes," Marianne said. She looked very small and weak, lying in her bed. All at once, she smiled and her eyes brightened. "But biology's not always bad. You know I'll be here when you get back from the Ice, right?"

"Yes," he'd said, and brushed his lips across hers, and turned toward the barking outside.

No matter how remote, colonies need law and order like anywhere else. Someone has to hold people accountable and keep the criminals at bay, right? You'd think a judge who travels with an execution chamber and a prison ship would be feared throughout the Colonies, but Judge Morell quickly discovers that's not true of everyone in this interesting tale by multi-award winner Kristine Kathryn Rusch . . .

THE HANGING JUDGE

KRISTINE KATHRYN RUSCH

They called her a hanging judge, even though no one got ever got hanged. However, Judge Esmé Morell did travel with an execution chamber deep inside the prison wing of her small ship. She used that chamber—and the threat of that chamber—more than all of the other judges on the circuit.

At conferences, at judicial review, she justified her position this way: The Anzler Colonies were still a group of colonies, loosely tied. None had great prison facilities, most didn't have the resources to house prisoners. No one seemed to agree with her, but she didn't care. She didn't get in trouble, although she occasionally had to justify a decision.

She didn't worry about it. Instead, she did her job—she went to the outlying colonies, stayed a month or two, listened to cases, passed judgment, then came home for a month or two, got some sleep, and then repeated it all. None of it made for a great personal life, but it did make for a fantastic public one.

And one of the things she liked the very best was that moment at the space port, when she and her four armed guards stepped off the ship. Inside the small port—and outside Latica, they were all small ports—the crowds would often wait for her in the narrow passageway between the docking bay and the interior of the port. Those crowds would always watch her warily. Sometimes, she could actually see the words, "The Hanging Judge," as she walked past the gossips.

Everyone thought they had something to fear from her, and some days, she liked to believe everyone was right.

The hanging judge's ship was smaller than Jeremiah Keegan expected. The hanging judge herself was smaller, too. He liked that she was small; it made things easier. However, he was concerned about the size of the ship.

He stood in the center of the crowd, gathered, like crowds always did, to see a ship from Latica land. Latica, the first colony, the biggest, the richest, the farthest away, actually had the money—and the resources—to build ships like this.

Shaped like the original ships, but with more up-to-date equipment, these ships had the quality of myth, at least in his mind. He'd expected this one to house half the colony of Pavonne, when in point of fact, maybe one-hundred people could fit inside.

Not that he had a hundred people for today's action. He barely had twenty, and not all of them were here. Some were in the arrivals wing, others at the far end of the crowd, and two should've entered Port Command Central right now. Port Command Central sounded so important, but it was usually one person struggling to fight off sleep. So few ships came to Pavonne that Port Command Central often had someone on call instead of monitoring the equipment.

Keegan's heart pounded, and his entire body shook. He'd never taken a stand on principle before—at least not one of those stands that could end in someone's death. He shoved his hands in his pockets, felt the coolness of the ancient laser against his skin, and knew that the moment when he could call everything off was passing.

The hanging judge walked by, flanked by four gigantic bodyguards in full body armor, dark and black and intimidating. Somehow she didn't get lost in the middle of them, even though she was a foot shorter, a little rounder, and wearing no armor at all.

Was that an intimidation thing? A confidence thing? Or something else? He'd heard that they were finally developing new tech in Latica, stuff that replicated the nanotech their people had left behind two hundred years before. No one had been able to do it until now, not because the tech was lost, but because development was resource- and energy-intensive, and those things were always in short supply.

Maybe the judge wore one of those skinny nanothings under that old-fashioned suit of hers, with its great coat and thin pants. Or maybe she just had the confidence of the virtuous. Maybe she was oblivious to everything but her own opinion.

That's what he hoped. That's what he'd heard. But that wasn't his problem. That was Andrea's. Andrea got the judge. He got the ship.

They'd do the rest on their own, if they could.

Even if his people all died, as he'd said at the last meeting, at least the Anzler Colonies would understand the importance of the cause.

Six months of planning got Andrea Leidinger to the place she was now. Standing front and center in Arrivals, dressed in her new suit actually purchased by the government of Pavonne, three tiny laser pistols—if guns this small could be called pistols—hidden on her person.

The one that bothered her the most, attached by a small pocket inside her right sleeve, felt twenty times larger than the others. Twenty times larger, twenty times more conspicuous, twenty times more important.

But no one checked for weapons in Pavonne because everyone had weapons. Even though Pavonne established itself fifty years before, it had done so on the largest island in the Clearwater Sea. So beautiful, so perfect, so threatened by damn near everything on Anzler's sixth moon.

Other colonies had started on this moon and failed. Pavonne had made it, but with lots of death, and lots of hardship, no thanks to Latica. It wasn't until the Pavonners—no one dared call them Founders, since the Founders were the Originals, the ones who settled Latica—had figured out how to build the Clearwater barrier that the violence from the native species tamed down.

Not that anyone really believed it. And everyone knew that if they ventured outside that barrier, they could die in less than an instant.

Unless they were prepared.

She waited near the doors. Her job was to be the beautiful face of the welcoming committee. That was if anyone cared to record the arrival for some kind of news feed. If anyone actually thought the arrival was newsworthy, actual reporters would've been here. They had no idea what was planned.

The actual reporters would end up using a feed because the hanging judge's presence in a colony wasn't news at all. It took all of Leidinger's strength not to look over her shoulder at her accomplices. They had the side and back doors guarded. They also had an escape route in place, one that would startle the local authorities.

No one ever did anything big at this tiny port. Big events didn't happen in Pavonne, at least not so far. The cases facing Morell on her docket were—at their core—all domestics. Someone killing family, friends, co-workers, usually in a mass, sometimes accidentally.

And the only reason the judge showed up for those instead of doing them via private feed from Latica was simple: somewhere in the past, someone had mandated that no one could be put to death in any of the Anzler Colonies without actual in-person contact. Contact later got defined as a trial of some sort, even though the witnesses, the evidence, the actual *case* all got presented in absentia.

She watched the judge stride past the crowd without noticing any faces inside it. The judge didn't leave the protection of her bodyguards for the entire journey, which wasn't a surprise.

Leidinger had watched dozens of recorded arrivals from this judge, and they all followed a pattern, a pattern the judge herself mandated. She wouldn't meet or greet local officials inside the port. She would have a formal meeting (with video) hours after her arrival. She did, however, need a local to guide her to the place that would be her home for the next month or two, and she also needed someone she could order about.

Everyone seemed so surprised at how happy Leidinger was to accept that assignment. Apparently, no one wanted the job. Or maybe no one had taken Leidinger as the kind of person who liked taking orders.

Everyone, apparently, saw her more clearly than she realized. So they really wouldn't be surprised when she violated protocol.

She almost laughed out loud. Violating protocol.

What she was doing was so much more than violating protocol.

But she was going to do it anyway.

*

Once every five years, Judge Morell got Pavonne duty, and once every five years she remembered why she hated it so much. The landing in the tiny port, the long walk of shame (as she privately called it), and afterwards, what awaited her? A mediocre dinner at the "best" restaurant in Pavonne with the current colony governor. Fortunately, this time, it was a rather entertaining fellow named David Chamberlain, whom she'd met in Latica more than once. *That* at least was something to look forward to.

This next meet-and-greet was something she *didn't* look forward to. She couldn't quite escape the "hellos," that each colony wanted to inflict on her, no matter what. So she did them her way: rude and tough.

She glanced at the young earnest woman who had agreed to be her factotum. The poor creature wore a clearly new suit that was at least four years out of date, in Latica styles anyway. She looked uncomfortable as she waited, a fake smile pasted on her reasonably attractive face.

If Morell did her job correctly, that smile would be the last smile on the young woman's face for at least a month. The Hanging Judge had a reputation to maintain, after all, and it wasn't the nicest reputation.

Morell nearly smiled herself. *Nice*. No one used that word for her. To the best of her recollection, no one ever had.

Which was one reason why she was so very, very good at her job.

Keagan slipped out of the crowd, and headed to the side door hidden into the wall. He tapped in the code, then held up his left thumb and marveled as the door's scans registered him as a port employee. He hadn't been anyone's employee in more than a decade.

But his people were doing their job. They'd spent six months planning for this.

He stepped inside the door, then held it open just a little. Two other members of his team joined him. They would capture the ship, while the rest of the team would get the judge back on board.

Of course, they'd discussed rushing the ship when it arrived, and he was now glad they'd decided against it. Even as he held that door, he could see the crowd dispersing.

Only a few members of that crowd even cared about the judge. Most of them were hangers-on, folks who took time out of their day to greet any ship that came to Pavonne. Not that they had many opportunities to do so. With the exception of the supply ships that came from Latica twice a year, the circuit judges and the occasional visiting politicians were the only official arrivals. Once in a while, some private ship came in, bearing visitors or extreme hunters or "explorers." The "explorers" angered him the most. He wanted to ask each and every one of them why they assumed no one in Pavonne was smart enough to explore every solid surface of this moon.

But he didn't. He liked to say he kept his opinions to himself, but he didn't do that either. He shared them with like-minded folk, which was why he was here right now. With like-minded folk, letting the door ease shut, and then heading down the narrow corridors to the back of the ship.

Docking was such a complicated procedure. Lots of locks and clamps and requirements. Some connection between the port and the ship. In the larger ports, like Latica itself, some decontamination procedures, and a few laws that allowed a shipboard search without a warrant.

And on the dry run for this part of this trip three months ago, he'd convinced all of the port workers that the informal rules in Pavonne had changed. Now Pavonne inspected vehicles that arrived from other places.

No one questioned it, especially visitors from Latica. Latica types expected rules. He suspected the judge expected rules as well.

Particularly since she was here to enforce them.

He nodded at his colleagues as they walked quickly toward the only dock in use.

This part of the mission had a timetable, which he established.

It was now up to him to make sure the timetable got met.

The smile Leidinger had pasted on her face was a sham, but she had no idea how to make it real or even realistic. She smiled, but she felt like some feral creature baring its teeth, instead of someone happy to be doing her job.

As the judge approached, Leidinger took a silent deep breath and braced herself. Part of her didn't believe that the judge would follow protocol. Because if the judge didn't follow it right here and now, the entire plan would go awry.

Then the judge stepped in front of her group of bodyguards. She didn't bother to paste a smile of any kind on her own face. She just grimly came forward, hand extended, as if she were about to touch something unclean.

Maybe she was.

"Judge Morell," Leidinger said in her warmest voice, "welcome to Pavonne."

The judge moved her tiny hand forward, about to brush fingertips as she had done a thousand times in other greets. But Leidinger didn't let her. Leidinger grabbed the judge's hand tightly, and pulled her close, just as she had practiced.

And, as she had practiced, the little laser pistol slid from its pocket into her right hand. She raised the pistol to the judge's ear, and stuck the edge inside. She'd learned, through all her practice, all her study, that the pistol was almost impossible to forcibly remove from this position, without it going off.

One bodyguard hurried forward.

"Don't even try it," Leidinger said. "You attack me, the judge dies. You will all stay back and let me take her out of here."

The bodyguard glanced down at the judge. Leidinger could see the judge's face reflected in the clear wall ahead of her. The judge didn't look frightened, which was too bad. Leidinger wanted her to be scared.

Leidinger still was.

"We've been through this before, Raul," the judge said to her guard. "Don't worry."

The guard nodded, and Leidinger tried not to smile. She had thought the judge might say something like that. The judge had been taken hostage three times before. All three times had been in a makeshift courtroom after or before a verdict, when the judge seemed vulnerable.

All three times had been attacks of the moment, impulsive and out of control. Leidinger had seen vids of all of them, and in every case, the hostage-taker was panicked long before grabbing the judge.

Leidinger wasn't panicked. Even though she still felt terrified, the terror was one of meeting expectations now, not of dying or of losing or even of failing.

This terror was a familiar one, the one she'd had before exams, on the first day of school, on her interview for this very job.

The judge smelled of lavender and sweat. She didn't move, but remained clasped in Leidinger's arms, not fighting. The bodyguard backed off.

"You're coming with me," Leidinger said to the judge. "And I'm not going to drag you. I'll shoot you first. So make sure your legs cooperate."

Leidinger moved backwards for just a moment, then her own team flanked her and hurried with her toward the exit near the back. When they'd reached it, she removed the laser pistol from the judge's ear, and shoved the judge at Barry Culver. Culver grabbed the judge, slung her over his shoulder, and ran down the hall with her so fast that no one else could keep up.

Behind Leidinger, screams, shouts, and threats. Then they muted as the doors slid shut.

Almost done, Leidinger thought, then checked the laser pistol to make sure it wouldn't go off accidentally, and slipped it back in her sleeve. Then she took off after her group, hoping she could catch them.

The last thing she wanted was to get left behind when the ship took off. She didn't want to imagine what would happen to her then.

One by one, the security feeds winked out. Governor David Chamberlain stood up from his desk and stared at the blank walls in front of him.

The judge arrived, tried to fake a handshake, and then got taken captive. He didn't recognize the woman who had captured her. He did recognize—even from that brief instant he saw on the feeds—how well planned this attack was.

He tapped the security console on the left side of his desk. "You got all that right?" he asked his security chief.

"Yes, sir," she said. "We're doing what we can. The feeds got cut at the port."

As if it were a real port, with real security. It was no more secure than the local hotel was. Latica collected taxes from Pavonne, but didn't grant any of the colony's requests for improvement. The main reason so few ships even came here was the size of that damn port. It couldn't accommodate most vessels that traveled between Anzler and its moons. Even the judge had to take a smaller ship just to come here, and she always protested.

I can't take as many prisoners back, she would say before her visits here. As if she ever took prisoners anyway. The cases she heard that ended in a guilty verdict almost always ended in death rather than lifetime imprisonment in the facility near Latica.

Chamberlain tried to shake nasty thoughts of the woman out of his head. He had to respond like he would to the kidnapping of any other citizen. Only he wasn't going to. Because he didn't want word out that the hanging judge could be kidnapped—that anyone could be kidnapped in Pavonne's port.

He did his job. He let security know they had his fullest authority to do what they needed to end this crisis. He also let the Government of the Anzler Colonies in Latica know that the judge was in trouble.

Then he dithered for just one moment. Personal dithering. Petty dithering.

In the end, he decided to keep the reservation at Pavonne's best restaurant. No sense tipping off anyone that the judge wouldn't make it.

Besides, he needed to eat. No matter what.

Morell's teeth rattled as the big buffoon carried her through the narrow back corridors of the port. His sharp muscular shoulder dug into her stomach and his hands had a disturbingly impersonal grip on her thighs. For the first time since she'd become a judge, she regretted her small size. If she'd been as big as this idiot was, no one could have slung her over his shoulder like so much dirty laundry. Her legs were so short that she couldn't even kick him in an effective part of his anatomy.

She knew better than to beg him to put her down. Begging automatically placed her at a disadvantage. So she just bounced along, trying to remain as silent as possible, although the jostling occasionally made her grunt involuntarily.

She had no idea where this crew of ruffians was taking her, but it probably wasn't anywhere she wanted to go.

She went over scenarios in her mind—these were probably friends of the accused who wanted something from her. Or people related to others she'd condemned. Violent types who should be stopped and whose gene pools should dead-end.

Of course, she hadn't gotten that dead-end gene pool idea approved in Latica either. They kept calling her radical there.

She wondered if they would call her radical now.

Not that it mattered. What mattered were the next few hours. She had to decide if she was going to try to negotiate with these idiots, lie to these idiots, or suffer these idiots silently.

Right now, they hadn't done much more than make her teeth hurt, cause all the blood to rush to her head, and embarrass her in front of half of this backwater colony.

As long as they didn't really harm her, she might actually survive.

Timing was just about spot on. Keegan opened the prisoner exchange door on the judge's ship. He could see the exfiltration group bringing the judge now. She was draped over Culver's shoulder, her short hair pointing downward. Surprisingly, she wasn't fighting.

Keegan was vaguely disappointed; he'd expected a fighter.

He held the door open, somewhat amazed at how smoothly the plan was going. He'd put on an environmental mask before boarding the ship, put an airborne sedative into the environmental controls from the cargo bay, and had knocked out what crew there were within seconds.

He'd locked the crew in the prisoner wing, and upped the oxygen levels everywhere. The crew would wake up slowly, but they wouldn't be able to stop him.

Then he put his pilot on the bridge, let his experts take a peek at the controls, and waited.

Smooth, smooth, smooth.

Something had to go wrong soon. Law of averages.

Then Culver arrived with Judge Morell.

She was awake, her head rising in surprise as she realized where she was.

"Where do you want her?" Culver asked.

They hadn't decided this part. Did Keegan want her near the bridge? Or in the prisoner wing?

It would be much more interesting if she were on the bridge, but then she'd need to be trussed up. Still, they had the equipment here. He could bring her up there.

"So you're the idiot in charge," she snapped. "You do realize you won't get very far in my ship."

Her voice grated already. Keegan hadn't expected that. Decision made.

"Put her in the cell next to the execution chamber," he said.

It was in the prison wing, but not part of the prison wing. From what he'd seen of the specs, it could be used as solitary if need be.

"You'll never get away with this," she said, not bothering to ask what he was trying to get away with.

He patted her face just a little harder than he should have. "The melodrama doesn't suit you, Judge," he said, then nodded at Carver to lock her away.

"Governor," his assistant Teresa Spencer said, "Latica wants you to make sure this group doesn't leave Pavonne. They'll send you some assistance."

Chamberlain rubbed two fingers along his forehead, almost wishing for a headache to begin. He deserved a headache. The situation *called* for a headache.

"Do they want to tell me *how* I'm going to prevent them from leaving, since I never got the funding for the security fleet that I asked for?" he said.

"I—um—asked, sir," she said, "a bit more politely, but I did ask. They want you to shut down the port, make sure nothing takes off."

He laughed. He couldn't help himself. The officials from Latica had clearly never come here. The port was a small-scale version of Latica's port from seventy-five years ago. No security upgrades, no staff to speak of besides maintenance, and certainly no one monitoring the space traffic.

He knew better, though, than to try to tell a bunch of bureaucrats— who couldn't be bothered with much more than a "verbal understanding" mixed with an "oh, yeah, pay your taxes" —that some of the tax money had to actually return to a colony for that colony to thrive.

There was only so much a place could do on its own, especially after all of its resources went into the Clearwater barrier, patrolling the borders, and making sure that some of the food in the hydroponics bays actually made it into the colony proper.

But that was an argument for another day. Side issues, those horrid bureaucrats would tell him. They'd command him to fix this problem.

"Inform them we're doing our very best," Chamberlain said.

"Sir?" she said. "We're not doing anything right now."

He raised his head and looked at her. He had forgotten how young she really was—unlined skin, wide brown eyes.

"What do you suggest we do, Spencer?"

She took a deep breath, then let it out. "I can order port security to take the conspirators into custody."

And put them where? He almost asked. *The jail we have is full of murderers, awaiting the judge's final decision.*

But he didn't ask. Instead, he smiled. "Good thinking," he said. "Let's do that."

The ship lifted out of the port with surprising ease. Keegan stood on the bridge, watching as the ship headed to a point just outside of the range of Latica's fleet of ships.

Then he contacted the Government of the Anzler Colonies:

"I have Judge Morell," he said. "I will negotiate for her release."

"Or what?" the Assistant to the Chief Executive said.

The response startled him. He'd expected someone to ask him what he wanted.

"Or we will execute her," he said.

"Hm," the Assistant to the Chief Executive said. "Give me a minute."

Too easy. It was starting to bother Keegan. He had his crew search for fleet ships, search to make sure that Latica's meager defense weapons weren't trained on the ship, search to make sure they hadn't been followed off Pavonne.

They hadn't. They were alone out here.

The communications array chirruped. Keegan nodded at his navigator, who opened communications.

"Sorry to take so long," the Assistant said. "The Council says you should go about your business."

"Excuse me?" Keegan asked.

"Execute her, keep her, steal the ship, we don't care," the Assistant said.

"You—what?" Keegan asked. "You haven't even asked who I am. What I want."

"As I said," the Assistant spoke firmly. "We really don't care."

Then he shut off communications, and try as Keegan and his people might, no one would respond to his hails. No one. Not on Latica, not on Pavonne.

"What the hell is this?" Keegan asked.

"Wish I knew," his navigator said.

Every conspirator they could find—all three of them—got rounded up and placed in Pavonne's overcrowded jail. Chamberlain wished he could be more excited about that, or the fact that seventeen people had escaped on the judge's ship.

Orders came from Latica: Don't let the ship land on Pavonne again. Not that the ship was trying. It remained a blip out in space, hovering there, probably as confused as everyone else was.

Chamberlain wasn't confused, not really. He finally had an order he could follow. He could keep people out of Pavonne. Every colony in the system got a defense grid when the colony reached a certain size. It hadn't been upgraded in forty years, but he'd consider its use against the judge's ship a test, if he had to.

Although he doubted he'd have to.

What kind of kidnapper slinked back to the port he'd left from? If anything, those bad guys would wait until they got what they wanted or some other place took them in.

Which meant they weren't his problem anymore.

Judge Morell finally had a reaction. Pure, unadulterated fury.

"What do you mean they aren't going to negotiate for me?" she asked the twerp who had kidnapped her.

He stood outside the execution cell, looking smaller and less powerful than he had when he stood in the doorway. She could attribute this to the fact she no longer had to raise her head at an odd angle to see him, but she doubted that was what was really going on. He seemed smaller, because he was smaller.

He was too dumb to realize this had to be a ploy.

"Let me on the comm," she said. "I have an emergency code.

Once they understand that you're not kidding, they will resolve this."

Maybe Government were already planning a raid. Maybe they had a team that was going to rescue her. But if they did, wouldn't they be a little more careful about telling the twerp they didn't care? After all, that could mean he might kill her.

He reached around to the control panel near the door to the execution area. "Give me the information."

Maybe that was what this was all about: her code. They could use it to—what? Get into judicial files? Pretend to be her? That seemed to minor and too subtle for a crew this unsophisticated.

She gave him the codes, then waited. It took longer than she expected, but finally the Chief Executive's voice echoed in the relatively small space.

"Esmé?" he said. "Did they release you?'

"Why would they do that?" she snapped. "You won't negotiate with them."

There was a long silence, and then the Chief said, "You're still a hostage?"

"Yes," she said tightly. "Of course."

He made a grunting acknowledgement. "Did they force you to contact us?"

How could she answer that? She was being held under duress. "They want to negotiate."

"Yes, I know, Esmé," he said. "But you see, we don't."

She wasn't sure she understood him. This had to be a bluff. "Of course you do," she said. "What will it cost you?"

"Time," he said too quickly for her satisfaction. "Resources. Money. All of which are in short supply."

Her breath caught. She'd heard those words before. She didn't like them. Or the reasonable tone he was using.

Or what he was implying.

"Do you value my life so cheaply?" she asked.

"Esmé." Now he sounded patronizing. "This isn't cheap. Every scenario will cost more than . . . ahem . . . um . . . well, you've made this very calculation yourself."

She froze.

Bastard. He *was* using her own words against her.

What is one life? She would say. *Especially one that had cost so many others? We could imprison that life, spend precious resources on it, feed it, sustain it, and get nothing for it. Or we could make sure it doesn't cost us any more than it already has.*

"I haven't done anything wrong," she said, then wished she could take the words back. They sounded defensive.

"I know," the Chief said. "You're collateral damage. These people who believe that crime solves everything—well, you have to understand. We must deal with them in the most efficient way possible."

"I don't have to understand anything," she snapped.

"Oh, Esmé," he said. "I know you understand. This is your policy, after all."

And then the signal cut out. She looked at the hostage taker. He looked at her.

This was a joke, something done to teach her a lesson, something that would end right now.

"What do you plan to do?" she asked him.

He shook his head, sighed. "They've barred us from Pavonne, and we can't go to Latica now. There's nowhere really close, and you don't keep this ship stocked."

She didn't. It was for short journeys only.

And executions, of course.

"So," he said, sounding defeated already. "I guess we're going to have to figure out what we have, figure out how long it'll take to get outside the colonies, figure out what it'll take to get there."

More fuel than they had. More food than they had. She knew that, but she wasn't going to tell him.

His gaze met hers. She sensed panic, and the beginnings of conviction.

"I guess," he said, "it's like the Chief said. It's a matter of resources—and in that instance, some lives are worth more than others."

And some were worth nothing at all.

She sat back in the execution cell and closed her eyes.

It's math, really, she used to say when someone confronted her about her reputation as a brutal hanging judge. *When you do the math, you always make the best decision.*

Always.

Except when you're not the one making the decision.

Like right now.

No journey to the stars could begin without a starship, and so we continue our journey with a tale about one of those without whom colonization of the stars will never happen: a colonial ship pilot, called upon to take an adventure and sacrifice life at home, until he begins realizing the cost. Did he make the right decision? Would you choose the same? What would you do if you had the option to flip the switch? Jamie Todd Rubin's story touched my heart. I hope it moves you as well.

FLIPPING THE SWITCH

JAMIE TODD RUBIN

The switch in my head is broken. Try as I might, I can't switch the emotions off.

In all my years of ferrying colonists to the stars, I'd never spent much time wondering if they ever missed Earth. I could turn off my emotions like flipping a switch on the instrument panel. Flip the switch again and my emotions are back. Psychologists called it a disorder, but it's a prerequisite for any starship pilot, and it virtually guarantees you a job in the space corp. Without worry or care, you can focus fully on the critical tasks at hand.

So I never gave a second thought to the colonists I carried to the stars. Just as it never occurred to me that switch in my head could fail. But try as I might I can no longer switch it off.

Nighttime was better in our tiny studio apartment. Darkness concealed the grimy alley beyond the two barred windows. The stench that rose from pools of murky water below those windows seemed less oppressive when the sun was down. And with the lights out, you couldn't see the cracking apartment walls closing in on you. Despite the comforting darkness, I couldn't sleep. I curled up to Selena, resting my hand on her round belly, her skin stretched tight and smooth.

The job had finally come through. In less than a year, I'd be leaving Earth as a full-fledged starship pilot. I'd be doing my part to ferry those who could afford a ticket away from the depressed planet to any one of a dozen brighter futures on colonies amongst the stars. It wasn't ideal, of course. Selena and the baby would stay behind. But the pay was good, and it would afford them a better lifestyle. For the first time in our lives, we might do more than just scrape by. We wanted to believe this. We were young and in love and we thought that would be enough to carry us through anything—and it *was* a job, one to which I was particularly well-suited. I don't think either of us really understood the time-altering implications of the job.

I felt a thump inside Selena's belly, as if the baby was showing her approval. It touched my heart as surely as I'd felt it with my hand. As a starship pilot, I knew that in a race against anything else, light was the inevitable winner. As a soon-to-be father, I wondered if this was really the case. Didn't love travel faster than light?

For as long as I could remember, darkness had ruled our lives. I would never have guessed that beginning on that day, light would take over, shaping our lives, defining the relationship between Selena and I; between me and my daughter. Little did I imagine that I would increasingly become an intrusion in her life even as she remained an oasis in mine.

At six weeks old, Gillian looked so different from when she was born that she might well have been another baby. It was hard to imagine that another six weeks would pass before I'd see her again.

Selena was understandably distant the day I left on the first trip. "She'll be grown up when you get back," she said, her features hardened into indifference.

"She'll be eight," I said and immediately realized it was the wrong reply.

Selena pulled Gillian closer, swaddling her tightly within the sling that hung across her breasts.

I kissed the soft spot on top of Gillian's head, intoxicated by her fresh smells, creating a memory garden of her scents. During the loneliest times en route, when I lay in my bunk trying to sleep, I intended to wander though that garden, picturing what Gillian might look like, what she was doing, what she had become. I wasn't sure I could bear to be away from her for a day, let alone six weeks.

I took one more look around the tiny apartment, drab and dreary in the light of day. "You should start receiving my pay as soon as I'm gone. You know what to do with it, right?"

"I know what to do. Safe flight, okay?" She leaned in and kissed me passionately for the first time in weeks.

"Wilco," I said smiling. I turned to little Gillian. "I'll bring you back a souvenir, honey," I said. She cracked a little smile at me.

Then I flipped the switch.

For the next forty-five days, I piloted the *Dertorous II*, a near-light passenger vessel powered by a subatomic black hole. The ship served as transport for several hundred colonists on their way to the Alpha Centauri system. Most of these stars had no habitable planets. Instead, colonies had been carved into massive asteroids, which provided just as much protection from the star's radiation as an atmosphere could.

Upon our arrival, we were granted twenty hours of shore leave. I found a gift shop and picked out a burping bib for Gillian. But before I paid for it, I realized that Gillian would no longer be an adorable infant when I returned. I left the shop empty-handed.

The outbound trip might have been exciting for me but for flipping the switch. I was emotionally idle. I didn't fret or worry over Selena and Gillian. Yet neither could I savor the full emotional impact of the journey itself. I kept myself busy chatting with my crewmates, occasionally making conversation with a colonist, but mostly throwing myself into learning the ropes from the Captain.

Our commander, Captain Tanner, was a good mentor. It was her third trip to the Alpha Centauri system, and she talked as if it might be her last.

"After just three trips?" I asked.

"All you rooks think that way. Six weeks round trip. After a while, you stop thinking in terms of the time that passes out here and start thinking in terms of the time that passes back home. Three trips amounts to less than half a year. But we're talking about eight-

and-a-half light years round trip, three round trips, and all of them at 99.99% C. That's more than a quarter of a century back home."

"Not me," I said, scanning the engine instruments. "I want to see what's out there."

"At the price of giving up everyone you love?"

"Pulling them up, that's what I'm doing. My wife will live better than she's ever lived before. My daughter won't know the squalor that I've had to live in." The truth was I didn't think about them. Out of sight, out of mind.

"Maybe," the captain said, "but it will cost your wife her husband, and your daughter her father." I can't imagine that I smirked, but something in my expression caused the captain to frown and say, "You don't believe me?"

"No, ma'am."

"Did you ever ask yourself why none of the passengers come back?"

"They're out looking for a better life."

"We're all looking for a better life. Relativity: that's the reason they don't come back. We are time travelers, all of us, skipping years in weeks. What we go home to . . . it's too painful."

I did a quick scan of the instruments and then glanced out the viewport. The distorted light was hard to look at, dizzying but not painful.

The glow of the instruments threw dark shadows across the Captain's face. "Well," she said softly, "maybe you're different."

We didn't talk much about it after that. I realized that while everyone in the space corps could flip the switch, some chose not to. The captain was clearly someone who didn't. I missed Selena and Gillian when I thought about them, but I just didn't think of them much. I enjoyed piloting the starship, but, even there, it was hard to say it was exciting. In flipping the switch, I couldn't pick and choose what I felt. It was all or nothing. The voyage out was mildly exciting. Returning home was a little less exciting. It wasn't that I didn't look forward to going home. I just didn't look forward to flipping the switch.

We began picking up broadcasts from Earth, and once we'd slowed enough to lower the shields that protected the ship, I was briefed on what had happened on Earth in the eight years I was gone. None of it seemed surprising. Some things were better, some were worse. I'd never been on a vacation before, but I was feeling what I imagined I would if I had been away on holiday.

Included in the briefing was a note that Selena would be waiting for me at the spaceport when I arrived.

I flipped the switch at the last possible moment. When all of the passengers had debarked, all of the checklists complete, I left the *Dertorous II* behind and dashed into the spaceport. There, at the end of the gangway Selena waited, a soft smile on her face.

Beside her, half hidden in Selena's skirts, stood a shorter, more childish version of Selena. Same high cheekbones. Same brown eyes. Same dark hair, done up in ponytails tied with wine-colored ribbon. "Hi, Daddy," she said, wrapping her arms around my waist.

At that moment, I felt my heart melt right into her eight-year-old hands. Overwhelmed, my chest grew tight and I found it difficult to breathe. I picked up Gillian, squeezing her so hard she squealed. "Did you bring me a present?"

Then I realized I'd made a mistake. I'd run out of time to find another gift and hadn't thought about it since. Now I had to face an expectant eight-year-old with empty hands. "I'm sorry," I said.

Selena said nothing, her eyes filled with tears—not of joy, but of anger. If Gillian was upset, she didn't show it. But I was crushed. How could I have been so selfishly forgetful?

On our way home, Gillian told me all about her school and her friends and the house and her bike. I drank it in. But the smells, those wonderful baby scents were no longer there, and some kind of spell had been broken by my wretchedness. What kind of man abandons his family the way I did? Sure, it afforded them a better life, but at what cost? Selena's silence magnified my distress.

Home, as it turned out, was in a suburb, across the river from the city--and it was an actual house, albeit a small one. Despite Selena's anger, this did my heart good. The money I earned had gotten Selena and Gillian into substantially better surroundings, despite the fact that the worldwide depression continued to deepen.

I tried to put it out of my mind, but did not flip the switch. I needed to feel these things. This was my penance. And besides, Gillian was eight years old. I had two years before I returned to space. I planned to use them to feel the world around me, to fill the emotional void of the last six weeks, to get to know my daughter.

*

They say time flies when you become a parent, so imagine being a parent and a starship pilot traveling at relativistic speeds. When I left on a trip, time melted away and Gillian grew up before my eyes in a way that only other pilots understand.

My second trip took me to an ancient M-class fireball orbited by a fledgling science outpost. We ferried a set of scout colonists who would share the potato-shaped asteroid with the scientists. All were eager to get away from Earth and seek out a new life. I wondered, fleetingly, if they realized what they were leaving behind.

We traveled further than my first flight, seventy days round-trip. I thought about home more on this trip than the first one, but that's because I decided to experiment and flip the switch once we reached our halfway mark. After that I thought about Gillian all the time. By the time we got back home, I felt like I was suffering from a kind of addiction withdrawal—until I saw Selena waiting for me.

Sudden relief overwhelmed me, the kind you experience tumbling into bed after a long day's work, knowing there are hours and hours of sleep laid out in front of you. She wore an elegant one-piece, the kind we used to see the rich folks wear on their way to the theaters. But something was off. Selena had aged and it was beginning to show. In the two months I'd been gone, she'd gained twelve years of lines in her face, twelve years of sag and decay. My god, she'd turned fifty earlier in the year! I was still in my late thirties.

I looked around.

"Where's Gillian?" I asked with a kind of overeager desperation.

"At school," Selena said. Our arms entwined and her head rested against my shoulder as we walked.

"What time does she get home?"

Selena stopped walking and gave me a look. "School, Zach. University. She's on the other side of the country."

My heart sank. A wave of nausea pummeled me. I was desperate to see my daughter and she was thousands of kilometers away. It was then that I realized what Captain Tanner had tried to explain to me on that first trip. Flipping the switch built a dam, blocking off a sea of emotion. The problem was the basic tool: a switch, not a valve. There was no flow control. Flipping my emotions back on converted that potential emotional energy into kinetic energy all at once.

The emotions prevented me from masking my disappointment, and I could see how that hurt Selena, but she said nothing more about it.

Selena was in a new house—new to me anyway. It was farther north than the old house and substantially larger than the first one. Its furnishings were elegant, clearly the result of professional decoration. I hesitated to walk on the imported tile floors that led from the foyer through a sunken living room and into the bright kitchen that overlooked a wooded backyard. I brushed my finger across the surface of a bookshelf and it came up dust-free. Nanites, Selena explained. They came out at night and carried away all of the dust.

"How do you do it?" Selena asked, kicking off her shoes and curling up into an egg-shaped chair.

"Do what?"

"Turn off your emotions, flip the switch."

"I don't know," I said, "it's just something that I've always been able to do."

"But is it really like flipping a switch? Is there some mental trick you perform and—click!—no emotion?"

I thought about it for a moment. "How do you move your finger?" I asked.

Selena tilted her head, her eyes studying me with an unnerving, quizzical stare. "I guess I just will it to move."

"That's how I flip the switch. It's like willing your finger to move."

"Are you doing it now?"

"Of course not."

She stared through me, past me. "I wish I could flip the switch . . ."

Later that night, I called Gillian. "She goes by Jill now," Selena warned me.

Seeing her on the screen was like looking back in time. At twenty-two, she was only slightly younger than her mother was when we first met. I saw in my daughter an image of the woman with whom I'd fallen in love some fifteen years ago. Fifteen years relative to me, anyway.

"Hey, Dad, how was the trip?" Her unintentional impersonation of Selena's voice was perfect. I wanted to reach out through the screen and hold her, tell her how much I missed her. She was growing up—had grown up—without me.

We talked for a while as Jill caught me up on the last twelve years of her life; how she'd been accepted to the school in California; how she'd majored in something called sentient psychology; how she'd be graduating in just a few months. There were some gaps, and I wondered what she was leaving out.

"Will you be at the graduation?" she asked.

"Of course I will."

"When do you go back?"

I hesitated for a moment, wondering if Selena hovered nearby. "Two years," I said. "It's always two years between flights. Family time and all. But on the bright side, I've been promoted to captain. I'll be in command of the next flight."

"Good for you, Dad," she said. I could tell she wanted to say more but held back. "Gotta go. See you soon."

Before bed, as I was recounting the call to Selena, she said, "I can't live like this anymore, Zach." There was a calmness about her, a peacefulness in her expression, a softness that seemed to melt away the hard lines of her face. It was as if she were somehow detached, as if she had learned to flip her own switch.

I started to speak, but Selena put a finger to my lips.

"You'll be here for two years and then you'll be off again, and for who knows how long. Look around. You've given us everything we could have hoped for. Everything but you." My heart jumped to my throat as she continued: "My life is going by without you. Jill's life is going by without you. She seems ambivalent about it, but she's used to your absence. I suppose I am, too. But I can no longer live like this, okay?"

She may have been calm, but I felt frantic. I thought back to those colonists, eager to leave the Earth behind and wondered how I could not have seen then what I saw now—each time I went away, I lost more of my connection to home—more of myself. I still loved Selena desperately, and when she said no more, it was as if the roots of our love, buried deep in my heart were ripped away with an angry violence. I tried to argue with her and wanted desperately to flip the switch, but I knew it would only make things worse.

Within a few weeks, we put through the paperwork. There was no bitterness, no pointing of fingers. We attended Jill's graduation together. Jill introduced us to a young man she'd been seeing. There was talk of marriage, and I was happy for her. I promised to visit often, whenever I was back on Earth.

And when it was all over, I headed home, but Selena did not come with me. We went our separate ways. I tried to be happy for her, but it still hurt. Dreading the dark feelings that I knew would linger for weeks and months, I finally flipped the switch.

This was not the future I had hoped to see, and I grew itchy for my next trip, eager to leave this place and come back to a happier time.

This trip—my first in command—took me to Sirius, a binary star system that included a mismatched pair of white stars. Forty-five days to get there and forty-five days back. I was still five months short of my fortieth birthday when I returned home. Nearly two decades had passed on Earth.

It sunk in a bit more once I'd flipped the switch back on.

My granddaughter's name was Zoe, and I met her a few weeks later when she arrived for a visit with Jill and her husband (my son-in-law!)—a trim, rugged-looking young man by the name of John Osuna—to celebrate my homecoming. Zoe was ten years old and it was very hard not to think of her as my own daughter. She had a strong resemblance to Jill, but she'd inherited enough of her father's features to ensure she didn't look much like Selena at all.

We chatted. Conditions had improved on Earth. The depression had started to recede into the ocean of the past, leaving behind it a transformed world. Slowly, things were recovering.

"It's like the economy has been hibernating these last few decades and is just now waking up to the spring thaw," Jill said, and there was wisdom in her words. It took me a few days to realize why.

"How's your mother doing?" I asked Jill one evening.

"Good. Remarried. Happy."

The remarried part, though not unexpected, still stung. I turned my attention to Zoe, who was playing in the den with a model starship I'd brought for her. Jill was peeling carrots. "She adores you, you know? Zoe, I mean."

"She hardly knows me."

"She knows you're a starship pilot and that gives her a certain amount of bragging rights with her friends. She's a lot like you . . . Dad."

Her subtle hesitation brought an awkward realization to the foreground: *My daughter was two-and-a-half years older than me!* Though it hardly seemed possible, she had lived more years than I, had more life experience than I did. As a father, I felt a creeping paranoia that perhaps I wasn't needed any longer; that'd outlived my purpose.

"I worry about her sometimes," she continued, "She can do it, you know. Turn off her emotions. They say it skips a generation. I'm afraid that she'll follow in your footsteps too closely, run off to the stars. Hardly age."

We must have been thinking the same thing, because she gave me a look. "What it is you look for out there, Dad? What's so important that you've spent most of your life away from your family?" It wasn't exactly anger in her voice.

"A better life," I said. "For you. For Zoe. For your mother."

"Our life isn't out there," she said.

"You don't know what things were like, how we lived."

"Maybe so, but I know what it was like to grow up without a father. Things are different now, Dad. Look around. We're doing just fine. We're happy with the life we've got. We'd be even happier with you in it."

It wasn't until that moment that I knew that I was searching for something out among the stars. Jill was right. Their lives were better than I could have dreamed possible. But I was no longer a part of that life. The lure of the stars called out to me once again. I tried to hush it by doting on Zoe. She was absolutely wonderful. She warmed my heart.

A few nights later, I was in the backyard with Zoe, looking up at the night sky. She would point to a star, I'd name it, and she'd ask, "Have you been there?"

Sirius was bright in the sky that night, and I pointed to it and said, "See that one? That's Sirius. I've been there. If you look carefully, you might even see me, still floating around up there."

"Don't be silly, Grandpa. You're here."

I tasseled her hair and said, "Of course I am." But it wasn't where I belonged. The siren song was calling me again, and I knew that in two years, I'd answer that call.

*

The call came three weeks before my second trip to Alpha Centauri. Jill sounded frantic. Selena had been killed in an auto accident near her home in France. There was a pressure in my chest as I heard the words. I didn't want to believe them. First the memories: our first date; our wedding; the day Gillian was born. That dam I'd constructed dissolved, emotions flooding like a surging river overflowing its banks and spreading its cold waters into the dry, empty spaces of my heart. But now was not the time. Not three weeks from the trip.

I flipped the switch.

At first, nothing happened.

Fear spilled into the flood like black oil. It was a lot like those nights, when I was a youngster, and I'd wake up from a dream, unable to move. Regardless of my brain screaming commands at my arms or legs, they wouldn't budge—at first.

I felt dizzy. My face was warm and beads of sweat accumulated at my temples while a bitter taste filled the back of my tongue. This couldn't be happening. Not now. I took a breath, tried to calm myself, much as I tried to do when I was a youngster. And then I gave the switch a single, violent tug. The world of emotion went dark and I could relax.

A funeral was planned for the following week. On the shuttle across the Atlantic, I allowed myself to feel some of the pain again. I tried making sense of it all, tried to understand how someone so young could be taken away so suddenly. But then again, Selena wasn't so young, she was seventy-two—it was I who had barely aged, thirty years younger than she. When I flipped the emotions off again—this time without any trouble—our life together, Selena and I, seemed like someone else's, a past life, something I'd seen in the holos, or read in a novel somewhere.

The funeral took place on a blindingly bright day at a small cemetery on the northern coast of France, a warm breeze carrying the pungent smell of the sea off the water. I stood with Jill and John and Zoe during the ancient service that Selena had insisted upon. Afterward, I sought out her husband, Matthieu, and tried to come up with words of condolence that somehow fell flat. Even as I took Mattieu's hand, I could see the discomfort in his eyes. It was something I'd never really noticed before. *You don't belong here*, it said. *You don't belong in this time.*

That night at the inn, after John had taken Zoe to find something to eat, Jill lit into me.

"You were never there for her," she said. "You were always running off to the future, running away from what you had at home. You never saw what it did to her. She hid it from you." There was a gleam in her eyes that I recognized. Jill was holding back her tears. "She *waited* for you. Every time you went away, she waited. She was in love with you from the start, but that wasn't enough for you, was it?"

"I loved your mother very much," I said.

"But you loved something else more, didn't you? You still do." Her voice cracked, her face crumpled into her hands. "*And you abandoned her for it!*"

I knew then that Jill was right, but I also knew she was no longer talking about Selena. It's one thing for a man to love something more than his wife, but what kind of man loves something more than his daughter? There was nothing I could say in response, but she didn't give me a chance.

"Zoe will not be like that. I won't allow it. She thinks the world of you, and wants to be a starship pilot. Well, I won't have it. I won't have her abandoning her family the way you abandoned yours. She won't listen to me, but she'll listen to you. You need to talk her out of it. You need to convince her that it's not worth it.

That I could never do.

I adored Zoe and knew she had to follow her heart. I could never tell Jill how proud I was that Zoe's heart might lead her to the stars, but it was the truth. From the shadows, I heard echoes of my grandfather's voice quoting Shakespeare, "To thine own self be true . . ." Zoe had to be true to herself, just as I had to be true to myself. Yet I could not bear to live with my daughter's resentment, either. There was only one choice I could make.

Rather than wait out the two year cycle, I volunteered to cover a trip to Tau Ceti after the scheduled pilot decided to retire. I might not be able to talk Zoe out of becoming a starship pilot, but I didn't have to be around to cause her or Jill any more pain. Jill wouldn't speak to me when I told her my decision to leave early. Zoe seemed thrilled for me.

"That's your longest trip yet!" she said, circling the star on the chart she kept on her wall. I watched her, watched her excitement, and for just a moment, I thought that maybe I could stay behind. Within my granddaughter was the spark of what I had and seeing it through her eyes might not be so bad. It would be awfully difficult to leave her behind to grow up without me. But despite everything I wanted for Zoe, I owed it to Jill not to interfere any further.

"My longest trip yet," I repeated, staring at Zoe's star chart. But whereas she might have been thinking of distance, I was thinking of time.

Tau Ceti, now that was a voyage! We were only the third ship sent out with the improved Sarkisian drives which brought us within five-nines—99.999% C. Twelve light years in about three weeks! And the star itself! Its yellowish light set aglow a halo of dense dust scattered throughout its orbital reach. It was the most magnificent view I'd ever seen in my life, and, when I flipped the switch on in order to feel the local sun's full effect, I felt as if I stood before the gateway to heaven.

Almost as quickly, I descended into the pit of hell.

Jill's words came back to me, still stinging after three weeks, the more so having repressed the emotions for so long. I couldn't bear it, not in the glory of this work of nature spread before me. So I flipped the switch off—except nothing happened. It simply didn't work. The emotions: awe, anger, fear, shame, all of them crashed in upon me and no matter how hard I tried, I could not will them back.

Abandon hope, all ye who enter.

The three week return trip was sheer agony. I replayed in my mind all of my choices, caught up in the game of "if only . . ." I mourned over the loss of Selena, and bitterly regretted what I had done to her—to us. And Jill's words . . .

Each day I tried to flip off the switch, always with the same result. I once heard that the definition of insanity was trying the same thing again and again and expecting different results. I was terrified I was losing my grip on reality.

I tried thinking of Zoe. She was just like me. She understood me. She had the gift, as Jill had pointed out. I realized that it was a mistake not to say anything to her. Zoe needed to know what she was getting into. I needed to warn her and decided to make that my first priority when I arrived home. The switch might be broken, and my emotions might be running wild, but I knew that seeing Zoe's face, hearing the excitement in her voice, would be my anodyne. It was her face and voice that got me through those remaining weeks—weeks that remain, to this day, the most horrific in my life.

We arrived back at Earth, and though it had been only three weeks since I'd lost control of the switch, it seemed as though I'd never really had control to begin with.

Distracted, deep in my thoughts as I passed through the spaceport, I didn't recognize Jill when she called out to me.

"Dad?" she said as I passed by, my gazed fixed on the long concourse.

I stopped and turned to face her. For her, twenty-five years had passed. A quarter century! And I wasn't there for a minute of it. Not for the first time, I questioned my true motives. What good was providing for a family you were never there for?

"Gillian?"

She put her arms around my neck. "I'm so sorry, Daddy."

She drove me to her house and John greeted me. He was looking trim and gray, but I clearly recognized the man who'd been married to my daughter for more than thirty-five years now. At dinner, they told me about Zoe.

"She became a starship pilot, like her grandfather," Jill said.

I was stunned. I didn't know what to say, but Jill smiled and touched my arm. "It's okay. It's what she wanted to do. It's what makes her happy. When you are a parent, all you really want is for your kids to be happy, right?"

Jill and John went on to tell me that they had four grandchildren— that made me a great grandfather four times over! Two of them were Zoe's kids, and the other two were Sam's kids. Sam had been born a year after I left.

"Do you see your grandkids often?" I asked.

"We see Ella and Darin all the time," Jill said. "But Zack and Tasha went with Zoe and Ryan into space."

The company was now allowing pilots to bring their families with them. With more and more people going to increasingly distant stars, allowing families to travel with the pilots kept turnover to a minimum. But what really struck me was something else:

Zoe named her son after me.

I felt consumed with the need to see my granddaughter—as a grownup, as a starship pilot, as a kindred spirit. I quizzed Jill and John on where she had gone, but they weren't certain. All they knew was that it was far away. They would never see her again.

"But it doesn't have to be like that," I said. "My next trip is in two years. I can pick and choose now. I can pick something that is equally far, and we can meet her back here when the trip is over! My heart was pounding with excitement.

"*We?*" Jill said.

"I can bring my family now. You can come with me."

The look that passed between Jill and John hinted at what was coming. "That's not our life, Dad. We're happy here. We're retired. We get to see Sam and the kids often. We like our life."

"But Zoe—"

"We said goodbye to Zoe when she and Ryan and their kids left. We knew it was for good."

"But—"

"You have your reasons for going, Dad. You always have. We have our reasons for staying."

It took some digging, but I found out where Zoe had gone and when she'd be back. As a senior captain, I had my choice of flights. There was a ship scheduled to leave to Betelgeuse, and it was mine if I wanted it. The question was: *did I want it?*

I could leave instructions for Zoe. Jill would see to it she received them. If she followed them, she could arrange to arrive back on Earth within a year of my arrival back from Betelgeuse. But Betelgeuse was six hundred light years away. Even at five-nines, it meant more than five years in space. And of course, twelve hundred years would pass on Earth. Not only would I be saying goodbye forever to Jill and John, I'd be saying goodbye to just about everything I'd ever known. On the other hand, it was my opportunity to venture farther into the future than I'd ever thought possible. And there was at least a chance that I would get to see Zoe again.

I agonized over the decision, wishing that I could flip the switch off, knowing that if I could, it would be an easy decision to make. I thought back all those years ago when Selena and I first considered starting a family. All we were trying to do was little more than scrape by.

I had a daughter, a son-in-law, both successful, both happy. I had grandchildren. I lost Selena, and perhaps Zoe too, but, even so, they saw benefits from sacrifices we made. It slowly began to dawn on me that I had right here on Earth everything I had hoped for when I'd left in the first place.

The next morning, I told Jill and John: "I'm staying."

Later that day, I scribbled out two letters. The first was to the space corps, asking them to put through my retirement papers, effective immediately. I did this not without sorrow, but without any regrets.

The second was to Zoe:

Dear Zoe,

Each night I look up at the stars and remember the time when you were just a young girl and we stargazed together. You pointed to Sirius, and I told you that if you looked carefully, you might still see me up there. "Don't be silly, Grandpa," you said, "You're here!

When I gaze up at the stars now, I imagine that I can see you, wandering around up there, raising your family, living your life as you have chosen to do. I wish I could be up there with you, but my place is here now. I wanted you to know, however, that you were right. A person can be in two places at once. For as surely as I see you voyaging to distant stars, I also feel you in my heart every day.

By the time you read this, I'll be long gone. But maybe I'll linger in your heart as you have in mine.

All my love,
Your Grandfather

There's a switch inside my head over which I once had complete control. Flip it off and my emotions would wink out like a light cut off from its power source. Flip it on and all of those cares and worries snapped instantly back in place.

Now that switch is broken. Try as I might I can't switch it off.

Thank goodness for that.

Someone has to go and prepare planets for colonist's arrival. In some cases, this will consist of advance teams of volunteers or government officials, in others, perhaps laborers will be recruited. In the case of our next story, those laborers are prisoners working off their hard time. The service in the brick fields is far better than other options, however. Unless, of course, one of your fellow inmates wants even more . . .

THE BRICKS OF ETA CASSIOPEIAE

BRAD R. TORGERSEN

I checked the primitive gauge on the kiln. The gauge's needle hovered steadily in the red.

"Still too hot," I said over my shoulder. "Gotta wait another day."

"That's nice," said my fellow inmate, Godfrey. "So what do we do until then?"

"You dig," came the reply from Ivarsen, our lone guard. Like the rest of us, he wore a broad-brimmed sun hat and wraparound sunglasses to protect against Eta Cassiopeiae's blinding rays. Unlike the rest of us, his shorts and shirt were khaki—instead of prisoner orange—and he had a holster on his hip holding a high-power pistol.

In the two planetary years since I'd been assigned to Ivarsen's care, I'd never seen him draw that gun. But with how Godfrey had been acting since his arrival one week ago, I wondered if even Ivarsen's patience had limits.

Godfrey vented his unhappiness in four-lettered fashion.

"Kid," I said, "How in the world did you ever make this detail?"

"I've got a winning personality," Godfrey said, grinning.

I shook my head at him, disbelieving.

Lisa Phaan, our only female inmate, gave me a knowing glance. She didn't think much of the kid, either.

"Prisoner Ladouceur and Prisoner Godfrey on the shovels," Ivarsen said. "Prisoner Phaan on the dumper. Wait here while I drive it around."

Our guard turned and walked away into the white glare of mid day, the broken and rocky landscape shimmering behind him.

Godfrey leaned close to me and said, "Why don't we just snuff him?"

I turned and looked at the huge-bodied youth, my eyebrows raised.

"And do *what*? It's two hundred kilometers to anywhere. The sun will kill you before you get thirty. Besides, Ivarsen has a chip in his body that monitors his vitals and stays in constant contact with a Corrections satellite. All the guards at these remote projects have one. If his vitals stop, the satellite gets alerted. Then the cavalry comes."

"Bull," Godfrey said.

"You really want to find out?"

The kid kept looking at our guard while Ivarsen receded into the heat.

"Look," I said, "is it really that bad? Time served here counts triple what it counts on The Island. They feed us and give us shelter. We're not at the mercy of the elements. Why ruin it?"

Godfrey turned and looked at me, hands balling. "Screw you," he said, and walked away.

I shook my head, wondering if I'd ever been that incomprehensibly belligerent when I was in my twenties. Then I went over to slap shut the ceramic door that covered the kiln's thermometer.

As indigenous brick kilns went, ours was pretty standard: a four-meter-cubed box constructed from cut-rock slabs. It sat on the eroded central peak of a shallow crater whose expanse had been populated with automated mirrors. Currently, those mirrors aimed skyward. But when we put a batch of bricks into the kiln, and the computer angled all those mirrors towards the small hill at their center, the kiln lit up like a bug under a magnifying glass.

Depending on the season and the weather, the kiln could take a full day to fire up—and the days on Eta Cassiopeiae's fifth planet were very long, especially at this latitude.

In the meantime, there was always more clay. And the new settlements along the polar coast always needed more bricks. In a world with no large flora and relatively little accessible iron, what else was there to build with?

The supply niche would have been filled commercially, if the prison system hadn't gotten there first. The work was arduous and filthy—the kind of soul-mending stuff reformists had been foisting on the incarcerated for many centuries, going all the way back to Earth.

On Eta Cassiopeiae Five, nobody in their right mind wanted to be this close to the equator, so the colonial government farmed the work out to Corrections. Thus everyone was kept happy—even us cons.

It sure beat the crap out of The Island, where there were no rules and it was literally every man for himself. I'd lasted just long enough to decide that The Island was a slow death sentence, then made an appeal to a Corrections Magistrate on one of their random, heavily-armed inspection tours Corrections occasionally made. They'd liked me, so I'd been given the chance to go to work.

And work I'd done. Happily. Eagerly. With a full stomach and boots on my feet, and no fear that the gangs were going to roll me up in the middle of the night and poke holes in me. Or worse.

A mechanized grumble broke me out of my reverie.

I turned to watch as the dumper came rolling down the dusty main lane between the mirrors. The huge truck ran on a hydrogen fuel cell and was our primary means of transport; vital to weekly operations.

Wet clay, extracted from the hills two kilometers to the east, had to be moved via dumper to the forming pit. Once formed and dried, the "green" bricks were put on ceramic pallets which again went into the back of the truck for movement to the kiln. Fired and cooled, those bricks remained on pallets until they were moved to the staging area to await pickup by monthly roadtrains headed north. Empty pallets came back from the settlements on roadtrains headed south, to be filled again. And so forth.

Nobody was allowed to drive the dumper except Ivarsen, who kept the truck's coded keycard on his person at all times.

When the truck came to a halt, Ivarsen leaned out and yelled, "Everybody in back!"

We trooped to the ladder on the side and climbed up and over, then down into the extra-large bed where two single-person shovels sat. They were called shovels because the hydraulic arm on the front of each unit was attached to a large scoop designed to dig hundred-kilo hunks of clay out of the ground.

There was nothing to say while we rode out of the crater and started on the packed-earth highway to the eastern hills. We just gazed out the back of the bed, the tires kicking up a column of dust, each of us enjoying the movement of air which partially alleviated the ever-present heat.

Once we arrived at the dig, Lisa climbed up on top of the cab while Godfrey and I slid into the bucket seats on our respective shovels. Ivarsen used controls in the cab to lower the aft lip of the dumper's bed to the dirt, and then Godfrey and I caterpillared out and attacked the scarred hillside.

Clay is not the same thing as mud. I'd learned that my first month on the job. You had to look for the phyllosilicate deposits, then clear off the top layers of worthless dirt and pry out the heavier stuff underneath. It came in various stages of plasticity, depending on how much moisture a given dig retained between thunderstorms, and we could hydrate it using a cistern back at the forming pit.

A familiar, pungent odor filled my nose as my shovel's scoop bit into the ground. I worked the scoop's hydraulic controls until a decent hunk had been pulled free, then motored back to the dumper and threw my load in. I did this two more times and stopped to watch Godfrey struggle for his first shovelful.

It was his third time, and the kid still didn't get it. He was punching his scoop into the hillside like a jackhammer, knocking crumbled clay loose until it threatened to engulf the front of his machine.

I motored up to him and yelled over the whine of the hydraulics, "Finesse, man! Gradual and steady! Push in slow, lift out slow."

"I'm trying!" He yelled back. "Tractor's a piece of effin' crap!"

I wanted to tell him it wasn't the machine that was a piece of crap, then thought better of it.

"Here," I said over the noise of both engines, "watch me."

Godfrey backed off while I drove up and eased my scoop into the beige-gray mass. The load pulled free with relative ease, I spun my shovel on the axis of its treads and moved away to let the kid continue.

His next few attempts were almost competent.

I sighed and kept working, the day wearing imperceptibly on while we filled the dumper with clay. Lisa used controls on the top of the dumper's cab to operate the dumper's claw arm, re-arranging our shovelfuls as the need arose, and ultimately picking up and depositing each shovel back into the bed once we had enough clay to take back to the forming pit.

Ivarsen watched us the whole time, standing off from the dig by about ten meters, hands on his hips. His head didn't move, but I always had the impression his eyes were constantly sweeping from behind his sunglasses, like radar.

Once we'd secured the shovels and the dumper's claw arm, we climbed back into the bed and Ivarsen went back to the cab. The drive to the forming pit was as silent as the drive from the kiln, and I idly scratched dirt out of my hair, thinking again about my imminent parole. The government of Eta Cassiopeiae Five was finally going to make me a citizen again. It was odd to think I'd spent my entire thirties locked up—the bitter wage of a mistake I'd long since learned to regret.

I wondered what kind of life I could now make for myself, beyond firing brick. With my legal file as checkered as it was, my options were limited. Maybe I could talk to the asteroid miners again? They always needed help. Could I get a felony waiver?

Such thoughts continued to occupy me until we arrived at the forming pit.

Lisa plucked the shovels from the bed before Ivarsen up-ended the entire thing into the slaking ditch. There the clay was allowed to bathe in rainwater from the nearby cistern. Each of us took a turn under the spout before we left; the closest thing we had to a shower.

Again Ivarsen watched us from a distance, never moving except to take a tug off the canteen normally slung across his shoulder.

Afternoon wore on into evening, and EC5's three small moons—captured asteroids, really—rose into the sky. Looking up at them, I imagined the miners and engineers working all day and all night, all planetary year long, turning those moons into way stations for the big colonial ships that would bring more people from Earth, once EC5's biosphere had been sufficiently beefed up. Two, maybe three more human generations. Someday EC5 would be a garden.

But not yet.

We drove back to our hooches in silence. Hungry and exhausted.

Dinner was the usual: pre-sealed trays of farm-grown meat and veggies—yielded from genetically tweaked crops and livestock, on account of EC5's not-quite-Earth-normal soil and mineral content. Eventually there would be genetically-engineered forests in the hills and mountains surrounding the farms, and men would build with wood again.

Until then, the world needed bricks, which meant the world needed *us*.

With night fully upon us, Ivarsen activated the electric fence cordoning off the prisoner hooches from the guard hooch. Like most nights, I found the familiar hum from the fence's transformer to be oddly soothing.

I faded into oblivion.

Morning came.

This time the kiln was sufficiently cool. Needle in the green.

Lisa used the dumper's claw arm to lever the kiln's huge door out of the way—like the angel rolling aside the stone at the crypt of Jesus—and we all walked in to inspect our work. Even Ivarsen seemed to take genuine pleasure in seeing the finished bricks all lined up neatly on their stacked ceramic pallets, ready to be sent north and laid into homes, shops, offices, apartments, and everything else that needed building.

Lisa and I showed Godfrey how to check for cracks and damaged bricks, which we'd separate from the rest when we used a shovel— now modified with a fork on its arm—to lift each pallet from the kiln and place it carefully near the dumper.

The kid just grunted, saying, "Whatever," and began examining the kiln's contents. He did it with the enthusiasm of a six-year-old being made to eat asparagus.

Lisa followed me out of the kiln while I went to get my canteen. Constant hydration was an ever-present necessity this far south.

"Ev," Lisa said as she leaned close to me, "I'm so sick of getting stuck with these morons."

"Yeah. Must be slim pickings these days. Pretty soon Corrections might have to start drafting civilians for the brick brigades."

Ivarsen, who had been getting out of the dumper's cab, laughed mightily. "That'll be the day! Imagine how much they'd have to pay union workers to come out here and do what you guys do for free."

"*You're* union," I said, with sarcasm.

"Damn right," Ivarsen replied, thumping his chest with a fist.

We shared a smile between the three of us. Then came a sudden yelp from the kiln, followed by the sound of a pallet collapsing and bricks tumbling.

"Lord . . ." Lisa said, rolling her eyes.

We hurried back through the kiln entrance to find Godfrey hopping up and down on one leg while he held the other foot. Obscenities peeled from his lips.

Lisa, Ivarsen, and I almost fell over—it was that funny.

"Stop laughing," Godfrey fumed.

"Kid," I said, "One man's pain is another man's pleasure."

Godfrey grimaced sourly as he prepared to give me a verbal broadside, but then he stopped.

All the pallets were rattling violently.

"What the—?"

A booming rumble shuddered through the floor of the kiln.

"Quake!" Ivarsen yelled.

Really? I'd not been through one of those since I'd been a boy.

What happened next was a slow blur.

Stacked columns of pallets swayed like hula dancers.

Lisa was screaming and trying to get to the door, only she kept having her feet knocked out from under her.

One of the columns tilted too far, and collapsed against the side of the kiln. Then another.

Godfrey managed to keep his feet, his mouth hanging open and his eyes gone stupidly wide. The column next to him started to give— this time, towards the middle of the kiln.

Ivarsen's reaction was so fast I didn't even realize what had happened until both he and Godfrey were on the floor, sliding out of the path of the collapsing bricks.

One of the walls popped thunderously, and a new crack split wide from floor to ceiling, shining a shaft of light crossways to that which already flooded in from the main door.

Two more columns of bricks went down.

And then . . . silence.

Lisa and I were coughing spastically on the dust that had filled the kiln. I discovered I'd been sitting on my butt the entire time. Heaps of whole and broken bricks were everywhere, and I got to my feet to move around to where I thought I'd last seen Ivarsen and the kid.

I got there just in time to see Godfrey crown Ivarsen with a brick the size of my forearm. Our guard crumpled.

"What in the name of—" I said.

But the kid moved quickly, snatching the pistol out of Ivarsen's holster and pointing it at me while he used his free hand to explore the pockets of Ivarsen's shorts.

Lisa froze when she came around the corner and saw what was happening.

"You stupid idiot," I said to Godfrey. "Ivarsen saved your life."

"Ladouceur, you and Phaan get against the wall."

Lisa and I didn't move until Godfrey thumbed the pistol's safety and pulled the hammer back. Then we raised our hands and backed into the shadows as Godfrey came away with the keycard for the dumper.

"You won't make it," Lisa said deadpan. "The chip is already sending its alarm to the satellite."

Godfrey scoffed. "Pig 'aint dead. Just knocked out."

I looked at Ivarsen's still form, and thought I saw thick, dark fluid running from the back of his head where Godfrey had hit him.

"If he dies," I said, "then we're dead too."

"You, maybe," Godfrey replied. "I'm out of here."

"Where are you going to go, kid? There's no native forage on this land mass. And they can track the movement of the dumper. You'll be—"

"Shut up, Ladouceur. Maybe you like being a slave. Not me. I'd rather take my chances."

Finally, the rage that had been rising in me, boiled over.

"Damn you, I was getting *paroled*!"

Godfrey considered this while sidling towards the doorway. He looked back at Ivarsen, then to Lisa, and then to me.

"Sorry man," was all he said.

Then he was gone, and Lisa and I were rushing to Ivarsen's side. The guard's heart still beat, and his lungs took in air. That was good. But the deep laceration on his head bled profusely, and I dared not explore it for fear of finding pulp where there should be skull.

Lisa ripped open Ivarsen's shirt, and we tore off pieces to use as a temporary bandage.

Outside, the dumper's electric engine started up. We heard its large tires crunch on the dirt as Godfrey drove away.

Lisa was cursing and started to rise to her feet, but I stopped her.

"Let him go. We've got more immediate concerns."

She thought for a second.

"We can take him on the shovel. It will be fastest."

I nodded—there was a first aid locker in Ivarsen's hooch. Could we get to it in time?

Godfrey had gone off-road and disappeared over the southern hills by the time we got Ivarsen back to camp. I drove the shovel while Lisa sat on a pallet we'd cleared, which now held Ivarsen's unmoving body. The pallet was perched on the fork of the shovel's hydraulic arm, and I did my best to avoid bumps. At ten kilometers per hour, it took precious minutes to motor out of the crater and follow the trail along the rim wall to where the hooches sat.

I set the pallet down and Lisa leapt off, running into Ivarsen's hooch to get his cot. It wasn't a perfect stretcher, but we managed to get him onto it, moving him into his hooch so he'd be out of the sun.

Lisa helped me rummage through the first aid locker and apply a more suitable bandage to the head wound.

Next I checked his pupils with a flashlight, alarmed to see that one of them had gone as wide as the iris would allow.

"Lord," I said.

"Is it that bad?" Lisa asked.

"Bad enough. We need Ivarsen's satellite phone. If he doesn't get a medevac soon, he's as good as dead."

"I think the phone was in the cab of the dumper," Lisa said. "He always kept it there when we were working."

Lisa and I looked at each other. Neither of us needed to say what was on our minds.

When the SWAT guys got here, it wouldn't matter what story we told them. All they'd find was a dead Corrections officer, and two live prisoners. And that would be that. Meaning me and Lisa. Done. And Godfrey, when they tracked him down, as surely they would. We'd all be lucky if they sent us back to The Island. More probably, we'd be shot.

I stood up from Ivarsen's side and stomped out into the glaring sunlight, sweat making my shirt damp, and my eyes squinting in spite of my sunglasses. I screamed and kicked the treads on the shovel. Years of patient effort. Down the toilet. Thanks to a dumb kid.

I'd have kept screaming, except that I thought of Ivarsen, and how he'd deserved this even less. Me, I'd lost my life a long time ago. And deservedly so. But Ivarsen had been a decent man. Such a waste!

I went back inside to find Lisa rummaging furiously through Ivarsen's other things. Our patient's breaths had become quicker, more shallow, and a sheen of sweat covered the exposed areas of his skin. I unzipped his sleeping bag and threw it over him for a blanket, then went to help Lisa. She was obviously looking for a backup phone. Surely they wouldn't issue Ivarsen just the single unit?

The only thing we found was the remote for the mirrors in the crater.

Lisa threw the remote to the floor in disgust, but I picked it up and walked outside, staring up into the cerulean sky. Lisa came out and looked up with me.

"What?"

"How many satellites watch this region?" I asked.

"Heck if I know."

I kept looking. Then I quickly strode to the crater's rim wall and scrambled up its side until I was standing on the top and staring down into the circular field of mirrors.

The remote had several preset codes. I chose the toggle for manual movement. The circular thumb pad in the middle illuminated, and I depressed it, pushing first to the north, then to the south. Out in the field, the little servos on the base of each mirror began to whine. The mirrors obediently leaned to the south, then back to the north.

Okay . . .

I programmed in a repeating series of motions, pressed the SEND button, and then dropped the remote into my pocket and watched the mirrors begin their slow dance.

Lisa nodded, catching on. "I hope someone is paying attention, Ev."

The day wore on, and we stayed in the guard's tent. Lisa occasionally sponged Ivarsen down with a wet rag, and I ran checks on his vitals every fifteen minutes as well as checking his pupils. The dilated one stayed dilated, and I wondered if the man wasn't just a vegetable already.

Out in the crater, the mirrors kept spinning and swiveling.

There was no sound, other than the occasional wind across the camp.

Evening came quickly. When I checked the supply bunker I discovered that Godfrey had been there before us and taken most of the cases of meals. He'd at least been that smart. But without water I knew he'd be getting thirsty real soon. And unless he found a natural spring, or we got some rain, he'd be in a bad way before the following day was out.

I allowed myself a small amount of satisfaction at the thought of Godfrey dying for lack of water, then heated two trays for Lisa and I and went back into the tent.

I almost dropped the trays when Ivarsen's head turned to look at me.

"Ladouceur," the man said, whisperingly.

My relief could not have been more obvious. "Good Lord, Ivarsen. I thought you'd gone to mush on us."

"Can't—" he said, then stopped. "Hard . . . to think."

"Can you drink water?"

". . . Try . . ."

Lisa put her canteen to his lips and gave him a sip, which he kept down. Giving him too much would be worse than giving him none at all, so we waited and watched while he blinked randomly.

"Godfrey?" Ivarsen finally asked.

"Gone," I said. "He took the dumper, your gun, and most of the food. And your satellite phone. I've got the mirrors in the crater waving around, hoping to attract some satellite attention. Like it will do us any good after dark."

"Good . . . idea."

He went silent again for several minutes.

Then, "Ev . . ."

It was the only time he'd ever used my first name.

I leaned over him. "Yah, boss?"

"Not your fault . . . have to . . . tell them."

"Just hang in there. You're not dead yet."

"Will be . . . soon."

Lisa held Ivarsen's hand. Her expression was agonized.

"Lisa," Ivarsen said. "Find my . . . PDA."

Lisa and I bugged our eyes out at each other. We never knew he had one!

Reading our surprise, Ivarsen said, "Access panel on the . . . solar power battery."

Lisa and I both raced out into the gloaming light, finding the big battery for the camp. We pried off the service plate with our fingernails. The little PDA was perched out of sight, just inside and to the left.

Lisa grabbed it and we charged back to the hooch, freezing when we looked at Ivarsen's face.

His eyes were still open, along with his mouth. But his chest no longer drew air.

We did what we could for Ivarsen's body, then despondently trudged for our separate hooches, figuring there was nothing to be done but to sleep, and wait.

To my surprise, Lisa stopped me and motioned me towards her door.

Raising an eyebrow, I went with her into the hooch. It was amazingly neat and orderly, right down to the dirt floor having been lined with used meal trays—as makeshift tiles.

She sat down on her cot and I took a seat next to her, the lights from EC5's three small moons shining through the mesh walls around us.

"Months? That was all?" Lisa said.

"Yeah," I replied. "Three. I was getting real short."

"I can't even think about parole yet."

"Shoplifting?" I said, smiling at my own joke.

"Drugs," Lisa replied, not smiling. "I used to be a pharmacist, back in the world. Got hooked on my own product, you might say. Started dealing. Stupid. Got caught. Wound up detoxing on The Island. Almost killed me. But at least I got clean."

"That sucks," I said, turning serious.

"You ever been addicted to anything, Ev?"

"Not really. I'm a teetotaler." And that was the truth.

Lisa shuddered. "Don't. Don't ever."

I'd never seen her more stone-cold serious.

"Yes ma'am," I whispered.

And that was all I could say

Silence filled the dark. This was more personal information

than Lisa had ever shared with me before. I felt we were both in particularly uncomfortable territory.

"Do you think we'll be executed?" She asked.

"Yes," I said. "Corrections doesn't play around when it comes to one of their own going down in the line of duty. On my last brick site, I saw a guy actually try to take out the guard with a shiv. Guy was crazy to do it. The guard emptied a whole clip into the perp. Corrections never even did an investigation. The hurt guard left on a medevac, and we three prisoners who remained, all got split up. That was when they sent me here. To work for Ivarsen."

Lisa's head hung to her chest for an undetermined period of time, and when she looked back up at me I saw wetness on her cheeks. Which put a lump in my throat, for her sake. I suddenly felt stupid for telling her about the prisoner who got shot—like she really needed to hear that from me at this moment. *Idiot.*

I sighed and looked at the floor. It wasn't fair. She was young. And, apparently at last, clean. As a pharmacist, she was educated too. She deserved a fresh start. But wouldn't get it.

Just like me.

For no particular reason that I can recall, I slowly leaned down and pressed my lips to hers. Just a peck.

She surprised me in that my kiss was returned warmly.

"Thank you," Lisa said.

"No, thank *you*," I said.

We held hands as we sat on her cot. The most intimate contact I'd had with any person in years.

Then, she asked, "What about you, Ev?"

"Huh?"

"You now know why *I'm* in. But what about you?"

My hesitation must have been palpable.

"Sorry," she said. "I didn't want to pry. I just figured—"

"It's okay," I said. "I suppose you oughta know."

I breathed in and collected my thoughts.

The younger me had had a problem with his temper. I'd kept it under wraps when I was in school, but after I got out, I'd gone through a few different jobs because I couldn't keep my lip zipped in front of the boss.

Then came the day on the work site when one little jerk of an engineer had decided to get up in my face. He'd been smaller and smarter than me, and he'd let me know exactly what kind of loser he thought I was. Insults turned to screams, and before I knew it I'd knocked the man onto his back and began beating him with my wrench. Hard, vicious strokes. The kind of blows a man doesn't just get up and walk away from.

They told me later that the other workers had to pry me off the engineer, who was pronounced dead at the scene before the constabulary cuffed me and took me away to Corrections. I can still remember sitting in the back of the wagon, bawling my eyes out. *What had I done?*

Dad had tried to keep me from doing time. He'd spent what he could for legal help. But it didn't matter. I'd killed another human being. Eta Cassiopeiae Five might have been frontier territory, but you didn't just murder a man—in hot blood or cold—and walk away from it unscathed.

Back on Earth they had people to spare. On EC5? No way. Especially not when the victim had been educated.

There weren't any levels or degrees of punishment with Corrections. Once the government deemed you a threat to society, it was The Island. Goodbye. Civilization officially washed its hands of you.

I still remembered the look on Dad's face when they loaded me onto the transport. He'd been sure he was never going to see me again.

I'd spent every day since regretting what I'd done. And learning to be a different person as a result.

The whole time I told my story, Lisa listened intently. Then she said softly, "I'm sorry, Ev."

"I'm sorry too," I said. "But not for this."

I bent my head down and kissed her again.

"Wake up, Prisoner Ladouceur."

I didn't move. I felt like last night's cold fish.

"Prisoner Ladouceur, on your feet!"

A gloved fist slugged my shoulder, and suddenly I was tumbling out of my cot, shaking. Morning light streamed into the tent, and I found myself face-to-face with four armed Corrections SWAT officers in mottled fatigues.

Lisa was nowhere in sight. Had they hit her hooch first?

"Chip worked, huh?" I said, realizing the time had finally come.

"Yes," said the tall, black-skinned SWAT who had sergeant's stripes on his arm. "But we were already on our way when officer Ivarsen expired. That idea you had, about the mirrors . . . pretty ingenious. Nobody remembers Morse Code anymore. Except for the computers. When the satellites started picking up your S.O.S. flashing over and over again, it was obvious something had gone wrong."

I looked down at my nude self, and then back at the sergeant.

"Do I need to get dressed, or can we finish it here?"

"Excuse me?"

"Come on. Bullet to the head. It'll be quick. Justice will be done."

The sergeant's white teeth grinned like the Cheshire cat's.

He held up Ivarsen's PDA.

"Don't worry. I think your alibi is good. Officer Ivarsen apparently thought well of you, and Prisoner Phaan too. He had a feeling Godfrey was bad news. Ivarsen's last few logs pretty much state that Godfrey was going to pull something. Too bad we can't put Godfrey up against a wall. He definitely deserved it."

"You found him?"

"Idiot rolled the dumper. Doing ninety kay over broken terrain. No safety harness. Thrown from the cab and crushed. Not much else to do but toe-tag the remains."

"Huh. Can't say he didn't have it coming. So what happens now?"

Ivarsen's logs made all the difference. It was like having a character witness speaking from the grave. That, combined with circumstantial evidence, put Phaan and I in the clear.

They split us up, of course, and sent us to separate sites to finish our original sentences.

Parole came, and I was released back into civilization.

I stayed at my sister's house while I looked for work. It was as discouraging as I'd expected. Even the asteroid miners didn't want me.

But I had to do something—I didn't like the idea of hanging around sis's place, endlessly mooching.

Dad finally came to visit one weekend. He hugged me harder and longer than he ever had in my whole life. He listened to the whole story, about my time on The Island, about the brick sites, about Ivarsen's death. Then he looked me in the eye from across the living room coffee table and suggested I apply to Corrections.

"You've got to be kidding," I said.

"Not at all," Dad said. "This Ivarsen guy, you said he seemed at ease around your crew? Ran the place like it was just another job? The man was obviously an ex con."

I hadn't thought of that before. Ivarsen had seemed too decent to be a criminal.

But then, so were Phaan and I.

The next day, I did what Dad suggested. To my surprise, they picked me up without question. And after twelve weeks at the Corrections Academy they sent me out to run one of the brick sites.

It was interesting being on the flip side of things. I found I actually liked being back in the desert with its blinding sun and fresh air and shimmering desolation. I'd missed it.

Planetary months rolled into a planetary year. Then two. Paycheck after paycheck. With no out-of-pocket cost for room or food, my savings began to pile up. Enough for me to seriously consider my future.

Using my PDA, I got on the Corrections network one night. Within a few minutes, I found Lisa Phaan's file.

She'd been telling the truth about the drug stuff.

But every record since her incarceration showed her clean and included continued reports of good behavior.

I remembered the pleasant sensation of her lips on mine.

Could we have something? Or was I just fooling myself?

Snapping my PDA off, I determined that I'd find out.

Meanwhile, there was always more clay. And there were always more bricks.

Sometimes human colonists themselves can be away so long, they begin seeing the Earth as a romantic, hopeful place different from what their ancestors who founded the colony might remember. In a reverse of our other stories, a bit of a Moses-esque promised land mythology arises amongst a religious sect of isolated colonists in regards to the Earthly home they left behind, driving some of them to live for one goal: to return home. But what if home is not the place their legends recall?

THE FAR SIDE OF THE WILDERNESS

ALEX SHVARTSMAN

One way or another, I'm nearing the end of my journey.

The spaceship is quiet now, except for the low rumble of the engines. It took me days, but I found all of the speakers which were filling the cabins with a cacophony of alarm bells. I pried each speaker open with a knife and cut the little rubbery wires, until the last of the infernal things had finally been silenced.

Deprived of its voice, the ship is blinking lies at me via the console screen. *Warning: low fuel levels. Warning: engine maintenance required. Warning: life support system failure imminent.* I once thought of the ship as a friend, a steed sent by the Creator to be the tool of our deliverance. Somehow, the Deceiver found its way in, wormed inside of the ship's machinery, and is doing whatever it can to break my spirit and thwart me from reaching paradise.

I place the decrepit postcard on top of the screen, covering the red blinking letters, then wrap myself in an extra layer of clothes against the steadily cooling air.

*

On the world of Kemet, we spent our days scavenging. Our tribe traveled to a section of the caves we hadn't been to for a while, long enough for fresh moss to grow on the rocks and tiny gnawers to repopulate. And then we'd make camp and collect the moss and trap the gnawers, and eat for a few days, until food became difficult to obtain and we had to move again.

In the evenings, as we huddled around the fire, Mother and other elders would tell stories.

Mother taught me that, a very long time ago, everyone used to live in paradise. She told me about the world of plenty, the world of blue skies and white clouds, where gentle sunlight bronzed the skin, and the air was thick and smelled of flowers. Countless generations lived in paradise, and they did not know hunger or fear.

She told me about the Deceiver, who whispered from the shadows. It filled people's hearts with pride, and desire, and wanderlust until they built flying machines powerful enough to puncture the sky. They thought themselves equals of the Creator as they crossed the void and spread out across the stars, but all they really accomplished was to deny their children paradise. And the Deceiver rejoiced.

When I was eight, I once hiked to the barren surface in search of the wonderful place from my mother's tales. I walked around for most of the night, until the pale reddish glow of our sun appeared in the East. Soon it would scorch the surface, make it too hot for a human to survive outside. I barely made it back to the caves, sweating and sunburned, choking on the sparse, dusty air. I did not find what I sought, and I began to doubt her stories.

When I confessed my doubts to Mother, she didn't chide me. She reached into her pack and retrieved a bundle wrapped in many layers of cloth. Inside was an ancient picture, a postcard, covered in plastic.

"This is the only image of paradise that survives on Kemet," mother said.

The tribe had a handful of items from before the colonists landed on Kemet. Mostly simple gadgets, built well enough to survive the centuries: flashlights, water purifiers, and drills. But I've never seen anything like this. I reached for the picture with great care.

A bright yellow sun reflected off azure water, more water than I could ever imagine collected in one place. Next to the water grew a cluster of trees, their branches reaching proudly toward the sky. And although the picture was very old and faded, the colors in it were still brighter than anything on my world.

"There is a better place in the universe," Mother said. "A better life. We must never forget this; never surrender our values and our culture, and never descend into barbarism. Then, one day, the Creator will welcome us home."

I cast doubt from my heart and resolved never again to let the Deceiver weaken my faith.

The ship came when we were studying.

Every day, the young ones had to spend two hours on reading and writing and math and all manner of other subjects. Like so many of my friends I often lost patience with learning about things that did not matter on our world, couldn't help fill our stomachs. Mother was patient with me. She explained that we must rise above our circumstances so that one day the Creator would look upon us with pride, forgive our ancestors' transgressions, and bring us back into the fold.

It was while we struggled to memorize the periodic table of elements that there was a rumble and the walls and ceiling of the caves shuddered, shaking loose a shower of pebbles. It felt like a quake, but came from above and not below. When the noise ceased and the shaking stopped, we rushed to the mouth of the cave. Outside, there was the most beautiful thing I had ever seen.

The ship rested on its side wedged between rock formations, its gleaming silver surface out of place in our world. There was a faint glow around the hull, which made the ship look like it had a halo. I knew right away that this was the Creator's gift, the carriage to bring us home to paradise.

We approached the ship and it opened to us, like a desert flower at dawn. Inside, there was death.

We found five bodies inside the ship, and one woman who was still alive, in her quarters.

She was feverish and sick, and we could do nothing except tend to her and make her last days a little more comfortable. I volunteered to stay with her, despite the dire warnings she issued in her rare moments of lucidity. The strange smells and textures of the ship called to me and were too alluring for anything to scare me off.

Her name was Beata and she was an explorer. Her ancestors left paradise at the same time as mine, four hundred years ago, but they landed on a much more hospitable planet than Kemet, and kept on developing their technologies.

This ship was designed to travel from one human colony to another, so that Beata's people could reconnect with their long-lost cousins. She said that they had been to several worlds before something went wrong. There were no people alive on the last planet they had visited, and the crew became sick very soon after taking off. Beata believed that they were exposed to the same virus which must have killed the original colonists, and she begged me to stay away from her lest I contract the disease and pass it on to the rest of my tribe.

Confident that the Creator's favor would protect me, I stayed and questioned Beata about paradise. She said that we came from the planet called Earth and that it was no utopia. Our ancestors poisoned its air and polluted its water, and that's why they had to leave for the stars.

I didn't believe her. Beata's people never lost their technology, or their pride. Their lives weren't harsh so they never found the strength to deny the Deceiver. Their bodies and spirits were too soft and the Creator never forgave them like he did us; that is why I didn't get sick despite spending days in a small room with Beata.

We talked of distant worlds and wonders of space. I told Beata of our life in the caves and she was horrified. She said that her people could help, could carry us to a more hospitable world. That her scout ship was automated, and would eventually return to her home world, and that she would record a message for them once she felt strong enough. But she was getting weaker and weaker. Near the end, she ordered the ship to transfer control to me, and asked me to record the call for help.

We burned Beata's body and scattered the ashes on the same plateau where we burned the bodies of the other explorers, so that Beata could be with her friends in death. That's when I told the others that I could pilot the ship.

It was a lie, of course. Not even Beata could pilot it. Learning that skill took a lifetime of training on her world. All I could do was give the ship's onboard computer basic commands and hope that its machine brain could interpret them right. But it wouldn't do to let the others know this. The Creator had chosen me to lead them home.

*

Twelve of us boarded the ship. It was too small to house the entire tribe, and so the elders decided to send only the young. I wanted so badly for Mother to come, but arguing for this would not have been fair or wise.

She hugged me tight when I was ready to go. Hope and pride shone on her face. She handed me a small bundle. "So you'll never lose your way," she said, her voice trembling.

I claimed the captain's bunk, placing my few belongings in the compartments by its side. Then I unwrapped her gift. It was the postcard, her most prized possession. The yellow sun beckoned to me from the photograph.

"Fly, ship," I implored and the engine roared to life, lifting us toward the arms of the Creator.

Life on the ship was better than the life in the caves. There was a machine that produced an edible paste that was tasteless but filling. Little screens could be made to play music and moving pictures, and the time passed by quickly while we discovered sights and concepts that were previously unfamiliar.

I maintained the illusion of control.

"Take us to paradise," I whispered to the ship when others couldn't hear me.

Unspecified parameters, the ship would answer.

"Earth. Fly us to Earth," I begged.

Unable to alter flight plan, the ship would say.

I knew that surely, with time, I could convince it.

"This place is not what you promised," said my tribesmen when the ship had landed.

Outside, grains of frozen water danced in the frigid air. Everything was covered in white, except the area around the ship where the engines melted the water and uncovered black patches of wet dirt. Beata had said that the ship would travel to planets with known human colonies, but if any people had lived in this inhospitable place, they had long since moved or died.

"The ship needs to rest," I told my people. "It cannot make such a long journey all at once."

They accepted my explanation. We let the ship rest for a while and wandered the alien landscape. Our feet left deep indentations in the frozen water.

There were people on the next world. Millions of lights illuminated cities so large that their outlines could be seen from space. Was this the world of Beata's people? We were eager to meet them.

They fired weapons at us before we even landed. Missiles exploded against the sides of the ship but weren't powerful enough to penetrate the hull. On the ground, war machines rolled toward us from every direction and continued to fire. These people did not see us as long-lost cousins. I asked the ship to carry us away and it complied.

Maintenance and minor repairs are required, the ship blinked at me from the console display.

"It will be all right," I patted the great mechanical steed. "Take us to Earth and the Creator will see to it that you arrive there safely."

We hopped across a dozen different worlds.

We swam in shallow lakes under the light of three moons and walked in fields of wild flowers each twice as tall as a man. But every time we landed on a world with other humans, I refused to open up the ship. The encounter on the war planet had made me cautious, and I couldn't risk the possibility that some bad people might covet our ship and try to take it away.

The ship was asking me for repairs more insistently now, but it was a good and true steed, and it soldiered on despite the fact that I could do nothing to assist it.

That is when we arrived on the world of the purple sun.

The ship landed in an idyllic valley. The purple sun shone above the land of plenty, which burst with a medley of bright colors. Plants swayed gently in the warm breeze. A peaceful, clear spring was lined with trees, their branches weighed down with large, juicy fruit. We explored the valley and the orange grass under our feet felt like the softest blanket.

It was several hours after the landing that strangers emerged from beyond the trees. I was alarmed, but they didn't appear hostile. They wore soft tunics and looked healthy and beautiful. They spoke in a sing-song language we did not understand, but there was kindness in their eyes and smiles on their faces, and soon we were no longer afraid.

We spent nearly two weeks in the company of the Betawi people, and were beginning to learn their language and customs. I enjoyed our stay as much as the others did, but was also impatient to continue the journey.

"Why should we ever leave?" asked my tribesmen. "This world has everything we could ever hope for."

"It's beautiful here," I said. "But it's not our home. The Creator awaits us on Earth. Surely this pleasant oasis is another test of our determination, our faith."

But they wouldn't listen. Not a single one of them would return with me to the ship. I was shocked at the ease with which the others gave up our quest. I would take any risk, give up anything to reach paradise, but my friends were eager to trade the Creator's favor for the promise of comfort this planet offered them. I pled and threatened, all to no avail.

I waited for several more weeks, in hope that time would teach them wisdom. But they were genuinely happy on this world, welcomed and loved by the Betawi, and soon doubt began to creep into my own heart.

I couldn't allow the Deceiver to gain foothold within me again. So I left the others to their new abode and continued the journey alone.

There are so many stars out there, more than one could count in a lifetime. Which one of them holds my salvation?

I have seen more wonders than I could have ever imagined growing up in the caves of Kemet. I have visited dozens of planets: heavens and hells and everything in between. I delivered my people to the far side of the wilderness. Will the Creator reward me for my faith, my stalwart willingness to press on, or punish me for abandoning them there?

I stroke the brittle surface of the postcard. Mother told me, many times, of the blue and white jewel suspended against the black velvet backdrop of the cosmos. More than anything else in the world, I want to see it for myself.

The Deceiver cannot defeat me. Countless generations of my people subsisted in caves but never lost their faith, or their humanity. Their faith kept them going through the worst of it, and the Creator blessed them and called them home. My faith is stronger yet, and The Creator is kind, and will surely allow me a glimpse of paradise, even if only from the distance.

I watch the stars from the viewport of the ship that is dying around me, and I wait.

This anthology might not exist had I not discovered this story. It was reprinted in an anthology Orson Scott Card's Intergalactic Medicine Show, *published by TOR in 2008, and it knocked my socks off. These colonists are just trying to find a new life for themselves, instead they find new life forms that bring new dangers and new fears to life. Autumn Rachel Dryden has since become a dear friend, but this story still moves me as much as it did when I first discovered it. Welcome to the world of scupps and undrus. Welcome to Respite.*

RESPITE

AUTUMN RACHEL DRYDEN

The wagon rumbled and crunched over the scupp shells in the sand. Each time Ann and Edward felt one of them crack under the wheels, they shuddered. The hatching could begin at any time.

The two of them sat silent and tense on the hard wagon bench, their simple black and white clothing a sharp contrast to the dun of the beach dunes and the purple shells thrusting up through the sand all around them. Ann clutched her swollen belly protectively, though she knew she would not be able to save the babe within if the scupps hatched before the wagon reached the shelter of the cliff caves.

"We left too late," Edward said. It had become a litany of sorts.

"We'll make it," Ann replied, because they had to try.

Edward whipped the scaled backs of the placid undru pulling the wagon. Ann could have told him it would do no good; the beasts were doing the best they could already. He glared at Ann's belly before quickly looking away. His look cut Ann to the core. *He's wishing I wasn't here with him, slowing him down. He wishes we had never tried to have this child.*

"And if the babe comes early?" His teeth clenched.

"I'm still glad we're having a child, Edward."

"I don't think you will be after we've been eaten alive by thousands of flying crab-things, shooting out of all of these scupp shells. Especially if we might not have been eaten if you hadn't slowed us down with a premature labor."

"I'm not going to go into labor. Edward, why are you being so hateful?" If I'd known you were like this when I met you, you wouldn't be the father of my baby.

"That should be obvious to the whole world, Ann. We're doomed out here, and we're alone, and if you weren't pregnant none of this would be happening." His arms gestured to include the horizon. Ann thought that he was pushing things a bit. The hatching would happen whether she was pregnant or not.

"May I remind you that I didn't get pregnant all by myself?" She felt her cheeks flush. "And that the main reason we came to Respite was so that we could have freedoms denied to us on Earth—such as having children? That used to matter to you, Edward."

"Freedom is no use if you're dead."

"I'd rather die free than live in the kind of bondage we were under on Earth. I'm still glad I came."

"The scupps are glad too. You'll be a nice meal for them, I'm sure." His lips tightened into a thin line. He didn't look at her. She stared at him, shocked. This place was changing him. And not for the better.

"That was completely uncalled for. You don't have to take your fear out on me."

"So now I'm a coward? I'd like to see the man who *wouldn't* be afraid in my shoes."

"That wasn't my point, Edward. I'm frightened as well. But tearing each other up is not going to solve anything, or help us survive this. I haven't given up yet. But I need you to not give up either."

Edward said nothing more, but his lips were still tight and he began to whip the undru again. Normally Ann would defend the animals, but in this case it was either her or them, and she was tired of Edward taking it out on her. Let the undru have their turn. They had thick scales after all. And whatever Edward might do to their bodies, their hearts could not be touched by him. If only humans could protect themselves so well.

For a long time the two sat silently on the bench, not looking at each other. Ann wanted to just close her eyes. Every direction she could see only dismayed her more. Under them, ahead and behind, there was nothing to look at but the endless purple shells sticking out of the sand. To their right, eastward, the sand eventually changed to brown hills covered with drooping, dying grass. To the west lay only the sea, salty and warm, harboring its own menaces. Overhead the sun shone harshly down from a wheat-colored sky, refusing to hide any of the ugliness around them.

Ann missed their little farm. It hadn't been much, but to her it was the whole world. A few acres tilled and planted, a small, struggling crop of grain, some chickens. They hadn't even had a real house; they lived out of the back of the wagon, and put a canvas cover on it during storms. It had been adequate, or so they thought. Houses and other niceties would have to wait until there was enough food to fill their mouths and that of the offspring soon to come. If any survived.

When the colonists had left Earth, all they knew about their future home was that it was compatible with Earth's atmosphere and climatic conditions. It had only been a number on a map of stars. They had been granted one small, aging starship with which to limp through the light years until they reached their home. The colonists had felt grateful to get it, and did not complain. The resources aboard the craft were barely enough to support the lives of the hundred people on it, even in stasis, but they managed to reach their destination. As a symbol of their new home, each of the colonists chose new names for themselves: plain, old-fashioned names. Like the Quakers or the Puritans on Earth. It was a way to return to simpler times. The landing was less than a year ago, but there were perhaps twenty women already pregnant. Ann was the farthest along.

What a privilege to conceive and bear children when she wanted, with whom she wanted. To live a simple life, free of mindless machines and the hive mind of an omnipotent government. Though the scupps were quite a trade-off to make.

As if reading her thoughts, the babe within her somersaulted. Ann gasped and clutched her stomach, then laughed. The sensation was so odd. No matter how often she felt it, she never got tired of the reminder that there was life within her womb.

Edward glared at her and said, "How can you laugh at a time like this? We could die, Ann. I thought you realized that."

Ann sobered a bit, but couldn't help saying, "Edward, if there is ever a day in my life in which I cannot laugh, that is the day I will die."

The wagon jerked, much harder than usual, and Ann grabbed Edward's arm for balance. Then the wagon was still. The undru strained, trying to pull the cart along, but it wouldn't budge. Edward cursed under his breath and hopped off the bench, looking at the wheel. It had cracked on a sharp stone sticking out of the sand. The axle was broken. There was no way to fix it.

"We aren't going to make it," Edward said. He was staring at the broken axle. Finally, he sat down and began to weep. Huge, racking sobs, tearing through his body. Ann had never seen Edward express so much emotion. Carefully she climbed down from the high wagon bench and joined him. She put her arms around him and said nothing for a time; just held him. Ann's eyes were still dry, which surprised her. If anyone had told her even a year ago that she would one day be cradling her husband, her strong man, in her arms while he sobbed his heart out to her and she remained unaffected, she would have laughed in their face. Yet the truth was undeniable. She was stronger than Edward.

She realized that she had always been stronger than him, but had never before admitted it, even to herself. Instead she had borne his weaknesses alongside her own strength, defending him, excusing him. What must the other colonists have thought of me? Knowing that I was married to a weakling, yet unable to see it? Perhaps that was why Edward had been so eager to establish their farm so far away from everyone else. Alone with her, he could be with the one person who did not despise him. But I do despise him. Now, when it is too late. Our fate is already sealed, and by my hand as much as his. Yet I must go on. I must be strong, for both of us.

After she felt he had had enough time to get himself together, she said, "Come on, Edward. We need to go."

"Go where? How? There's nowhere to go. We'll never make it."

"Edward, stop it. You're giving up. We still have the undru. And I can walk if I have to. The cliffs can't be too far off. Maybe a day's walk or so. We'll make it."

Edward just put his head in his hands in reply. Ann sighed, then got to her feet and went over to unhitch the placid, patient undru. They were native to Respite, and had taken the place of Earth oxen, which did not thrive on this planet. They were large, reptilian beasts with short stubby tails and a broad bony plate across their head. They looked more like dinosaurs than anything else, but they were quite gentle and easily tamed. They had stiff overlapping scales, like chain mail, covering most of their body, a natural protection from the claws and jaws of the myriad tiny scupp hatchlings. When the hatching took place, the undru would squat down and curl into themselves, exposing their scaly backs and nothing else to the onslaught. At least, Ann assumed that would happen; she had seen the undru, when frightened, do that in the past. The colonists had not yet been on Respite long enough to really know what to expect of many of the animals on it.

Only one colonist had seen a hatching and survived; he had managed to find shelter in a hole in the ground, blocking it from the inside with rocks as the scupps swarmed all around it. The scupps were purple buzzing flying discs the size of Earth locusts, that had lots of tiny black claws and a mouth like a crab, except that crabs didn't fly and eat people. The man, Daniel, had returned to the cliff caves that were the landing base of the colonists and told his frightening tale.

He had been exploring the coast in an area where none of the colonists had yet been, when one morning he noticed a few purple spots in the sand. He examined a few, and found that they were all large shells, shaped like clams or oysters, larger than a man's head, buried in the sand, and burrowing to the surface. Over the next few days, the shells stuck farther and farther out of the sand until they were completely exposed on the surface. There were now thousands of them. Then they hatched open, revealing the swarming death within that shot towards the sky in a cloud.

He was lucky to survive, in his hole in the ground. The others who had gone with him had not been so lucky. Only their bones remained to show they had ever existed.

Word was sent to all the outlying farms to watch for the scupp shells and stay away from the coasts, and to return to the cliffs as soon as possible, since no one knew how widespread the hatching would be, or how many more times it would happen that season. For some reason, the scupps seemed to stay out of caves during the one hatching that Daniel witnessed. The theory was that because the caves were bare rock there was nowhere for the scupps to burrow to hibernate and transform, before again rising to the surface. The shells could be cracked with a hard blow, but there were too many for that to be effective. The colonists in the cliffs were experimenting with ways to kill the scupps before the next hatching, but so far had been unable to find anything that worked.

Ann and Edward received the warning, but Edward insisted that they were far enough inland that they were not in immediate danger. Besides, the grain would be ready to harvest in a couple of weeks. They were probably okay to wait until their crop was ready to go back to the cliff caves. Ann reminded Edward that they had to cut back to the coast to reach the caves; the nearest inland route was many miles longer and impassible for the wagon; a road had not yet been cleared through the thick vegetation. Edward was confident that they could make it, though, so they had stayed. And I stayed with him. I could have left; could have made him leave. But I didn't. I thought he was the strong one then.

Yesterday morning, Ann found a purple spot on the ground near their well. Edward examined it and their worst fears were realized; it was a scupp shell, barely peeking through the earth. Immediately they threw their few belongings together and loaded the wagon, catching the chickens as fast as they could. They had been traveling steadily ever since, even through the night. They only stopped for brief intervals to rest and water the undru. As they traveled, the shells became more and more plentiful. Now, as Ann looked about her, most of the shells were at least three quarters of the way through the sand. How much longer did they have? Would it be long enough?

She tied their water skins and some of their blankets on the back of one of the undru, to serve as a sort of saddle. Undru weren't ordinarily ridden by humans; their backs were a bit too broad and their scales were intensely uncomfortable to sit on. Ann felt that in this instance she had no choice. She couldn't walk far or fast enough to beat the hatching, and needed to ride.

"Edward, I need you to help me mount." During Ann's exertions, Edward hadn't gotten up. He simply sat, staring at a scupp shell near his feet. Now he rose wordlessly and helped Ann clamber up the back of the undru. When she was sitting unsteadily on the beast, he stopped moving again. "Let's go, Edward." He seemed drained; the anger was gone, but so was his will to live, apparently. Why wouldn't he fight?

"Edward, I don't want to leave you behind. You are my husband."

"Some husband I've been to you."

"We don't have time for this right now. We've got to get going. If you aren't going to help yourself, help your child. The baby needs you to not give up."

"It won't matter whether I give up or not. The end result is the same."

"It *will* be the same if you don't get moving. Help me, Edward."

He said nothing, but his lips were once more in that tight line she had come to hate. He turned away. Ann finally let herself get angry. "All right. Stay here then. I'm taking the undru. No reason for innocent creatures to die along with you. Goodbye." And if the child is a boy, I'm not going to name him Edward.

She tugged on the reins of the undru she was riding, and it started plodding northwards again, its companion rumbling forward with them. They were still yoked together. She had thought about leaving one behind for Edward, but the yoke was too heavy for her and he hadn't seemed to care enough to take it off himself.

"Wait. I'm coming." Edward ran up beside the undru.

Ann was relieved. She really hadn't wanted to leave him behind.

Now that they were moving again, Edward seemed to be more like his old self. He had always preferred action to sitting still. That was probably why he had become a colonist in the first place; to avoid stagnation.

She looked down into his face, wondering how he was feeling. He avoided meeting her gaze. He knows that I'm the stronger one, and he can't deal with that. Has he always known that?

The afternoon passed very slowly. There wasn't anything to do but look at their doom drawing near. No time to stop and cook a meal, so there wasn't anything to eat. The undru was very uncomfortable to ride, and at intervals Ann had to dismount and walk beside Edward. Then she would get out of breath and start to feel dizzy, and Edward would help her remount. Ann had been ill much of the pregnancy, and traveling so near to her time wasn't helping matters at all. She wanted so desperately to just give up and lie in the sand, regardless of the consequences.

But I can't do that. Not when I have a child who is relying on me.

In the evening, the pains started.

Ann didn't notice at first because she hurt all over anyway, but by full dark she could no longer put it out of her mind: her back was aching deeply, and she was starting to feel contractions. Edward was right. The babe would come early. She was afraid to tell him about it though, for fear of his reaction. He had been so strange lately.

I don't know if I can trust him to stay sane long enough to reach the cliffs anyway, much less if I tell him that his prediction came true. So with each contraction I'll hold my breath and try not to show him my pain.

The hours continued to pass with agonizing slowness, Ann's rhythmic pain the only thing marking the passage of time. At one point, she didn't know when, she felt her waters stream down her leg and soak the blankets on the undru's back. Ann had stopped thinking clearly a while before that. She hadn't slept in two days now, and with labor on top of her exhaustion, there wasn't much room in her mind for thoughts. She clutched the bony plate on the undru's neck to keep her balance, and half dozed even through the pain.

Edward seemed oblivious to what she was suffering. He kept his head down, looking at the shells in the dim starlight, walking beside the undru.

At long last, the sun rose over the ocean. It brought a welcome sight: the cliffs were ahead. Ann could even make out the cave openings, very small. Safety was within reach.

We're going to make it.

Then she looked down at the ground. The shells were completely out of the sand now, and lay like fat upright fans on the ground, with a seam showing at the top of each one. The seams hadn't been visible yesterday. That meant the hatching was soon, very soon.

"Edward?" The sound was faint coming from Ann's throat. Her pain was suddenly very strong. She felt herself sliding off the back of the undru. Edward caught her and eased her to the ground. Ann clutched her belly and writhed, screaming. The contractions were unbearable, a continuous unrelenting agony. My mind is going to fracture. I can't do this. Edward I can't do this. Help me.

She wasn't speaking out loud, wasn't even aware that she wasn't. She dimly heard Edward, from a long way away, say, "Ann. Ann, listen to me. The baby is coming. I'll help you with the baby, Ann. Can you hear me?" Yes. Edward. I hear you. But the words stuck in her throat as another contraction, the strongest of all, came. She could feel her child being born.

In a short time, or maybe a long time, Ann didn't know, she was holding her bloody child in her arms, with Edward leaning over her.

"It's a boy, Ann," he said. That part she heard. The baby cried, weakly. Then she heard something else. The undru were moaning.

The hatching was beginning.

Only a few feet away, Ann saw a scupp shell begin to rock back and forth. Everywhere the shells were moving. Edward jumped to his feet in terror.

"Oh god, Ann. We're too late. It's starting."

The undru began to lower themselves onto their knees, their heads pulling in towards their chests.

"Edward. Edward, listen." His eyes were wild and she didn't know if she had the strength to make him hear her. "The undru."

"What about the undru? They'll survive without my help. We're the ones who will die, Ann. We didn't make it, after all. I was right!" He started laughing. It was not a sane sound.

"Edward. Take the baby. Hide inside the undru." She pulled weakly at the knife on her belt. Edward had one too. At last he understood what she meant.

There was a moment that seemed to last an eternity in which Edward was obviously torn between making a run for the caves—so near!—leaving her and the baby to their fate, or staying to help his family, his flesh and blood. Ann held her breath and simply stared into his eyes, willing him to be a man, to do the right thing. Then he blinked and looked away from her, his decision made.

He whipped out his own knife and turned to the nearest of the two beasts. The undru were hooting and moaning, and trying to crunch into protective balls. The yoke prevented them from completing their crouches. Edward was still able to get to the softer underbelly of the near one. Thank god his knife was sharpened recently. A large red gash appeared where Edward slashed at the animal. He dug his hands into the side of the undru, ignoring its bellows and struggles to get away from him. He pulled out handfuls of steaming innards, gagging and coughing at the stench and the sight of the animal's viscera, then turned to Ann. As he picked her and the baby up, the shells opened, disgorging their contents in a violent spew towards the sun. He ran with her to the bleeding carcass, and began to pull open the tough side of the creature, to make a space for her. She tried to get him to take the baby and save himself, but he either didn't understand her or chose to ignore her, continuing to open the belly of the undru.

All at once, the sky darkened with teeming untold numbers of flying discs. They began to land on Ann, on Edward, on everything. As soon as one landed the disc sprouted claws, and a mouth. Then it began to feed on any creature in its path. The bites were excruciating, and Ann found herself writhing around in an attempt to beat them off her body and that of her son. They came off easily, but there were so many of them that she would be unable to hold them off for long.

Edward shoved Ann and the baby into the body of the animal. He barely got them in, Ann shielding her son with her body and trying to make sure the baby had air, before turning to the other undru, to slash its belly open and make room for himself. But he was too late. The undru had managed to complete its crouch, and now its scales were a defense against Edward's knife, as much as from the scupps.

He was forced to turn back to the first undru and try to squeeze himself into the opening that was already a tight fit for Ann. He couldn't get completely inside. The scupps began to feed on Edward's unprotected back. She desperately tried to make room for him, but he couldn't come any farther.

Edward bit his lips, but couldn't keep from screaming with the pain. He forced his body to remain still, to block the opening, protecting Ann and the baby. He could have run, but he didn't. Ann looked into his eyes. He hadn't been a coward after all, at the end, when it mattered. She should be the one dying, the one protecting him. She was the strong one. But she couldn't help feeling glad that she would live, despite her guilt at watching Edward die in her place.

"I love you, Edward." She had said it before. She realized now that she meant it.

"Love. You. Ann." The words were bitten out through the pain. Then one of the scupps burrowed into Edward's spine, and he suddenly went limp. His body blocked the scupps from coming further into the undru's carcass and feeding on Ann as well, but that wouldn't hold them for long. She had to think, to be strong still. Edward's death was not enough.

Ann sobbed inside the undru, holding her son, looking at her husband, his now dead eyes staring unblinkingly back at her. She forced herself to burrow deeper into the beast, retching with the stench and hot closeness and blood. She was up behind the ribcage now, and she pressed against the lungs and heart of the beast. She found the windpipe and tore it free, letting a bit more air into the cramped space. The scupps were eating behind her, she could hear them everywhere.

Nearly blinded by the darkness and the gore, her sense of hearing was heightened as never before. As she listened, the sound changed. The scupps were doing something different now. They were scraping against each other, shell on shell, rhythmically, hypnotically. The sounds of chewing stopped, changed to an odd vibrating hiss. The sound was frightening, but not as menacing as the chewing. She slid back down to Edward's body, or what was left of it, and peered out.

The scupps were changing. The little discs were now completely unfurled, and were more oblong than round, one side rough and shell-like, the other raw and unprotected. I must remember this and tell the others. When they are like this we can find a way to defeat them. As she watched, the scupps rubbed over and under each other, hissing, until two of them rubbed raw sides over each other and stopped, fastened together, with only the rough outsides exposed. Then others paired off, and more, until the ground was covered with very small versions of the large scupp shells, with only seams to show that what had once been two creatures was now one.

The scupp shells burrowed back into the earth, hiding themselves once more from view, as the cycle began anew.

Ann crawled carefully from the body of the undru. Its hide had protected her, but Edward had saved her. He was little more than a skeleton now, though his face had largely escaped the predations. He looked at peace to Ann. In fact, he looked strong.

She looked up at the cliff caves, and saw people pouring out of them, running to meet her, now that the scupps were no longer a threat. She sat, grateful that her journey was at an end, nursing her son, waiting for them to come. The thought that life had come from so much death was soothing to her, and she rocked her son in her arms and crooned to him as she nursed.

Nathaniel was the first of the people to reach her.

"My god. What happened to Edward? How did you make it? We couldn't quite see what was happening here. I wish we could have come to help you. We had no way to get past the scupps." He knelt beside her, concern on his face. The others examined the body of her husband, and that of the undru that had to die for her to live. The other undru was still alive, and trying to get up out of the crouch, but was hampered by the yoke and the dead weight of its companion. Two of the men removed the yoke and helped the undru to its feet, then loaded Edward's body carefully onto it, to take back to the cliffs for burial.

"Edward was very brave. In the end, when it mattered. He might have made it, if only he'd left me behind and run for it. But he stayed. He was strong for me. I was too weak. I wouldn't have survived on my own."

The others exchanged glances at this, probably wondering how to compare this new description of Edward with the way they had previously viewed him. Let them never know how he was during the journey. I will never shame his memory. His sacrifice is enough, his penance completed.

"We used the undru hide as protection. In future, we should all have hides with us to use as a shield, so we are never caught like that again. I saw how the scupps mate. They are vulnerable and soft on one side, just before they join together into new scupp shells. We can use that to our advantage. This planet can still be a good home for us, for our children."

"This is my son," she held him up for everyone to see. The first child born on Respite. The hope of the future. The source of her strength. "His name is Edward."

Not everyone who comes to a colony is seeking a new life. Some come with other motives. Josaiah Parker is one of those, and, in this case, his zealous enthusiasm brings dire consequences for himself and those who've followed him. Set in the universe of her Philip K. Dick Award nominated military science fiction series "Theirs Not To Reason Why," Jean Johnson's story packs a punch.

PARKER'S PARADISE

JEAN JOHNSON

June 13, 2417 Terran Standard

Josaiah Emmanuel Bartholomew Parker should have been a side-show barker. Instead, he was the charismatic head of the Parker's Paradise Colonial Expedition, and was even now conducting a very spirited bidding auction on who would get to have the right to be one of the first one hundred colonists to step foot on their impending new homeworld, on a site ". . . specially selected to be the single most beautiful view of our glorious new home!"

Sarah Draper, first officer of the refurbished, second-hand Terran United Planets Colony Ship *Sluggo's Motorboat*, didn't believe a word of it. Oh, he sounded sincere, and if a psi had scanned him for truth-telling, he probably would be judged as believing every single word. Sarah . . . didn't.

She shifted at her post, leaning against the upper balcony railing, a laser rifle cradled in her arms, a projectile rifle and a stunner clipped into their holders on the railing. Bored, she glanced to the side, where her partner, Gunner Greg Cueto, stood on the other side of the balcony on the upper level. Tall, lean and dark, hair twisted in spiky short columns, Cueto slouched with his rifle set on a swiveling pivot attached to the railing. The muzzle pointed up . . . but his forefinger and thumb were lined up with Josaiah Parker's head, and she could hear faint "Pkeww!" noises over the headsets linking the two of them.

Technically, there should have been six gunners on duty on the upper balcony, but Parker had insisted otherwise, citing it "wasn't necessary."

Nothing in this rapidly collated colonial expedition felt right to her. *The permits were garnered far too fast. We haven't spent enough time in orbit. There's not enough infrared readings to indicate a decent amount of foliage at the selected landing site, compared with the original charts. We haven't sent down more than five probes to cover an area five thousand kilometers wide—cheapskate—so we don't fully know what's down there. And the Captain is far too easily bribed.*

I honestly don't think the survey scouts are done with their drone-analyses of all potential hazards on this planet. And the planet's too heavy to safely land the ship and take off again. Not without a ready source of water nearby, but Parker wants us to land away from that lake and river. Yes, yes, the proposed landing site is both large and flat and low-vegetation enough to fit the Motorboat, but we'll run out of hose trying to reach water if we're not very careful.

Unfortunately, she wasn't the pilot, so she couldn't tell Parker to stuff it. Landing a CS was not like landing an orbital shuttle, something she could do. Colony Ships, based on V'Dan designs, had the capacity to descend through an atmosphere and touch down with minimum impact on a surface. They were huge, though, with great engines that shivered and thrummed through the deckplates despite layers of insulation and shielding.

Orbital shuttles ranged from a dozen meters to a hundred in size, but a typical Colony Ship was over a kilometer long, a third of that wide, and half again as high. The Motorboat was no exception. It was designed to serve as the intial base while the colonists worked on digging in and building their new homes, but could lift off—with enough hydrofuel—and retreat if a planet turned out to be too dangerous despite previous surveillance attempts.

On M-class worlds, ones with breathable atmospheres and habitable temperature ranges, the ship could be opened up directly and construction materials for housing and the like disembarked through the great cargo ramps lining the lowest decks. On worlds without breathable atmospheres, construction usually began at extendable airlock gantries so they could start building the initial ring-like foundation chambers for the colony's first dome.

Parker's Paradise was an M-class world with slightly warmer than average temperatures, a very breathable atmosphere with a slightly higher than average oxygen ratio, and—according to the reports Parker had shown everyone repeatedly—virtually no viruses, bacteria, or other assorted pathogens that were considered invasively compatible with the biology of the three most heavyworld-adaptable species: Humans, the felinoid Solaricans, and the chitonous, multi-legged, spider-like K'Katta.

"—Do I hear ten thousand and five credits! Ten thousand and five—ten and twenty! Do I hear ten and thirty, ten and thirty—ten thousand and twenty credits from Lord Frrrasten, our noble Solarican backer! Going once . . . ?"

Noble backer, my asteroid belt, Sarah snorted.

She wasn't the only one amused by that lie. Frrrasten was as dark-furred as the Human woman was dark-skinned, but unlike the ship's first officer, he had a dark heart to match. He knew who and what he was, a hunter-killer, a throwback to the ancient days. Part of him longed for the days when the strong took whatever they wanted from the weak by claws and by teeth. These days, one had to amass power through boardroom deals and bribes. By restling with laws, not with beasts. Gathering money, not goods.

He wasn't the most powerful at the boardroom deal; the Alliance was but one corner, one pocket of the Solarican empire. Elsewhere, he would have to follow the rules more carefully, but a fresh start on a new world, with all of a firstworlder's rights...land, and property, and power. A chance to ensure there *weren't* stupid restrictive laws. *How do these Humans say it? Big fish in a very little pond. A gamble, but worth the odds.*

"Going twice . . . ?"

His ears twitched at Parker's words. How he wanted to slash out the idiot's throat. He knew cons; he ran them as just another claw in hand, one of many such weapons to scratch for opportunities, tear down barriers, and climb for power.

". . . Did I mention these were for the first Firstworlder step? Yes, that's right, folks, I am selling my land rights to be the very first person on this planet as your colonial settlement leader, and will be instead choosing a patch of land after everyone else in this settlement has selected theirs. So...do I hear more than ten thousand and twenty credits?"

"Fifty thousand credits!" "—No, sixty!" "*Seventy*-five!" The bidding shot up hard and high once more in a babble of voices.

Lord Frrasten flattened his ears in annoyance, but let it drive up as people gambled their life savings on being the very first settler. He watched Joseph Parker smirk at the sound of all that desperation. There were a few others who were willing to gamble huge fortunes on making little dynastic empires for themselves and their cublings here on Parker's perfect new world . . . but none could match his wealth, or the gamble he was about to take with it.

First Footfall for the average settler meant gaining a large chunk of primary real-estate. But First Footfall for the settlement leader... *that* meant claiming the primary chunk of real-estate for the capital city, which would be built on the low plateau beyond the *Motorboat's* landing-ramps. *That* would be worth spending up to half of his own fortune in grabbing for that much power. *Let the grass-eaters bleat for their share of the meadow. I will take the mountain.*

He drew in a breath to speak. The ship's intercom whistled loudly, cutting through the bidding. It took a few moments for the rest to quiet down and listen, but that didn't stop Captain Sluggovisk from speaking over them.

"Attention, all hands. The Motorboat will be reaching the surface in three minutes. Post-landing procedures will be strictly followed, including a twenty-minute surveillance check by drone sweeps. If all goes well, the ramp will descend in time to greet the dawn...in a dramatic and glorious welcome-home to all the new colonists of Parker's Paradise."

The last was recited in a dry voice. Milo Sluggovisk was just as cynical as his first officer, however bribable. Frrrasten had gotten his personal entourage onto the ship without any security checks, thanks to the Captain's avaricious nature, though none of them were in this group of one hundred thanks to the luck of the lottery draw.

"Two minutes forty-seconds to touchdown. That is all."

"One quarrrter milllionnn crrredits," Frasten stated, cutting off the next round of bidding. His offer beat the last number by a cool seventy thousand. The awkward silence that followed made him purse his lips forward in a Solarican-style smile. He would have grinned Human style, baring his teeth, but knew that these Humans would assume it was a feral expression—he *felt* like a hunter jumping down on its prey, but he didn't want these furless sentients to *realize* it just yet. *The planet and its laws will be reshaped into a* hunter's *paradise . . . not a stupid grass-eater's.*

"Well, then, it seems we have our new First Footfall leader!" Parker stated, smiling warmly. Bombastically. "Let us bow our heads in prayer during the landing, shall we?"

Frrrasten flicked his ears carefully upright, rather than letting them flatten. He was not one to pray to any gods, false or true. But Humans could read ear-posture, too, for all their own were stupidly immobile. *First chance to make it an "accident" . . . you stupid, furless, grass-tongued, would-be Seer . . .*

"Feel like you're armed for bear?" Greg murmured half over his headset, half to her directly as their erstwhile "leader" began a prayer session.

"Only if it's a Parker's Paradise bear," Sarah shot back. "Wish we had more though."

"Paranoid much?" he asked, though her lanky shipmate didn't say it with any heat. He, too, didn't like this setup.

"Something about this doesn't feel right," she murmured, mindful of the passing of time. Down below, the Solarican won the bid.

"Heh, think you're turning into a precog?" Greg quipped.

"If I am, it's only a Rank 1 or 2. But better—*ack!*" The ship jolted. Staggering, she braced one hand against the railing; the floor had canted just enough to feel it in her inner ear. Touchdown wasn't completely smooth, it seemed; no doubt the soil underneath the landing struts had shifted under their weight. After a moment, the ship leveled itself. "Damned *shakk*-poor choice for a landing site."

"Let's hope the local fauna are friendly," Greg pointed out, slipping on a headset with eye-wires as well as earbuds and voice pickups. "I don't like how far we'll have to run the hoses."

Sarah donned hers as well. Hefting the laser rifle she grunted. "You don't like it?"

He eyed her. "Do you really expect that much trouble?"

"What do *you* think?" Sarah stared down at the civilians on the

main deck. Only Lord Frrrasten looked bored; the rest looked like
they had swallowed everything Parker was spewing.

"... To the God or Goddess whom many of us believe in, to
the whims of Fate and the Stars for the rest, and the determinism
and determination which have brought all of us together here on this
hallowed, heavenly sphere, this blessed new world, this new home,
full of hopes and dreams, angelic wishes and . . ."

*Nothing but bilgewater being poured over shaved ice, if you
ask me. With our luck, this really will be a peaceful landing, and
Parker's Paradise will be turned into a religious nut farm as more of
the "faithful" flock forward and pass their hard-earned credits on to
the nuttiest of the lot. Too bad, Parker; I'm not one of your faithful. I
have a job to do. And I'll do it with or without you.*

"*First Officer Draper, reporting in. What's the look of things out
there?*" she asked, adjusting her headset.

"*Lots of large biomasses moving about,*" the bridge tech, Ned
Chan-Trask, informed her. His voice was a soothing baritone in her
ears, if slightly dry. She could hear the beeps and clicks and faint
murmurs of the others manning the bridge in the background. "*Still
not sure how such big beasts can get around on such a heavy-gravitied
world. Which reminds me, don't forget there'll be a distinct drop in
any projectile fire once it clears the counter-gravity we're generating
in the ceiling weaves.*"

"*Any patterns to their movements?*" Sarah asked, seeing a blob of
transparent colors through her view of the hull. "*Numbers?*"

"*About thirty or so, most of 'em scattered. A few are in groups
or three or four,*" Ned added in her ears. "*It's warm outside, close
to thirty celsius, so the thermal scans aren't giving us much more
than that. Lux magnification shows movement, but not shape; they're
using the rocks and what looks like half-dried vegetation for cover.
Can't say if they're hostile or not, yet.*"

"*How's the rest of the 'congregation' reacting to Big P's flowery
speech?*"

"*Like converts who've seen the Devil, and are now at a two-
for-one Save Your Souls special at Sunday Mass, eyes glued to the
screens and hands clasped in prayer.*"

"Charming," she muttered, staring at the as-yet unopened doors.
"*All this new-paradise-planet shakk is unnerving me. Have we
extended the shield pylons yet?*"

The link fell silent as he put her on hold for a few moments, then he came back. *"Pylons are out, but the shields are off, as per our contract with Preacher Parker down there."*

"Idiot preacher. We're ready when you are."

"Understood. Operations out," Ned replied, ending the connection.

"Keep your eyes open," Sarah warned her partner. With Parker's stupid trust in his own drivel, there weren't many weapons present at this "momentous occasion" of claiming the planet for settlement. In fact, he actually used those words, right after she thought them. Thankfully, the ship's intercom whistled again, interrupting Parker's long-winded speech. He hastily brought it to a close just in time for Captain Sluggovisk's next words.

"Attention, all hands; preliminary surveys suggest it is safe to open the main landing bay. All hands, all colonists, prepare for First Landing. Remember the protocols, meioas. There are thirty-nine local lifeforms larger than your head within one quarter kilometer of the ship, and hundreds more that are head-sized down to insect level. Opening the bay doors in three . . . two . . . one . . ."

Sarah bent low over her rifle, peering through the sight as the doors opened.

Frrrasten squinted against the draft that whistled in the moment the far wall—in reality a huge door—cracked open and started swinging out and downward. Dust swirled in, sharp and tangy with unfamiliar smells. Not a bad set of smells, almost lemony, with a hint of pepper. He didn't trust it. The more Parker insisted this world was peaceful, the more it *seemed* that way . . . the less the Solarican trusted it.

The Captain's timing was impeccable, however. The dust had almost settled when a last bit whooshed up with the landing of the ramp on the ground. At the same moment, the local sun broke over the far horizon, blue-white and sharp when seen from space, but with a golden-red cast to it here on the ground. Off in the distance, a flock of something vaguely bird-shaped took wing, marking the sky with a half-dozen tiny, dark silhouettes.

If it weren't for the desert-like appearance of the landing site, with its sparse, half-dessicated bushes and scrubby tufts of grass-analogs, it would have indeed looked like a slice of paradise. The rising sun dead ahead didn't help with seeing details, but the moving shapes of the local fauna were visible. The felinoid noted how the different kinds were not only avoiding being too close to each other, but were eyeing each of the other kinds warily.

Some looked like lone hunter types. Others, the groups of three, were either herd beasts or pack hunters. He knew that curiosity, that sense of weighing the risks versus the potential rewards when in new territory. Frrrasten dropped his hand to the Terran-style projectile pistol strapped to his thigh.

"Sign here," Josaiah Parker stated, his face grass-eater cheerful but his eyes hunter hard, "and the very first step is yours, meioa."

Ears flicking, he lifted his other hand to the transaction pad. Pressing his thumb to the scanner square, he let the machine register his identity, authorizing the transfer of two hundred fifty thousand credits from the account he had linked to Parker's database for this moment. Once it was done, he released the pad and stepped forward.

Frrrasten paused at the very edge of the ramp, milking the moment for his own brand of drama, then deliberately stepped onto the soil of Parker's Paradise.

Nothing happened, other than a faint <u>crunch</u> from his boot striking the gritty soil.

He brought his other foot to land next to it, and a cheer spontaneously arose. His fellow colonists applauded. Lips pursed in a felinoid smirk, he turned, bowed more or less in Human fashion— wobbled and grunted from the strain of the extra gravity pulling down on all his bones—then the Solarican straightened again. Turning back to the rest of their newly claimed home, Frrrasten stepped forward.

He didn't go far, but he did leave plenty of room along the edge of the broad metal ramp for the others to join him. Excited, his fellow colonists hurried down the ramp, not quite pushing, but eager to follow in his footsteps. *Grass-eaters, assuming I'm their herder, and not their hunter.*

Maybe I will herd them for a bit, before I, what do the Terrans say? Ah yes, fleece them alive. Sheep, that's the type of grass-eater they are, more useful still alive than hanging in the larder. Eyes flicking over the colonists, he returned them repeatedly to the horizon, and the shapes lurking there. Some of them . . . were coming closer. *But are these hunters, or are they also sheep?*

*

"*Sarah, three degrees off dead ahead, starboard,*" Greg murmured over their linked headsets. "*You see it?*"

She nodded. "I do. There's a single off to the side—three hundred forty-ish degrees—that looks twice the size of it."

Off to her left, at the edge of her peripheral vision, she saw him shift a bit. He peered through his scope, then chuckled. "Okay, that has gotta be a Parker's Paradise bear. It's big, it's lumbering, and it's furry."

"If that's a Parker's bear, then those trio-of-things are Parker's pups," she shot back. "Parker's dogs? Parker's wolves?"

"Tell ya what. If they're friendly, we'll call 'em Parker's pups. If they're unfriendly, Parker's wolves," he joked back.

"Wolves actually tended to leave people alone," Sarah pointed out. Then grimaced. Parker had moved back as the colonists moved forward, and was now climbing up the access ladder to the second level. "Oh great, the bombastic bastard's coming up here . . ."

Ned's voice interrupted their banter. "*Heads up, everyone; they're getting close. Captain's keeping the other bays closed, just in case.*"

Both crewmembers fell silent. The odd trio of not-wolves moved closer, as did the not-a-bear. Even Joseph Parker noticed their approach, but then he now had the same fine vantage point for viewing the world beyond the doors as the first officer and her crewmate did. Grinning, he held up his hands. "See? See that, everybody? Even the local animals have come out of God's green glory to welcome us to our new home!"

Sarah snorted. His "green glory" was more brown and sere at the moment. Still, the animals approached with what looked like equal parts curiosity and wariness, their eyes on the one sentient farther out than the rest, the Solarican who might or might not be a crimelord.

As the beast approached, its hide mottled to blend in with the dull vegetation, Frrrasten held himself very still. He kept one hand still on the grip of his pistol, ears picking up the sounds of Parker's hired guards *finally* raising their stunner rifles. *If they were* my *guards . . .*

they'd be whipped until they bled, he thought, sternly controlling the urge to flick his ears and lash his tail. Any sudden movement might spook the native creature coming to greet him.

If they're grass-eaters and friendly, they might be tasty, and tameable, he thought, mind racing over the profit-making possibilities. New sources of edible protein are always a good market . . . particularly from a world where the local pathogens cannot infect us.

The bear stopped a couple yards from him, whuffed at the air, then slowly eased forward. No fool, the Solarican eased his weapon out of its holster. The not-a-dog's companions moved a little closer. Parker muttered something about ". . . making friends with our new neighbors," and Frrrasten lifted his free hand. He spread the claw-tipped digits slightly, letting the beast smell his version of fingers, but ready to withdraw it or attack in a warning slash.

An odd, almost musical whine rose up from the beast's throat. Three tones, two of them aligned in harmony but one slightly off-set from the others. Behind it, the other two not-dogs lifted their heads, tripart jaws gaping slightly. The second one yipped, the third one whined—and the one in front of Frrrasten lunged faster than even the heavyworld-bred hunter could react, snapping its mouth around the outstretched limb with an audible snap.

Frrrasten hissed in pain-filled rage and whipped out his gun, firing it with a trio of bangs that echoed into the landing bay. The thug-guards fired their stunners in pzzzt-flashes of energy. Hunter-red filled his vision even as the beast whipped its head back reflexively, ripping off chunks of the Solarican's hand that made him roar, one thought alone on his mind:

Death! DEATH to them ALL!

Blood fountained up and splattered out even as the retort of the gun echoed off the walls. Cursing under her breath, Sarah sighted on the animals beyond the range of those stunner rifles and pulled the trigger of her own weapon. It made no noise as the deep red light lanced outward. The laser scored smoking lines on tawny hides as several more beasts lunged their way, but it was hard to catch vital organs on creatures with utterly unknown biology.

The other beasts were very fast. Disturbingly so for the gravity. What had been a couple hundred meters were crossed with remarkable speed by the large, six-legged things. Screaming settlers bolted into the landing bay. The nearest trio, the Parker's wolves, staggered but did not go down; it seemed they were just a little too large for the current stunner settings to handle.

Three thugs were slaughtered by almost casual claw-wipes while they tried to readjust their nozzle cones for a tighter, more intense beam. Another had his yell cut off when the not-a-bear slammed its spike-tipped tail through his chest. The Solarican, Frrrasten, had emptied his gun and was now tearing into one of the beasts with teeth and claws, showing just how far his species had *not* come from their earliest, most primitive days.

Sweating, Sarah gave up on the ineffective laser rifle—the damned felinoid was doing more damage than she was! Tossing it aside, she fumbled the projectile rifle into place. Two shotgun clips tumbled out of her pockets and off the upper balcony before she got one properly loaded, and then the *BLAM* of the shells being launched echoed loudly off the hard metal walls of the landing bay.

Most of her targets were the incoming beasts. Half were too slow; the ship's shields, activated belatedly, pushed them out with a rippling shimmer that made her eyes twitch. The rest died on the rocky ground in front of the landing ramp, thanks to her and Greg. Turning her attention to the interior of the bay, she found the remainder finally knocked unconscious on the deck, along with several bleeding colonists.

Methodically, ruthlessly, the first officer used her vantage point to fire more long-range shotgun rounds into the stunned fauna, several rounds to ensure they stayed down. Shocked quiet followed, broken only by gasps and whimpers and sobs.

Parker, one of the few unharmed and unbloodied, stared down at the carnage. Sarah heard him swallow, glanced over in time to see him lick his lips…and dropped her jaw as he tried to sound jocular. *Jocular*, as if this bloody battle were nothing more than a jest!

"Well . . . I, uh, suppose . . . every Paradise has a serpent or two . . . ?" he offered, shrugging his unharmed, unbloodied body lightly.

Down on the main floor, with his limb tucked close to his body to staunch the bleeding and his pistol now empty of bullets, Frrrasten growled and picked up a rock. It was the only weapon in range that could reach the Human "*Grraa sha-shenn svaa!*" he spat in his native tongue, then hurled the rock at the stunned colonial leader. He snarled it in Terranglo, just to make sure eveyone got the point "*Die*, you lllllying *filth*!"

The chunk of stone smacked into Parker's chest. It wasn't the only one. A couple of the surviving mercenary Humans picked up rocks, too, and flung them with equally bloodied arms, shouting their own invective.

Joseph Parker flung up his hands in protest. "Here, now! I can hardly be blamed for *this*!—Ow! Hey! It's the ship crew's fault for not protecting us!"

Sarah's jaw dropped. If she'd had a rock, she would have thrown it, too. "You *paid* us to do everything the exact way *you* wanted!"

"I did no such thing!" he lied. "If you had only followed my instructions *properly*—!"

Furious, she fished an energy-clip from her pocket and threw it at him. It *thumped* into his temple, making him stagger. With a roar, the other surviving colonists charged up the stairs. More rocks were flung, forcing the spluttering man back, even as medical personnel came out of the lower airlock, rushing to help the injured. Parker retreated toward the upper airlock, only to backpedal as it hissed open, disgorging a clutch of equally angry colonists. *They* hadn't been injured, but they *had* believed in his lies.

Rocks were now the least of his worries . . . and Sarah wasn't even going to try to intervene, even if it technically was her duty as first officer to quell any possible violence against one of their passengers. *Rot in a Parker's Hell, you lying little sack of* shakk!

Frrrasten wasn't the only one who went after Parker, but he found himself pushed to one side as the crowd became a riot. It turned out to be a good thing, as he found himself confronted by a Human who had a Solarican medical kit. The pain in his badly torn hand was nothing compared to the rage of the crowd, however. Furious satisfaction filled his blood as he watched the would-be colonists attacking their so-called leader.

Somewhere in the scrum of punches and kicks on the upper level, someone found a cable and wrapped it around Parker's throat. Someone else pushed him off the balcony edge, and both colonists held the ends. He dropped, struggled, and slowly strangled to death while more rocks and curses and bits of whatever were hurled at him.

A wicked thought curled the Solarican's lips back from his teeth in a very un-Terran smile. "*I* know what to do with him!" he roared, catching the attention of a few. Parker was still twitching, barely alive. "*Burn him alive!*"

Ironic as it was, the idea caught like a flame set to dry tinder. The two crew officers on the upper deck didn't stop them as shouts of agreement went up and bodies scattered, looking for the means to get rid of Josaiah Parker. Within minutes, the rioting colonists had hauled in bundles of his belongings for fuel, and ignited the hastily made pyre on the bottom deck. Others dropped the now unmoving body of their putative colonial founder to the deck, and more hands lifted him up, shook him like a rag, and tossed him onto the rising flames.

Burning him here was the best place; the landing bay was lined with metal and would not catch fire . . . and someone up on the bridge must have agreed, for the fire suppression systems did not go off, leaving the bay rife with the stench of burning meat, bone, and plexi objects.

The pyre for Josaiah Emmanuel Bartholomew Parker seemed to be a point of catharsis. The mob soon dispersed, save for those determined to make sure the body fully burned, occasionally throwing more rocks into the flames. The shields continued to hold a perimeter, despite the way the noise and the oddities had drawn in more predators. They fought among themselves in a few bloody contests as the Colony Ship's shields held them off, but they didn't go away.

The *Motorboat* might have a hard time getting the hoses run out to the nearest body of water, and might even have to try a risky relocation attempt on low fuel—which would be shorter and easier than trying to relaunch fully into space—but the shields *were* holding. The tempers of the would-be colonists were another matter.

Frrrasten was still alive . . . and still had his First Footfall rights. With Parker's death, all of Parker's other duties fell to him. Hand throbbing, he drew in a breath, and roared for attention. Primatoid instincts triggered by that sound, the Humans froze and glanced his way, their eyes filled with worry that it was another local beast trying to attack..

"*Ennnough!*" he snapped, seizing their full attention. "Finish burrrning the body, and start taking carre of the wounnnded!"

Frrrasten ordered. "Lllike it or nnot, we *arre* settled on this worrld. *I* will lead you nnow. *No* false prrrromises! Parkerrr's World is *nnnot* a Paradise . . . but *is* ourrs!"

Holy shakk, *they're obeying him,* Sarah thought, blinking at the subdued obedience. *Well. Criminal lord or not, at least he knows how to lead.* Activating her headset, she contacted the bridge. *"Draper to Chan-Trask, everything seems to be calming down out here. What's the status inside?"*

"Lucky you," Ned replied, his voice terse. *"Three decks still have rioting. They're making crude effigies of Parker, and are pelting them with whatever they can throw while being dragged around on a rope—ah, stand by . . ."*

The intercom whistled loudly. *"All hands, this is Captain Sluggovisk. If you wish to burn your effigies of Parker, you will do so outside this vessel. You may do so within the protection of the ship shields, but you will* not *set fire to your effigies while still on board. Anyone who does so from this point forward will be shoved outside the shields and left to die. Parker was a lying bastard who deserved it, but this ship is the* only *thing protecting you from those monsters.* Do not damage it. *Captain out."*

Movement at the edge of her vision made Sarah snatch up her rifle. The shields were holding, but more of the local beasts were on their way. Demonic beasts, not angelic creatures. Making sure the gun was turned on, she braced herself against the railing and went back to standing ready to fire on anything that pushed its way through the ship's shields.

It was highly unlikely; those shields were designed to fend off ship-to-ship missiles. But at this point, the first officer of the Motorboat wasn't going to take any chances. This planet would be settled. There were too few uninhabited M-class worlds out there not to settle it, high gravity and nightmarish wildlife not withstanding.

I do wonder what they'll say about this whole mess, when the future students of this world have to learn about its Founding Day . . .

An example of people with the kind of motivation many of us might expect would lead to colonization, this story first appeared in issue 5 of Orson Scott Card's Intergalactic Medicine Show *alongside the debut story sale of fellow contributor Jamie Todd Rubin. Just as the Pilgrims fled persecution for the New World, so too did Samuel Yoder and his Amish family and community. But what happens when those who reject and fail to understand their traditions threaten their way of life?*

RUMSPRINGA

JASON SANFORD

The English arrived at the farm shortly before supper, their ship buzzing my draft horses and baling combine and kicking a cloud of hay dust into the dry air. Even though I wasn't impressed with the ship's acrobatics, my younger brother Sol, who'd been wrapping the hay bundles with twine, stared at the English with excitement. Knowing I wouldn't get any more work out of him, I stopped the horses. The socket in the back of my head itched in resonance to our new visitors, which I took to be a particularly bad sign.

The ship landed by the barn and three English stepped off. One, an older woman named Ms. Watkins, had served as New Lancaster's mediator between the Amish and English for the last three centuries and always respected our customs, as demonstrated by the plain gray dress she wore. The other English, though, didn't share her regard. The man behind Ms. Watkins wore a blue militia uniform, a definite slap at our nonviolent beliefs, while the teenage girl beside him was naked except for a swirl of colors obscuring her private parts. She gazed around the farm and smiled when she spotted me.

"What do you think they want, Sam?" Sol asked as he stared at the naked girl. I shook my head, even though I had a good idea.

A new comet had shone in the sky for the last few weeks, growing massively larger with each passing day. My father and I had discussed its looming impact several times. Now, as the English approached my father, I knew our concerns about the comet had come true. I handed the horse reins to Sol and walked over to join the conversation.

"Ms. Watkins," my father said, shaking her hand.

"Bishop Yoder," Ms. Watkins said. Then, turning to me, "This can't be Samuel? Last time I saw him he was just a little boy."

"Sam hasn't been a boy for almost five years," my father said without a trace of pride, just like any proper Amish man. "In fact, he will turn twenty-one next month."

"Ah, rumspringa," the naked girl said, rudely stepping between my father and Ms. Watkins. "I assume you'll be baptized on your 21st birthday?"

"I hope to be," I said, annoyed at an outsider asking such a personal question. In addition, these English surely knew exactly who I was. Their pretense of ignorance was merely another of their endless, convoluted games, although it would be rude to say that.

"Well, I hope you'll reconsider. After all, there's more to life than working a left-behind farm." The girl dimmed the colors flowing across her chest, allowing everyone a full view of her bare breasts. "It's not too late, you know. You can still seek forgiveness for any deadly sin that comes your way."

My father coughed awkwardly. Even Ms. Watkins blushed a solid, scarlet red, testimony to the modest personality proxy she'd downloaded before coming here. The militia man, of course, didn't respond and stared stone-faced at everyone.

"Rumspringa isn't a time to simply run around and sin," I said. "It's when one 'puts away the things of a child' and becomes an adult. Nothing more. Nothing less. And I'm well aware of what life has to offer." As I said that, I readjusted my straw hat, feeling the skull socket I would give anything to remove.

My father nodded to my words, indicating I had spoken a solid truth, then waved for Ms. Watkins and the others to follow him into the house. I wanted to follow but, glancing back at Sol, I saw he'd somehow tangled the horse reins in the baling combine's gears. By the time I reached him, one of the horses had kicked the baler, damaging the main driveshaft.

I groaned. It would take all night to undo the reins and repair the driveshaft. Wanting to join my father inside, I glanced over at Sol, who was backing the horses up to give the reins more slack. Luckily for me, when the English created antique machines for us with their nanoforges, they included the same repair gollums as on their own equipment. With Sol distracted by the horses, I reached my mind through my socket and accessed the baler's gollum. The driveshaft's metal flowed and reworked itself until the reins lay free in my hand and the driveshaft looked as good as new.

As Sol and I led the horses back to the barn, he glanced once at the baler. But he didn't say a word as we unharnessed the horses and washed them down for the night.

By the time we finished, the sun had set and the new comet glowed brightly across the sky. I led Sol into the house, where my mother intercepted my brother at the doorway.

"The men are on the back porch," she said as she led Sol the other way, to my brother's obvious disappointment. "There's chicken and mashed potatoes on the table, but it'll keep."

I nodded and headed for the back porch, fighting down a combination of pride at being considered a man and nervousness at why the English were here. The pride worried me the most—right after violence, our worst sin was *hochmut*. Before stepping onto the porch, I took a deep breath and calmed myself until I felt humble before God and life and the world.

"Sam," Ms. Watkins said. "Glad you could join us. Please, have a seat."

Ms. Watkins sat in a wicker chair, while several elders from nearby farms sat on a bench beside my father. I walked toward my father, irritated at Ms. Watkins offering me a seat in my father's house. Beside her sat the militia man, while the teenage girl leaned on the porch railing with her body colorings flowing to the slight breeze. As I passed the English, my socket buzzed slightly and I wondered what they were discussing among themselves. As if knowing my thoughts, the teenage girl smiled a most wicked smile and slid her tongue along the top of her red lips.

"We have been discussing a mutual problem," my father said, stroking his beard in irritation at the girl's behavior. "The comet will impact near here next week."

"How far?" I asked.

The militia officer, whose name holo read Captain Stryder, looked over. "Just over 500 kilometers from this settlement. As I told your father, there will be some modest damage at that distance—windows blown out, that type of thing—but your community should survive. Still, we need to do a temporary resettlement to be safe."

"Why are we just being notified?" I asked.

Captain Stryder didn't even blink. "Until yesterday, we didn't need to. A massive outventing changed the comet's course. Otherwise it would have impacted well away from here."

I nodded. New Lancaster was an Earth-size planet, but lacked sufficient quantities of water, with little standing liquid and only modest underground reservoirs. Since settlement began four centuries ago, periodic comet impacts had been used to terraform the still mostly deserted planet.

Captain Stryder looked at me with the calm, reassuring gaze generated by his militia leadership proxy. But despite Stryder's attempt to put me at ease, I didn't trust him. I also recalled his name from somewhere. But short of accessing my socket, I couldn't figure out what I'd once known about him.

"There really is no choice," Stryder said. "We'll move everyone to a safe holding location, then move you back after impact."

Assuming nothing goes wrong, I thought, filling in the unspoken words.

My father opened his mouth to respond, but before he could say anything, the teenage girl jumped up from the porch railing. "This is ridiculous," she said in agitation. "Why are we even discussing this?"

My socket again buzzed as, I assume, Ms. Watkins and Captain Stryder told the girl to shut up.

"No," she shouted. "These people depend on us for trips across the universe and machines and everything else, but they still don't want anything to do with us. Why do we bring them to each new world and babysit them? I'd say it was nostalgia, but who even understands that emotion anymore."

In the faint glow of the gas lantern, Ms. Watkins blushed while the elders looked away. My father, though, kept a steady face. "I don't believe you've been properly introduced," he said. "This is Emma Beiler. She is an expert." He paused. "On the Amish."

"I see," I said, struggling to find a suitable response. "How does one become an expert at such a young age?"

Emma snorted. "Watch your manners, boy. I'm 641 years old come September. Born on old Earth herself."

I was quite familiar with life extension, having witnessed it up close among the rich and powerful in New Lancaster's main city. A millennium ago, our Amish order decided that life extensions were not part of our *ordnung*, or rules of living. While there was nothing sinful about preserving one's life, extending it indefinitely was extremely expensive, more so to revert to a vastly younger age. This expense would have caused dissension in the community. In fact, I had no doubt that Emma's teenage body was an attempt to create jealousy among her much older-looking colleagues. I shook my head in sympathy. While I refused to judge Emma, the fact that she'd lived so long and understood so little of life saddened me.

"As I was telling our guests before you arrived," my father said, "we will send someone to their ship to examine the data on the comet impact. Once that's done, we will discuss this among the entire congregation."

Captain Stryder nodded. "We'll need an answer in four days."

I felt the far-too familiar buzz in my socket, meaning the English were heavily involved in discussing matters among themselves. Even without accessing their data streams, I doubted they had come here out of concern for our Amish settlement. I wondered what Captain Stryder and Ms. Watkins would do if we refused to leave.

As the English walked back to their ship, Emma glanced at me. For a moment her eyes looked old and sad, as if she'd lost something she'd give anything to regain. But then, with the flash of a new proxy, her eyes became young again and she giggled in her teenage voice.

After the elders left, I walked to the barn with my father to make sure everything was in order. Because of the excitement, I hadn't properly taken care of the hay baler, a fact my father pointed out almost immediately. Embarrassed, I picked up a rag while he grabbed the grease gun.

"What do you think?" I asked.

My father placed the grease gun's nozzle over a lubrication nipple and squeezed the handle. "I think it's suspicious. During your time with the English, did you work on their comet program?"

"No, I worked in high orbit on the nanoforge assemblies. But as part of my advanced training, I studied comet work." What I didn't tell my father was that everyone working the assemblies downloaded complete work proxies covering any possible job one might be asked to do. All I had to do was access the proxy in my socket, and I would become an instant expert on comet movement and impacts.

"That's good," my father said. "The elders and I will present this information to the congregation on Sunday. While God's will always prevails, any information you can provide—without using your socket—will be appreciated."

My stomach sank at his mention of the socket. While my father had lived his entire life among the Amish, he always knew far more than he let on about the English world.

"What if that's the only way to find out the information we need?" I asked.

"Then we don't need it."

I nodded, remembering my years among the English. Every Amish adolescent was expected to make his or her own decision about whether to commit to our faith. Like many of my friends, I'd wanted to see the life I'd be giving up. Unlike them, I stayed away for over four years, only returning shortly before my 20th birthday. I hadn't talked much with my father about my life among the English, or why I had returned, but I wouldn't be surprised if he knew a good deal about what I'd done.

My father finished greasing the baler, then placed the grease gun back on the tool bench, where he eyed the damaged horse reins Sol had jammed in the combine's gears. "Do you remember when I was chosen as bishop?" he asked.

I said yes. Our congregation cast lots to select our deacons and bishops, letting God decide who should be chosen.

"A few weeks after I was chosen, Ms. Watkins flew in to congratulate me. I didn't know what to say. Until then, all anyone had expressed to me was sympathy at the heavy burden I'd been chosen to carry. Still, Ms. Watkins meant no ill. She simply doesn't understand us. No English can. Do you see what I'm saying?"

"I believe so."

"I'm not sure you do." My father opened the access panel on the baler, revealing the clean, new-looking driveshaft.

I hung my head in shame. "I'm sorry. I shouldn't have done that."
My father sighed and rubbed his beard. "Sam, you need to understand. Before you are baptized, the community can overlook these transgressions. But after baptism, if you keep using that socket, they will shun you. I don't want that to happen. I know you use the socket to help out, but it's not allowed. Don't give in to temptation. That's your burden to bear, just as mine was being selected Bishop. Embrace the burden and God will show you the way."

I nodded. I started to ask my father if he knew what had been required of me to live among the English, but I couldn't stand mentioning this shame to him. "I don't trust them," I said. "Few of the English care about anyone but themselves. Plus, this planet is almost totally empty. They could have easily aimed the comet to a place where it'd pose no risk to anyone. They're up to something."

"All the more reason to see what you can learn. English claims to the contrary, they have less understanding of life than we do. Perhaps something has tempted them. If so, we need to know."

As we left the barn, I glanced at the sky. Just last night, the comet had been a object of beauty, a sparking exclamation of God's power in the universe. Now it was one more sign of humanity's ugliness, aimed directly at everything I cared about.

"Remember," my father said, patting me on the back as we walked in the house. "To the English, being chosen is an honor. Don't be like them. Don't be proud at being chosen."

Shortly before dawn, Sol and I woke up and fed the pigs and chickens. We then finished bailing the hay. I worked quickly, urging the Clydesdales faster and faster, unable to focus on the truth contained within this hard work. Instead, I continually glanced at the comet as it slowly disappeared below the horizon.

I finished my work around noon. After parking the baler in the barn, I walked by the water trough and noticed that the water flow had stopped. Because there was no rain on New Lancaster, we used large canvas water catchers in the foothills above our farms to collect the morning mists. Pipes carried the water down into large metal reservoirs for use in drip irrigation to grow crops and as drinking water for the animals and ourselves. While it rarely happened, the pipes sometimes clogged at different points. Not wanting to waste any more time, I told Sol to find the clog and remove it.

After washing up, I pulled on a plain gray shirt and pants, two suspenders, and my wide-brimmed, black-felt hat. I then harnessed a painted mare to our family's buggy and rode off to the English ship.

The ship sat on a nearby foothill, which rose five-hundred meters above the plains. A stubby native grass called thickens, which stored their own water like a cactus, grew along the top of the foothills. Thickens were extremely difficult to remove from the land and the main reason we didn't farm near them. Luckily, they only grew at higher elevations, where they could condense water from the nightly mists.

When I reached the English ship, I parked the buggy and hobbled the mare's legs. I also slipped on her feedbag. Thickens were toxic to Earth animals, and I didn't want her to be tempted.

Captain Stryder waited for me at the foot of his ship. "About time," he said in an arrogant tone. "I expected you this morning."

"I had to finish bailing the hay."

For a moment, Captain Stryder's personality proxy cracked as a smirk crossed his face. I knew what he thought: How could I bail hay with possible destruction heading toward us? But that just showed Stryder didn't understand the Amish, for whom everyday work was an act of devotion.

I followed Stryder inside the ship, where I was struck yet again by how few people were needed to run English technology. While we used hundreds of Amish to build a barn, Stryder only needed himself to run his entire ship. He led me through the empty ship to the bridge, where Ms. Watkins and Emma waited. As I sat beside them, Ms. Watkins shook my hand. Emma nodded in the overly polite manner of an automatic proxy, meaning her other personalities were off diving in a different socket-accessed reality.

For the next hour, Captain Stryder presented his data on the comet. A kilometer and a half in diameter, the comet had been directed toward the planet for the last century. While Stryder's data indicated our settlement wasn't vulnerable to the impact's electromagnetic pulse—aside from the unused repair gollums in our nanoforge-created machines—we would suffer minor air blast and seismic damage. That said, if the comet changed course even slightly, our settlement would be destroyed.

To make clear the danger we faced, Stryder proceeded to show me startling images from a recent megaton-range weapon impact. That's when I remembered where I'd heard his name before. Stryder's unit enforced quarantine, making sure no unapproved biomatter reached the surface and interfered with terraforming. The images of mushroom clouds now boiling before me came from his controversial decision to destroy a large, unoccupied section of New Lancaster after an unapproved animal species was released. As Stryder spoke with pride about that destruction, I wondered why he was involved in relocating us. Perhaps the militia figured Stryder's experience using megaton-range weapons helped him understand comet impacts.

The fact that I hadn't remembered all this until now made me miss my socket even more. Even the most basic of sockets could spin Stryder's facts and figures and words a billion different ways to see through his flash and bang to the truth of this matter.

"That's all very nice," I finally said, trying to keep the English sarcasm I'd picked up out of my voice. "I still don't understand why we weren't informed until now."

"The outventing," Stryder repeated, as if I were an ignorant child. "When I worked on the nanoforges, I downloaded a comet worker proxy. Based on what I know, any outventing big enough to cause such a large course change should have been easily predicted. I don't believe this happened by chance."

I was bluffing, since I'd never actually opened that proxy. While bluffing wasn't the most Amish of traits, I needed to know if Stryder was telling the truth.

Unfortunately, his proxy didn't waver. "That's perfect," he said. "Let's dispense with this charade. Download my data and use that little socket of yours. You'll see I'm telling the truth."

My socket almost screamed at the chance to access Stryder's information. Unfortunately, while my gut told me Stryder was also bluffing, unless I went against my community's rules, I couldn't be certain. I glanced at Ms. Watkins, who refused to meet my eye.

"Can you provide the data in a printed format?" I asked.

"It would comprise a hundred million of your printed pages."

My heart sank.

"That's what I thought," Captain Stryder said with a sneer. "I knew you would act this way. Distrustful. Outwardly humble yet inwardly proud. Wanting to explore the world beyond your precious

Amish, yet afraid of all we 'English' can do. Is that why you returned to your people? Out of fear?"

Not for the first time, I felt violated as a stranger accessed the memories which I'd long ago copied and uploaded. Instead of responding, I took a deep breath and reminded myself that the memories Stryder had access to had been sold years ago. They weren't the man I was today.

To my surprise, though, his words woke Emma from her socket-induced stupor. "Stop tormenting him. Provide the child with any analysis he needs. He wins, we win. We get to save these backward idiots and go home."

Captain Stryder thought about this and nodded. "Yes, this is a waste of my time. Do you have any old-grade computers in your settlement?"

"Yes, in the school house." Our order allowed a few higher tech machines for community use, in this case for accessing New Lancaster's weather and emergency net. While the school computer was more advanced than anything else in our community, it was still a millennium behind anything the English used.

"Perfect. Emma can download the data and enter it into your computer. Run a simulation. You'll see I'm telling the truth."

For a moment, my socket tingled as Captain Stryder and Ms. Watkins and Emma engaged in a ultra-fast and obviously high spirited argument. The communication ended with Emma apparently satisfied.

"What's the catch?" I asked. The English never did anything without payment in return.

"They said I can spend some time with the Amish," Emma said. "My research on you silly people is out of date."

I sighed but, seeing no alternative, agreed. For the briefest of moments Emma's eyes shivered as her socket downloaded the massive data on the comet, causing my own socket to ache for the power and ability it had once possessed. I muttered a silent prayer for God to deliver me from this temptation.

Instead of God answering, Emma blew me a kiss with her red, red lips.

Emma rode back to the farm with me. As the buggy creaked along the dirt road, she sat with her eyes glazed over as she dived her socket without even bothering to generate a cover personality to interact with me. I had insisted that Emma dress modestly, so she'd had the ship create a typical Amish outfit, in this case a full-length gray dress with long sleeves and a cape and apron. On her head she wore a black prayer covering, signifying, just like my lack of a beard, that she was not married. While Emma dressing as one of us annoyed me, I figured it was better than her running around naked.

We arrived home well after dark. After unhitching my horse, I turned on the faucet and found that the pipes were still blocked. After giving my horse some of our reserve water, I explained the situation with Emma to my parents and showed her to the guest bedroom. I then woke Sol and asked him about the pipes.

"I unblocked them," Sol mumbled, half asleep. "Thickens had gotten inside. But I cleaned them out and patched the pipe."

I told Sol to go back to sleep. I'd take care of the water problem in the morning.

At first light, I watered the animals with the remainder of our reserves, then hitched up the horse and loaded the buggy with all the tools I might need. The distant water collectors in the foothills glittered with moisture in the rising light. Obviously the nightly mists had arrived, so the pipe must still be blocked. While running the simulation on the computer was important, more important was getting water for the animals and crops. In New Lancaster's dry air, they could die from dehydration well before the comet impact.

Once the horse and buggy were ready, I walked back in the house. To my horror, Emma sat in the kitchen talking with my mother. I panicked—afraid Emma would insult my mother, or worse, reveal what I'd done among the English. To my surprise, though, my mother appeared to enjoy talking with her.

"Is everything okay?" I asked warily as Emma handed me a plate of bacon, eggs, and oatmeal, which she'd evidently cooked by herself.

"Everything's perfect," my mother said. "Emma's a delightful young lady."

I glanced at Emma, who was again dressed like one of us. I wondered if my mother remembered Emma parading half-naked through our house only two days ago. Emma's eyes flickered for a moment, and I realized she'd used yet another personality proxy to modify her behavior.

Not wanting to leave Emma alone with my parents, I told her we were riding up to the foothills to fix the water pipes.

"What about the computer sim?" she asked.

"We'll do it when we get back."

Emma shrugged and followed me out of the house, much to my relief.

The ride up was uneventful. Emma sat silently beside me, lost in whatever socket-derived world she wished to create. My own socket tingled to her presence and, as the buggy rolled slowly through the empty kilometers, I wished I could patch in with her. All I'd have to do was create a new personality to drive the buggy. I could then expand my mind into the endless connections and worlds used by all the English on New Lancaster.

As if knowing my thoughts, Emma turned to look at me. She seemed pleasant, and I assumed this proxy was the one she'd used with my mother.

"Why were you so anxious to get me out of the house?" she asked.

I started to yell at her—another habit I'd learned among the English—but the look in her eyes said she truly didn't know. Proxies could compartmentalize knowledge and memories, so a person with a particular proxy literally wouldn't know what they'd done only moments before with a different one.

"To be honest, I'm afraid you'll tell my parents what I did among the English."

She stared at me with uncertainty until her socket supplied the missing information. "You sold yourself," she said.

I nodded. The problem all Amish face if they leave the faith is that, according to the current standards of humanity, we aren't truly human. We lack sockets. When humans can create new personalities and emotions at the drop of a pin and have nanoforges to satisfy every whim and desire, what are the Amish, who've changed only a little across thousands of years?

As all Amish youth discover during rumspringa, an eighth-grade education can't compete with enhanced humans who can download libraries of information. While charity ensured that none of us starved—after all, what were a few crumbs to nanoforges—there was little hope for advancement in a society where only access to a socket ensured one's success.

Enter the devil's bargain. Any Amish kid could earn their own socket in exchange for the one thing we had which others wanted: Our lives. In an age where nothing about humanity was stable, where any person might possess a thousand distinct personalities, what the Amish owned were our experiences. Our beliefs. Our years of hard, physical work. Our secure love from growing up in a deep, nourishing community.

Most Amish youth refused to sell their lives and returned to their family farms. Not me. I not only uploaded my memories, I allowed others to experiment on me. The English exposed me to endless personality proxies and shared in my reaction. I became a woman, a baby, a genius, a warrior, an idiot, a bird, a whale, and more. For a bit of money, anyone could see through my naïve eyes as I reacted to each startling mental change.

After four years of this, though, I began to yearn for what I'd given up. Ironically, this nostalgia made me even more popular. Those who had everything had no way of missing anything. I tried to upload an explanation about the emptiness I saw all around me, how even if one connected into a million different lives these proxies were nothing but a distraction from life. However, no one understood. So I collected the scattered pieces and memories of my original life, stitched them together into a new/old personality, burned them back into my brain, and returned home to beg my God and community for forgiveness.

I didn't explain any of this to Emma. With her socket, she downloaded all the stored information about me and understood in an instant. "I'm sorry," she said. "Believe me, I understand."

Before I could ask her how she understood, my socket buzzed. I started to tell Emma no, but as I stared into her face I felt her utter sincerity. Asking God to forgive me, I opened my socket for the briefest of moments.

Emma's life flooded into me. I saw her as a child more than six centuries ago, growing up in Lancaster County on Earth. She too was Amish, and she too yearned to see the universe beyond her one patch of ground. Like me, she sold her memories and life, but unlike me she never returned, instead living and aging across the years until she immigrated to New Lancaster as an Amish expert for the government.

But even as I learned this, I also saw her anger and regret. She hated her life, hated the emptiness of a society of self-centered people who could create anything they wished for. Emma only wished for one thing and that was the one thing she couldn't have—to return to her family and community. Like me, she had created the proxy she now wore from the memories of her childhood and had embedded it into her brain by rewiring her very neurons. She used this hardwired proxy as an escape from her socket-driven life, or, occasionally, to interact with the planet's Amish. The rest of Emma's memories and personalities lived in her socket, connected forever and irrevocably to the very life they abhorred.

I closed my socket and said another prayer as I urged the horse up the gently sloping foothills. All the anger and hate Emma's proxies felt showed me how I might have turned out if I hadn't returned to the faith. I thanked Emma for sharing this, but instantly saw that the hardwired Emma was gone, replaced by a new proxy who sneered and called me a weak, backward idiot. I ignored her words and urged the horse to go even faster.

By the time we reached the water collection system, Emma was in rare form. She was so angry about her hardwired proxy giving me such a personal download that, as I unpacked my tools, she grabbed a knife and ran to the giant mesh nets which covered acre after acre of these hills.

"Screw Amish nonviolence," she said, dangling the knife under a section of mesh. "What'll you do if I cut this?"

"Repair it," I said. Emma smirked and sliced a long gap in the mesh. I shook my head and walked over to take the knife, but she wanted to fight for it. Refusing to do that, I simply ignored her. After cutting a few more nets, she hacked in anger at the yellow thickens growing beneath the nets then jammed the knife in the ground.

"That's why Stryder and Watkins will win," she said. "You won't fight them."

"One can still win without fighting."

Emma snickered, then zoned out as she retreated into the hedonistic paradise of her socket. While she zoned, I ran a rooter into the blocked section of pipe and pulled out a clump of thickens. While thickens grew all along these hills, I had never known them to clog the pipes. After estimating the distance to the clog, I grabbed my shovel and dug up the buried section of the nanoforge created pipe, which we'd been given in exchange for a crop of hand-grown tobacco.

The pipe had cracked and thickens had grown inside, attracted by the abundant water source. It took me two hours to clear them out, an amazing fact since I could see where Sol had cleaned out and patched this very pipe the day before. Obviously thickens grew explosively fast when exposed to large amounts of water.

Once the pipe was clear, I reached for my patch kit before realizing that was exactly what Sol had done the day before. Knowing I didn't have the time to keep returning to the foothills, I opened my socket and activated the pipe's gollum. Instantly the pipe sealed shut.

Emma emerged from her socket trance to tease me. "You're addicted," she said, "so don't you dare look down on me." She then disappeared back into her socket.

I didn't say a word as I drove us back to the farm.

Over dinner that night, Emma and I explained what we'd learned. After returning from the foothills, we'd had time for Emma to download the comet's data into the school house computer, where I'd run a number of simulations. Each one suggested Captain Stryder and Ms. Watkins were telling the truth.

"So there's no ulterior motive for wanting us to leave?" my father asked.

"I couldn't tell," I said. "But the information on why the comet is impacting nearby appears to be correct."

My father nodded. He ate another bite of chicken and looked out the window at the comet, which shone brightly across the darkening sky. "When the congregation comes over tomorrow for worship services, I'll tell everyone about this and suggest we evacuate until after the impact."

Before I could agree with my father, Emma spoke up in the pleasant voice which meant she was using her hardwired Amish-girl proxy. "Ms. Watkins and Captain Stryder are lying to you. They don't care about the Amish."

My father stared at his fork. "Excuse me?" he asked.

Emma stared at her plate, obviously embarrassed at having said anything.

"What do you mean, they don't care about us?" my father asked. "No offense intended, but I'm not sure you care either."

Emma nodded, and suddenly the arrogant, hateful Emma

appeared. "You are correct. Concern among my people changes like the wind. Are Ms. Watkins and Captain Stryder concerned? No. Ms. Watkins believes the Amish are needed for colonization because you provide an underclass we 'English' can look down on, making our powerful yet disjointed lives seem better in comparison. Captain Stryder's proxy cares only about defending English civilization and terraforming this planet. You're fools to trust either of them."

As soon as she finished speaking, Emma's eyes flickered and she blushed a deep red. "I'm so sorry," she stammered, standing up from the table. "Please forgive me." She then ran from the house. I explained to my shocked family how the English used personality proxies, which changed from moment to moment. I also explained that Emma had been born Amish and left during rumspringa. The personality we liked was created from the centuries-old remnants of Emma's Amish memories. My father nodded with a sad look on his face, as if we'd just witnessed a horrible accident but could do nothing to help.

"When you disturb the most basic things God has given us—emory, emotion, soul—can you call what remains human?" my father asked. "But that's for God to decide, I suppose."

I nodded, even as I wondered if my father would consider me human if he knew how much I resembled Emma.

The next few days passed quickly. After Sunday church services in our house, my father explained to the congregation about the comet and why he believed we needed to temporarily evacuate. The congregation discussed the situation for hours, but eventually agreed we should leave. My father and I volunteered to stay until the last minute to take care of the animals on the nearby farms while the rest of the families flew to a relocation camp four hundred kilometers away.

Captain Stryder wasn't happy with me and my father staying. Still, he said he'd spare a small AI piloted shuttle to pull us out at the last minute, as long as we accepted responsibility for our deaths if anything happened.

The next day the ships landed and our families boarded. Sol hugged me so long that I didn't think he'd board the ship. I also kissed my mother, who told me to watch over my father. They then flew away to safety.

That night, with the comet lighting up the entire sky, my father and I rode our buggy from farm to farm to check on the animals, making sure they had enough food and water and were protected from the coming blast. Now that we had time to talk, I mentioned how the thickens had grown into the pipe. He said he'd heard rumors they could grow explosively fast around standing water. He asked me how I'd fixed the pipe, to which I didn't respond.

"No matter," he said. "In the last week you have behaved very much like the man God intended you to be." He didn't say he was proud of me—that wouldn't have been fitting—but I still felt a sinful pride at his words.

We woke the next morning a few hours before impact. After a final check on the animals in the area, we bedded down our horse and waited for the shuttle to arrive. It did so with a mere fifteen minutes left before impact.

"We English like to cut it short," Emma said as the shuttle's door opened. "Life's boring without a little drama."

My father started to ask why she was here, but I saw the wild look in her eyes and told him to get onboard before she changed her mind. While I didn't trust this proxy of hers, I doubted she'd do anything to endanger her own life.

Naturally enough, I was totally wrong. Emma flew the shuttle directly toward the impact zone, buzzing so low over the foothills that I saw our buggy tracks from the other day.

"Where are you going?" I asked.

"I'm doing you a favor, Sammy boy. I downloaded your life last night and had a revelation. If I can't go home, I might as well save your worthless community."

My father glanced at me but remained silent. I was about to say something when I saw Captain Stryder's ship appear on one of the foothills, where it'd been hidden from view. Emma landed the shuttle by the ship in a small explosion of dirt and thickens.

The door opened and Emma jumped out. My father and I followed. Even though I didn't want to, I accessed my socket and learned we had eight minutes until impact. I nervously glanced at the comet, which burned in the sky directly over the horizon.

As we approached the ship, a door opened and Captain Stryder emerged. "What the hell are you doing here?" he yelled, his calm militia proxy obviously overwhelmed.

"I'm on to you," Emma shouted, hitting Stryder across the face. "I won't let you do it."

With a quick motion, Stryder reached into his tunic and pulled out a stun gun, which collapsed Emma into pain on the yellow thickens. He bent over to make sure she was alright, then looked at us and shook his head.

"I sincerely apologize for this," he said. "I knew she was unstable, but I had no idea her disjointment went this far."

"What are you doing?" I asked.

Stryder aimed the stun gun at us. "We don't have time to fight," he said. "I'm alone on the ship. If I hurt you, I can't carry all of you onboard to safety before the impact."

"We won't fight you," I said. "But what are you doing?"

Stryder wavered for a moment, then kicked at a thicken. "They're spreading," he said. "The damn things used to only cover places like these foothills, where the mists fed them. But as the planet grows wetter, they're starting to spread. What's the point of terraforming if a native plant spreads everywhere and keeps out our own vegetation?"

I stared for a moment at the thickens and thought about how hard a time we'd had removing them from a few isolated spots. I then remembered Stryder's role in removing any unauthorized biomatter which threatened terraforming. "You're going to destroy them," I said, even as my socket warned me there were only three minutes until impact. "You're going to vaporize the entire region, just like you did a year ago."

Stryder sighed. "This is the only group of thickens near a settlement. With the comet hitting nearby, we could burn the region away and say any harm to your settlement was merely unanticipated comet damage."

I glanced at Emma, who rolled in pain on the thickens. Any weapon strike big enough to completely destroy all these plants would also destroy our settlement. My anger rose at Stryder's arrogance in deciding the fate of our community, and I tensed to charge him. But before I could move, my father laid his hand on my arm. Stryder smirked. He obviously considered nonviolence a weakness. He gestured with the stun gun.

"Carry her onboard the ship," he ordered. "We need to be inside to be safe from the impact."

As I bent over Emma, my socket buzzed. On a hunch, I opened myself to her and a wave of information flooded in, everything from her uncovering Stryder and Watkins' plan to detailed sims showing Stryder using his ship's weapons to destroy everything within a hundred kilometers of these hills. As I watched our community explode, Emma suddenly smiled. One final, but critical, piece of information clicked into me.

I stood up and faced Stryder. "We're not going anywhere."

My father reached for me, but he didn't have to worry—I had no intention of fighting. Instead, I uploaded the access code Emma had just given me into Stryder's ship, sealing the main door shut. A look of panic crossed Stryder's face as my socket warned we were one minute to impact.

"Open the door," Stryder screamed, but I'd already scrambled the code. He aimed the stun gun at me and fired, sending pain coursing through my body. As I fell onto the thicken-coated ground, I glanced up at the comet, which appeared unmoving and eternal yet also ever changing.

As Stryder banged on the door in purest panic, the comet entered the atmosphere with a massive, eye-burning explosion. The fire reached above the distant horizon like God's hand embracing His own. As I passed out, my last thoughts were a prayer, hoping He would forgive my sins and pull me into the sweet night of His bosom.

I woke two days later in my own bed. At first I was disoriented and thought I'd entered a simulation of my parent's house, but when I tried to find my way out, I only felt my own body and senses. I rubbed the slight bump under the back of my skull. The socket was physically there, but the slight buzz I'd felt ever since installation was gone.

I stood up and looked out the broken window at the foothills. The distant hills were still covered in yellow thickens, and I saw the glint of water on the damaged water condensers. I then walked downstairs to find my parents sitting on the back porch with Ms. Watkins.

"Sam," Ms. Watkins said, standing up and offering me her chair. "Glad to see you up and about."

Remembering Emma's last upload and how Ms. Watkins had

been working with Stryder to destroy our community, I refused to take her seat. Ms. Watkins gave me a sour look, then shook her head and walked toward the barn, where a shuttle waited for her.

My father and mother quickly filled me in. After the electromagnetic pulse fried the sockets of Stryder, myself, and Emma, my father had pulled us behind the relative safety of the English ship. The seismic shaking hit a minute and a half after impact; the shock wave twenty minutes later. As we'd been told, the damage to the community was minimal at this distance, although ejecta from the impact pelted our crops rather hard.

Ms. Watkins and other rescuers arrived an hour later. Stryder was in bad shape—evidently he'd relied almost totally on his socket for storage of his memories and proxies. While Emma's socket, and my own, were also destroyed, Ms. Watkins said we should be okay because we had stable personalities hardwired in our neurons. As a precaution she'd sedated us, but said there would be no lasting effects—aside from having a dead socket in our head for the rest of our lives. She'd also half-heartedly apologized for going behind our backs in dealing with the thickens problem. While my father knew she didn't truly mean this, he still suggested several low-tech solutions for controlling the plants near the Amish settlement. Ms. Watkins had expressed interest in exploring those options.

"Do you trust her?" I asked.

"No," my father said. "But I trust God, and even you must admit He handled things rather well."

I nodded, still amazed my socket could no longer tempt me. While I'd been praying for this ever since returning to the faith, the fact that I couldn't go back to the English world now scared me more than anything. Seeing my concern, my mother hugged me and told me to go check on our guest in the spare bedroom. I nervously walked to the bedroom and knocked on the door. An excited voice told me to come in.

Emma sat on the bed, a black prayer covering in her hands. She quickly placed it on her head and smiled.

"Your mother let me borrow some clothes," she said, standing up. Her dress was loose and baggy, and she laughed as her apron slipped from her waist. "She said I could stay as long as I want. Guess I'll need to sew myself some clothes. Been a few centuries since I've done that."

   I took her hand and squeezed it, then hugged her tightly. I wanted to ask how much of all this her other proxies had planned and how much had resulted from God, or chance, or any of the above. But as I looked at Emma's happy face, I realized none of that mattered. Everyone else she'd ever been was dead and, in a strange way, both of our prayers had been answered. What else could we do but be content with the new lives we'd been given.

Sometimes the consequences for colonists might be more personal or interpersonal, depending on how you look at it. For David and his husband, Carlo, the chance to join a colony was seen by one as an escape and the other as salvation, but the end result is one neither had expected.

ELSEWHERE, WITHIN, ELSEWHEN

CAT RAMBO

For the past month, David had been dividing their possessions, separating things out from each other, sorting shelves of knickknacks into groups of his and Carlo's. All in the name of efficiency. Efficiency in order to speed the moment when he told Carlo he was leaving.

But he had thought he would be packing for himself, after saying goodbye to Carlo. He'd already figured out the essentials that would fit into the colony ship's weight allowance, assembled a few hardcopy books, Nana's lucky maneki neko cat, his great-grandfather's pocket knife, and his absolute favorite vintage Hawaiian shirt, Monty Pythonesque, pop-eyed dragons writhing on a background of opulent white clouds. He'd researched household necessities, reading through the message boards where future colonists chattered back and forth. He'd assembled lists of spices, and seeds for most of them, preparing for new ground, imagining himself a video hero, a pioneer readying to carve out a rugged, solitary life.

Instead he was packing for both of them, and Carlo was the one who was taking him along.

Unconscionable for David to begrudge Carlo's luck. Carlo had worked hard to qualify for a berth on the *Bon Chance*, a colonist's position. And wasn't he taking his spouse along, so they could start a family on the newly discovered planet? Many colonists chose to abandon planetary partners as well as lives.

Carlo hadn't even thought twice about it. He'd assumed of course David would come along on the one-way trip to the planet the marketing company had named Splendid. Assumed that his partner just as ready to transplant their relationship to a new world.

David considered a set of silver spoons. They clinked reproachfully as he returned them to the drawer. But who needed fancy dinnerware on the frontier? They could take so few objects, so very few things, things that they might never see again in colonial life.

He didn't think he would have chosen differently in Carlo's place—he knew it. He'd meant to leave Carlo behind. In fact, it was why he'd applied for the *Bon Chance* in the first place. It seemed an easy way to break up, to regretfully say that he didn't think he could take Carlo along. The government rejection devastated him. He hadn't even known that Carlo had applied too, until his husband said that night, "I've been accepted to the ship."

David stared at him across the table. He hadn't been able to collect the energy to make dinner, so he'd ordered in pizza. He'd even chosen a place they'd never tried before, a passive aggressive nudge that made him feel, shamefully, better. But Carlo didn't make his usual fuss about a new, unproven restaurant, had simply dug in as though he hadn't even noticed.

Who'd have thought Carlo, who hated untested things, who liked his life safe, would have opted to apply for the ship and the unexplored existence it represented?

David said, "Why didn't you tell me? Were you afraid I'd tease you about it?"

Carlo fiddled with the plastic cutlery, staring down at the knife and fork as though trying to figure out how to combine them. "We don't talk so much, anymore." He put the utensils down, one on either side of his plate. "The chance to mention it never came up."

David replayed several weeks of conversations in his head. Was Carlo accusing him of not letting Carlo speak? But that wasn't Carlo's style either. He didn't keep score, didn't make oblique accusations.

Had Carlo kept silent because he had been thinking along the same lines, of striking out on his own, or even with someone else, but changed his mind at the last minute?

"No, we haven't talked much," David said. "We should do something about that."

"We should."

They stared at each other helplessly across the table.

All along David had thought he'd be the one picked as a colonist. He hadn't planned on taking anyone but himself. Now things were entirely changed. Where he thought Carlo would be abandoned, he could have been. And, somehow worse, somehow even more humiliating, it never came into question whether or not they would go together. Whether or not they'd undergo the surgery that would allow one or the other to carry a child to term when they chose to start the family that they were, though not legally obligated to, strongly encouraged to populate the planet with.

Whether they'd continue being a unit.

He'd checked the passenger list to see if any of Carlo's former coworkers were going. That might have explained it. But none of the names were the one he most feared to see there.

Still, he couldn't let it rest until he asked, on Carlo's afternoon off, when they were sorting his closet into items to be given to friends and Goodwill.

"Is Ben going?" He threw a handful of silk ties, fluttering wildly, towards a box. They lay across it, rainbow snakes pondering an escape they had halfway achieved.

"No. I haven't seen him since that night. I told you. He transferred to another hospital."

"You said it didn't mean anything to either of you." David's jaw clenched with anger.

"It didn't." Carlo had given up any pretense of sorting. He turned to David, shoulders slumped as though already defeated, watching his face.

"It meant enough that he transferred, though. So he wouldn't see you anymore."

"We thought it would be best."

"You discussed it." The thought of them planning the future together, considering options, dizzied David.

Carlo said, "Do you want me to move out? We can't keep coming back to this over and over for the rest of our lives."

"No," David said. "It'll be different once we leave here." Once they left this place forever spoiled by what had happened, the apartment whose walls had grown small while David waited for his lover, knowing something was wrong, but not what, back before Carlo had first spoken Ben's name.

At the last minute, some new regulation assigned everyone going on the ship a counselor to help them with the transition. David went downtown to see his in a vast building of glass and steel that looked like an exposed spine.

After forty-five minutes wait, he was admitted to his appointment. Once introductions were over, he launched into the question that had haunted him all the way there. "Wouldn't it have been smarter to accept people in pairs? So you know that both partners will contribute, have the skills you need?"

The sandy-haired counselor had a tired smile above his lemon-yellow tie. He said, in a way that made David realize this wasn't the first time the question had come up, "We've tried that. Studies have shown that it's possible to be too efficient that way. It works better if we add some randomness to the mix, some people who aren't trained but are adaptable, can take on roles as needed. Spouses and partners are the best way to do that, rather than introduce an unaffiliated group."

"So the spouses are valuable for that reason," David said, half to himself.

"Of course they are," the counselor said. David could hear the patronizing tone buried deep under the words.

Everything got mixed back up together in the packing, the things they couldn't bear to leave behind despite the limits of the rules. The chiming clock Carlo had inherited from great great greats had to be abandoned, but not the teapot colored cerulean and gold that reminded David of his mother, which he justified by filling with seed packets. Small toys and books each had laid aside for future children.

David packed it all in the plastic crates provided for them; one cubic half meter each. He packed and repacked, trying to squeeze as much as he could into the space, worked out clever tricks of putting things inside other things, around things, rolling a shirt into a thin rope that could be coiled around the teapot to cushion it, until at night he dreamed only of packing, getting things into smaller and smaller boxes.

They were heavily encouraged to use the space for equipment, but no one did. It was a one-way trip, the colony, unless you made yourself such a good life there that you could afford a trip back.

He ignored the sullen anger smoldering in his stomach. He'd planned his studies in order to make himself valuable. Hardly his fault that new technology had emerged to make all his work with ansibles useless. No one needed old tech, made of inorganic metals and chemicals, once biotech took hold. Even as he finished up his studies, he knew himself obsolete. That knowledge nagged at him, till he felt frustration-frayed, no longer a complete person but a ragged cluster of resentment, filled with the sludge of a thousand wounds.

Sometimes he snapped at Carlo. He couldn't help it. He felt things more strongly than simple, calm Carlo. That had first drawn him to Carlo: that strength, that uncomplicated outlook on life. David was different, full of more complicated, nuanced feelings. They didn't look at things the same way. David kept track of the relationship's give and take in an internal algebra alien to Carlo's way of thinking.

He felt bad about it, but what was he to do? He didn't understand how people "let go" of such things. He tried his best, he really did, but resentment choked him at each slight, each ill chosen word or accidental triviality, like Carlo taking the last clean towel, even though David had laid it out for himself. Each instance grew into a perfectly formed little knot of negativity, collecting to coat him like barnacles, until he could only move in the way his heavy armor, made of anger and irritation and jealousy, permitted him.

It weighed him down. He thought, more than once, of telling Carlo to go on without him. Humiliating to have earned his place because of who he fucked, rather than his own merit.

He could stay on earth. Keep working and studying. Earn his own ticket. Plenty of companies readying to seed the systems discovered by the Hirsch probe ten years ago, a wave of ships stretching out over the next decade. But the competition was so stiff, so close, so hotly contested. There was no guarantee he'd make it.

So he followed Carlo. It didn't mean they be together forever, after all. A year or two tops of cohabitation. Long enough that it wouldn't seem like he'd come under false pretenses. Then he'd leave. Oblivious Carlo.

Not so their friends. David had confided his doubts about the relationship and his plans to sever it to more than one. David could see the question in their eyes when they came to see the pair off. He chose to ignore it, smiling brightly, waving. Keeping a possessive hand on Carlo's shoulder as they walked up the ramp into the shuttle taking them to the *Bon Chance* to begin their journey.

He put a good face on for the voyage. He volunteered for things. He spent most of his time in the holodeck's training room, learning skills that might come in handy in the colony. Three months and five days of stale, re-circulated air later, they arrived at Splendid.

The *Bon Chance* shuddered its way down through the atmosphere to land, rather than remain in orbit. David's heart lifted as they all watched the planet's surface coming towards them on the screens. The *Bon Chance* would land and become something new. He could do the same, be transformed by their arrival, made into something useful and interesting. And lovable perhaps, because it seemed to him that Carlo had brought him not so much out of love as from habit. Here in this new place, he could become someone new. Together he and Carlo could become something else.

The ship landed with a shudder that made everyone sway, even as they cheered. It would never see space again. Instead, it began to unfold and fall apart, designed to disassemble into its own little frontier city, every part transforming, recycling into something of use.

2500 people altogether in the colony's first wave. At first they clustered, familiar knots in this unfamiliar landscape where the trees grew twinned, and birdlike creatures breathed fire (or at least sprays of sparks), and where the rocks could speak.

Though they didn't know about the last of those until David's discovery.

Everyone had admired the phenomenon. Every once in a while, in this landscape, you found a boulder, a round of glassy stone, like an immense gem, colored red and violet and yellow, standing as high as David's waist. Gupta, the colony geologist, argued with Tompkins, the chief biologist, over whether they were organic or inorganic. When they finally cracked one open and analyzed it, the mystery intensified.

The boulders were made of layers of some substance that resembled glass, but was hard as gemstone. The combined layers, varying in color and thickness, produced an effect like lacquer, but filled with an interior luminescence that Gupta attributed to the structure of the crystals, which trapped light. He named the substance nacre when he discovered what lay at the core.

Buried in the boulder's center was one of the long-limbed simians that haunted the riverbanks, creatures with golden fur and deep violet eyes. They weren't intelligent, the initial survey had already determined. Somehow these rocks grew around them, used them to form themselves, in an unfathomable process.

They were so beautiful that no one wanted to break them up, even when they were located in inconvenient places, like the middle of a nascent wheat field. They used precious fuel and lifting equipment to gather them in an area that would someday, or so the chief town planner assured them, be a rock garden to rival any on earth.

In his role as a doctor, Carlo was busy every day. Too busy to ever see the rock garden. David had more free time. His more nebulous role consisted primarily of keeping Carlo fed, clothed, and comfortably housed. He'd gone by once or twice to see who Carlo was working with, but it had been clear more important things than entertaining his husband occupied Carlo.

He could have done useful things. Every hand was appreciated, but he chose to spend free hours in the rock garden, leaning against a boulder, and thinking about his place here. He'd found no confidante for his frustrations and ambitions during the voyage. So he'd come here, to a great round filled with red and amber and yellow and somewhere deep below, a lambent green like new growth.

You'd expect a colony to feel busier, but there were moments when you could swear you were the only person on the whole world. No one around to hear him, so he spoke aloud, rehearsing what he'd say to someone else after he'd left Carlo.

"What he did broke us," he told the boulder he leaned on. Sunlight played over its surface as it listened. "I couldn't trust him anymore."

He broke off to look down the hill towards the river. Three monkeys sat on the bank, the same sunlight touching their fur into a golden blaze. They cupped long-fingered hands to dip them into the water, drink from them, while they continued to stare back in his direction.

"I know he thought we'd start a family. But I believed this place would buy us time to pull away. Carlo could get used to not having me around. I could get used to not having him."

Because Carlo did do a lot, David had to admit that. But he

didn't think they'd ever mend what had happened. It lay between them like a poisoned wound, too tender to look at, let alone touch or speak of.

Perhaps if he could have said this to Carlo. He didn't know why he couldn't, why every time he tried to broach the subject, anger choked him into speechlessness. Instead, here he was, alone and talking to a rock.

A voice in his head said, *tell me more*.

The surveyors had missed several things, but the talking rocks were the most important. Not that they affected the colony's existence. It wasn't the first colony to find itself dealing with intelligent species missed by the surveyors.

The reason the surveyors had missed the phenomenon was the fact that it was not until they had been clustered together that the rocks began to speak, although they failed to explain what lay behind the previous silence.

Talking rocks. Not that they talked, exactly. They spoke in your head, in whatever language you spoke best, so Carlo swore they spoke Parisian French, but David heard it as standard English. Although the many rocks seemed indistinguishable and seemed to share information, a fact which led some to think them a hive or group mind, so if you spoke to one you spoke to all of them.

But David, like some of the others, thought that he could detect the traces of personality. He returned to that first one each day.

Carlo praised him for his discovery, saying, "Someone needs to figure out what they are. No one thinks they're dangerous, but how can we know that until we understand them? But don't touch them, don't go too close."

David could have predicted Carlo's attitude towards the planet, but it didn't prove the detriment he'd thought it would be. Carlo wouldn't touch or taste anything untested. He kept the planet away from him. But as a result, he didn't get the Pomegranate fever (called that for the redness it brought to the skin) that many caught from the stick insects nesting in the long grass's roots, and he nursed David tenderly when he shared the fruit that intoxicated for a few hours, then brought a two day long hangover.

Still, Carlo wouldn't come talk to the rock as David had. David thought perhaps this was a way to deal with his feelings, talking to the rock, as though it were confessor or therapist. But talking about his situation only made it all seem worse, let him go back to those old resentments and refer to them over and over until they were as fresh as the day he'd first gathered them.

He tried to gather information. But the rock didn't want to talk about itself. It answered questions with other questions. It wanted details of the colony life, details sometimes so personal David wouldn't have confided them to any human. He kept trying.

He did learn a little, although it was muddled and cloaked in semimystical terms. The rock claimed that they existed not just in this dimension but another, another that the humans were unequipped to sense, called Elsewhere. It referred to storing its mind and personality there, as though it was only a protrusion from that dimension.

He kept returning to their origin, asking questions. Questions that the rock would not answer, although he kept trying, rephrasing the question as though some new combination of words might unlock the secret.

But the rock kept asking him questions in turn. Asking him about his feelings.

He said one day, "Sometimes I feel as though I'm made of anger. If you took away that, there would be nothing left."

The rock was silent for so long that he wondered if it'd heard him. Finally its words seeped into his head. *We can show you what to do with it*, it said. *We can show you how to put it outside yourself. Is that what you want?*

He answered immediately, no question as to whether or not this was what he wanted. He wanted to put the anger outside himself, no longer have to deal with it. "Yes," he said.

You would need to learn to access Elsewhere, it said. *I could teach you.*

David thought this would excite Carlo, the thought that his lover would learn what the rocks could teach, would become an authority on this strange new technology. No other human would know how to do this thing.

But Carlo said, "That's going too far. You're exposing yourself to alien forces. It could hurt you."

David thought, *would it really matter to you? I would be out of your hair then anyway.* Two days ago, after yet another strained argument laden with unspoken resentment, David had made a bed for himself in one room, one for Carlo in another. Neither of them knew what to do with what they'd become. Perhaps this would be a solution to all that.

Carlo said, "I can't forbid you, of course. But I can ask you not to do this, surely." He stared at David, his eyes pleading.

David looked away, thought for a moment, as he mustered words, then let his gaze snap back to meet Carlo's. He said, "What you can't stand is the thought that I might actually become my own person. You're worried I might become more important than you to the colony."

"That's not fair at all," Carlo said.

It wasn't. But David ignored that. "I'm going to do this," he said. "I'm going to be the first human to do this."

You think we are wise, the rock told him, half statement, half question.

"You sit and think all day," he joked. "Surely that is the very definition of wise?"

We are trapped by emotion, the rock said. *You are to be envied, for your traps still allow you to move.*

This confused him, but he didn't dare ask any of the experts about it. They were angry that he'd gotten as far as he had, that the rock spoke to him when he was, he heard Gupta mutter, "a hobbyist." He'd seen it happen to the other spouses. They were pressured to start childbearing, begin the population process. Most of them had, resulting in a large number of pregnancies across the tiny city. Wherever he looked, David seemed to see someone waddling by.

David could have started a child at any point. He'd had the necessary augmentation, he could carry it after drawing on both his sperm and Carlo's as he'd been taught. The fact that he hadn't decided to do so yet, despite those silent expectations, set him apart as much as anything else.

But he and Carlo hadn't discussed it. Sometimes he caught a sad, patient look in Carlo's eyes but it only infuriated him, as though Carlo had said, "It's just a phase." David felt maneuvered and trapped. He hadn't agreed to bear children, hadn't expected the insistence that beat beneath the colony's expectations like a pulse, not heard but felt like a reverberation throughout it.

He laid his hands against the boulder. It was so beautiful, that rock. The layers of nacre covering it showed light in their inner depths, colored crimson and purple, shot through with threads of gold.

"What will you teach me to do?" he asked.

I will teach you what was taught to me.

"Who taught it to you?"

An Elder, the rock said, but the mind-picture that accompanied that word was not of an immobile lump like the boulder he crouched beside, but rather a flickering creature made of light and electromagnetic sinew.

"Is that what you will become in time?" he asked, heart beating quick with excitement. Why had he been so much more successful in coaxing answers from the rocks than anyone else? It wasn't so much that they refused to answer questions as that they diverted them. They'd answer a question with another question. You'd find yourself telling them things, things you'd never told another soul—how you lost your virginity, or that time in the drainpipe, or what you'd done to your sister's favorite toy.

He knew his friendship with this one was unusual, but this unusual? He spun a fantasy in which the colony acknowledged his contributions, his groundbreaking success, Carlo looking on with love and a trace of envy.

That would be satisfying. Vindicatory.

The rock said, *It is what I might have become if I had understood then. Now it is too late. I will teach you to make ___ of ___.*

He didn't know what either of those words were. The accompanying mental pictures only confused him. He pressed on.

It was difficult, of course it was. Anything easy wasn't worth it. Only the hard things were worthwhile. It meant trying to see colors that he'd never seen before, trying to imagine shapes that were inside out and right side up and inverted all at once, like watching a tesseract, a cube cubed. But as he worked at it, he began to glimpse the dimension the rocks spoke of.

He saw flickers there. He asked the rock about them. The rock gave him a picture of the golden apes that capered by the riverbank. *That is where they keep themselves*, the rock said.

When the lesson was over, a bit of nacre rolled in his palm. He'd made it himself, using the odd mental twists and turns dictated to him.

Made it out of emotion, by summoning the memory of joy. It shone like sapphire, but a sapphire filled with light, beautiful and amazing. He'd give it to Carlo, now that he knew the secret of the boulder.

But he wouldn't tell Carlo just yet. He'd perfect the art before he showed it to his husband.

Every day he came back to the boulder and practiced. His pockets were heavy with bits of nacre, but it wasn't enough, was never enough.

Finally the boulder said, *Remember what you asked me*?

"How to let go."

Now you begin, it said. In his mind it showed him certain other steps. He saw how to look down into his very roots and understand them in a way few other humans had.

So many resentments hidden away, some from early days, long nursed. Others more recent, piled high and deep and fresh. That sludge, accumulated from mulling over slights and insults.

It surged around him like a wave, pulling him under. Panic gripped him. He reached out, trying to transform the emotions. They were different than channeling joy or happiness or love. They pulled at him with inescapable hands. He could feel the rock regarding him. He could sense a cluster of the golden apes, watching sorrowfully, and he could feel intelligence in their gaze.

That surprised him, but the rock said, *They store part of themselves in Elsewhere, as we do. That is why your scientists never thought their minds complex enough to prove intelligent.*

So not just one intelligent species, but two? The surveyors would be upset by how far off they'd been.

He would have to tell someone.

But he could feel the emotions all around him, making it hard to think. He opened his eyes, or tried to. Something trapped them, lay over them. He could feel the nacre creeping over him, encasing him. Anger made solid. A prison of his emotion.

Suffocating him. Was this what the rocks were? Gupta had thought they somehow preyed on the apes, but in reality they were what the apes became when they did this.

The rock said, its mental voice tinged with sorrow, *You do not understand. As I did not understand.*

Understand what? David thought, but his lips could not move to speak.

Making it manifest is only the first step. After that you must let go, or become like me.

He felt a touch on his surface, on the part of him that was not completely covered. He heard Carlo's voice.

"Stop it! You've got to stop whatever's happening to him!"

And Gupta and Tompkins, arguing, the words indistinguishable.

Why did Carlo sound so frantic? This was for the best. David had never been able to let go of the anger. It had kept them apart, as surely as the layers of nacre would.

But there was warmth where Carlo's palm was pressed against his skin.

"I won't let this happen," Carlo said. "I love you, David. Don't leave me. Fight it!"

I love you, too, he wanted to say. *That's why this is for the best. I'll clear the way for someone who'll treat you better.*

Somehow Carlo was reaching into Elsewhere, touching him. And where he touched, the hard nacre melted, gave way.

But deep in its core was something unmeltable. Anger at the thing he tried to never think about. Carlo, telling him of the affair he'd had with a nurse. Ben. He'd told David it meant nothing, had been a mistaken impulse. Swore he'd never see the other man again.

Every resentment, he thought, had started there. That was the core of it all. Unless that was gone, nothing could slow the flow, to melt the layers of anger and resentment and frustration around him.

He could feel Carlo overcoming his fear and loathing, reaching out to his lover.

How brave of Carlo to try. How futile.

He felt an answering wash of love at the thought of his husband, reaching into an alien substance, to try to save him. Carlo believed in him. He didn't know why, but Carlo wanted him here. He hadn't brought David along out of spite or to rub his nose in his own uselessness. He was here because Carlo wanted him in his life.

Could he forgive him? Could he love Carlo as much as he deserved?

With the thought, the nacre softened further. Wherever their love touched each other's it was melting, somehow. And with that, he pushed harder, trying to batter through the wall, flinging his love against it. He found the core of hurt and anger and jealousy and pain. He didn't want to be one of the rocks. Didn't want to live immobilized by his emotions. He thought of the things he loved about Carlo, even the things that irritated him and made him fond all at once.

He was too full of anger. It wouldn't be enough.

He couldn't forgive him.

But he could. He could let go. He grappled with that hard lump, cracking flakes of it away. He'd made his own mistakes. He could let Carlo have made some too.

It was enough. It was enough to crack the core into a thousand pieces. Still there, but the edges were bearable now, somehow.

He blinked away the shards, feeling the layers crack, feeling them fall away. The anger was still with him, the resentments, the frustrations, but they were different now, as though he was looking at them from another point of view, while all around him faces gaped and he swam out of Elsewhere and found himself where he belonged, in his lover's arms.

In Simon C. Larter's action packed tale, a freelancer and his trusty A.I. respond to a distress call from an isolated colony ravaged by indigenous beasts, only to discover the situation is far from what they'd expected. Remember, future colonists, ignore warnings at your own risk!

INNER SPHERE BLUES

SIMON C. LARTER

No matter how you analyzed them, messages were fuzzy near the galactic center. Always. Didn't matter how many cycles you dedicated to decoding, minimizing noise, static gusted through communications like Jovian wind, blurring them and only ever allowing half the story through, if you were lucky. At least Yu Chen was lucky more often than not.

He paused and straightened when the ping sounded in his earpiece, letting the crowbar drop to the rock-strewn surface of the asteroid. It fell slowly in the low-grav, bounced lazily, settled. 'Go ahead,' he thought.

Another ping, followed by a burst of static, then the message. Chen listened, watching the slow wheel of the system's central star as the asteroid executed its ungainly, wobbling orbit, before cueing the transmission once more, and then a third time. Grace repeated the sub-aural tags as the communication replayed: *Keywords: colony, life-form, aggressive, assistance, rewards.*

Chen ran it through again, then bent to pick up the crowbar. 'Run the diagnostics one more time. Compensate for mag interference and G-bend,' he thought.

As if I hadn't done that already? Grace said. They said AI developed a distinct personality after a few years in service. It figured he'd gotten the snarky one. Maybe he brought it out in people. Or computers.

"Do it again," he said aloud. "And this time compare and correlate with the transmission from M20-1617-Delta. I don't want a repeat of that fiasco."

Grace sounded irritable. *I did that, too. What, no trust?* 'Just run another analysis,' he thought. 'Normalize and report on all potential errors and their probabilities.'

If a computer could roll its eyes, Grace would have been straining her ocular muscles. *Understood.*

The computation would have been done in microseconds, but, as an advanced AI, Grace knew when to keep silent. Chen bent to pick up the crowbar, muttering silent imprecations, and applied himself once more to the task of breaking the drill bit loose from the metallic deposit in which it was jammed. Robotics had allowed for wonderful advances in innumerable fields, but there was still no substitute for plain old elbow grease in some situations.

I heard that, Grace said.

Chen snorted.

Freelancing was no kind of life anymore, Chen thought. After a few decades of skirting the edges of civilization, picking up piecemeal work, trading in violence and mined exotics, the shine had started to wear off. Freedom from authority was a lifestyle benefit, but a hand-to-mouth existence could only remain exciting for so long. More and more, lately, Chen had found himself longing for a real atmosphere, a comfortable bed, and the predictability of routine. A man of his skills would be able to make himself useful on any number of the fringe worlds, wouldn't he?

"Run it by me one more time, Grace," he said aloud. Thought-communication was faster, certainly, but it didn't do to let one's vocal chords atrophy. Singing in the shower did only so much to keep a voice in practice. "And tell me again how we could be wrong."

Several different scenarios flickered behind his eyelids as Grace broadcast information to his visual cortex. He'd seen them all before, but since the debacle on M20-1617-Delta, he'd made it standard operating procedure to review distress calls a minimum of ten times before even responding. Depending on how long the jump between systems took, he'd review it several times more before dropping into orbit, too. Anything to avoid litigation, he thought. Litigation was always so awkward.

"What does the database have to say?" he asked, not for the first time.

Another flurry of images: colonists; a bubble town; quadrupedal indigenous beasts—all claws, fangs, and fur; dead bodies; crematorium chimneys. *It's too fringe for Central to investigate further. Colonists are members of a religious sect. They'd been warned not to settle, but ignored the communiqués. Problems ensued, naturally.* Grace had a knack for making her sub-aural transmissions sound annoyed.

Granted, Chen's newfound cautious streak had to be bothersome for an AI used to reaching nanosecond conclusions and moving directly to the execution stage, but there were situations that even superbly-programmed machines couldn't adequately parse. Intuition hadn't been rendered into code yet.

It all seemed straightforward. Still, Chen had seen too many inner-sphere communications go wrong to believe his first impressions of any given transmission.

Time to destination, twelve hours, thirty-six minutes, Grace said.

"Good. Wake me in ten hours." Chen dimmed the lights and relaxed against his pillow. "Earlier, if anything goes wrong."

I'll let your discorporated atoms know if we hit the galactic core, Grace said.

The planet glimmered gray and blue against the black recesses of space as the *Chance* oriented her thrusters and decelerated toward a synchronous orbit. Chen watched as masses of cloud moved against a vast sea broken only by the occasional brown-green patch—islands in a world-spanning ocean. The pressure of the restraint straps eased, then disappeared as Grace cut the reverse thrusters, the *Chance* settling silently into orbit.

'Let's find out what these colonists want us to do for them, shall we?' he thought. 'Open a channel to the main settlement.'

A brief quiet ensued, during which Chen watched the slow swirl of clouds below. He'd seen some stunning sights in his time near the core—glittering clouds of stellar ejecta, dead star cores with molten mineral crusts, micro-black holes shining synchrotron beams every which way—but the sheer beauty and variety of planetary systems never failed to amaze him.

The silence stretched. Clouds swirled. Chen waited.

"Uh . . . Grace?" he said.

They're not responding.

Chen blinked. "No response at all? Are they still there?"

The equipment is functional. They're receiving the hail, but aren't opening the channel.

"That's a first."

I tried the emergency channel too, but it's set to auto-respond with a 'No assistance required' code.

"Then why the distress call? Are the operators on coffee break."

Grace offered no response other than a silence that could only be characterized as "frosty." Chen had yet to figure out how she managed that, being a mere silicon neural network. "Do you think we're too late?"

Catastrophic colony failure unlikely.

"And you can't scan them through the atmosphere."

No.

Chen stood and headed for the galley. "Coffee sounds good, actually. Keep trying to open that channel."

Of course.

The scent of freshly-brewed caffeine began to permeate the cabin as Chen walked back toward the beverage unit. Stimulant inhalants were all well and good, he thought as he curled his fingers around the warm mug, but sometimes the old-fashioned methods offered comforts lacking in modern forms of delivery. Returning to his chair at the console, he took a long sip and settled in to wait.

Nothing. An entire two hours of nothing. Chen had nursed two cups of coffee, speed-viewed three lectures on the history of galactic imperialism, and indulged in a lengthy shower, but the colonists had remained frustratingly silent. The cams trained in the direction of the settlement showed nothing but slowly milling clouds, broken by the occasional glimpse of green. Presentiments of disaster had been flitting through Chen's brain for the past hour. That and possible overcaffeination combined to make for a vague nervousness that refused to dissipate no matter how many mantras he chanted.

He exhaled slowly. The cloud-strewn expanse of ocean shimmered placidly below him. Chen tossed back the dregs of his cold coffee and tucked the mug into the netting on the side of his seat. "All right, Grace, enough waiting. Take us down, but keep the channel open."

Gentle acceleration pressed Chen back in his seat. In the viewscreen, the planet swelled. He breathed deeply, deliberately, and watched the near-uniform grey blur of the clouds resolve into sharp-focus peaks and valleys.

And then they were pushing into the atmosphere, the subtle red of thermal glow creeping at the edges of the monitors as friction heated the shields faster than the ship's computers could compensate for the distortion. A diffuse river of white flowed past, flickering, streaked with grey, a turbulent blindness. Chen had seen it a hundred times, each of them disconcerting.

Grace tickled his subconscious with an offer of mild sedation—standard procedure. He rejected it—standard procedure. Let younger spacers ride the waves of chemical hormone modulation—Chen was old enough to believe in the value of the endocrine system. Millenia of evolution couldn't be *that* wrong, after all. There was only so much a silicone-based intellect could understand about biological phenomena.

I heard that, Grace said.

The main colony structure came into view by degrees—the clouds dissipating slowly as the *Chance* descended, streamers and wisps of cloud seeming to graze the viewscreen, blurring the distant dome of the energy shield. Grace reversed thrust, slowing them and banking into a long, slow loop over what was now revealed as a sizable complex of buildings arrayed in a spoke-and-wheel pattern around three central plazas dominated by large, circular pools of water. Broad avenues radiated outward, lined with tall trees and high, waving stands of grassy plants.

Not a single human was visible.

"Grace?"

The buildings are heavily insulated. Thermal scans aren't returning anything useful.

"Take us in closer."

The *Chance* angled into a steeper bank, bringing them down to just a few hundred meters above the shimmering energy field. Chen magnified the view until individual fronds of foliage could be seen on the trees, but the only visible non-plant life forms were occasional small, rodent-like creatures that scurried into the shadows whenever light broke through the clouds. The gleaming white stone of the sidewalks were carved with wide, spiraling designs that looked for all the world as though they'd never seen the passage of a single bootheel. Everything appeared spotless.

Everything appeared abandoned.

"Are they underground, do you think?" he asked aloud.

Scans indicate significant underground cavities, but I get the same results from the surrounding jungle. Appears to be a function of local geology.

"And still no response to the hail?"

None.

The *Chance* was now passing over the landing platform outside the energy barrier. Chen twiddled the controls on his chair's armpad, zooming the cameras for a better view. It wasn't encouraging. Between the rust spots like lesions on the steel grating, the broken signal lamps, and the vegetation that had grown across at least a third of the pad, it looked as though it hadn't seen use in years.

"When was the last known resupply shipment, Grace?"

The colonists discontinued resupply shortly after settling. Self-sufficiency is apparently one of the prime tenets of their faith.

"Can't fault them for that," Chen mumbled. He'd been operating on the same principle for two decades, now. "Suppose there's no need to maintain a landing platform you don't use. Still," he said, "I don't like this. We should have seen someone by now."

There could be another explanation.

"What, they all nap at this time of day? Prayer time at the temple? Ritual indoor food fights?"

They continued their circuit above the colony. A movement on the screen caught Chen's eye. 'Lock on that,' he thought, and the screen image shifted suddenly, zeroing in on a small, robotic cleaner unit that had just exited its dock at the base of one of the buildings. Chen watched as it whirred across the sidewalk, scooping up invisible flecks of dirt and pausing now and then to perhaps work at some recalcitrant stain, until his view was blocked by intervening buildings, the *Chance*'s flight path carrying him onward. The camera panned back out, and now Chen could see thousands of the tiny cleaner bots hurrying to and fro, scrubbing the pathways and roads of the empty city.

"Well, if something disastrous *did* happen here, the evidence certainly wouldn't last long," he said.

Within minutes, the bots had fulfilled their programmed directive and scooted back into their docking stations, the avenues of the city returning to sterility once more. Street after empty street passed under Chen's camera's lens, the only movement the slow swaying of the vegetation, the furtive darting of the rodentia. By the fourth circuit, he had had enough.

'Set us down on the landing platform on the next pass, Grace,' he thought.

The *Chance* slowed and settled as they looped around for the last time, dipping lower, until the waving tips of the jungle were bare meters beneath the star-hardened skin of the spacecraft. And then, with a gentle burst of reverse thrust, a hiss of hydraulics, and a slight lurch, Chen's ship touched down. The engines' steady *thrum* faded. Metal ticked and creaked as gravity asserted itself. Chen released the restraints and stood, stretching.

"Right," he said. "Now how do I get through that energy shield?"

Despite his many experiments with nullifying agents, cleaners, and absorbent filters, the air in Chen's rebreather still tasted of plastic. If the fringe-jumpers' message boards were any indication, he wasn't the only one with this problem. Stabilizers notwithstanding, it appeared as though some mildly distasteful interaction between polymer, oxygen, and human tastebuds was inevitable, despite the prodigious number of AI cycles that had been dedicated to the problem.

I—

'Yes, I know you heard that, Grace,' he thought, smiling. 'But you'd be famous the galaxy over if you could find a solution for it.'

A frosty silence. Again. She couldn't fix the plastic taste of rebreathers, but she could certainly imbue a non-response with the scent of disapproval. Perhaps she could patent that.

Very funny.

'I thought it was.'

The humid air was an almost physical force, palpable even

through his en-suit as Chen walked down the ramp. He gripped his rifle firmly, scanning the undergrowth on either side of the landing platform for unexpected movement. Unfamiliar sounds filtered through the earpieces on his helmet—strange tweets and chirps, dry rattles, the swish of vegetation in foreign winds, the far-off susurration of waves on a distant shore. His boots raised tiny clouds of pollen with each step. The desiccating inserts in his gloves were working overtime in the tropical heat.

'So what do these problem carnivores sound like?' he thought.

Grace broadcast directly to his auditory cortex. It was a low, grunting sound, a bass rumble that grew to a high-pitched shriek, the kind of noise that, if heard in the dark of an alien jungle, would freeze a man in his tracks. Chen rolled his shoulders.

'I'd really rather not hear that first hand,' he thought. 'Do me a favor, Grace, and tell me if anything larger than a Chihuahua approaches.'

Naturally.

He checked the energy stores in his rifle for at least the fourth time, exhaled slowly, then stepped out and away from his ship, toward the city.

The vines draping the platform and walkway curled and gripped the grating, claiming it for their own. Thin, vegetative feelers, rippling in the desultory breeze, gave the plants a questing air as Chen passed, as though they were scenting an intruder. Part of the walkway had succumbed to rust and collapsed, the steel gone, flecks of ceramic coating disappearing into the thick humus coating the jungle floor. If it weren't for the faintly-glowing barrier at the end of the walkway and the sterile perfection of the colony beyond, Chen would have found it easy to believe that civilization, here on this forgotten planet near the core, was succumbing to entropy, an uncaring world absorbing and discarding humanity like so much refuse. He walked on.

This close to the shield, Chen could feel it in his gut. The vibration in the air reached through his en-suit to shiver his skin, the hair on his arms and legs prickling with the proximity. He reached for his belt and grabbed the transmitter.

'Go ahead, Grace.'

He held the device up, moving it close to the wall of force. His fingertips tingled. Somewhere beyond his perception, electronics flickered and produced a localized emission intended to nullify the barrier. The forcefield glimmered briefly, beginning to fade...then snapped back again. Chen reached his free hand toward it, only to feel an uncomfortable tingling in his fingertips.

'Grace?'

It changed frequencies. She sounded annoyed.

'So follow it.'

I'm trying. It's started to autorange.

Chen frowned. 'Any recourse?'

Give me a minute.

He glanced over his shoulde at the jungle. The vegetation writhed, ever-shifting. For a brief second, the sun broke through the cloud cover to slash light across the landscape. The autodim of his visor kicked in, but still Chen had to blink away the afterimages. In the full-strength sunlight, the trees seemed to stand taller, their branches straining skyward, as though the entire landscape were inhaling.

He turned back. The arm holding the transmitter began to cramp. Chen switched hands, raised it again.

Hold it still, Grace said snappishly. Then, *Wait.*

'What is it?'

Movement approaching rapidly, two-eight-zero degrees. Large mammal.

Chen whirled, slipping the rifle from his shoulder and holstering the transmitter. "How close?"

One hundred meters, closing at 18 meters per second.

"Dammit, Grace!" He burst into a run. The *Chance's* ramp looked a kilometer away.

How about you try frequency-matching a random algorithm with—

"Oh, shut up," he gasped. "How—?

Fifty meters.

"I'm not going to make it."

No.

Chen skidded to a halt, dropped to one knee, and brought the rifle stock to his shoulder. 'Power up, Grace. Weapons online.'

Behind him, he heard the engines hum to life, a steadily increasing vibration that trembled the platform. But over the bass rumble, he could hear a crashing in the jungle, approaching fast.

Twenty meters.

Ten.

The space of a breath.

And then a huge, tawny form bounded from the foliage and sailed onto the platform. A flood of adrenaline sharpened Chen's vision, quickened his heartbeat.

The beast was sleek, its fur short, dappled. Muscles bunched and rippled in its shoulders as it paused, its massive head raised, nose twitching as it scented the air. Claws like scimitars clacked on ceramic-coated steel. Chen swallowed as its eyes, dark and luminous, fixed on him. Its head cocked.

A familiar surge suffused Chen's chest. He felt a grin stretch his lips as excitement and fear commingled, his breathing speeding, deepening. He was on his feet. The rifle sight zoomed, locked on the base of the thick neck. His trigger finger tightened.

The big cat blurred into motion. Recoil jarred Chen's shoulder once, twice, three times. Energy pulses sliced the air. An impression of bared teeth and glistening gums. So close!

A sledgehammer blow slammed Chen's side, and he found himself flying, the world doing a slow cartwheel before his eyes. A flicker of platform, ship, colony, jungle, platform, ship...impact.

Blackness.

Light.

Green foliage waved in staccato visual bursts.

Chen sucked in a deep breath. His arms twitched. Sudden sound; recoil pushed the rifle into his shoulder. He bolted upright.

Blinking, he stood. His head felt loose, perceptions flickering like old film. His limbic system screamed of danger.

Instinctually, unthinking, he flicked the switch on his rifle for blanketing fire, then held down the trigger. A blinding sheet of energy streamed from the barrel of the weapon, pulses too fast for the eye to follow scything everything within reach. Backpressure sent him stumbling backward, his rifle jolting upward, energy bolts tearing rents in the clouds above.

Silence. He was sitting down, back against a tree. A red light on his rifle blinked insistently—charge drained. Looking down, he realized his finger was still clenched tight on the trigger. A deep breath. Chen pried his hand free, let the rifle droop.

An insistent something intruded on his thoughts.

. . . *Chen! Yu Chen!*

He looked up. "Grace?" he said, then swallowed. "What . . . ?"

It's still alive. Sixteen meters, forty degrees. And there's movement in the colony.

"The . . . colony?"

Yes, the colony. Hang on.

A sudden prick jabbed at the base of Chen's neck. He inhaled sharply, squeezed his eyes shut. Artificial adrenaline and painkillers spiked his system as Grace triggered the en-suit's built-in medtech.

Better?

'Yeah. Thanks,' he thought. 'Now run that by me again?'

Hostile is sixteen meters at forty degrees, alive, not moving. Colony showing activity. Party approaching.

"Brilliant," he muttered. "Now they show up."

Chen levered himself to his feet and shouldered his rifle. He drew his pistol. 'Who's coming to see us?'

Twelve colonists. Various ages. Hostile still not moving.

Chen grimaced. The painkillers would only last so long, he knew; tomorrow would be brutal. He grasped his weapon with both hands and began to run.

Wait, Grace said. *More hostiles. Six of them, four hundred meters and closing. All directions.*

Chen bolted.

Leaves slapped against him as he pushed through the thick foliage at a dead run. Vines grabbed his ankles. Ahead, the rusted white of the platform came into intermittent view.

Three hundred meters.

He erupted from the jungle into the relative clear around the platform. A jump, a plant of one foot on a fallen log, a flying leap onto the stained grating.

Two hundred.

From the corner of his eye, Chen could see a small party approaching the platform walkway from within the barrier. He turned his head slightly. The man in front—tall, gray beard protruding around a slimline breathing mask—raised his hands as he approached the forcefield. It shimmered and drew back. The party passed through.

One hundred.

He turned back toward his ship's ramp, putting his head down. It was close. He would make it.

"Hold, traveler!"

Chen stumbled, slowed.

Fifty.

"What?"

The tall man raised one arm. "Hold!" he said again.

Thirty.

Chen spun, his pistol at the ready.

The jungle swayed and rustled and discharged six massive, muscled carnivores. They leaped with exquisite grace onto the landing platform and walkway before Chen, sextuple death machines with eyes and fangs aimed toward him. He felt the prickle of their attention in his spine. Pink tongues protruded between razor teeth.

'Acquire targets, Grace,' he thought.

A thin hum of hydraulic actuators indicated the repositioning of pulse emitters. But the *Chance* boasted only four. Two felines against one slim pistol. Chen shrugged inwardly. It would be quick, at least. Perhaps he could save a few of the colonists with his actions.

'Return to Central when it's over, Grace. Reintegrate.'

It's not done yet, she said.

He smiled as he drew a bead on the nearest beast. "All right, then."

The voice cut above the whine of the *Chance's* engines, a sharp bark of authority. "Traveler, I said *hold!*"

Chen eased his finger back from the trigger and exhaled through his teeth. The animal in his sights blinked and yawned. Its jaws were cavernous. When its eyes opened, it fixed Chen with a bright gaze and settled onto its haunches.

Footsteps approached. Chen spared a glance over his shoulder, saw the tall man approaching, a small knot of people hanging back behind him.

"Traveler." His voice was gentle. "Stand easy."

"Easy?" Chen echoed. "Staring at imminent death?"

The man's voice seemed weary. "You have it wrong, traveler. There is no death here."

"Tell that to my ribs."

"You misunderstand."

Chen snorted. "Then help me sort it out."

A firm hand landed on his shoulder. "Gladly."

The man stepped past him, hands spreading wide. He moved toward the felines, smiling. Chen blinked, then darted forward, grabbing at the tall man's arm. "What are you doing?"

"Nothing I haven't done before, stranger."

Gently, but firmly, he pulled free of Yu Chen's grasp and walked toward the big cats. Nonplussed, Chen watched, the barrel of his pistol wavering, as the man moved forward. The nearest beast stretched, its spine curving, claws scraping furrows into steel, its eyes fixed on the approaching figure. Lips pulled back from teeth. Chen half-raised his gun.

And then, with a languid slump, the cat lay down on its side, raising its head to nuzzle the tall man's hand. The long tongue flicked out to lap at the extended wrist as the man ruffled the fur behind the tufted ears. Chen looked on, his jaw making a solid attempt to unhinge itself.

'Grace?'

Her response, when it came, seemed tinged with the machine equivalent of chagrin. *I got nothing.*

"Uh . . ."

"You see?" the man said. "The *leoniyes* pose no threat to us, or you."

"But" —Chen took a deep breath, winced at the sudden pain that radiated along his ribcage— "one attacked me!"

The man's face darkened. "Did it?"

"It knocked me halfway to the outer clusters!"

"It hit you?"

"Yes!"

A raised eyebrow. "Then where are the claw marks?"

"Where . . . ?" Chen looked down at his en-suit. It was rumpled, yes, slightly stained, but intact. He glanced to where the reclining cat's claws had raked furrows in the steel of the landing platform, then back to the side of his suit.

"If it had wanted to kill you, we wouldn't be having this conversation." The man offered a small smile. "It was . . . playing."

"You're serious."

"Yes."

'Grace?'

It . . . computes. It appears he's speaking truth.

"But . . ."

A movement off the right of the platform caught Chen's eye. He pivoted, snapping his pistol into position. His injured ribs grumbled portents of tomorrow's pain. Foliage decimated by a full-auto burst from a CD-600 pulse rifle swayed and rustled. A broad, blood-streaked face pushed through the greenery, mouth agape, tongue lolling.

"Oh," the tall man said, a world of disappointment condensed into a single syllable.

The big cat pulled itself forward, out of the clutching foliage, its muscled forelimbs bunching, straining. Its hindquarters followed. Chen's stomach dropped three stories.

The animal's hind legs had been shredded. Deep, cauterized channels had been plowed in its flesh, energy pulse holes burned through muscle and bone alike. It moved with a pathetic limp, its hindlegs twitching and flopping ineffectually. A high keening noise burst from its throat when it saw the group on the platform. The assembled felines, standing, responded in kind, their sympathetic wails penetrating.

A soft huffing sounded behind him. Chen turned. The tall man's companions—a motley group of men, women, and one child—were staring at the injured beast. The child, a girl, began to cry quietly.

"There, Marya," the man said, brushing past Chen to go to the girl's side. "Do not weep. All will be well."

The girl pressed her face into the tall man's stomach, her small frame shaking with sobs.

"Stranger," the man said, regarding Chen once more, "I must ask that you leave." Cordial his words might have been, but there was no mistaking the anger in his tone.

Chen took a deep breath, then another. He clenched his teeth. "There was a distress call . . ."

The tall man blinked. "Pardon?"

"The distress call said—"

"Friend, we sent no distress call. We ask nothing from Central, save our independence."

"It said," Chen went on, anger clipping the edges of his words, "you were suffering breaches. The cats were killing people."

"Ah." The man looked down at the girl, brought his hand up to stroke her hair. A smile ghosted his lips. "I see."

"What?"

He released the child, bent to murmur something in her ear, then turned toward Chen. "That signal," he said, "is more than a decade old."

Chen blinked at him. His mind hit high gear.

A ten-year-old signal? Inner sphere distortion. It had to be. But hadn't he checked for that? He'd run the message more times than he could count.

'Grace?'

Silence.

"Grace?"

The communiqué wasn't date-stamped. She sounded defensive. *Interference.*

Chen squeezed his eyes shut. Not again. Had he really made the same mistake twice?

Really?

When he opened his eyes, the colonists were staring at him. The big cats on the platform were staring at him. The dying feline in the jungle was staring at him. Somewhere in the center of his chest, a hard, small knot of self-judgment stared at him, too.

Perhaps, Chen thought as he heard the uncomfortable apologies spill from his lips, it was time to retire after all. Surely one of the fringe worlds could use a man of his skills.

Surely.

'Damn those inner-sphere transmissions,' he thought.

Indeed, said Grace.

Early colonists' adventures may indeed become the foundation of legends for the generations which follow. In Jennifer Brozek's tale, a grandmother regales her grandchildren about when colonists and aliens struggled over water, and it took a child to lead the way to understanding.

DUST ANGELS

JENNIFER BROZEK

Dac smiled a brave smile at Ken then closed the stockroom door with a finality that reminded her that this room, this safe haven, could also be their tomb. She heard her husband riveting the boards in place as she turned and saw twelve sets of excited, terrified eyes watching her.

There should be more, she thought. Then shook her head of iron gray hair. The rest would be hidden in other homes. She could not protect them all. However, looking at the children before her made her realize how frightened they were and how much they needed her to be a safe haven in the storm. She smiled at them. "Look at you. Snuggled down like it was story time."

"We get a story, don't we, Dac? Momma promised."

That was Sho Whelan with his ginger hair and almond-shaped dark eyes. The youngest here at five.

Dac nodded. "Of course." She stepped through the room, weaving her way through the cluttered room of shelves and makeshift beds, to the rocking chair that the children had automatically left empty. "But today's story will be special."

"Why?"

The rumble of something exploding too near for comfort silenced the room. Much of the excitement disappeared in the growing fear of what could happen. Dac smiled, turned in a flamboyant arc to get the children's attention back on her, and sat down.

"Because this story is true." Dac settled into the old rocking chair, a relic from another world, and put the pulse rifle to the side—within reach but out of the way. She held up her hand to forestall the next question bubbling up. The children were polite and well-mannered but it was an extraordinary time and tempers ran hot.

"When we came to New Montana on one of the first colony ships, our town was simply called 'Haven.' Nothing more. Nothing less." She watched Sho's face screw up in confusion and glanced to the other children. They knew where this was going. Every child over the age of five knew . . . and still they leaned forward, eyes bright.

"But . . ." Sho stopped himself and looked around at the other children, knowing that sometimes his questions upset them.

Dac smiled. "Why is the town called 'Angels Haven' now? That is what this story is about." She raised her gloved hand. "And how I got this."

Sho's eyes widened as he stared at That Which Should Never Be Mentioned.

"Are you ready?"

Again, something either hit the ground with tremendous force or landed too close for comfort. The ground rocked with a roaring sound from the north. Dac kept her face as neutral as possible and continued on without waiting for an answer. "This is the story of the Dust Angels and how they came to be. The first thing you need to know is that my name wasn't always Dac. It was Elsa . . ."

Haven, for all its hardship, was a godsend. The years on the colony ship had taken their toll. Far too many people died from illness in the close quarters. More became insane. We need fresh air and sunlight or we die. Just like all living things. Of course, I was born on the colony ship. I didn't see sunlight until we left the safety of our quarters. Mom being pregnant with me is what got my parents on the ship to begin with.

When we landed, New Montana was in the last stages of terraforming. Ships towing asteroids of ice were still months and months away. There was no Lake Degrasse or Lake Tyson. The polar caps were barely a blip on the screen. Those came later. When they did, it saved the planet from failure.

Did you know, once it was a crime to waste water of any type? It was sacred. First offense, imprisonment and hard labor. Second offense . . . exile.

We only had three ways to get it: a protected water table deep in the ground, the recyclers from the colony ship, and moisture farms. The protected water tasted the best. I was a little girl, just older than you, Sho, and my main chore was to collect water from the well. It was a cranky old thing with a pneumatic pump but it worked. I just had to make it work with a bit of sweat and quiet swearing. You know how stiff pumps get, even when they're powered.

Haven wasn't like it is now. There was no grass or trees or bushes. It was miles and miles of dirt, dust, and rock. I would see whirlwinds of dust called 'dust devils' by my parents. I never really agreed with the term. They didn't looked evil to me. They looked like the wind playing in the dirt. We don't get them anymore. Not since the lakes were created and integrated into the terraforming.

One day something fell from space. A meteorite we thought. Not unheard of and, despite the light in the sky, the explosion wasn't so bad. It didn't really hurt the buildings. Then again, plaststeel is awful hard to hurt. The thing it did do was break the recycler from all the ground shaking.

This was somewhere between devastating and a catastrophe. Everyone had to ration water more than before. No showers. No washing dishes unless it was with third-use water. And, besides drinking water, the crops got the most of it. Or we would've starved. It was hard. The land was hot, hard, and thirsty. It made all of us like it.

Suddenly, water carrying was so much more important. I didn't realize how important until the Dust Angels came. We didn't know what they were . . . and they didn't know what we were.

My parents were worried about the water. That much was obvious even back then. Would we have enough for the animals? Would we have enough for the crops? Would we survive? Every colonist knows that a newly terraformed planet is a risk and a challenge. The rewards of land, space, a place to call your own, meant the danger of living on the edge for decades.

Things got worse when the animals began to die. My brother, Paul, found the first of the dead animals. You wouldn't think those big steers with their horns and bad tempers could die. They could. They did. I found out about it by overhearing my parents talk in hushed tones of terror.

Is there anything more interesting than something that frightens your parents? I see those looks. Of course not.

Danger or no, we all still had chores to do. My water carrying doubled. I was bringing all of the water in from the pump. Why the pump wasn't closer to the house, I didn't know. But, at the time, if it hadn't been so far away, I probably wouldn't have found out what was killing the herd.

I first saw it while I was headed out for water. I thought it was a dust devil. A big one. But it didn't move with the wind. So I followed it, watching. That's when I saw the eyes. They looked like glossy stones against the dirt. I didn't know what it meant. Then I saw it go to the grazing pasture. The herd ran from it but one of the smaller females wasn't fast enough. The dust devil landed on her, and next thing I knew, the cow was dead and the dust devil looked fainter . . . but redder.

It was red with the cow's blood and every other fluid in her.

I dropped my buckets and ran home.

Lord help me, I told my parents what I saw. I didn't know what was going to happen. If I had . . . No. That's times past. That door can't ever be closed. My father grabbed his pulse rifle and my brother, Nels, came with him. I showed them where it happened. They sent me home with the water. I didn't stay home. I had to go get more water. Or so I told myself.

Really, I just wanted to see.

What I saw was my brother murdered before my eyes. What I saw was a dust devil become a blood devil, filled with my brother's lifeblood. What I felt was terror and sadness. I wanted to know why. So I followed it. I kept the water carrier with me. I thought I would be able to fend it off with those heavy buckets.

I followed that dust devil all the way back to where the meteor had struck. I watched it hover above the unfamiliar ball of metal and rock in a hole far shallower than I thought it should be. I didn't know what meteors looked like. I didn't know I was looking at a space ship. Not at first.

But then I saw the dust devil rain blood down upon the ship and, while I watched, the rock melted away and the metal sphere healed itself, and the dust devil became something more. A whirlwind of glittering wind. Things clicked over in my mind.

That's when it occurred to me that perhaps the dust devil wasn't a monster. Maybe it was an alien and it just needed water. Water was so precious. And I had two buckets with me. I gathered my courage to pick up one of the buckets from the harness and bring it over to the hole. I faced the heat of the earth, and my fear, and poured the water into the hole.

The alien sensed it and rushed over to the water, sucking it all up from the ground. While it rained the water on metal sphere, I hurried back to the other bucket and picked it up. When I turned around, the alien was there. Right there. I froze. I didn't know what else to do. I closed my eyes and waited to die.

Instead, the bucket got lighter. I opened my eyes and saw the alien was clear again. It was so pretty and I was so young. I did what most children do: I tried to catch one of the sparkles. Instead the alien caught me; caught my hand; caught my mind. Because, as it had filled itself with the water in my bucket, its primary need was taken care of. It's secondary need came forward—the need to know the land.

While my brother was being killed, my father was searching the hills for the monster we knew was out there. That was how he found me. One hand holding a bucket. One hand stuck in an alien made of wind and jeweled eyes. I know this because I was seeing through the alien's eyes. I begged with all my heart for it to spare my father. I could feel its thoughts, so different from my own. But there was one thing that it understood—family.

Even as my father ran at it, futilely shooting it with the pulse rifle, it understood that there was more to this planet than it first knew. It had not seen us as sentient . . . or even living. The whole time my father railed at it, punching the wind, trying to free me from its grasp, the alien learned from me. It learned my fear and sorrow. It learned it had killed one of my family. It learned that we communicated in a different way than it did.

Then, as my father fell to his knees and begged the alien to spare my life, I felt the first touches of direct communication. The request to use my voice because it had none. I agreed. I didn't know what else to do. I'll remember until my dying day what those first six words were: "Sorrow. Apologies. Mistake. Water needed. Please." I repeated this three times.

That was it. When the alien used my voice, my eyes glowed with its light. My father stopped his begging and listening. His only answer was to ask it to let me go. The alien did, finally understanding what father wanted. When it did, it retreated to its ship. I fainted.

When I woke up, I was back at the house, in bed. My hand was bandaged up. I couldn't see or feel it. Not at first. Then I remembered what had happened. And I remembered so much more of what I understood from the alien. I knew I needed to tell my parents.

Half of Haven seemed to be in my house. They were all arguing about what to do. Most wanted to destroy the metal sphere. Father was of two minds. It had killed Nels but it had let me go. When I came out of my room, they wanted to push me back in. I fought them. The aliens . . . the dust angels as I had started to think of them... needed our help. The dust angel was horrified at killing another sentient creature. It had not met one like us before.

It was mother who made everyone listen to me. The alien had let me go. It hadn't hurt me that much. It had learned from me. The alien needed water and then it would leave again.

But where to get the water? No one knew how much water it needed. And no one knew what would happen if it didn't get it. But we needed water to survive. It was a problem the colonists had never faced: a new alien species and a need for the same resource of water. No matter what happened, we were on our own.

While they were arguing, I slipped out of the house. I could feel the dust angel calling to me. I thought enough ahead to bring out a pitcher of water with me. I was in the yard with the dust angel when my parents discovered me gone. We waited for the colonists to discover us out in the front yard. While we did, I tried to explain the problem with the water. How rare and precious it was. The dust angel seemed to understand and was still sorry about the death it caused.

Once everyone found me and the dust angel, I let it use my voice again. There was a conversation but it was a long time ago. Decades. Mostly I remember them talking about the water and how much was needed. Father asked about Nels and the dust angel offered a life for a life. Its life in particular.

It wasn't a mistake that I was generous with the dust angel to begin with. My parents refused to take the life of the dust angel. It's because of my parents' compassion that Angels Haven still stands. In the end, the colonists agreed to share the water. It would be tough on both sides, but it didn't need to be one or the other. No one had to die for the other to live. Resources could be shared and that is the way we've lived ever since.

Dac's voice was soft as she told the tale of Angels Haven. She only raised it when she had to; when the fighting got too loud or when the bombardment came too close. New Montana was a fertile and valuable planet—one worth fighting for.

"Sho, bring me the water." She watched while the redheaded child did as she bid. He brought her the sealed pitcher. She accepted it with both hands, knowing that soon her left hand would be useless again, and put it on the box next to her. Watching the excitement rekindled in the children's eyes, she put her hand to the pouch on the long thong around her neck. It was something she never took off. The older kids knew what was coming.

"You know that in times of real danger . . . the kind of danger that we of Angels Haven cannot face alone, we go to ground. You've heard us speak of it. We did when the UA came. We did again when the Corporation came. You weren't alive then but you've heard tell of it."

Bright eyed and awed, Sho could only nod.

"Now, I'll show you why." Dac opened the beaded bag and poured a single clear gem from it. It was five centimeters in diameter and gleamed with an inner light that shimmered like ice crystals. "This came from the dust angel. After my parents refused to take its life, when it understood what my parents thought it was offering, it decided to stay and protect Haven from all comers. It gave itself to the planet because it took from the family, my family. It exchanged its life with its people to protect us. This is only one reason we leave a bucket of water outside each night."

While she spoke, she let the beaded bag fall into her lap. Holding the gem in her good hand, Dac pulled the glove off her other hand, revealing the desiccated flesh. She held that hand up for everyone to see. She held it there for a moment, letting curious eyes drink in what had been hidden for so long. She knew it looked dead, mummified. The sight no longer horrified her. The glove was to protect her fragile skin.

"This is the hand I first touched the dust angel with. It didn't know what it was doing would hurt me. I didn't know what it was doing would allow us to communicate."

She looked at Sho. "Dac isn't a name. It's a title: Dust Angel Caller. With this hand, I can talk with our guardian." She paused and looked at each child in turn. "Eventually, someone will need to take my place. It is a small sacrifice for something so important to our community." She was pleased to see that more than half of the children, some her grandchildren, still looked her in the eye.

Dac put the gem into her withered hand and clenched her fingers around it. There was still pain but it was better than the forthcoming numbness. She dipped her hand with the gem into the water and closed her eyes. When she pulled her hand out again, a small glittering whirlwind rose out of the gemstone.

Dac opened her eyes but light shone out. "The family heard my call. They come. They are here now. Heed. You are protected. The pact is upheld." She was vaguely aware of the gasps of surprise and awe from her charges.

Dac closed her hand and her eyes. "Thank you, dust angel. The pact is upheld." She put the gem back into the beaded bag as one of the older children took what the empty pitcher before it fell from Dac's lap. Already the numbness spread through her hand. There was nothing she could do about it. Perhaps in a year she would have limited use of it again.

The silence of the storage room echoed the sudden silence outside. The dust angels were doing their work. Soon Ken would free them from this room and every sacrifice made would be worth it.

A light touch to her withered hand—felt more as a pressure than anything else—made Dac open her eyes. Sho was there, stroking her deadened flesh, looking curious. "Does it hurt?"

"Only for a little bit. Then it doesn't hurt at all. Not anymore." She spoke the lie with a smile, knowing one of the children listening would need to take her place soon.

Maurice Broaddus is known for his gritty urban fantasies set amongst The Knights of Breton Court, *where Arthur legend meets inner city Indianapolis. He departs with a tale of missionary soldiers and a psi ops priest investigating stolen property, a kidnapping, and an infection of her people . . .*

VOICE OF THE MARTYRS

MAURICE BROADDUS

A mist rose from the cool waters stretching out in front of me. For all of my training, open water terrified me. I viewed open water the same way I thought of God: majestic and mysterious from a distance; holy and terrifying when caught up in it. My body trembled, an involuntary shudder. The migraine following my regaining consciousness meant I was at least alive. Then I vomited, confirming it. My biomech suit was a self-contained unit long used to handling my various excretions.

Even in the gloom of the graying twilight, my surroundings danced on the nearly artificial aspect of my holo-training sequences. The large fern leaves, a shade too green, undulated in the wan breeze and water dripped from their undersides to splatter on my visor. My arm clung to a piece of bobbing driftwood, a pillow tucked under it and clutched to in my sleep. Water lapped just under my chin, but my seals were intact. A tired ache sank deep into my bones and I suddenly felt my true age. Remaining the physical age of twenty-seven every time I re-upped for another tour with the Service of the Order factored into my decision for continued duty. Vanity was one of the many sins I worked on.

I tapped at my wrist panel. The action caused me to slip from my precarious perch. I re-adjusted myself, half-straddling the shard of log, and bobbed in place. The seconds retreated, collapsing into a singularity of eternity as I waited for it to lock onto the beacon of my orbiting ship, the *Templar Paton*. I used its navcom signal to map my position relative to our colony site. The terrain's image splayed across my visor view screen. I paddled toward the shore.

Memories returned in fragments. Thundering booms. Balls of light. Clouds illuminated against shadowy skies. Ground explosions scattering people. Heat. The confusion of artillery bursts. Targets acquired. Chasing someone. Shots fired. A shelling run toward me. Bolting across a field. The sudden pressure in my chest.

Falling.

My biomech suit sealed me off from the world, shielding me from the errant breeze or the rays of the sun on my skin. It filtered sound through its receivers, the noise of which became muted when navcom channels engaged. The world appeared to me on my visor, scanned and digitized. Set apart, I was a foreign intrusion and like any other pathogen, the world organism raised up antibodies to fight off my presence.

I pushed through the thick canopy of leaves whispering in the breeze. A series of sinkholes replaced the metal cabins where our camp had been. Our fields burned to the ground with methodical thoroughness. Animal carcasses torn asunder by blade, the occasional limb scattered here and there left to rot. Insects worked over them in a low-lying cloud. The ways of death and reclamation were a constant throughout the universe.

Even without the proximity detector, I knew I wasn't alone. Despite the isolation of my suit, my psi ops enhancements functioned at high alert. A Revisio. Their eyes, too big for their head, studied us with their critical gazes, a mixture of curiosity and mild disdain. Their skulls smooth and higher, they carried themselves with an invisible burden. The Revisio sentry skulked about the remains of our camp. Turning over scrap metal, scanning the rubble, it hunted me. It. Once a mission required judgment protocols, thinking of those about to be judged as an "it" made the work easier.

Despite its deceitful bulk, the biomech suit moved with great stealth. Dampeners reduced its external noise to near nothing and its movements were as fluid as my own. It no longer mattered that I had lost my rifle. For up close work, I preferred my combat katas.

Though I came upwind of it, the native turned at my approach. It ducked the wide arc of my kata, the edged baton bashing only air. It tried to bring its spear to bear, a lazy gesture I blocked. I spun into it like an unwanted tango partner, thrusting my biomech-enhanced elbow into its gut. I grasped its wrist, praying the thumb lock I had it in was as painful to its physiognomy as a Terran's. Wrenching its arm up and behind it, I ignored the snap of its bone, and held it long enough to deliver another couple punches. The creature slumped in my grip.

"Where?" I asked. This Revisio had no understanding of my language at all. That was why psi ops lieutenants were attached to mission units. Besides security, we provided translation. The metal cap, a socket on the back of my skull, pressed into its place within the suit. Repeating my question, I projected my intent. Spatial concepts were the most difficult to process between cultures. Few saw life the same way. The universe, our place in it, was a matter of perception and perspective. Where did he come from? Where were my compatriots? Were there any survivors? The questions were meaningless, but my intent clear. In the end it was about brain chemistry and interpreting signals. A complex swirl of thoughts bubbled beneath a barrier stifling my efforts. Had it been trained, it would have shut me out entirely. Along with its derisive sneer, I managed to perceive the direction from where it traveled.

The issue at hand became what to do with the native. We entered *hostile relations*. Once those conditions were met, military protocols were in effect. Casualties were expected.

I would pray for his soul.

My fears for this mission were being realized.

This wasn't how this was meant to be, but this was the only way it could end.

They dubbed the encampment Melancholia as the cyan sphere of the gas giant they orbited filled the sky. The name had more of a ring to it than its designation CFBDSIR2149. The crew cleared a space for this camp along a crest overlooking a lake. Hastily constructed sheds broken down from the self-contained modular sections of the supply shuttles surrounded a central fire. Test batches of Terran agriculture grew outside our camp, green sprouts rising from dark earth. A thick grove of trees, lush with leaves the span of an arm's breadth, encircled our site. A mist swept across the ground. I longed to take off my helmet and smell the foliage for myself, but that would've broken mission protocol. Once deployed to the field, infantry had to maintain preparedness at all times. I patrolled in my suit. I slept in my suit. I wept in my suit.

"Magnificent isn't it," Novice Wesley Vadair pulled his blond hair back into a ponytail. Three days of beard growth stubbled his long angular face. His eyes squinted in an involuntary muscle spasm, but no one ever commented on his facial tick.

"What is, sir?" Novices were little more than glorified civilians, but he had mission command.

"The view. The potential. You can practically feel it on your skin. Well, I suppose *you* can't." He slapped my back in an all too familiar way, not that I felt it within the suit. He meant to convey a camaraderie we didn't share. "Professional hazard, I suppose."

He was already tap-dancing on my last nerve. "Is this your first colony plant?"

"That obvious?"

"If I could detect excitement levels, your readings would redline."

"Good. Excitement is contagious." Novice Vidair began walking, waving an invitation to join him.

"Then it's a blessing I'm in this suit, sir."

"I welcome your cynicism. I'll win you over, you'll see. I'm going to do things differently than other colonies. My dad was a planter, I grew up in a colony like this, so it's in my blood."

"Familial hazard, I suppose."

"See? We're going to get along great, you'll see. This colony won't be burdened with dogma. It will be more about community . . ."

The novice went on to describe his vision, sprinkling it with all of the popular jargon and buzzwords of the day. Community. Conversations. Authenticity. But I knew this story would end the way it always did.

My parents were the vanguard of "indigenous leaders" novices aimed to raise up. They were killed in their colony. I forgave their murderers. At their funeral, I mouthed my prayer over and over. "They know not what they did."

Other indigenous leaders took me in and raised me. Then I

witnessed how such colonies worked from the other side. Coming into our neighborhood, planters demanded that we act like them, speak like us, until there was little left of us, in order to receive their gospel. Eventually their colony plants dotted the land like grave markers.

I joined the Service of the Order on my sixteenth birthday.

"What do you think?" the novice drew me back to full attention.

"Permission to speak freely?"

"Always."

"I've heard it before. If you didn't believe that, you wouldn't be a planter. But planting is what it always is."

"What is that?" the novice asked.

"A wealthy culture sending out well-intentioned missionaries using the gospel to impose themselves on indigenous cultures to create satellites of themselves."

"You make us sound like . . . cultural bullies."

"It's a push or be pushed universe, sir."

"And what's your role in this process?"

"I'm *your* pusher."

I followed Novice Vidair from the settlement into the valley. He spouted the right words, but I had the evidence of history. My own history. Once in the Service, the Order selected me for Jesuit Training School, officer candidacy. I faced grueling studies in advanced mathematics, Latin (because all alien cultures need to be fluent in languages long dead on Terra), stellar cartography, astrobiology, logistics, strategy, game theory, and tactics. Part of me suspected the reason they took such a special interest in me was because I was reclaimed, a story of redemption they could point to. I was that rescued urchin from the streets with a tragic story. They could pat themselves on their backs for having saved me from the fate of my people. My parents.

"They know not what they did."

The valley was a potential utopia, but I knew that our leaders back home saw only desirable natural resources and a strategically positioned planet. The gas giant CFBDSIR2149 absorbed most of the radiation emitted by the solar system's star, lowering the amount of UV radiation, so fewer mutations followed. It slowed evolution, leaving fixed gene patterns. Life took the hand it was dealt and would be required to play for a long time. Whatever life forms that dominated here were frozen mid-step on the evolutionary ladder, easy kings of the food chain, but the transplanted flora and fauna displaced native species with ease.

"We're almost there," Novice Vidair said. "You can see me in action."

"Sir?"

"What do you know of this planet?"

"It's the moon of CFBDSIR2149 of the AB Doradus Moving Group. The planet itself is a gas giant," I said.

"Yes, yes, a rogue planet ejected from its system, cradled by its neighbor. But what understanding do you have of life on Melancholia."

"I . . ."

"Look over there. We call them Species A."

A group of natives milled about a cave entrance. Long simian arms rippled with burly musculature. Thick brows ridged deep, inset eyes. A hulking brute stopped and sniffed about, his protruding jaw set and resolute as if he'd had a bad day out hunting. Picking up a stone, he hurled it in our direction. We didn't budge. Satisfied, he joined the group of other males guarding the entrance.

"Aren't they magnificent?" He spoke of them the way I spoke of my cat back home.

Despite their primitive appearance, they were more human than I felt. Stripped of my culture and my people, not much of me remained. I wore the emptiness that came with a life of obligation and duty without passion and meaning. My neural pathways had been re-routed to accommodate the cap. I could sync up with a computer in order to download information, language matrixes, and action protocols in an instant. My physiognomy recalibrated with each tour of duty, slowing my aging process and knitting tired muscles back together. I hated and resented the Order as much as I loved and needed it. The Order gave me life and purpose. The Service left me without scars, physical ones, that is.

"Do they . . . speak?" I asked. "It doesn't appear that they have reached the level of development necessary to grasp the intricacies of the gospel."

"Now who sounds elitist? I'm sure they have some sort of proto-language. If we can teach the gospel to children, we can reach these noble savages. We have an opportunity here, a people in the early stages of their development. With our help, their culture, yes, their entire civilization can be made in God's image. We will avoid the mistakes of the past."

The colony buzzed with excitement at the caravan's approach. Taking point, I escorted Novice Vidair. Fraught with possible misunderstandings, first contact protocols were the most dangerous part of the mission. Novices were trained to be opening and welcoming, but service members were trained to watch for and deal with threats. My parents had paid the ultimate price for the short-sightedness and arrogance of novices.

A delegation of four rode beasts similar to hairless horses. Three of them were armed with spears, with daggers tucked into sashes girding them. The last of them wore a tunic of animal skin. This aliens' musculature was smoother, closer to resembling ours. In my experience, the more a life form mirrored ours, the more nervous I became. Violence was our way, no matter where we found ourselves in the universe. My rifle, displayed but trained at the ground, showed that we had teeth. It helped establish trust as they knew what they were dealing with. Novice Vidair all but applauded with joy at their approach. With every step forward, the novice nipped at my heels. I placed my open hand in the center of his chest to scoot him behind me.

"Greetings," the head of the processional said. "I am Majorae Ha'Asoon."

As he dismounted, I processed the sounds through my linguistics database. My cap thrummed while reading and deciphering the intent of his words. I relayed the message's content.

"I gathered as much. 'Hello' is 'hello' on any world." The novice smirked at me with dismissive disdain.

"'Hello' is only 'hello' if not followed by weapon fire." My cap continued to process their language. Given enough of a sample with my psi impressions monitoring the emotional intent of their words, the cap sped up, relaying translation in near-real time. I conveyed the greeting on behalf of the novice.

Majorae Ha'Asoon turned his back to me to address Novice Vidair directly. "On behalf of the Revisio, we welcome you. You are not of . . . here."

"We are of a far off planet called Earth," Novice Vidair said with the tone of a parent telling their child a fairy tale.

"You, too, can travel the stars?"

"We detected no signs that you had such technology." The novice glanced towards me to confirm. I nodded.

"We don't require vessels to travel. We are star stuff. Flotsom carried in the void," Majorae Ha'Asoon said.

"I don't understand," I said.

Majorae Ha'Asoon kept his back to me. "Yet you recognize us?"

"You look like the natives, the ones we have called Species A. Except . . ." Novice Vidair said.

"Different. We, like you, are from another world. We, unlike you, have a natural claim to the *Derthalen*, as we have called them."

"What claim?" I asked. The steel of my tone caused Majorae Ha'Asoon to shift to his side, keeping me within his peripheral gaze and making a smaller target of himself. His guards moved in predatory lurches. I swung my rifle to my side.

"The right of first. We are children of the blue planet."

"We detected no life on CFBDSIR2149," Novice Vidair said.

"Perhaps not life as you measure it. We are . . . what would you call us? A virus?"

"You look pretty big for a virus," I said. My cap continued to whir, locked in a processing loop, as if under a cyber attack of some sort.

"Floating unicellular things. I suspect as you would measure it, each strain you would consider an individual."

"Some sort of communal intelligence," Novice Wesley Vidair said with that too-excited glee of his. "Fascinating."

"This virus business, I still don't understand," I said.

Majorae Ha'Asoon sighed. "It's simple. We were carried here on the backs of asteroids. The *Derthalen* made for natural hosts. Understandable since we are from the same star stuff. Once we take over, we mutate and spread. Each generation of the virus is a mutant strain of the last. The course of the infection has physical side effects, too."

"I noticed. You appear smaller," I said.

"No, you don't understand. They . . . we have evolved." Majorae Ha'Asoon gestured to his men. "Look around you. We're not running around naked as beasts. Our form allows us a certain resonance with the minds of others."

My cap tingled again. The Revisio's "resonance" functioned

as a low level kind of telepathy. Each of them had the equivalent of my cap, though theirs operated naturally. Communicating with each other, gleaning information from us, interfering with my cap, it explained why they were so familiar with our ways. It also made them more of a threat.

"This is utterly fascinating. We've suspected and explored that potential in our own kind. There is so much we could learn from one another," Novice Vidair said.

"We had hoped you were a peaceful party," Majorae Ha'Asoon said.

"We are, I assure you."

"You are well armed for peace." Majorae Ha'Asoon cast a sideways glance at me.

"Experience has taught us to be cautious when exploring new worlds and contacting new peoples. Not all missions end . . . diplomatically."

I thought of my parents.

It was an Easter Sunday service. A group of "seekers" entered to learn more about the Scriptures. Seeker were my parents' favorite kind of people to talk to as they were open, questioning, and thinkers. But the seekers were actually members of the *tarik*, a group of faithful believers from a competing sect, armed with an array of weapons: guns, break knives, ropes, and towels. Towels. Because they planned for a lot of blood. No one told me what happened, only that my parents were killed in the line of duty. But the full truth resided in the reports which I had access to once I joined the Service of the Order. The *tarik* read from the Scriptures before the assault began. They tied my parents' hands and feet to the chairs.

"When you oppress the weak and poor of your own world, trampling their freedoms, there are consequences. For the oppressed and the oppressor," the tarik *leader said.*

They video recorded their handiwork, which I have never watched despite it being still available in the archives. The power of the stark words in the reports, combined with my imagination, was enough: ritual slicing of orifices, disembowelment, emasculation, decapitation. One hundred thirty-two stab wounds total. You never know what you really believe until those beliefs are tested, in that moment when you put your life on the line for them. My parents believed in a loving and just God. But I forgave the killers. I forgave them.

"If you got business with them," I leaned forward, letting him see the full bulk of my armament, "you handle it through me."

"Stand down, lieutenant," Novice Vidair said. "We're all about meeting new friends."

"Yes, heel," Majorae Ha'Asoon said.

I re-gripped my rifle, doing my level best to resist the urge to cram the butt of it into his . . . its . . . inviting jaw.

"We would welcome a conversation of equals." Majorae Ha'Asoon made a point of once again turning his back to me.

"Indeed. I look forward to it."

Majorae Ha'Asoon bowed slightly then hopped on his beast. With a swirl of his hand, he led his men away.

"That went rather well," Novice Vidair said.

"We need to prepare for an attack," I said.

"I appreciate your hypervigilance, but that's not the way to follow up a first contact."

"Did we not hear the same thing? They are a colony, too. An entrenched one from what I gathered. And we are a threat to them."

"Lieutenant, nothing of the sort was said. Perhaps we can establish a trade of some sort with them. Crops, maybe. We have much to offer them. And them us."

"I know a scouting party when I see it. They were taking our measure." I stared at him full on. "And make no mistake, I have killed enough people in the service of the Order to know how this story ends."

"Then perhaps all of the blood on your hands has made you paranoid. We serve God's will."

That was the problem with many novices. They existed in a bubble of privilege. They were used to people deferring to them simply because of their special calling. People were done no favors by being raised up coddled. It made them soft. People needed to fight off things: germs, people, life. It built you up. If you didn't . . . I thought of Species A, the *Derthalen* as the Reviso called them. Not even allowed to name themselves.

"God's will or not, this expedition will face troubles. My job's to handle them."

"You don't understand, this could be the miracle from God that we were looking for."

"Excuse me, sir?" I said because "what the hell nonsense did you just spout" would have gotten me court-martialed on the spot.

"You feared that Species A might not be cognizant enough to receive the gospel."

"A notion you dismissed."

"Yes, before we learned of Species B. Perhaps we were meant to evangelize Species B in order to bring the message to both them and Species A."

"But the Revisio are a virus."

"Exactly. Imagine the gospel spread by viral transmission. It would make our task so much easier and our stay shorter. The Lord's ways are not our ways. Just like our ways have you obeying the orders given you. My orders."

The Lord sure could bring out the stupid in some folks.

It all came down to the story we lived by. If the metaphor of that story could be changed, the individual could be changed. An ungodly people deemed less than human. Our people, holders of secret knowledge and power, could trade the Scriptures for land and resources. Evangelism encouraged by way of blaster rifles. *My* blaster rifle. The people traded one sin-soaked culture for another; forced to change their language, their names, their gods, their cultures. Suffer a slow death by assimilation. The story always ended the same way.

"Your . . . orders." My set jaw began a slow grind, like I chewed on something distasteful. I peered down my nose at him. "Allow me to correct any misconceptions you may be laboring under: I'm not here to wipe your nose. I'm not here to diaper your behind. I don't cook, clean, or sew. You think I sings and dances real good, too? You need to get out of my face and let me do my job."

Novice Vidair squinted at me. His facial tick intensified when he was angry. "Lieutenant, you are confined to your quarters for a day."

"I thought I 'always' had permission to speak freely."

"Until you cross the line. I give some people enough rope for them to hang themselves."

His order probably saved my life.

This wasn't how this was meant to be, but this was the only way it could end.

*

I tracked the trail of the attack party back to a series of looming structures, ominous shapes of deeper shadow in the night. I wasn't even sure what my mission was anymore. I had ignored my action protocols. I hadn't signaled the *Templar Paton*, not with a status update or report. I moved on instinct. I couldn't call myself investigating the native culture, though the biomech sensors recorded and logged everything. Without knowing if my party was even alive, I couldn't claim to be on a rescue mission. And if they were dead, the Order wasn't about vengeance.

The Service, however, was all about God's judgment.

Flexing my arm and wiggling my toes, I tested each extremity to make sure everything still worked. I craned my neck to each side, popping out the kings, certain that I should just name the knots in my shoulders since they accompanied me for so long. The pain focused me on the task at hand: I had bastards to kill. In Jesus' name.

Having lost nearly an hour finding a suitable blaster rifle, I crouched behind a fallen tree. No breeze moved the leaves. I detected no sounds of birds or any other night life I had gotten used to; as if the structure's very presence stilled all life to a respectful silence. The main building seemed carved from the very mountain itself. With its massive foundation and heavy fortifications it could have been a temple or a citadel, the high arch of its entrance and formidable walls meant to convey a mixture of awe and intimidation.

Twin sentries patrolled the main archway. The entranceway lit by a series of torches, illuminating an area leading up to it that provided no cover. Even at full sprint I couldn't cover that distance and subdue the guards without raising an alarm. I skulked through the dense forest, circling the castle. At its side, a rivulet emptied into the lake below. Perhaps it was simply an underground stream, or a natural sewage line, either way my heart stuttered at the prospect of wading through it to make my entrance.

The force of the water's current slowed my progress, each lugubrious step an act of determined will. Steadying myself against each tunnel wall, the water rose past my thighs. My visor digitized my surroundings as much as it could through murky dimness. The lights on my biomech suit didn't penetrate the pitch. The cramped space pressed in on all sides, with no way to measure when my journey would end or if my progress would be halted by watery death. But I kept walking. Faith buoyed my steps. I had to believe in something, have a hope to grasp on to. No amount of faith could still the apprehension that gripped me as the water lapped my helmet. I only had a few more steps before the water overtook me. I couldn't help but re-think my plan. It made sense why this passage wasn't well guarded. Only a fool would chance this.

Water filled the entire passageway. The biomech suit continued to circulate air as the emergency supply automatically kicked in. A timer on my visual display counted down how many minutes of air I had left.

I continued to march deep within the compound. Scant seconds of air remained. Shafts of light stabbed the darkness ahead. I gulped one last breath of air. The passageway opened into a bay of sorts with a grate above me. I punched handholds into the wall to scale my way to the top. I bashed though the metal mesh and pulled myself up. The biomech suit was designed to augment its occupant's efforts, but the work began with my own exertions. I collapsed, sprawled out along the floor while my re-breather unit replenished itself.

The room was a mechanical closet of sorts. Heat baked the room, a cauldron of molten metal rotated. Levers and switches cranked away. The way the cauldron revolved, its contents' heat could be used to warm the complex or be hurled as a distance weapon. I left it for the structural engineers aboard the *Templar Paton* to puzzle out. The floor was connected to the walls, rigged to fall into the antechamber below in case of emergency. Advanced thinking. It began to make sense, even to my simple infantry mind. The Revisio, no matter how advanced, how evolved, couldn't just drop tech into this world. Life on their own planet precluded them from building anything. To build they had to have, well, thumbs. They were essentially advanced minds. They may have evolved the Derthalen, but it would take a while to get their technology to the point where they'd have the tools necessary to advance their world. But it wouldn't take long. Within a generation or two, they'd rival us. I could only imagine what they'd do on our world with our tools and technology.

Scrounging a loose bolt, I tossed it against the door. I listened for a few moments before I retrieved it and threw it again. A guard opened the door. I expected as much. It stood watch against anyone going into the room, not coming out. I yanked him inside. Another soul I would have to pray for. Later.

Flickering pools of amber from torches created puddles of shadow throughout the long hallway. The biomech wasn't designed with indoor stealth in mind; however, it was built to carry armaments. I crept along the shadows as best I could, setting a charge as I went, praying none of the natives decided to turn down this way. I followed the sounds of garrulous chatter and laid two more charges. I may have lacked Samson's strength, but blowing a support wall would collapse a room or two if it came to that. I hoped my escape wouldn't come to another trek through the crawlspace. I took a measured breath then plunged into the room.

The room ran the length of a banquet hall, ringed by long tables. Behind them, male and female Revisio wore simple tunics of animal skins. In the center of the room, game roasted on spits. Musicians played in the corner while two women danced. Guards stood at attention by each table. My entrance halted the revelry. I fired once above Majorae Ha'Asoon's head. My blaster scorched the wall before I trained my weapon on the leader. "Where are my people?"

"Is this more of your diplomacy?" Majorae Ha'Asoon sipped from a tall cup, unflustered.

"You have our diplomat. I, on the other hand, am not . . ."

". . . very diplomatic. Do they not have manners on your home planet? You barge into our great hall uninvited and accuse us in our home."

"Our rules of etiquette don't extend to those who lay siege to a peaceful camp, destroy our property, and make off with our people."

"You talk to us of peace? You come to this world armed with no regard for our plants and animals. You comport yourselves in the way of your world, imposing them on ours."

"As you have with the *Derthalen*?"

"This is our moon. Our dominion."

"I'll ask one last time, where are my people?"

"We have . . . exchanged ideas. They have been welcomed into our tribe. There have been some . . . complications."

"They better be unharmed."

Majorae Ha'Asoon nodded and a member of his guard departed. The others shifted positions, not grouping to surround me, but taking up more defensive postures. I eyed on the nearest exit. Majorae Ha'Asoon's attention focused on my weapon, studying my suit with the glint of greed in his eyes.

The guard led Novice Vidair to the area just before Majorae Ha'Asoon. The novice averted from my gaze, studying the ground. It had been not even half a day since the attack, but the novice's belly distended. His face gaunt, flushed with a grayish pallor, his eyelids had swollen shut. Wizened fingers dug into emaciated arms, scratching at the red splotches that ran along them.

"Are you okay, Novice Vidair?" I asked.

"They infected us." He upturned his hands. Maroon pustules blossomed on his palms like tumescent stigmata. When his eye spasmed, the muscle contraction tightened his entire face.

"We didn't know what effect our introduction would have on your kind," Majorae Ha'Asoon said.

"You mean as you force yourself on us," I said.

"Your kind no longer embraces change."

The full implications of what he intimated settled in. Perhaps we had evolved as far as we were able. I swept the room with my rifle, stilling the slow encroachment of the guards. Their movements were subtle, professional. "We resist you."

"We're the future. We build. We create. We define. We have no need of your *God*. Or your Order. We have studied your Scriptures and one 'truth' intrigues us." Majorae Ha'Asoon returned to his meal. He waved his knife about, light glimmering from its edge. "Your chosen people were called to wipe out nations and peoples before them. That is where we find ourselves. Our story destroying the one that came before it. That is the 'gospel' message you have brought us."

I watched the glint from the knife. And thought of my parents.

The first shot of my blaster burned a fist-sized hole in the center of Majorae Ha'Asoon's chest. My next shot took off a quarter of the nearest guard's head. I fired and fired, backing toward Novice Vidair. Before I could turn to shove him toward an exit, he leapt on my back.

"Too late for us." His fists slammed into my neck attempting to divorce my head from my body. My biomech suit shuddered with the impact of his unanticipated strength. "We are joined. Not one of them. No longer us. We order you to join us."

I reached around and flung him from me as if tearing off a shirt I no longer wanted. Veins thickened and bulged along his neck. Peering with overly vesseled eyes, blood trailed from their corners like thick tears. He raked fingers across my suit, desperate to open a gash.

I raced down the corridor, pursued by a mad clamor of hoots and cries as the guards were let loose from their leashes. Back-tracking to the room I entered from, I barred the door and disabled the room dropping mechanism. My people had been biologically compromised by a hostile contagion. The Revisio had genocidal intent toward the *Derthalen*. Nothing remained of this mission except judgment protocols.

"They know not what they did."

I placed my remaining charges around the massive cauldron.

Synchronizing the timers, I gave myself a thirty second window. I no longer cared if that allowed me enough time. God would see me through if I was meant to labor on. I dove for the grated opening into the waiting water. The torrent whooshed me along, flushing me from the compound like so much unwanted waste. The vibrations of the explosion rattled the passageway. I prayed the rough tunnel's integrity would hold, as the only death I imagined worse than drowning was being buried alive while I drowned.

The hillside shook, its contraction excreting me toward the lake. I dug my biomech enhanced hands into the earth until I came to a halt. The remains of the building collapsed on itself. I doubted there would be any survivors, but I would wait. Each step became more difficult as the extensive damage to my biomech suit caused power loss. Eventually, it would be inoperable. I will salvage what I can, but I needed to send one final report. With my suit compromised and the vector of the Revisio's transmission unclear, I submitted myself and this world as under bioquarantine.

From the cover of forest undergrowth I could study Species A, the Derthalen. A pod of them groomed one another, the adults sheltering the young. No one escaped agents of change. If God was already at work in their culture, as we purport to believe, then these people have earned the right to find their own way.

As have I.

In her action packed tale, Jaleta Clegg examines hazards which might arise for human colonists if indigenous life forms were unexpectedly sentient, in this case plants. Those who go ahead to prepare the way at potential colonies must survive these hazards or die trying . . .

ONE-WAY TICKET TO PARADISE

JALETA CLEGG

My first day on Eden wasn't the paradise I expected.

"Ma'am, remember your breathing mask before stepping outside," the pilot reminded me as I stepped off the shuttle.

I snapped the mask in place without comment. I knew far more than he did about such things. I was one of four environmental systems techs assigned to the new facility. Our job on Eden was to prepare it for the first wave of colonists, due in another six months. If one breath of free air killed me, it didn't bode well for the colonists.

I jogged through Eden's dense jungle. The fresh air tasted much better than the recycled shuttle air. The world hadn't evolved animals yet, only plants and insects. I was tempted to explore, but duty required me to check in first.

The research facility spread up the side of a hill, the main glass atrium reflecting the morning sun. Levels split off either side, like branches of a tree. Four greenhouses sat on the far side of the facility. Jungle foliage crowded the base of the building, deciduous forests surrounded the greenhouses and upper levels. A narrow strip of land divided the two. It looked as if someone had hacked off the jungle right at the base of the hill. I hitched my duffel higher on my shoulder as I hiked the trail to the building's main doors.

The plaza in front of the doors was new, a ragged line of bare earth along the edge. A thin film of yellow dust covered the plascrete surface. Footprints disturbed it in a path leading straight to the door. I stooped, running my finger through the yellow particles. They were all different sizes from sand grain-size down to a fine powder. A plume of yellow floated from the nearby plants. Pollen, I didn't need a botanist to confirm it. If this was the normal level, the air filters were going to be murder to clean.

I joined the end of a line waiting to get through the airlocks into the main building. Standard protocol on a new world was to keep the world out until it had been tested. The colonists would be inoculated against any ill effects of the contaminants until they could adapt to the new world. So far, only a handful of worlds had proven too dangerous to colonize.

I stepped into the airlock with the tail end of the group. Air rushed past us, blowing away any loose particulates. The inner doors whooshed open.

Sound exploded around me, people talking and arguing, equipment haulers groaning under heavy loads, footsteps echoing on the hard floor of the atrium. Outside, I'd had the wind and insect chirps. I was tempted to turn back and exit the airlock doors, but I had to report in, so I hunched my shoulders and wound through the crowd to the appropriate table.

I spread my hand on the id scanner. "Talia Korman, environmental tech."

The harried man behind the desk barely verified my credentials before shoving an id card across the table. "Women's dormitory, level three, left and all the way to the end. You're assigned to the greenhouses. They want you there as soon as possible. The filters are gummed up again."

A gangly man took my place at the table as I took my card and stepped away. I headed up the stairs in the middle of the space. The fibermat in the level three hallway showed traces of yellow powder. I made a note to recommend adding foot scrubbers to the airlocks.

I found the dormitory room and used my id card to open the door. Four sets of bunks lined the far wall with lockers and cabinets between. I picked an unoccupied bunk as far from the others as I could. The last time I'd had this many roommates, I'd ended up sleeping in a janitor's closet instead. I don't like people much, never have.

The main greenhouse lay beyond another set of airlock doors at the end of the hall. A short enclosed passage separated the two buildings with branches leading up and down the hill to connect the other greenhouses. I entered the main one. Standard procedure had two greenhouses dedicated to crops, grains that would keep the colony functioning. Botanists experimented with varieties and growing conditions to test crop viability in the new conditions. The main greenhouse was used as a garden for the preliminary crew as well as an experiment for the botanists for all the other flowers, fruits, and vegetables the colonists might want. The last greenhouse, the one most separated from the others, was where they grew native plants, testing for edibility and toxicity.

Judging by the luxuriant growth surrounding me in the main greenhouse, Eden would prove very successful as an agricultural world. I stopped to sniff some yellow flowers spilling from a hanging pot.

"The greenhouses are closed to staff, at least for the rest of the week."

I turned from the flowers to face the man who'd accosted me. "I'm Talia Korman, environmental tech assigned to the greenhouses."

The man wiped sweat from his balding head. "Good. The filters are down again. That cussed pollen gets into everything no matter what we do. Wreaks havoc on our pollination programs. We've had to dump the tomato seedlings five times now. It mutates them in the weirdest ways. Brun Heimner, chief botanist for this project."

He didn't offer his hand to shake. I didn't mind.

He walked as he talked. "Filters are on the far side. We keep scrubbing them and switching them out every twelve hours, but the fans keep clogging up. Suits are in the airlock next to them for when you go outside. We've got vines climbing up the filters. The things grow three feet an hour. If I could figure out how they do it, I'd make a breakthrough in plant genetics."

I followed at his heels. It was all standard, just like the last six assignments I'd had, except for the sheer amount of particulates. And the vines. I'd never had to hack fast growing vines off the equipment.

The fans were silent and still when we reached the far side of the greenhouse. Brun tapped the controls mounted on the wall. "We had to shut them down. Kept overheating. We've got the tightest filter they'll give us installed." He swiped his hand over the fan blade. It came away yellow. "If you can figure out how to stop it, I'll put you in for a commendation."

"I'll see what I can do."

He hurried away as I ducked under the fans to check the filter screens.

I spent an hour scrubbing the four sets of double filters then slipped them back into the vents before flipping on the fans. Warm air, rich with the smell of the jungle outside, blew across my face. I debated for a moment about suiting up to go outside before deciding to save it for later. I hated the suits. Maybe I could get away with just a mask. I headed up the hill to the grain greenhouses.

Brun stalked the aisles of the first one, three assistants scurrying at his heels. The flats of grain seedlings looked sickly, twisted and yellowed where they weren't black and rotting. Brun waved his hands over the ruined plants. "We're going to have to replant the entire crop. Try the spelt this time, and the corn hybrids." He caught sight of me near the entrance and gestured for me to join him.

A sour smell wafted from the decaying plants. I rubbed my nose, trying not to breathe it in.

"I want triple filters installed," Brun said when I reached him. "And an extra set with fans in the airlock room. The native pollen kills anything we plant in here. You'll need a laser cutter when you go outside. We've got shrubs taking over the air intakes. They don't grow as fast as the vines, but they have thorns long as your finger. Watch out for the ants, too. They're symbiotes with the bushes. As soon as you start burning, they'll swarm."

"Are they sure this world is worth colonizing?" I couldn't help asking.

Brun glared. "They're just plants and insects. Get moving. The upper greenhouse is in even worse shape. The only grain we've managed to get beyond sprouting is rye, and it's infected with some nasty fungus. This world hates grasses. We may have to use cassava or potatoes instead of grain. We're supposed to start animal trials next month, but we have nothing to feed them."

"Maybe they can eat the vines."

Brun shook his head. "Toxic sap. Wear thick gloves and disinfect when you're through. Make certain every bit of leaf or stem stays outside. These things sprout from even the smallest fragment. I don't want them inside the greenhouses."

I nodded and went to work.

The bushes outside the vents on the top two greenhouses were as bad as Brun said. Vicious insects the size of my thumb boiled out of the growth as soon as I fired up the laser cutter. Between them and the thorns on the bushes, I was very glad the suit was reinforced carbonite fabric. It was hot and the bottled air tasted stale, but I wasn't stung or scratched. I burned the bushes to the ground and spent a while zapping stray ants. Most of them scrambled into the surrounding forest, forming long snaking lines of bright red bodies and multiple legs flickering in the sunlight.

I smashed my way along a faint trail outside to get to the lower greenhouses. The forest ended abruptly just above the garden greenhouse. Bare earth showed in a ragged strip about five feet wide. The jungle began on the other side. It was like a neutral zone between two warring nations. I shrugged away my uneasiness over the strange situation, then checked the oxygen level of my tank. They were just plants.

The flickering force blade on the pruners made short work of the twisted growth of vines. I cut them back an extra twelve feet. I didn't want to have to suit up and prune every day if I could avoid it. The plants didn't attack me with insects like the bushes, but they left wide smears of sticky green sap across my suit. I swiped a glove over the mess. I'd have to scrub the suit before storing it. More tedious work I didn't want to do.

I walked down the faint trail to the lowest greenhouse, crushing plants underfoot as I went. The vents of the building were surprisingly clear despite only one set of filters on the fans. The yellow dust clung to the blades, but not as thickly as at the other greenhouses. I swiped a gloved hand over the filter, knocking most of the pollen off. A swarm of fluttering white-winged creatures swooped over my head, circling in front of the vents before drifting up and over the roof of the greenhouse.

I used the airlock of the lowest greenhouse, glad I didn't have to hack and burn any more plants. I stripped off the suit, careful to avoid the green smears from the vines. I hung the suit in the cleaner, sealing the door before starting the sterilization cycle.

The greenhouse was a riot of luxuriant growth. I paused near the closest flat. Squat plants with fleshy leaves sprouted curled vines like springs. I touched one. The coil flicked straight, snapping against my cheek. I wiped a smear of yellow sap from my skin.

"You want to wash that with soap."

I looked to the side where the voice came from. A young girl about ten standard years old watched me with solemn gray eyes. She kept her hands behind her back as she talked. "It's better not to touch anything in here until you know it's safe. I can tell you're new."

"Thanks." The yellow sap was starting to burn on my face and my fingers.

The girl tilted her head towards the door leading back to the main building. "There's a sink over there. Everyone's supposed to scrub before leaving this greenhouse."

She followed me through the maze of native plants to the sink. I scrubbed the burning sap away while she watched. I was torn between shooing her away or pumping her for information. The weird array of plants had me curious. I'd never seen anything like most of them. She stood in silence, waiting for me to finish. I decided as long as she didn't babble, I could stand her company, at least long enough to find out what she knew.

"How long have you been here?" I asked as I dried my hands.

She shrugged. "Since the building went up. My father is the colony governor."

I shoved the paper wipes into the trash. They'd be recycled into compost for the greenhouse.

I leaned against the sink waiting for the girl to speak. She studied me in silence, her face serious. I gave in after a long moment of listening to the plants rustle in the artificial breeze.

"What can you tell me about these plants? Besides don't touch."

A small smile twitched across her mouth. "The peonies are my favorites. They don't do anything dangerous. This way." She trotted across the greenhouse, weaving between the trays of plants. "I'm Nione. What's your name?"

"Talia."

"I saw you cleaning the filters. Is that your job?"

I nodded. "Environmental tech in charge of the greenhouse filtering systems."

"Watch out for Brun. The colony plants are dying. That makes him angry."

"I noticed."

Nione stopped at the edge of the greenhouse beside a bush covered in puffy pink flowers. "He yells a lot, but he's still nice. He gives me his dessert most of the time. I call these peonies. Listen." She stroked the petals of one flower. A low hum rose from the plant. "Try it." She reached to stroke a second flower. A different note joined the first.

I touched a flower. The petals were soft and silky under my finger. A third note joined the others. Nione giggled. We stroked more of the pink petals. The entire bush sang, the sound growing louder as we touched the soft flowers.

"I've never got it so loud," Nione said.

We both smiled as we fingered the flowers.

Something smashed into the greenhouse right above us where the roof curved down to the wall. The song died as if cut off. I ducked as more thuds sounded overhead. I glanced up. The white-winged creatures I'd noticed earlier were smeared across the glass roof, their insides leaking blue liquid. The bush rattled though the breeze barely touched it.

"That never happened before," Nione said.

"I'd better clean those off." The blue liquid etched trails over the glass panes despite the coatings meant to protect them.

Nione nodded.

"Meet me here tomorrow?" I asked. "I want to know what you know about these plants. And this world." None of the things I'd seen were mentioned in the skimpy brochure I'd been given.

"Will you get in trouble?" Nione asked.

"Will you?"

She shook her head before scampering to the airlock leading to the main building. I decided I could like Nione. She didn't talk much and wasn't as obnoxious as most children I'd encountered. I touched a pink flower with one finger before leaving to suit up again. The bush rustled. A single note floated on the air.

I'd been on Eden only a week when I was first attacked.

I was trudging up the trail to the grain warehouses, laser torch in hand. I stepped onto the bare strip of dirt between jungle and forest.

Ants boiled from the shrubs on the up-hill side. I froze, one foot poised above ground that heaved and twitched as the insects plowed through the loose soil. I'd never seen so many in one place. They swarmed around my legs, climbing up to my knees. I set my foot down. Bodies popped and crunched. The swarm changed direction, circling around me and the dead ants.

They stopped moving all at once, as if someone flipped a switch. Antennae flickered. I stood in the middle of a rippling sea of red bodies. Thousands of beady little bug eyes bored into me, as if sensing me for the first time.

I swallowed a knot of sudden apprehension. I sensed a vast intelligence studying me like I'd studied these ants. I backed a step, tiny bodies crunching under my boots. My thumb rested on the trigger of the laser torch. I wondered if it had enough power to burn a path back to the airlock.

The ants tumbled forward, like a wave washing towards my feet. I hit the trigger, scrambling backwards towards the dubious safety of the greenhouse. Their jaws clicked as they advanced. I burned the front ones, but the rest kept coming. The press of their bodies covered the blackened corpses with a tide of red.

Something stung my shin, right above my boot. I glanced down. A knot of red bodies clung to my suit, jaws working at a hole in the carbonite. Their jaws snipped through the toughest fabric we had. I stomped my leg, trying to shake them off. They clung tighter, never even pausing in their chewing. One wriggled inside. I screamed as its jaws clamped onto my leg. I swept the laser torch perilously close to my foot as I burned the ants off. I slapped at the one inside, feeling it crunch under my glove.

The swarm boiled out of the forest after me. I cranked the power on the laser torch. It did little good. The things just kept coming. The laser torch sputtered, its power drained. I threw it into the heaving mass. It disappeared under their squirming bodies and flashing jaws.

I ran for the airlock. Ants crunched under every bootstep. They climbed my back, chewing their way through the tubing. They severed the oxygen feed to my helmet. I couldn't breathe. I reached for the release catch. A knot of red ants landed on my face mask. I swiped at them with one gloved hand, crushing them into pulp. I couldn't take the helmet off, but I couldn't breathe with it on. I staggered. The mass of ants under foot made the trail slippery, treacherous. If I fell, they'd devour me.

Several ants crawled inside my suit. Their bites burned like acid. My lungs ached for air. I was too far from the airlock. Ants swarmed over my head, their feet scratching at the thin layer of protection keeping me from their snicking jaws.

I stumbled, falling to my knees. I couldn't reach the emergency com button. I was going to die under the swarm of ants on a planet supposed to be free of peril. I screamed in rage as I smashed ants with my heavy gloves.

They drew back. I stopped, hands poised over a suddenly empty patch of ground. The ants milled around the edge of the forest, a red tide shifting restlessly. I popped the latch on my helmet, drawing in deep breaths of air. Drifts of yellow powder poured from the jungle. A swarm of white flyers spiraled through it. I swear they directed the pollen onto the boiling mass of ants. I coughed on a lungful, feeling it burn in my chest.

The ants retreated into the shelter of the forest. The flyers circled. Yellow pollen fell like rain. Leaves rustled despite the lack of breeze. I crouched in the barren strip between the two forces. Sweat dripped from my nose.

The sun beat down. The flyers drifted into the jungle canopy, wings fluttering like scraps of paper. My nose itched. I lifted a glove to scratch, but stopped when I saw the smears of greenish body fluids from the smashed ants. I didn't want that on my unprotected face.

I got to my feet. Every bite burned with the ants' venom. I had to treat them soon. I limped towards the safety of the greenhouse.

I only made it two steps before the forest growth started quivering. Ants, more than before, boiled from the trees, launching themselves into the jungle. Yellow pollen erupted in clouds from the jungle plants. White flyers exploded from vines, swirling over the red mass of ants. I tucked my face into the crook of my elbow in a vain attempt to filter my breath.

I ran for the airlock. Ants smashed under my feet. Flyers tangled in my hair. Yellow pollen coated everything with a slick powder. I slid and staggered through the mess. My legs burned from bites. A flyer landed on my arm, extending a long stinger from its abdomen. I knocked it away. The ants boiled over it, burying it under a flood of red bodies and wicked pincers.

I tumbled to the ground, tripping over something. I rolled through the mass of ants, staggering to my feet as quickly as I could. Not fast enough to avoid several bites to my unprotected face.

Something pierced my neck. It felt like a lance of fire from the laser torch. I slapped a hand over the pain. Broken wings fluttered away. My hand was smeared with blue fluid.

I crunched through a tangled knot of ants and flyers. Pollen coated everything with yellow. I staggered, trying to keep to my feet despite a sudden attack of dizziness. More flyers swarmed around me. I swatted blindly, my gaze fixed on the promised safety of the airlock. Only a dozen more steps.

A wave of ants poured over my feet, surging up to my knees. I kicked and stomped. I was not going to die on Eden, killed by ants and moths. I staggered, falling to the side.

The airlock door cycled. Two figures in white suits stepped out. Fire blossomed from nozzles in their hands, sweeping the path clear of insects. The ants retreated into the undergrowth. The flyers spiraled into the air. I breathed in pollen and coughed.

The lead figure crouched beside me, flames pointed into the forest where the ants lurked. I caught sight of Brun's frown through his face mask. "Should have left your mask on."

"Couldn't. They cut the oxygen." I fumbled the words through swollen, numb lips.

"Never seen a swarm this bad." Brun clicked off the fire before slinging the flamethrower over his shoulder. The second person kept sweeping flames around us, driving the insects back.

Brun reached for my arm. He pulled me to my feet. I had to lean on him. My legs were swollen and aching with the ants' poison. The moth sting on my neck burned and throbbed. We limped to the airlock, guarded by the one thing the insects seemed to fear: Fire.

Brun paused only long enough to strip off the protective suit. I sagged against the wall. Poison slipped through my body. Strange burning triggered muscle twitches. The taste of overripe fruit filled my mouth. Halos of bluish light flickered around the wiring conduits.

"Are you listening?" Brun leaned over me. The brush of his hand on my arm sent surges of electricity sizzling over my skin. Numbness spread behind the electric shocks.

I mumbled. My tongue and lips were too swollen to form words. "Infirmary, now."

I swayed in his hold. His assistant grabbed my other side. The ants and flyers smashed themselves against the glass walls of the greenhouse. The docile plants we'd brought with us wilted, their leaves streaked with brown. The plants outside, lush and green, whipped branches and vines though the air was still.

Brun paused at the door. The tunnel stretched to the main building, walls intact, but the floor bulged as the ground beneath heaved.

"Ants?" the assistant asked. I'd never learned his name, never bothered to care.

Brun shrugged. "It's not safe in the greenhouses. We have to chance it."

A vine slapped the roof behind us. The unbreakable glass pane shattered. Shards rained over the dying off-world plants. The jungle vines slithered inside, vines twisting as they sprouted new leaves and coiled tendrils. A swarm of white winged flyers fluttered through the hole.

"Move it!" Brun shoved me through the door into the tunnel.

Ants boiled up between the floor plates, filling the tunnel. They crawled over us, as if we didn't matter. They filled the doorway into the greenhouse. The bushes whipped their branches wildly outside, flinging thorns at the sides of the tunnel and the greenhouse. The metal frame of the building screeched as it gave way under the assault of plants and insects. I stared over my shoulder as my feet fumbled towards the main building. The greenhouse collapsed. Vines trailed every direction, burying it in moments. Ants climbed the vines, blurs of red that left dead black spots behind where they bit the fleshy stems.

"Fighting," I managed.

"The ants and moths, I know," Brun hurried us through the airlock into the main building.

I shook my head. "Plants. They know."

He stopped, staring behind at the destruction. A cloud of yellow blocked the windows. "The plants are sentient?"

I closed my itching eyes and nodded. Their poison spread through my tissues, ant bite fighting moth sting. And in my head, thoughts not my own fought for dominance. No words, plants didn't need them.

The ceiling panes of the atrium imploded with a thunderous crash. Screams filled the hallways, followed by clouds of yellow pollen.

Brun dropped my arm, running for the center. His assistant paused only a moment before abandoning me, too.

I tottered on shaky legs. The jungle fought the forest. We were caught in the middle. We were a minor nuisance. They lanced our building as if it were a boil full of pus. I heard them in my head. I choked on air full of dust and pollen. More walls collapsed. Vines twined through any opening. Moths fluttered. Ants flooded through cracked floors. I stumbled forward, not sure where I headed, only that I had to keep moving.

"Talia? What happened?" Nione appeared from a shattered doorway. She clung to my hand. Her face swelled from a sting, angry welts stretched under her skin.

"Attack." I swayed.

"Who?" She swung her head frantically searching.

"Them." I pointed at a swarm of moths fighting ants. "And them." I stomped on a plant sprouting up through the floor.

"Don't!"

Her sharp tone stopped me, foot raised over the seedling. I shuffled back a step. The seedling was a jungle tree, already knee-high and growing fast. I rubbed my swollen eyes that didn't see right. Nione's skin was turning green where the poison streaked. Tiny swirls of vines twined through her hair. Half of me rejoiced at the sight, the other half snarled in anger. No, not me, the poisons inside me. The human piece of me whimpered in terror.

White wings fluttered overhead. Nione spread her arms wide, welcoming them. I shifted back, afraid of their stings. They ignored me, moving toward the sounds of screams coming from a room ahead.

I staggered up the hall, unsure where I headed, only that I had to keep moving. Nione skipped at my heels. Moths danced behind her. Pollen filled the air with yellow. Lights exploded as power surged and pulsed. Ceilings smashed open as vines pulled them apart. Floors cracked and bulged from the ants and roots surging beneath. Bodies sprawled in the rubble, swollen and disfigured by stings and bites. I stepped over them with care. My balance was off, my head swollen and spinning.

We reached the communications room. I stopped in the entrance, swaying as I fought to stay on my feet. Roots tangled through the power conduits. A frond from a tree branch dangled from a crack in the roof. Nione's father, the governor, stood in the center surrounded by smashed and broken equipment. He looked up from the mess at his feet. His eyes were wild.

"We have to report. Someone attacked us." He spread his hands through the yellow dust that powdered every surface.

"Not someone," I said, my voice cracking and hoarse. "The plants."

"Plants don't attack. Plants can't think."

"These do." The two factions pressed on my mind, filling my thoughts with growth. The jungle was winning. The forest retreating. For now.

The governor lifted one hand in a futile gesture. Bites and stings marked his flesh. "We failed. I failed. The colonists will die." He closed his eyes.

I reached for his hand, needing the human contact to keep hold of my own humanity. The remnant of myself clung to a single thought. The colonists would arrive soon. They had to be warned away. They had to be saved.

I dug in the twisted storage cabinets, pawing through the ruined equipment despite the seeping wounds on my hands. The jungle throbbed in my head, demanding my surrender. I ignored it, like I did people most of the time. The demand faded.

The governor stood in the center of the room, face slack. His eyes were empty now. Nione danced with the moths around him, more plant than human now. The poison had changed her.

It changed me. Patches of green marked my skin. But patches of brown sprouted, too, bark from the forest where the ants had left their marks. I shifted smashed electrical boards. Something collapsed in the atrium. No one screamed, not anymore. I pulled a case from the back of the storage cubby. I flipped open the latches. The emergency beacon inside was cushioned in foam, still in one piece. I turned it on just to be sure. The colonists had to be warned. They had to be saved. I packed the beacon back in the case.

"We should go." I hefted the case. Where would be safe? Not this building. Another crash sounded from down the hall. The jungle plants tore the human construct apart, piece by piece.

The governor, I couldn't remember his name, struggled to fit words together. "Shelter. By the landing pad."

I shifted the beacon to one hand, taking his hand in my other. The emergency shelter would be small enough that maybe the jungle hadn't noticed. It would be stocked with food, water, the basics. We could wait there, leave the beacon listening for the colony ship.

The man stumbled beside me. Nione skipped in circles around us, singing wordless songs to the white-winged creatures dancing around her head.

"Eden control? Please answer."

I scrambled out of the hammock I'd strung between two trunks. The beacon crackled with static. Had I imagined the voices?

"Eden control, please come in."

I knelt on the earth between the massive trees. I flipped a switch on the beacon. "Hello?"

"Is this Eden? What happened? We can't get a reading on you."

I grimaced. The colony building and greenhouses were gone, utterly destroyed by the plants. The landing pad suffered the same fate. The emergency shelter stood at an angle, half buried in dirt but still accessible. Five of us survived. The governor, I'd dubbed him Sam, had completely lost his mind. He followed me like a puppy, digging in the dirt and singing nursery rhymes to himself.

Nione and two younger staff had become hands for the jungle. Their skin was green, more plant than animal. Their hair turned to coils of vine. They watched me sometimes, standing for hours, just staring. They didn't speak to me. They weren't who they had been, they'd changed too much.

I caught glimpses of others sometimes in the leaves of the canopy and between the massive trunks, but they weren't human. They'd never been human. The plants learned, copying our form and the ability to move untethered to the soil. The jungle had spread up the hill where the colony greenhouses once stood.

I'd checked there once. A few imported plants thrived, most were dead. The jungle insects fluttered over them constantly. I wouldn't be surprised if the jungle figured out how to incorporate watermelons and tomatoes into its arsenal. I didn't dare eat the fruit I found on the peach tree. It was deformed, like the tree, changed by Eden's touch.

"Are you there?"

"You have to go back. Don't land."

Static crackled between us for a long moment.

"What happened?"

"The plants, they're sentient. They attacked. Wiped out the colony."

"We'll send a shuttle to pick you up."

"No." My denial was quick and certain. I rubbed a bark patch on my arm. Eden had tainted us. And if Eden's rulers got loose among the docile plants of other worlds? Humans didn't stand a chance. "Put Eden under quarantine. Don't let anyone land here, ever. Set up warning beacons. Tell them it's plague or radiation or whatever. Just don't let anyone land here. And don't ever, ever let anything leave."

"Explain it to me."

I did, all of it. I hoped they'd listen. I hoped Eden would be banned from contact. All it would take was one seed, one plant. I hoped whoever was in command of the colony ship would listen and believe.

The plants had our technology. They'd figure it out eventually. Humanity had to be prepared for when the plants moved in.

Erin Hoffman, best known for her Chaos Knight fantasy series from PYR, takes a departure here to look at colonists and humans through alien eyes. How would our world, lives, and goals look from that other perspective? Here's one possibility . . .

THE GAMBRELS OF THE SKY

ERIN HOFFMAN

Kelara is a galaxy.

Her sunstar shape is familiar, myriad spreading arms an everlasting roof of light. But she is not the idea of a galaxy, the abstraction or distant quantum impression—she is every star, every planet, every cosmic duststorm that burns or bubbles in the vast elemental nothing. She is precisely 1,125,899,906,842,624 of these bodies. In a remote corner of her an electrical storm is brewing as five supernova collide in spectacular fashion. Elsewhere, there is an arrangement of stars whose hydrodynamic currents suggest a kind of consciousness, and she is pleased.

Subroutine terminated.

The words faded in and out from Kelara's left eye as her ego came back online. Beside her, Ilar opened her eyes, disengaging from the link.

"This is passable. You lean too much on g-type systems."

"Galaxies are not my specialization."

"We are looking for passion independent of specialization, Kelara. You know that."

"Really. I thought the synod was interested in obedience."

Ilar flickered, an ultraviolet rumination across her shoulders that indicated she was aware of but unmoved by Kelara's insolence.

"When will I be moved to another assignment?"

"When your simulation is complete. The green district is quite looking forward to your findings. And they are concerned that Ma Emi is getting old." The colonists aboard Hypatia might be most interested in uncovering Ix Relics or novel genetic structures evolved on Zakalwe, but a token effort at least would be made to absorb the culture of the indigenous Bissbanians. Kelara was the token, and recognized her disinterest in the project as evidence of Hypatia's low estimate of Ma Emi's value.

So she ignored Ilar's rebuke. "Will I be assigned a human?"

"Humans are not your specialization." Unspoken: species preference in a simulant is immoral.

"They should have put someone on the bubble who had a passion for the Bissbanians."

"That would have represented a contaminating conflict of interest."

"Like my being assigned a human?" Kelara said.

"Yes." Ilar remained unmoved.

"And yet the synod desires passion."

"It's called 'work' for a reason, Kelara."

The Brain is Wider than the Sky

A small piece of Kelara is a goldfish.

The goldfish is not an unnoticeable tax on her resources, but it is close. It operates in space sanctioned for personal use, not like Bruce. The fluid mechanics of the water surrounding it are more interesting to simulate, but the goldfish is alive, and so its patterns have an ineffable charm. She was not enough of a philosopher to tell you exactly what differentiated them, a turn of meaning slender as syllable from sound, but different they were.

There was something in the goldfish that fascinated a deep part of her; something about its simplicity coupled with how it retained integrity. Perhaps she should, as Ilar had often suggested, invest in some philosophy training. Yet intuition said that the human philosophies were incomplete, and she found android—especially simulant android—ones unbearable.

Size measured in synapses was a funny thing. She could run herself and the goldfish simultaneously, or herself and Ma Emi, or the goldfish and Ma Emi. But not Bruce and herself. Or Ma Emi and Bruce.

Kelara had no real idea of Bruce's integrity, though he had been set up well in theory. It was too risky to simulate him here on the transport from mainship to the bubble, and so she had to content herself with the goldfish, its sensations, its reactions. A kind of meditation on its identity kept her busy until the pockmarked black lettering of the John Muir hove into view.

She dismissed the goldfish as the transporter docked, and unfastened her restraints moments before the light bonged to announce that she was allowed to. The ship complained, threatened, but she ignored it. If the synod could ignore Ilar, and Ilar could ignore her, she could ignore a ship.

The humid green scent of the bubble flooded her nose as she stepped off the gangplank. And another scent, an unfamiliar one, coming from the pale blue smoke that spiraled up out of the mud hut at the end of the brushed-steel pier.

Ma Emi was baking. That's what the humans would have called it anyway. Kelara had never seen her bake. She wished she had been able to record the patterns during the process that led up to the baking, but was also perversely pleased that her meeting with Ilar had made her miss it. Let the humans wait. If they were just going to shove another Bissbanian at her for her next assignment, she had no real interest in wrapping this one up. In a way, here she was among a fellow alien: Ma Emi, despite her people's intensely social nature, denied contact with her fellow indigenous population; and Kelara, denied contact with human colonists: her creators, her ancestors.

The door to the hut was open, but Kelara knocked on the threshold anyway. A soft whistle drew her inside. Ma Emi was opening shelled animals with a long knife. They belched vapor as she split them open. More already sat steaming on her low table; she'd made over two dozen, far too many for one of her kind to eat. Kelara reached back in her mind for the name of the crustaceans—ourani, she thought. Believed to grow bravery in children, they were rarely eaten by adults. Ma Emi must be experiencing maternal urges. As a Ma, she would likely never have had children of her own, but if not for the bubble, she would have lived in a village and been part caretaker to the children of her sisters.

Ma Emi finished splitting and scraped the opened ourani into a bowl that had been lined with purple seaweed. Then she brought the bowl to the table and folded herself down next to it. She gestured with a webbed hand.

"Can you eat?"

"I can pretend."

"Pretend, then."

They ate, and Kelara extended her perception array perfunctorily. There was little new data; her projections that Ma Emi was baking to assuage her desire for a brood proved correct, but the hypothesis had been so simple as to border on insulting. She activated her Ma Emi simulation, and fell into the rhythms of speaking as if she were another Ma of a neighboring village.

A Narrow Fellow in the Grass

Kelara is a small boy named Bruce. He is nine years old. His favorite thing is an ancient homeworld artifact called Super Mario Brothers. He is playing it in the spidergrass of the patch, a hundred meters or so of dry land that holds the hut out of the swamp.

Bruce is fixated on this level of the game, an underwater one. He has beaten it before, but he's never gotten all of the coins. It's a secret level, which makes it even better. But the coins are hard to get, and he hates the white squids. He might even hate them more than snakes. He'd come on across a snake once in the spidergrass, a giant one with a yellow head, and he'd had nightmares about it for weeks.

Thinking about the snake distracts him, and he doesn't swim fast enough. He gets sucked to the bottom of the screen, and he dies.

He's mad, but only for a second, because a noise from behind makes him jump up, afraid it's a snake. But it's not. It's a tall thing, as big as his mom, and it has eyes and hands like she does, but it's covered in scales, and deep cuts on either side of its neck puff in and out as it breathes. It is way, way scarier than a snake.

Subroutine terminated.

Kelara turned then, met the dark pearlescent spheres of Ma

Emi's eyes. The nanosecond that it took to disengage from Bruce's simulation was too long to activate and project perception routines.

There's a Certain Slant of Light

Kelara is herself. She is trying to convince Ma Emi that Bruce should not be reported.

Even as Kelara and the synod studied Ma Emi, Ma Emi studied humans, and their android tools. She would know as she saw Kelara hunched in the grass, talking to herself, that she had an unauthorized simulation.

"Please don't tell them. Please," Kelara said.

The Bissbanians, who called themselves Elun after their own name for their mudball of a planet, did not have a concept of "please". Kelara was relying on Ma Emi's exposure to humanity to convey the strength of her request. Possibly she was also telling Ma Emi that she, Kelara, was the only friend she had.

"Why did you simulate a human child?" Ma Emi asked. She sat on the floor of her hut with a feathered chicken-like beast on her lap, stroking its feathers. "Why not an Elu child?"

There was no good answer, and Kelara thought Ma Emi knew it. "I've been working on him a long time." It was true, and also not an answer.

"And what happens when I tell them about him?"

"They'll delete him."

Ma Emi looked at her. The amphibious eyes of the Elun were notoriously difficult to read, even for another Elun. Underwater they could communicate emotion with pheromones, so there was little need for facial muscles, but here above the water they were nearly unreadable.

In Emi's eyes, she tried not to think of the yellow-headed snake. It was difficult. It had actually been difficult to not think of the snake ever since he'd had that incident. She knew this meant that Bruce's identity had contaminated her already, had probably compromised the assignment, but she didn't care. Kelara looked away, and tried not to imagine the snake.

A kernel of fear had developed in him, rare and arising as they sometimes did. The image had passed in front of him early in the simulation, had echoed off a cluster of neurons and formed a pattern that he could not eradicate on his own. And since he had been thinking of it when he saw Emi, it had escaped out of him and into her.

"I have no children of my own," Ma Emi said. "I never will."

Kelara looked back at her. The eyes, dark and light around the edges as a fine sherry, bored into her like the distance in the look of death.

In Anthony Cardno's tale, when a deep space communications hub loses the satellite which provides their only communications link with Earth, the team must scramble to make repairs. Then a deeper threat appears on the horizon. Can they finish their mission and make it back to safety in time?

CHASING SATELLITES

ANTHONY R. CARDNO

How the hell did this happen!"

Zimmerman was ranting at Werder, the new kid, when Milne reported for his shift in the communications hub. One of the tallest humans on Orpheus, Zimmerman would tower over the shorter, stockier Werder even if the kid hadn't been sitting rigidly at his console.

"How the hell did what happen?" Milne asked, around a yawn born of too little sleep. Parenting a tween-age child on Orpheus was no easier than it would have been back on Earth.

"We've lost contact with Earth," both men replied, the anger in Zimmerman's voice in rough counterpoint to the timidity in Werder's.

"How long ago?" Stifling his second yawn, Milne crossed to the beverage station for some coffee. Wu, his shift partner, was already there looking equally exhausted. Milne cocked an eyebrow at him, silently asking *another heavy drinking night*? Wu's strained smile was answer enough.

"Six hours." Werder's answer went a long way to shaking Milne's lethargy. Wu's eyes widened a bit, too.

"Six hours! You didn't call me. Who did you call?"

"Zimmerman." Werder shot a sideways look at his trainer. Zimm puffed his cheeks out like he was going to interrupt, then thought better of it. "He said it was probably just solar interference on their end, like the last time, and that I should log and monitor it. So I did."

"Okay, but for six hours? You didn't think to call it in again after, say, hour two? The last time this happened, it only lasted an hour and a half."

"I . . . uh . . ." Werder turned slightly red, making the freckles on his face stand out even more, and mumbled something Milne had no problem understanding.

"You. Fell. Asleep." He put the half-made coffee down with a bit more force than he'd intended and stalked to his own console, bringing it online with a series of swift, sure finger movements. "Kid, transfer me the data, so I can figure out how much of a problem we have."

Werder grimaced, hunched his broad shoulders, and started tapping at his own console haltingly. Milne tried not to roll his eyes; the kid knew the layout and presets of the console but was clearly flustered by Zimmerman's reaction. He cast a quick look at Zimmerman and Wu. "And what have you two been doing since you got here? Why is Werder's the only console up and running?"

"Trying to figure out what the hell the kid was thinking, falling asleep . . ."

"Give it a rest, Zimm." Wu's voice barely made it out of the beverage station, every word tinged with hangover. "We've all done it. Even you."

"Not for six hours!"

"Let it go!" Milne had no patience for Zimmerman's posturing. Of course Zimm's reaction was over the top. He was the one who had proclaimed Werder ready for solo-shifts. Part of the problem was rushing kids out of school and into training. A necessary downside to where they were as a colony. "We need to figure out what to do, not waste another hour berating the new kid."

"No, I'll take care of that while you're fixing this."

Milne sprang from his seat and snapped to attention at the new voice, mirrored by Werder. Zimmerman was a second slower, and Wu came to attention with only a slight wobble and without spilling his coffee.

Commander Foley stood in the hub's doorway, arms crossed and an unusual—but not uncalled for—scowl on her face. Werder went pale and blushed at the same time, something Milne thought a physical impossibility. Foley walked in and pulled the door shut behind her.

"Situation."

"Commander, the kid here dropped the ball," Zimmerman began.

"Not you." Foley interrupted, and Zimmerman's mouth stopped moving. She turned to Werder. "You."

Werder's mouth worked soundlessly for a moment. He cleared his throat and started again. To his credit, the kid didn't stammer once he got going.

"Sir! At 0100 hours, the communications channel with Earth read normal: not much chatter but coming through clear. Thirty minutes later, there was no chatter at all and a staticy background. Per protocol, I logged the interference. At 0200 hours, the static had increased, so I called Lieutenant Zimmerman. He reminded me of the previous comm-break's cause and ordered me to continue monitoring and logging."

"Why didn't you call Lieutenant Commander Milne?"

"Sir, as you know, Lieutenant Zimmerman is my trainer and immediate superior. As he was not overly concerned about the break, I thought it inappropriate to interrupt Lieutenant Commander Milne's night with his husband and daughter. Family First, sir!"

"Respecting the Prime Rule." Foley had a slight smile. "Very good, as far as it goes, but six hours is an unrealistically long time to monitor a comm-break without a follow-up report."

"Sir, Lieutenant Zimmerman is correct that I shirked my duty. By 0300, I had fallen asleep at my console. I have no good excuse for . . ."

"We'll discuss that later." Foley turned to Milne. Behind her back, Werder visibly deflated. "Status?"

Milne sat back down and reviewed the data streaming in from Werder's console. A scan of just the first hour's worth of data showed something Werder should have noticed and that the others certainly would have.

"The problem's not with Earth or solar activity. The freakin' transponder satellite isn't where it's supposed to be." He slapped both hands on his console in frustration. "I can't pinpoint where it is, but I can tell it's moving erratically. We could lose it, but even if we don't, it's too far out of position to do us any good even when Earth is in proper alignment again."

"Solutions?"

"None that are optimal. If we try to course-correct it from down here without knowing exactly where it is . . . we're as likely to send it spiraling into the void as crashing into the surface of Orpheus."

"And if we don't resume communications," Foley shook her head, "Earth will assume we finally succumbed to the more hostile elements of this planet and write us off."

"As if they haven't done that much already," Wu grumbled. "Ten years, not a single supply ship. Just encouragement to thrive until they can spare resources. Thanks for nothing, homeworld."

Milne knew that Wu was not a negative person except when nursing a killer hangover. Foley knew it, too, and she rounded on him.

"Stow the fatalism, Lieutenant. It's unbecoming of an officer in front of the ranks."

"Is that true?" Werder's eyes were wide. "I've grown up here because Earth refuses to send help?"

"It's complicated, kid." Despite being best friends, there were times Milne would like to smack Wu upside the head with a blunt object. "Look, you're military now. You're going to hear things the civilians may not know yet. Discretion is key. Think about how that news would affect the colony. Family First, right?"

"Yeah, Family First." Werder didn't sound as enthusiastic about the Prime Rule at this moment.

"Suggestions." Foley brought the conversation back on track.

"Only one I can think of." Milne took a deep breath. "We go up."

"Zimmerman to hub, we have achieved orbit."

The shuttle had been equipped with enough tracking sensors and automatic relays for the hub to know exactly where they were, but verbal verification made the crew feel better and assured the folks on the ground that they were still alive.

"Locking trackers onto the transponder satellite," Wu reported. Zimmerman was piloting, Wu was locating. Milne would make repairs, if necessary, before they repositioned the satellite to the optimal position.

Zimmerman refused to move the shuttle until they had a set destination.

"Got it!" Wu sent the satellite's new coordinates to Zimm's console. From the data, Milne could see the satellite was moving slowly away from them.

"The shortest route is in the opposite direction." Zimmerman grumbled.

"Better than circling the entire planet," Foley said from the hub. "Turn around."

They moved in a controlled stationary rotation and then on minimal thruster power based on Wu's input. Milne watched his console and waited for the forward external cameras to pick up the satellite so he could begin damage assessment.

"We have camera-visual," he announced moments later, manipulating and transferring images from the cameras to the hub before the shuttle was in range for actual line-of-sight confirmation. The quicker they analyzed the situation, the better.

"Damage?" Foley asked over his headset.

"Checking now . . . " Milne kept his focus on the visuals streaming across his console. ". . . one distended antennae for sure, hard to tell, but I think it can be corrected." He zoomed in for a close-up, cleaned up the image as much as possible, and transmitted it. "Several dents all in the same basic area surrounding the antennae. No other surface damage visible from this angle."

"Eye-visual confirmation," Zimmerman interrupted.

Milne had not noticed the slight increase in speed Zimmerman had applied to close the distance faster without overshooting.

"We will have close contact for extra-vehicular activity in three minutes."

Milne bit back a comment about how easy it was for Zimmerman to say that, since it would be Milne going out there.

"Dents and broken antennae," Foley cut back in. "More escaping ring debris?"

"Looks like it," Milne confirmed. "We'll know in a moment if what we're seeing is the worst of it."

"Does everyone realize today is the tenth anniversary of the crash?"

Werder's voice caught them all by surprise. They'd almost forgotten he was in the hub with Foley. In the morning's commotion, the anniversary had slipped Milne's mind, but how, he didn't know.

"And your point is?" Zimmerman barked into his headset. "We're kinda on a time limit up here, kid."

"Debris escaping the ring brought the *Poitevin* down. We haven't paid much attention to the ring since, resources being limited, so how do we know this isn't an annual event, like meteor dispersal?"

"It's worth looking into, Ensign." Milne was impressed that

Werder had made the connection before the rest of them. Maybe the kid did have a future in this line of work. "Think you can analyze the stored transponder records from the past decade and find a pattern? Might help in repositioning this thing if it's still working."

"On it!" There was a slight click as the kid muted his headset so he could work his console without interrupting communications between shuttle and hub.

A private message popped up on Milne's console. NICE JOB. Effusive praise from Foley. Milne typed back: SOMEONE DID THE SAME FOR ME ONCE, and then, with a small nod, set himself to figuring out what tools he was going to need to salvage the antennae.

The antenna was in worse shape than it had appeared from a distance, and Milne sweated some of the repair work. In the EVA suit, with all the tools attached to him via leads, he didn't need to worry about sweaty palms or things flying out of reach. Sweat dripping in his eyes was the problem.

He rewired the antennae and bent the metal back straight again. If anyone was annoyed by his occasional grunts or sighs, they wisely kept it to themselves and left him to his work. Still, it was taking too long.

When it was time to screw the antennae rod back into the base, it took three tries to get it to thread correctly. Each time it stuck, Milne bit back a curse and took a breath before unscrewing and trying again. If he jammed it and couldn't get it loose, the mission was a bust.

On the third try, it stuck for a moment, and then slipped past like he had stripped the threads. That time, he did shout an expletive, louder than he'd intended. Four alarmed voices asked if he was okay.

"Fine, fine," he answered. "I thought I screwed up, but the antennae is reattached and okay." He paused, and then uttered a sad laugh. "Heh, get it? Screwed up? While screwing the antennae in?"

"Lieutenant Commander, how much more work do you have to do out there?" Foley's voice was measured, but Milne knew she was concerned when she addressed him by rank.

"Let's run the diagnostic on the antennae," he answered, "before I start looking for other problems. If it's not working, there's no sense checking for other damage. Wu, ping a signal to the antennae."

Milne waited in silence. Without visual displays, he had no way of knowing if the satellite received the signal.

"Pinged and pinged back," Wu said moments later with noticeable relief. "I sent the usual connection protocol, and the satellite responded appropriately."

"Hub, are you reading anything from the satellite?"

"Affirmative," Werder answered. "Reading static, but much less than last night."

"So the patch job isn't perfect, but at least the antenna is working." Milne took a moment to collect his thoughts. "Commander, I have a suggestion."

"Go ahead."

"We should start broadcasting the message we recorded now. We know the transponder's not malfunctioning, we know the antenna is at least temporarily fixed. By waiting 'til we bring the satellite back into optimal position, we're taking a chance. Based on the remaining static Werder is hearing, let's not risk it. Even if it's not beamed directly at Earth, at least it'll be there for ships to hear."

"Ensign Werder," Foley ordered, "Begin transmitting the message. Shuttle, check to be sure it's going out."

Milne pushed back from the satellite, extending his tether so that he was in the path of the outgoing signal. The problem with these tight-beam transponders was that the recipient had to be in virtually direct line with the source, no matter how far away, to receive the signal. Within a moment, Commander Foley's prerecorded voice came over Milne's headset.

"THIS IS COMMANDER FOLEY OF ORPHEUS COLONY, FORMERLY OF THE ESS POITEVIN. IF YOU HEAR THIS, OUR TRANSPONDER SATELLITE IS FAILING AND WE'VE LOST COMMUNICATIONS WITH EARTH. PLEASE RELAY THIS SIGNAL. OUR COLONY IS NOT IMPAIRED OR FAILING, BUT WE NEED HELP REESTABLISHING COMMUNICATIONS WITH . . ."

There was more to the message, but it cut out suddenly.

"Milne! Get out of there!" Werder's voice cracked mid-shout, and Milne had the urge to slap his hands over his ears at the kid's volume. "Shuttle! Reel him him!"

"What the hell are you on, Werder?" Zimmerman interrupted.

"Satellite sensors are picking up a debris storm in the ring, headed out-bound! Coming your way, now!"

So much for the statistical analysis. Milne finger-toggled the suit thrusters and pushed towards the satellite, even as he felt the tug of the tether line pulling him in.

"Milne, what are you doing?" Wu's words came over in a rush.

"Grabbing the satellite! If we can pull it out of the way, we can take it with us, circle around, and reposition it!"

"Screw that!" Zimmerman replied. "We're getting out of here now! Wu, pull him in double-time!"

Milne laid his hands on the satellite shell and felt for a good grip before Zimmerman hit the thrusters and pulled him away. The tether and the satellite pulled against each other. His grip held and the satellite started to follow him.

And then all hell broke loose. Small bits of debris zinged past his face-plate. He pulled his head back, closed his eyes and held his breath, waiting for an impact that didn't come. He opened his eyes again and watched more pebbles pass, imagining he could hear the whistle the way someone who narrowly avoids being shot hears the whine of the bullet as it misses. The sweat on his forehead poured faster as his heart-rate soared. He blinked rapidly to clear the sweat and stop the sting. But his grip still held, and the satellite moved with him as the tether brought him closer to the shuttle.

The amount of debris passing him increased in frequency, speed and size. Debris ricocheted off of the satellite shell and dispersed in every direction, although the shell itself protected him from the rebounds. It wouldn't take much to puncture both layers of his suit. He whispered goodbyes to his family. The others were putting out so much chatter he doubted they heard.

The satellite vibrated as larger debris struck and Milne tightened his grip. How much further to the shuttle? They'd been reeling him in forever. A sharp pull from behind jerked him sideways, and one hand slipped off the satellite. "What th—?"

"Milne!" Wu sounded panicked. "Debris tore your tether! Let go of the satellite so we can haul you in before it rips through!"

Milne bit back another curse. The choice was taken out of his hands as a large piece of debris caromed off of the shell, straight "up" from Milne's position, while the satellite pulled to his right, away from Orpheus. Once his hands were loose, the tether yanked Milne towards the shuttle. More debris hit the satellite dead on, pushing it farther out of reach and out of orbit.

As he was pulled backwards, more debris impacted his suit, surely creating minute tears in the outer layer. Thankfully, nothing punctured the inner layer. Yet. He twisted so he could see the shuttle.

"Stay still!" Wu yelled. "You've got about two strands holding you to us and a couple of feet to go! On my mark, curl into a ball and you'll slide right into the airlock!" The pause was the longest of Milne's life outside of waiting for Aleksander to accept his proposal. *There aren't enough stars in the sky to swear by,* Alek had responded. There were more than enough stars around Milne now.

"MARK!"

Milne pulled himself into a ball, gripping his knees with his hands. He sped up slightly and forced his eyes to stay open so he could see the upper edge of the airlock gliding past him. He untucked as the door slid shut. Several pieces of debris ricocheted off the closing door and into the room, one pinging off his visor and starting a spider-web effect. Milne held his breath and waited for the door to be shut and the tell-tale hiss of oxygen filling the airlock chamber before he released it. The visor hadn't completely cracked, but the suit would never be usable again.

He was out of the suit and barging through to the bridge in seconds, leaving the suit crumpled up on the floor. Zimmerman swore under his breath, fingers flying across his console to determine the fastest, safest landing vector.

Wu turned from his console long enough to punch Milne hard on the arm. "You deserve a punch in the face, but we don't have time to set any broken bones. Not that it'll matter, since there's a good chance we're crashing."

Milne slid into his seat, buckled up, and accessed his own console. He was still getting data streamed from the satellite as it slid further and further out of range; still broadcasting.

"Zimmerman, what are you seeing that we're not?" Werder was all calm and professional now. "We've lost the satellite data-stream."

"Yeah, well, we've lost the satellite, so that makes sense." Zimmerman barked. "There's a ton of debris headed our way, and the pieces are getting larger. We've got a problem if we don't get down fa—"

The shuttle shook with the impact of something large. All three men grabbed their consoles. No alarms sounded to indicate a hull breach. The shaking stopped after a moment, and Zimmerman resumed a course to take them home in one piece. The shuttle continued forward and down towards the atmosphere.

There was another impact, a stronger one. Milne gave a sideways glance to Wu's console, catching the bright red of the impact on a schematic of the shuttle, surrounded by yellow markings for smaller impacts they were not feeling. The number of yellow markers worried him. Enough smaller impacts could be as troublesome as a few larger impacts. Smaller debris could also settle into the engines through the exhaust panels.

Milne returned his attention to his own panel. The signal from the satellite continued to diminish in strength as the distance between them widened. He boosted the gains as much as he could, and the signal flared for a moment. The satellite was moving off at a different direction from the majority of the debris exiting the ring. That could be a blessing, in that the satellite would not suffer any further immediate damage, but also a curse, as the new trajectory was pushing it farther out of line with Earth. As the signal weakened, he tried to think of other ways to boost the connection. At least they'd started broadcasting. Other colony ships might drop out of warp in a location to pick up that signal and relay it back to Earth.

The cabin lights went red. Klaxons sounded, warning of an imminent breach of the outer hull.

"Personal protective equipment NOW!" Zimmerman shouted over the alarms, just as Foley's voice came over the radio.

"Shuttle! Scuttle mission and bring yourselves down immediately!"

"As if we had a choice." Wu grumbled before toggling his mic open to the planetary frequency. "Werder, give me a beacon to lock onto, outside the colony. Screw looking for a soft landing; we're gonna be lucky to land at all."

All three pulled on protective suits and then continued working their consoles: Zimmerman trying to pilot away from the larger pieces of debris heading their way, Wu laying in coordinates for a landing that would keep them well away from the colony itself if they came down explosively, and Milne collecting and relaying the diminishing data from the satellite.

Zimmerman cut off the alarms and the chamber, still washed in red light, was eerily quiet.

"We know we're in trouble. We need to hear each other better," he said to no-one in particular.

With the alarms off, the number of direct hits and partial glances the shuttle was taking from the debris became more noticeable. Milne had hoped they were heading away from the storm, but it seemed like they were now in the middle of it. Every reverberation through the shuttle shook them in their seats and made them tense up expecting the breach alarm and their suits to seal.

The breach alarm never came, but the shuttle took its most violent hit yet, and a different alarm sounded.

"Engine rupture!" Zimmerman shouted.

Milne could feel the shuttle swinging around as forward momentum ceased. Another piece of debris hit the rear end of the craft. "Thrusters?"

"Firing," Wu answered. "Werder, forget that beacon. We can't control our descent beyond what the thrusters are capable of." He paused, swore. "And we're leaking what little fuel we have left. There's a good chance once we hit the atmosphere, we'll be leaving a flaming trail for you to find us by."

"Get yourself to the ground," Foley responded instead of the kid. "We'll be waiting."

Hands worked consoles feverishly. Wu tracked the fuel. Zimmerman fired the thrusters, pushing them down into the atmosphere. Milne gave up tracking the satellite data and tracked the debris storm, which they passed out of as they moved closer to the planet.

They could feel increased resistance on the shuttle as they entered the atmosphere. The shuttle became harder for Zimmerman to control even before the fuel reserves ran out.

Milne switched his sensors over to positioning data, to figure where the shuttle would come down. "We'll come down outside the colony by several miles."

"But not on anything soft," Wu added.

"Not in that location, no." Zimmerman concurred.

"Foley is on her way out to your projected landing site," Werder's voice came over the line. "We've mustered every crewmember we can."

"Hey, kid," Zimmerman interrupted.

"Yeah?"

"Sorry I was so hard on you. And so easy, too. Shoulda spent more time teaching, less time blaming."

"You'll have plenty of time to make that up, Zimm." The fact that Werder addressed him by his nickname wasn't lost on Milne. "And the rest of you, too."

"Still, just in case." Milne chose his next words carefully. "Tell our families we love them, and you do everything you can to keep comms running in case Earth ever does get in touch. Got that, Werder?"

"Yeah." Werder sounded resigned. "Yeah, I do."

"Good. Now stop talking to us, and let us try to set this thing down without a big explosion, okay?"

"Yes, sirs."

And then there wasn't time to think, just react, as the ground drew closer.

Zimmerman pulled the nose up and they landed on the shuttle's belly. But the shuttle had been built for controlled vertical landings with landing gear deployed, not for landing like an old Earth aircraft.

Milne passed out as the shuttle began an uncontrolled skid across the flat plateau in front of them.

He came to in a hospital bed, wrapped in bandages. His blurry right eye opening after several blinks; the left forced closed with something heavy and unmoving. Something immobilized his neck, but he tried to look to his right anyway. A headache spiked behind his eye in response to the movement, and he gasped.

"Welcome back. It's been a rough few days." Werder moved into his line of sight.

"F . . ." Milne tried to speak, but his mouth was too dry.

"Your family's right outside. Doc had a feeling you'd be waking up soon. You and Wu have been recovering at about the same rate and he came to an hour ago."

"Z . . ." Milne tried to speak again.

"I'm sorry. We got you and Wu out before the fire got to you, but Zimm . . . he was crushed by his console. I . . . I'd rather let Foley give you all the details. I'm gonna get your family."

Milne grabbed Werder's arm as he turned away. The kid spun to look at him.

"S . . ." Milne tried again.

"Satellite's gone, man. But we got a ton of extra data from it thanks to the boost you gave the signal before it slipped out of range. It was still broadcasting. Maybe someone'll hear it and chase it down. Meantime, our days of chasing satellites are over. Can't afford to risk any more lives up there. We're here, this is home now. Let me get Aleksander and Renee. Family first, right?"

Milne nodded, and let Werder leave. Family first, he thought. Orpheus Colony would survive, thrive, or fail on its own. This had always been true. But now it would be a known reality. At least the planet was hospitable, the colony strong and secure. With the comm satellite gone, they could put their energy and resources into exploring the world they were trapped on.

Milne's daughter pushed through the door and rushed the bed before Aleksander, trailing behind her, could rein her in. Milne grunted with the impact, and his good eye blurred with tears. It hurt, but it was a good hurt.

Alerted by a biologist, the Director of Native Relations between humans and the slythii discovers details that affect their burial ceremony and must find a way to interfere to save lives. Nancy Fulda is a Hugo and Nebula Nominee and has been honored by Baen Books and the National Space Society for her writing. Her story here asks some interesting questions while taking some unique twists and turns.

SOARING PILLAR OF BRIGHTNESS

NANCY FULDA

The knock at Adrian's office door was brief, tentative, and mildly desperate. Reluctantly, he set aside his research and called, "Come in!"

The handle swung downward, and a young biologist from the colonial research institute poked her head around the door. "I'm sorry to bother you. I know you must be very busy . . ."

"Not at all," Adrian lied. He read the name on her ID badge. "Come in, Brenda, and tell me what the slythii have done this time."

Not, Adrian reflected sourly, that the inevitable conflicts between the human colonists and their alien hosts were ever truly the *aliens'* fault. The slythii were an herbivorous race, quadrupedal, and almost annoyingly complacent. About the only crime they'd ever committed was the accidental blockage of traffic by milling around on public roadways.

The roadways in question, it turned out, had been built along a series of culturally significant hunks of rock bordering the canyon wall. Adrian, incensed on the aliens' behalf, had shouted down several overzealous traffic cops and complained to the colony leadership. He'd expected to ruffle a few feathers, get the roadways removed, and return to his quiet field studies of slythii culture.

Instead, he'd ended up with a desk job and the lofty title of

"Director of Native Relations," which hadn't been his intent *at all.*

Adrian sighed, set his coffee mug among the scattered documents on his desk, and wondered how sunrise had come so quickly. The planet's rings, arching overhead like gold-dusted ribbon, had already caught the glowing edge of dawn. Another hour, and his day would vanish in a morass of trade negotiations, political inquiries, and activist outcries over native mineral usage.

Brenda emerged from behind the door's expansive bulk, tucking her hair behind her ear. "It's, um . . . not exactly about the slythii."

"Well, that's something."

"It's about their death rituals."

Adrian froze, all aspirations of returning to his research draining away. "What about the death rituals, exactly?"

Brenda held up a small, flexible data strip. "I—we . . . sort of recorded one of them?"

Adrian gaped, swallowed, and managed to avoid breaking into a cough. "Are you sure?"

"That it was a slythii Ascension? Oh, absolutely. You can hear them keening on the recording." She added hastily: "We weren't trying to eavesdrop. Professor Fazzolari asked me to set up a three-day surveillance for *tchuno* spores. But when I looked at the video . . ." She broke off, wilting. "It was an accident, I swear! We didn't know there was a Deceased in the area. You don't think this will start an interspecies incident do you?"

Her expression of abject terror was distressingly genuine.

"Brenda, the slythii are neither aggressive nor politically inclined. Learning that an Ascension was observed by outsiders would—" *be a grave violation of the trust they placed in me* "—merely displease them. Let me see the data strip."

She handed it over. Adrian activated the built-in holoprojection, skipping to the time stamp she indicated.

A wooded hillside glowed above his desk. The planet's rings, majestically multipartite, illuminated the gathering dusk. A raw-throated wail rose from the speakers.

For several seconds nothing happened. Then, beyond the far line of treetops: a soaring rush of light. The column blazed like a conduit to heaven, bright enough to make Adrian wince. A hiss of wind against the treetops, a distant sonic echo, and the glow faded.

A slythii Ascension. The recording matched native descriptions perfectly. As near as Adrian understood, through his admittedly imperfect mastery of the slythii tongue, the giant, tranquil aliens believed that deceased souls resided for several weeks within the hardened carcasses of the dead. Taloned avians called *ghondui* attended the body during this time, driving away scavengers and preparing to escort the dead slyth's spirit into the greater life.

Adrian had always presumed the rushing light that supposedly accompanied the soul's ascension to be a metaphorical exaggeration. Apparently, it was not.

"Play the recording again," Brenda said. "Frame by frame, at high magnification."

Adrian did so. Frowned. Scrolled back and froze the playback during the brightest frame. Light surged in the motionless image, rising behind the trees, spreading with an almost chemical quality. Amidst the ripples atop the column, grainy with magnification, floated six hazy figures. Creatures. He was inclined to call them gargoyles.

Wrinkled heads, tightly sealed eyes; taut, stout bodies beginning to unfurl from a fetal compression. Corrugated wings, vengeful beaks. Slime-encrusted feathers dripping with liquid light.

"Blazing stars," Adrian whispered. "What are those?"

Not the rising spirit of a dead slyth, certainly.

"They're immature *ghondui*," Brenda said quietly. "I ran the image through our biological correlation programs. Bone structure, relative limb length, feather distribution... there's no room for doubt."

"*Ghondui*," Adrian murmured, appalled. "Guardians. That's what the word means in slythii. Supposedly, adult *ghondui* guard the bodies of the dead until their spirits are ready to ascend."

"Then why," Brenda said—and the gravity in her tone implied that *this* was why she'd come to him— "are the supposed guardians of the dead brooding their young in the carcasses of the Deceased?"

"I don't know," Adrian whispered.

He stepped the playback forward, frame by frame. The *ghondui* spread their primordial wings, fanning from the glowing apex of the geyser. They were almost impossible to spot, even in the slow-motion recording. To slyth standing on the ground, eyes dazzled by the brilliant eruption of light, they would melt invisibly against the faded slate of the heavens. Unseen.

"There are wasps back on Terra," Adrian said, "who lay eggs in the bodies of dead spiders. The hatchlings feed off the corpse until they're mature enough to take flight."

Could enterprising birds have taken a similar evolutionary leap, learning to lay their eggs in slythii corpses?

"You mean," —Brenda's eyes were aghast— "The entire slythii religion is based on a parasitic relationship? Those big, stupid birds lay their eggs in the dead, then guard the corpse until . . . until some sort of chemical reaction shoots the hatchlings beyond the reach of ground predators?"

"It appears so," Adrian said reluctantly.

'Big, stupid birds' was perhaps an ungenerous description of the *ghondui*. According to the initial survey team, the *ghondui* were rather intelligent—possibly even sentient, although they'd shown no interest in communication. Sentient or not, they were knobby-skinned, bad-tempered, and approximately three times the size of the raptors found on Terra.

"Are you going to tell the slythii?" Brenda asked.

"Tell them what? That the blazing light their corpses emit has nothing to do with spiritual ascension? That carnivorous birds are using their dead as incubation chambers? That their entire religion is based on a hideous fallacy?" Adrian leaned back in his chair, surveying the display with an expression Brenda would surely interpret as a glower.

Silence stretched between them.

"I don't know," Adrian said. He shut down the data strip, fervently wishing that he, like the junior biologist standing in front of him, had a superior whose desk he could dump the problem on. "Death rituals are the heart of the slythii culture. Attacking the convictions they're based on could result in unpredictable, species-wide effects." He spread his hands in indecision. "I'd like to keep this data strip. I'm afraid you'll have to make a new recording for Dr. Fazzolari."

"Of course." Brenda nodded. She retreated toward the hallway, but paused halfway through the door. Turning, she said: "I'd want to know, sir."

Adrian glanced up, puzzled.

Brenda continued. "If my species had spent two millennia believing a lie. If someone had evidence of the truth... I'd want to know."

She blinked as if astonished at her own statement, muttered a timid farewell, and fled.

Adrian tossed the data strip onto his desk.

Should he tell the slythii? *Could* he tell the slythii? Most cultures did not take kindly to attacks on their religious precepts. On the other hand, as an ethical man, how could he not?

"Ah'drahn?" Adrian's head jerked up at the slythii pronunciation of his name. Rukha's mottled head poked through the open doorway. The Native Relations complex had been built to slythii proportions— double-wide by human standards—but Rukha's torso blocked all view of the hallway. His snout bobbed with excitement. "It is time."

Adrian rose, strangely reluctant. He did not wish to view a slythii interment; not today. Not with the data strip glaring like a baleful eye from his desktop. But he was the first human to be accorded such honor. More, the Deceasing was blood-kin to Rukha. He would insult his friend if he refused to come.

So he tucked the data strip into his pocket and slid his chair back into position. He pulled his government-issue taser from the bottom drawer of his desk and strapped it into his thigh holster. Slythii were not aggressive, but that did not make them non-dangerous. They tended to treat humans as one of their own, jostling to assert physical dominance. Since the average slyth massed as much as a small elephant, this could prove hazardous for the humans. Adrian had learned that, in moments of extreme cultural disconnect, it was useful to have a way of evening the odds.

Rukha was halfway down the hallway, his head ducking to avoid the light fixtures, by the time Adrian stepped out of his office.

The slythii were a leathery-skinned species, with blunt, ridged snouts that made Adrian think of box turtles. Rukha's shoulders spanned most of the hallway. A less enlightened slyth might have brushed into passers-by, crushing them against the wall and inadvertently breaking bones. But Rukha had been interacting with humans almost as long as Adrian had been interacting with slythii. He was the closest thing they had to an ambassador.

On the front steps of the building, Rukha paused. He bent his neck until one wide eye hung near Adrian's face, and spoke in the rasping tongue of the slyth.

"Djudin," he said. *Great friend.* "My lungs are heavy."

"I am not surprised," Adrian answered in the same language. "Gazhii is the first of your brothers to depart."

"It is not that. Death is no cause for sorrow. But Ghazii has not always honored the old ways. I am afraid no guardian will come to ease his passage."

Adrian's tongue snagged in his throat, caught in the gap between two impossibilities—uttering the comforting words that were a lie, or uttering the truth that would dishonor the dead.

Adrian temporized. "I am sure that what is right and proper will happen."

Rukha heaved a slyth-sized sigh. "You are a good friend, Ah'drahn. You do not lie to me. Yes. What is right and proper will happen." He stepped onto the gravel access road, headed toward the tree-line.

No, Adrian thought, following. *I am a poor friend. I should have the courage to tell you things you do not want to hear.*

But trying to talk science with a slyth was difficult on the best of days. Adrian's pointed questions about slythii reproduction, for example, had been greeted with blank stares.

Where did the young ones come from? From the forest, of course. Rukha and his brothers did not find it unusual that juvenile slyth should creep like foundlings from the underbrush, no parents in sight, to join the herd. Gender and reproduction were foreign concepts, unrelated to the slyths' immediate lives, and hence uninteresting.

Adrian and Rukha trudged past rustic buildings, winding deeper into the forest. Equipment sheds and research outposts loomed through the trees.

"You are thoughtful," Rukha said as they stepped off the high-traffic pathway and onto a subtle slythii trail. "Have you no questions for me today, Ah'drahn? You are always full of questions."

Adrian hesitated. Should he tell Rukha about the data strip? Slythii appreciated bluntness, and Rukha certainly had a right to know the truth. But Adrian didn't want to bring up the data strip right now. The slyth would be distressed if he knew an Ascension had been recorded.

Perhaps he could approach the topic obliquely, leaving the data strip out of it. Laying the groundwork for future conversations.

"Have you ever wondered," Adrian said at last, "Whether it

would be such a bad thing? If no guardian came to collect Ghazii's spirit, I mean."

"Your thoughts sit strangely, Djudin. Of course I do not wonder."

"What if I told you that the guardians are parasites? That they're feeding of the bodies of your dead?"

"Then you would be tragically mistaken," Rukha said, unperturbed. "I do not wonder about such things, Ah'drahn, because my ancestors have already done so. This thing is known. A Truth-seeker has written it."

"Written?" Adrian said, surprised. "On the stone pillars, you mean? The cliffs that run parallel to the roadway?" The strange engravings, like hairline fractures across the rocks, had puzzled human colonists for decades.

"The very same." Rukha emitted a rippling sigh. "I will try to explain. I am a *hlath-ha-zhanai*, a seeker of Truth. It is the closest role we have to your scientists. It is the reason I choose to concern myself with your people, when other slythii do not.

"Someday, when the change begins to take over my body, I will leave words of value for my people. I will condense the massive sea of data about your strange, starfaring people into powerful statements of truth, and I will engrave those truths on one of the pillars. You are a complex species. I believe I will need two or three sentences."

"That's all?" Adrian asked, startled. "After an entire life spent studying humanity, you'll only write down a few statements?"

"I will write that which is of value," Rukha affirmed, "and allow the rest to pass into oblivion."

"What about everything else?" Adrian demanded. "Your studies, your years of effort? Why bother acquiring knowledge, merely to let it be forgotten?"

"That which is of value remains," Rukha replied placidly. He swung his head around to regard Adrian with one bobbing eye. "I have noticed that your people place great stock in information, as though knowledge were a treasure to be hoarded."

"It is," Adrian said. How could he say this in a way Rukha would understand? "Knowledge is the most precious of acquisitions."

"You humans . . . you carry many details that are not useful." Rukha stretched, as though searching for words. "I will use an example. We once discussed fruit, and the reason it falls from the tree, yes?"

"Because of gravity. Yes."

"And what is this 'gravity,' according to your scientists?"

"A phenomenon by which objects attract each other."

"And the cause of this attraction?"

"The interactions between atoms."

"Why should the atoms behave in this way?"

Adrian faltered. "They just do."

"Ah," Rukha's head lifted, the slythii equivalent of a smile. "You have described the phenomenon in iteratively more complicated detail, and yet you are no closer to answering the original question. When the talking is finished, you and I must both accept that this truth merely <u>is</u>."

"It's not about explaining fundamental truths," Adrian objected. "It's about understanding our world. Knowledge of gravity helps our engineers design ships like the one that brought us here."

"And yet most of your people are not engineers."

"Of course not."

"Why are they then taught of this 'gravity,' Ah'drahn?" Rukha appeared to be truly curious. "How do their choices flow differently, because one has put a name on the reason the fruit falls?"

Adrian felt strangely out of footing. How had this conversation turned around on him so quickly? "Look, you can't guess in advance which knowledge will be useful. Some is, some isn't, and your best bet in life is to learn everything you can about, well . . . everything."

"No one can understand everything, Ah'drahn. It is foolish to try. It leads to incomplete knowledge, which is more dangerous that ignorance."

"I don't understand."

"Ignorance leads to indecision, a dangerous state. But incomplete knowledge leads one to err with conviction, a far more hazardous event. This is why each Truth-seeker devotes his life to a single topic: To ensure that his writings will be of value."

"Like the writings about the guardians?"

"Yes. A good example. If I did not know that the guardians escort the souls of the dead, I might mistake them for carrion birds and drive them from my brothers' shells. This would be a great tragedy." Plod, plod. Thump. "This is what I mean when I say your science is not useful. Why preserve trivial masses of data, when only the culminating conclusion matters?"

It was the most information Rukha had ever offered about the philosophy of his people. Adrian's mind spun.

The engraved stone pillars were not, as Adrian had previously supposed, a collection of cultural histories. They were a blasted set of alien commandments; imperatives stripped of all meaning or justification, pressed in stone and left to dominate the lives of all who followed.

"So that's it?" he demanded, appalled. "You're going to accept the conclusions of a slyth who's been dead for thousands of years?"

"The *hlath-ha-zhanai* would not have written truths of which they were not certain. Unless something has changed, as it did when your people descended from the sky, there is no need to duplicate past efforts."

"But what if they made a mistake?"

"That which is of value remains," Rukha said firmly.

The narrow trail continued. Soon they were stepping on eggshell-thin fragments, a clear sign that they had reached the slythii burial grounds. The *Kahn-ti*, as they were called, stretched across two full hectares of forest, littered with fragments of exoskeleton; ominously devoid of bones. As they picked their way beneath the thinning tree canopy, he spotted the mottled brown husks of the Deceased, nestled like boulders among the tree trunks. Above them, crooning tuneless songs among shadowed branches, weaved the bright yellow eyes and curving beaks of the *ghondui*.

The sight sickened Adrian. The clawed, yellow-eyed guardians were not wise spiritual mentors. They hadn't come to escort the dead into the greater life. They'd come to plunder them.

At the far edge of the fields, a crowd of slythii had assembled. Rukha shoved through the mass of bodies, asserting his right as the Deceasing's blood-kin. They had emerged together from the forest, along with five others, scraping through the underbrush on their tummies, with eyes and ears still tightly closed. Among the slythii, that bond was as precious as sibling relationships on Terra. Perhaps even more so, as there were no parents to care for the foundlings.

Rukha came to an abrupt halt. They had come to the place Rukha's brother had chosen for his death.

The Deceasing lay in a heaving huddle, nearly encased by the flaky crust of a hardening exoskeleton. His neck and legs, curled in against the torso, were already fused in place. His lungs, wheezing, powered rippling bellows along his rib cage. Beneath the hardening slime, cracked patches of skin wept like a tree stripped of branches in springtime. Ghazii's mucus pores, dormant throughout his long life, had begun to create his coffin.

Above him, attracted by the sweet scent of his decay, clustered a dozen yellow-eyed guardians. They hissed as Adrian approached, a grating rattle that seemed to settle in his spine. That hiss was an honored sound among the slyth; a sign that the guardians prepared to escort the Deceasing to the greater world. Adrian heard only the sound of a parasite preparing to maim.

It doesn't matter, he told himself. *Ghazii will be dead either way. Where's the harm if the creatures feed off his body?*

The Deceasing had spotted them. The mottled head lifted, a long wheeze indicating the struggle to draw breath. His body shifted, cracking the shell in several places to let the sap bleed through.

"Rukha." Ghazii's voice—half-whisper, half-cough—revealed the strain of his transformation. "I thought you would not come."

"I delayed to fetch the human, Ah'drahn."

Ghazii's lungs created an unpleasant sound. "Who was it that crawled with you from the forest, him or me? Fine ways you have of honoring your brother."

"He is more interesting than you."

Adrian, accustomed to the blunt honesty of slythii conversation, recognized the affection that ran beneath the words. Rukha would miss his brother greatly.

Ghazii coughed and blinked to clear the worst of the mucus from his eyes. "It is not long. I feel the change within."

Rukha brought one eye close to Ghazii's bleeding face. "I will greet you again in the greater life."

"Pah!" Ghazii's desiccated snort was loud enough to startle nearby slythii. "Back," Ghazii wheezed. "I cannot breathe in this crowd. You—" his murky gaze fell an Adrian. "You stay."

Ghazii's brothers murmured at this breach of tradition, but complied with the will of the Deceasing. Adrian stepped into the open space, close enough to touch the forming shell with his fingers had he chosen to. There was something about the crust of hardening slime along Ghazii's body. Something familiar . . .

"You do not believe the ways of our people," Ghazii said. "Do not answer. I have sensed it. I do not believe them either. I have spent my life defying the ancient customs, and claimed I took no thought for the greater journey." Ghazii's voice lowered. One round eye pinned Adrian with its gaze. "But to you; you who does not condemn me for denying the will of my forefathers... to you I may confess this: I am afraid."

Ghazii's voice was hardly more than a whisper. He closed his eyes and grew still. A gasping sigh crept through his teeth, the sound of lungs being emptied by the constriction of inner webbings; of airways being closed off forever.

Ghazzi's brothers returned in a wave of flesh. They thrust their heads at Ghazii's congealing corpse, rumbling encouragement which he may or may not have heard. The flow of mucus increased, hardening unimpeded now that muscles no longer writhed beneath the exterior.

Adrian, watching at a distance, jolted in surprise. The way the shell thickened; the way the contours settled . . . "Blazing novas. It can't be!"

He pressed between lumbering shoulders to reach the encrusted body. He studied the slime in horrified fascination.

Rukha's words haunted him. *Incomplete knowledge is more dangerous than ignorance.*

Adrian, studying the slythii for so many years, had overlooked the obvious. He had never asked the most important question: Biologically speaking, why would a species create a protective shell around its dead? What possible evolutionary advantage could it offer?

Overhead the guardians stirred, feathers stretching like funeral shrouds. Rough-edged squawks cut the air as they jostled for position above Ghazii. Yellow eyes peered downward, intent.

Adrian watched the scene in a kind of frozen horror. It would have been so easy for Ghazii's brothers to defend him. The *ghondui's* claws, edged enough to shred human flesh, could not have pierced Rukha's leathery hide. But Ghazii's brothers just lowered their heads, beginning to keen in a complex pattern of pitches that resembled music.

They did not know that Ghazii wasn't dead.

How could they know? They had never heard of a chrysalis. No one had told them that life forms could exist in a comatose state—without food, without oxygen—while biology wrought its magical change upon the body.

"Rukha," Adrian said, urgent. "Rukha, the guardians must be kept away from Ghazii!"

The branches overhead erupted in screeching. A single guardian, large and bedraggled, separated from the others and dropped to the ground. It began to crawl along Ghazii's body, pecking, testing, poking . . .

"No!" Adrian shouted, switching, in his alarm, to his own language. "Don't you understand, he'll be killed! He'll never emerge from the chrysalis . . ."

"Calm yourself," Rukha reprimanded mildly. "The guardians have come for Ghazii after all. My lungs are filled." He took a breath and trumpeted in praise of the dead.

Adrian pulled the data strip from his pocket, even though he knew it was too late. Even if he could make Rukha watch the recording, even if Rukha could be convinced . . . the guardian was about to deposit its eggs. There was surely a window of opportunity, during these few precious minutes before the shell hardened. Once the ghondui's eggs were sealed inside, there'd be no way to get them back out.

Adrian's groping fingers, still fumbling with the data strip, brushed against his taser. He snatched it from the holster and targeted the guardian.

Windows of opportunity cut both ways. If Adrian could keep the creature from ovipositing for just a few minutes . . .

All right, Rukha, Adrian thought. *You say the only knowledge that matters is knowledge that affects actions? Well, this knowledge is affecting my actions. Here, now.*

He compressed the trigger.

The guardian screeched, stiffening. The slythii snorted, stamping in dismay as the guardian convulsed and flopped onto its side.

Rukha, in the sudden panic, was the first to realize what had happened. He had spent more time with humans than the others. He had seen tasers function, and knew that this odd, outstretched motion of a human arm could immobilize a distant object. The look he gave Adrian was beyond outrage.

"What have you done?" Rukha hissed. His massive forefoot struck Adrian's hand with numbing force. The taser flew from his grip, sliding across the ground. "Ghazii was lucky to earn a guardian! Now his spirit must walk in eternal sorrow."

"Rukha, listen!" Adrian shouted to be heard above the noise from the slythii. "The guardians aren't what you think. The Ascension isn't what you think."

How could he explain? He didn't know half the words he'd need in the slythii language; many of them didn't exist.

Adrian lifted the data strip and triggered its holo-display. A blazing pillar appeared in high magnification freeze frame. No spirits, there. Just six immature *ghondui*, glowing from the chemical reaction that had propelled them into the sky. It was not hard to imagine how the event had been mistaken for something ethereal.

"Look. Look here," Adrian said, raising the display.

But Rukha was attacking.

Slyth often expressed feelings physically. This, however, was no minor display of annoyance. Rukha was enraged, rising high on his hind legs, weight preparing to drop.

Adrian dodged the crushing feet, scrambling toward the fallen taser. Rukha, hissing in fury, lowered a broad foot onto the weapon, splintering it.

Adrian dodged behind a pack of slythii, gaining respite as Rukha turned to nose the stirring guardian. The paralyzing effect of the taser had almost worn off. If the milling slythii would just trample that parasite instead of crooning at it like deranged hens . . .

But the slythii breathed snorts of relief, stepping anxiously aside as the guardian rose and fluffed its feathers. It produced the eerie, rattling hiss characteristic of its kind and clambered again onto Ghazii's chrysalis.

Adrian rose, ready to lunge at the guardian, but a massive foot pressed into his back, pinning him to the ground.

"I'm trying to *help*," Adrian gasped, struggling. Once the guardian inserted its eggs beneath the hardening shell, Ghazii's death was certain.

The foot lowered, making it difficult to breathe. Its owner—one of Ghazii's many brothers—lowered his head and said with calm but implacable conviction: "Do not interfere."

Adrian tried again, lifting the data strip. Its little holoscreen was still running, white fountain blazing beyond the dark shadows of treetops. If they would just *look* . . .

"No more weapons."

With a bone-jarring strike, the slyth knocked the strip from his hands. The device struck a rock, flickered, and went dark against a splatter of mud.

Adrian glowered. What good was proof, when no one would listen?

Poor Ghazii would never complete his metamorphosis now. His two-phase life cycle had been truncated, abruptly, at the completion of the larval stage. So apparently, had the metamorphosis of every other slyth in this community. The chrysalides, every single one of them, had been commandeered by the parasitic *ghondui*, a circumstance that was unspeakably ominous at the species level. Where were all the post-metamorphic slythii? Were there even any left? And how much longer would it take before juvenile slythii stopped creeping from the forest to replace the ranks of the Deceasing?

Adrian's chest felt the strain of the slyth's foot, pressing him downward. By craning his neck, he could see the *ghondui* atop Ghazii's chrysalis, pecking, poking, prodding.

Ah, Ghazii, what might you have become?

That loss, the loss of learning what a post-metamorphic slyth looked like, cut more deeply than any of the others.

Adrian grabbed a jagged rock and slammed it into the leg that held him pinned. The slyth roared and pulled back. Adrian slid out and darted toward the chrysalis.

One good hit . . . If he understood the guardians' territorial patterns, no other guardian would claim Ghazii's body. If Adrian could just get to the thing . . .

He ducked beneath the startled legs of one slyth, slipped between the trampling feet of another . . . only to be knocked backward by Rukha's head, swinging with bone-crushing force. Adrian flew sideways, ribs snapping; his spine struck a rock with a terrifying *crack*.

Pain shot through his lungs. Adrian tried to rise, failed, and reluctantly confirmed that his legs no longer responded. He lowered his throbbing head and swore vehemently.

The medical team back at base might be able to salvage his spinal cord, if he could be transported safely. On the other hand, there seemed to be a lot of blood running down the gritty surface of the stone. A very awful lot of it...

Rukha's head appeared in front of him, still bobbing in anger. "I do not understand you, Djudin. Why have you—" A sudden pause. "Ah'drahn, are you injured?"

In that odd, dispassionate way slyth had, Rukha's feelings vanished beneath the need for action. "You are not well. We will bring you to your people."

"It is not safe to move me," Adrian said. "Send someone to fetch them."

Rukha nodded and stepped away.

Adrian's gaze flicked to the chrysalis. The guardian moved across it in frantic bursts, pecking and vibrating its tail. It was not the range of motion Adrian expected from an ovipositing female. The longer Adrian watched, the more certain he became: The creature was not laying eggs.

It was copulating.

Adrian gaped. The behavior made no sense . . . until he realized that no biologist had yet observed what hatched *out* of the eggs the guardians laid. The colony was only a few decades old, and with an entire planet to explore, no one had bothered much with the temperamental avians.

Adrian's vision was blurring. His heart thudded from blood loss. He struggled to make sense of it all.

A four-phase life cycle: egg, larva, chrysalis, adult. Such patterns were common enough, across the known planets. Genetic exchange usually occurred at the adult phase, but what if . . .?

What if reproduction occurred *across* the phases, instead?

The pattern spread before him like a complex diagram. A complex life cycle: juvenile slythii hatching from guardian eggs, scuttling through leaves and underbrush toward the scent of the herd. Deceasing slythii entombed within their mucus shells, using pheromones to attract a mate. Within the chrysalis, a genetic miracle; new creatures formed from the bones and tissues of the old. Young guardians bursting from the chrysalis in a brilliant geyser of light, ready to mature and, someday, lay eggs that would begin the cycle anew.

Rukha returned, snout hovering too near to focus on. He murmured something about the medics and the colonial office, but Adrian didn't have the strength to care.

The slythii Truth-seekers had been right. Ghazii's soul *would* ascend along with the guardians who would form from his body. And Adrian, in his arrogant certainty, had almost destroyed it. If he had prevented the guardian from copulating, Ghazii's life cycle would have ended with a barren chrysalis.

Adrian's head was swimming. He must have lost a lot of blood. Dimly, he lay his head against the rock and let the last of his illusions slip away.

The Saggitarian colonial hospital was not built to slythii proportions, and so Rukha, when he visited, was obliged to stick his head through the open window. There were no apologies. It was not the slythii way.

When the doctors finally cleared Adrian for minor excursions, he took his still-wobbly legs straight to the colonial research institute. More specifically: to Brenda Vickington, whom Adrian had commandeered from Professor Fazzolari for a little biological legwork.

"You were right," she said as soon as he walked through the door. "The genetic scans match perfectly. *Ghondui* are a post-metamorphic stage in the slythii life cycle."

She handed him the data readouts and, for good measure, a few ultrasound pictures of baby slythii wriggling inside guardian eggs. "Do you think they retain memories?" she asked wistfully. "When they emerge from the chrysalis, I mean. Do they remember their life as a larva?"

"The slythii believe so. I'm rather inclined to believe them, these days." A more interesting question was whether all six emerging guardians shared the same memory set, or whether the metamorphic slyth's experience was somehow divvied among its descendents. Since the *ghondui* resisted all attempts at communication, the answer might well remain a mystery.

Two months later, when Rukha began scratching his Truth-seeker's wisdom on the ancient stone pillars, Adrian watched in fascination.

"I don't suppose you're going to tell me what it says?"

Rukha, forefeet propped on the rough surface of the stone, paused in his work to stare downward. "What purpose would that serve? You are not a slyth."

"Curiosity, I suppose."

"Curiosity is leads to incomplete knowledge."

". . . which is more dangerous than ignorance. Yes. I understand now."

"You should write it down. For your people."

Adrian laughed, caught off guard. "I doubt they would pay much attention to me. Anything I write would surely be swept away in the tides of history."

Rukha turned placidly to his work. His spine rippled, the slythii equivalent of a shrug.

"That which is of value remains," he said.

Grandmaster Robert Silverberg is a living legend with fans all over the world and has the awards to prove it. But his fiction has rarely touched on his own Jewish heritage. In this classic, he examines colonial life for Jewish colonists when indigenous aliens form a unique bond with one of their own . . .

THE DYBBUK OF MAZEL TOV IV

ROBERT SILVERBERG

My grandson David will have his bar mitzvah next spring. No one in our family has undergone that rite in at least three hundred years—certainly not since we Levins settled in Old Israel, the Israel on Earth, soon after the European holocaust. My friend Eliahu asked me not long ago how I feel about David's bar mitzvah, whether the idea of it angers me, whether I see it as a disturbing element. No, I replied, the boy is a Jew, after all—let him have a bar mitzvah if he wants one. These are times of transition and upheaval, as all times are. David is not bound by the attitudes of his ancestors.

"Since when is a Jew not bound by the attitudes of his ancestors?" Eliahu asked.

"You know what I mean," I said.

Indeed he did. We are bound but yet free. If anything governs us out of the past it is the tribal bond itself, not the philosophies of our departed kinsmen. We accept what we choose to accept; nevertheless we remain Jews. I come from a family that has liked to say—especially to gentiles—that we are Jews but not Jewish; that is, we acknowledge and cherish our ancient heritage, but we do not care to entangle ourselves in outmoded rituals and folkways. This is what my forefathers declared, as far back as those secular-minded Levins who three centuries ago fought to win and guard the freedom of the land of Israel. (Old Israel, I mean.) I would say the same here, if there were any gentiles on this world to whom such things had to be explained. But of course in this New Israel in the stars we have only ourselves, no gentiles within a dozen light-years, unless you count our neighbors the Kunivaru as gentiles. (Can creatures that are not human rightly be called gentiles? I'm not sure the term applies. Besides, the Kunivaru now insist that they are Jews. My mind spins. It's an issue of Talmudic complexity, and God knows I'm no Talmudist. Hillel, Akiva, Rashi, help me!) Anyway, come the fifth day of Sivan my son's son will have his bar mitzvah, and I'll play the proud grandpa as pious old Jews have done for six thousand years.

All things are connected. That my grandson would have a bar mitzvah is merely the latest link in a chain of events that goes back to—when? To the day the Kunivaru decided to embrace Judaism? To the day the dybbuk entered Seul the Kunivar? To the day we refugees from Earth discovered the fertile planet that we sometimes call New Israel and sometimes call Mazel Tov IV? To the day of the Final Pogrom on Earth? Reb Yossele the Hasid might say that David's bar mitzvah was determined on the day the Lord God fashioned Adam out of dust. But I think that would be overdoing things.

The day the dybbuk took possession of the body of Seul the Kunivar was probably where it really started. Until then things were relatively uncomplicated here. The Hasidim had their settlement, we Israelis had ours, and the natives, the Kunivaru, had the rest of the planet; and generally we all kept out of one another's way. After the dybbuk everything changed. It happened more than forty years ago, in the first generation after the Landing, on the ninth day of Tishri in the year 6302. I was working in the fields, for Tishri is a harvest month. The day was hot, and I worked swiftly, singing and humming. As I moved down the long rows of cracklepods, tagging those that were ready to be gathered, a Kunivar appeared at the crest of the hill that overlooks our kibbutz. It seemed to be in some distress, for it came staggering and lurching down the hillside with extraordinary clumsiness, tripping over its own four legs as if it barely knew how to manage them. When it was about a hundred meters from me, it cried out, "Shimon! Help me, Shimon! In God's name help me!"

There were several strange things about this outcry, and I

perceived them gradually, the most trivial first. It seemed odd that a Kunivar would address me by my given name, for they are a formal people. It seemed more odd that a Kunivar would speak to me in quite decent Hebrew, for at that time none of them had learned our language. It seemed most odd of all—but I was slow to discern it— that a Kunivar would have the very voice, dark and resonant, of my dear dead friend Joseph Avneri.

The Kunivar stumbled into the cultivated part of the field and halted, trembling terribly. Its fine green fur was pasted into hummocks by perspiration, and its great golden eyes rolled and crossed in a ghastly way. It stood flat-footed, splaying its legs out under the four corners of its chunky body like the legs of a table, and clasped its long powerful arms around its chest. I recognized the Kunivar as Seul, a subchief of the local village, with whom we of the kibbutz had had occasional dealings.

"What help can I give you?" I asked. "What has happened to you, Seul?"

"Shimon—Shimon—" A frightful moan came from the Kunivar. "Oh, God, Shimon, it goes beyond all belief! How can I bear this? How can I even comprehend it?"

No doubt of it. The Kunivar was speaking in the voice of Joseph Avneri.

"Seul?" I said hesitantly.

"My name is Joseph Avneri."

"Joseph Avneri died a year ago last Elul. I didn't realize you were such a clever mimic, Seul."

"Mimic? You speak to me of mimicry, Shimon? It's no mimicry. I am your Joseph, dead but still aware, thrown for my sins into this monstrous alien body. Are you Jew enough to know what a dybbuk is, Shimon?"

"A wandering ghost, yes, who takes possession of the body of a living being."

"I have become a dybbuk."

"There are no dybbuks. Dybbuks are phantoms out of medieval folklore," I said.

"You hear the voice of one."

"This is impossible," I said.

"I agree, Shimon, I agree." He sounded calmer now. "It's entirely impossible. I don't believe in dybbuks either, any more than I believe in Zeus, the Minotaur, werewolves, gorgons, or golems. But how else do you explain me?"

"You are Seul the Kunivar, playing a clever trick."

"Do you really think so? Listen to me, Shimon. I knew you when we were boys in Tiberias. I rescued you when we were fishing in the lake and our boat overturned. I was with you the day you met Leah whom you married. I was godfather to your son Yigal. I studied with you at the university in Jerusalem. I fled with you in the fiery days of the Final Pogrom. I stood watch with you aboard the Ark in the years of our flight from Earth. Do you remember, Shimon? Do you remember Jerusalem? The Old City, the Mount of Olives, the Tomb of Absalom, the Western Wall? Am I a Kunivar, Shimon, to know of the Western Wall?"

"There is no survival of consciousness after death," I said stubbornly.

"A year ago I would have agreed with you. But who am I if I am not the spirit of Joseph Avneri? How can you account for me any other way? Dear God, do you think I want to believe this, Shimon? You know what a scoffer I was. But it's real."

"Perhaps I'm having a very vivid hallucination."

"Call the others, then. If ten people have the same hallucination, is it still a hallucination? Be reasonable, Shimon! Here I stand before you, telling you things that only I could know, and you deny that I am—"

"Be reasonable?" I said. "Where does reason enter into this? Do you expect me to believe in ghosts, Joseph, in wandering demons, in dybbuks? Am I some superstition-ridden peasant out of the Polish woods? Is this the Middle Ages?"

"You called me Joseph," he said quietly.

"I can hardly call you Seul when you speak in that voice."

"Then you believe in me!"

"No."

"Look, Shimon, did you ever know a bigger sceptic than Joseph Avneri? I had no use for the Torah, I said Moses was fictional, I plowed the fields on Yom Kippur, I laughed in God's nonexistent face. What is life, I said? And I answered: a mere accident, a transient biological phenomenon. Yet here I am. I remember the moment of my death. For a full year I've wandered this world, bodiless, perceiving things, unable to communicate. And today I find myself cast into this creature's body, and I know myself for a dybbuk. If I believe, Shimon, how can you dare disbelieve? In the name of our friendship, have faith in what I tell you!"

"You have actually become a dybbuk?"

"I have become a dybbuk," he said.

I shrugged. "Very well, Joseph. You're a dybbuk. It's madness but I believe." I stared in astonishment at the Kunivar. Did I believe? Did I believe that I believed? How could I not believe? There was no other way for the voice of Joseph Avneri to be coming from the throat of a Kunivar. Sweat streamed down my body. I was face to face with the impossible, and all my philosophy was shattered. Anything was possible now. God might appear as a burning bush. The sun might stand still. No, I told myself. Believe only one irrational thing at a time, Shimon. Evidently there are dybbuks; well, then, there are dybbuks. But everything else pertaining to the Invisible World remains unreal until it manifests itself.

I said, "Why do you think this has happened to you?"

"It could only be as a punishment."

"For what, Joseph?"

"My experiments. You knew I was doing research into the Kunivaru metabolism, didn't you?"

"Yes, certainly. But—"

"Did you know I performed surgical experiments on live Kunivaru in our hospital? That I used patients, without informing them or anyone else, in studies of a forbidden kind? It was vivisection, Shimon."

"*What?*"

"There were things I needed to know, and there was only one way I could discover them. The hunger for knowledge led me into sin. I told myself that these creatures were ill, that they would shortly die anyway, and that it might benefit everyone if I opened them while they still lived, you see? Besides, they weren't human beings, Shimon, they were only animals—very intelligent animals, true, but still only—"

"No, Joseph. I can believe in dybbuks more readily than I can believe this. You, doing such a thing? My calm rational friend, my scientist, my wise one?" I shuddered and stepped a few paces back from him. "Auschwitz!" I cried. "Buchenwald! Dachau! Do those names mean anything to you? 'They weren't human beings,' the

Nazi surgeon said. 'They were only Jews, and our need for scientific knowledge is such that—' That was only three hundred years ago, Joseph. And you, a Jew, a Jew of all people, to—"

"I know, Shimon, I know. Spare me the lecture. I sinned terribly, and for my sins I've been given this grotesque body, this gross, hideous, heavy body, these four legs which I can hardly coordinate, this crooked spine, this foul, hot furry pelt. I still don't believe in a God, Shimon, but I think I believe in some sort of compensating force that balances accounts in this universe, and the account has been balanced for me, oh, yes, Shimon! I've had six hours of terror and loathing today such as I never dreamed could be experienced. To enter this body, to fry in this heat, to wander these hills trapped in such a mass of flesh, to feel myself being bombarded with the sensory perceptions of a being so alien—it's been hell, I tell you that without exaggeration. I would have died of shock in the first ten minutes if I didn't already happen to be dead. Only now, seeing you, talking to you, do I begin to get control of myself. Help me, Shimon."

"What do you want me to do?"

"Get me out of here. This is torment. I'm a dead man—I'm entitled to rest the way the other dead ones rest. Free me, Shimon."

"How?"

"How? How? Do I know? Am I an expert on dybbuks? Must I direct my own exorcism? If you knew what an effort it is simply to hold this body upright, to make its tongue form Hebrew words, to say things in a way you'll understand—" Suddenly the Kunivar sagged to his knees, a slow, complex folding process that reminded me of the manner in which the camels of Old Earth lowered themselves to the ground. The alien creature began to sputter and moan and wave his arms about; foam appeared on his wide rubbery lips. "God in Heaven, Shimon," Joseph cried, "set me free!"

I called for my son Yigal, and he came running swiftly from the far side of the fields, a lean healthy boy, only eleven years old but already long-legged, strong-bodied. Without going into details, I indicated the suffering Kunivar and told Yigal to get help from the kibbutz. A few minutes later he came back leading seven or eight men—Abrasha, Itzhak, Uri, Nahum, and some others. It took the full strength of all of us to lift the Kunivar into the hopper of a harvesting

machine and transport him to our hospital. Two of the doctors—
Moshe Shiloah and someone else—began to examine the stricken
alien, and I sent Yigal to the Kunivaru village to tell the chief that
Seul had collapsed in our fields.

The doctors quickly diagnosed the problem as a case of heat
prostration. They were discussing the sort of injection the Kunivar
should receive when Joseph Avneri, breaking a silence that had lasted
since Seul had fallen, announced his presence within the Kunivar's
body. Uri and Nahum had remained in the hospital room with me; not
wanting this craziness to become general knowledge in the kibbutz, I
took them outside and told them to forget whatever ravings they had
heard. When I returned, the doctors were busy with their preparations
and Joseph was patiently explaining to them that he was a dybbuk
who had involuntarily taken possession of the Kunivar. "The heat
has driven the poor creature insane," Moshe Shiloah murmured, and
rammed a huge needle into one of Seul's thighs.

"Make them listen to me," Joseph said.

"You know that voice," I told the doctors. "Something very
unusual has happened here."

But they were no more willing to believe in dybbuks than they
were in rivers that flow uphill. Joseph continued to protest, and the
doctors continued methodically to fill Seul's body with sedatives and
restoratives and other potions. Even when Joseph began to speak
of last year's kibbutz gossip—who had been sleeping with whom
behind whose back, who had illicitly been peddling goods from the
community storehouse to the Kunivaru—they paid no attention. It
was as though they had so much difficulty believing that a Kunivar
could speak Hebrew that they were unable to make sense out of
what he was saying and took Joseph's words to be Seul's delirium.
Suddenly Joseph raised his voice for the first time, calling out in a
loud, angry tone, "You, Moshe Shiloah! Aboard the Ark I found you
in bed with the wife of Teviah Kohn, remember? Would a Kunivar
have known such a thing?"

Moshe Shiloah gasped, reddened, and dropped his hypodermic.
The other doctor was nearly as astonished.

"What is this?" Moshe Shiloah asked. "How can this be?"

"Deny me now!" Joseph roared. "Can you deny me?"

The doctors faced the same problems of acceptance that I had
had, that Joseph himself had grappled with. We were all of us rational

men in this kibbutz, and the supernatural had no place in our lives. But there was no arguing the phenomenon away. There was the voice of Joseph Avneri emerging from the throat of Seul the Kunivar, and the voice was saying things that only Joseph would have said, and Joseph had been dead more than a year. Call it a dybbuk, call it hallucination, call it anything: Joseph's presence could not be ignored.

Locking the door, Moshe Shiloah said to me, "We must deal with this somehow."

Tensely we discussed the situation. It was, we agreed, a delicate and difficult matter. Joseph, raging and tortured, demanded to be exorcised and allowed to sleep the sleep of the dead; unless we placated him he would make us all suffer. In his pain, in his fury, he might say anything, he might reveal everything he knew about our private lives; a dead man is beyond all of society's rules of common decency. We could not expose ourselves to that. But what could we do about him? Chain him in an outbuilding and hide him in solitary confinement? Hardly. Unhappy Joseph deserved better of us than that; and there was Seul to consider, poor supplanted Seul, the dybbuk's unwilling host. We could not keep a Kunivar in the kibbutz, imprisoned or free, even if his body did house the spirit of one of our own people, nor could we let the shell of Seul go back to the Kunivaru village with Joseph as a furious passenger trapped inside. What to do? Separate soul from body, somehow: restore Seul to wholeness and send Joseph to the limbo of the dead. But how? There was nothing in the standard pharmacopoeia about dybbuks. What to do?

I sent for Shmarya Asch and Yakov Ben-Zion, who headed the kibbutz council that month, and for Shlomo Feig, our rabbi, a shrewd and sturdy man, very unorthodox in his orthodoxy, almost as secular as the rest of us. They questioned Joseph Avneri extensively, and he told them the whole tale—his scandalous secret experiments, his post-mortem year as a wandering spirit, his sudden painful incarnation within Seul. At length Shmarya Asch turned to Moshe Shiloah and snapped, "There must be some therapy for such a case."

"I know of none."

"This is schizophrenia," said Shmarya Asch in his firm, dogmatic way. "There are cures for schizophrenia. There are drugs, there are electric shock treatments, there are—you know these things better than I, Moshe."

"This is not schizophrenia," Moshe Shiloah retorted. "This is a case of demonic possession. I have no training in treating such maladies."

"Demonic possession?" Shmarya bellowed. "Have you lost your mind?"

"Peace, peace, all of you," Shlomo Feig said, as everyone began to shout at once. The rabbi's voice cut sharply through the tumult and silenced us all. He was a man of great strength, physical as well as moral, to whom the entire kibbutz inevitably turned for guidance, although there was virtually no one among us who observed the major rites of Judaism. He said, "I find this as hard to comprehend as any of you. But the evidence triumphs over my scepticism. How can we deny that Joseph Avneri has returned as a dybbuk? Moshe, you know no way of causing this intruder to leave the Kunivar's body?"

"None," said Moshe Shiloah.

"Maybe the Kunivaru themselves know a way," Yakov Ben-Zion suggested.

"Exactly," said the rabbi. "My next point. These Kunivaru are a primitive folk. They live closer to the world of magic and witchcraft, of demons and spirits, than we do whose minds are schooled in the habits of reason. Perhaps such cases of possession occur often among them. Perhaps they have techniques for driving out unwanted spirits. Let us turn to them, and let them cure their own."

Before long Yigal arrived, bringing with him six Kunivaru, including Gyaymar, the village chief. They wholly filled the little hospital room, bustling around in it like a delegation of huge furry centaurs; I was oppressed by the acrid smell of so many of them in one small space, and although they had always been friendly to us, never raising an objection when we appeared as refugees to settle on their planet, I felt fear of them now as I had never felt before. Clustering about Seul, they asked questions of him in their own supple language, and when Joseph Avneri replied in Hebrew they whispered things to each other unintelligible to us. Then, unexpectedly, the voice of Seul broke through, speaking in halting spastic monosyllables that revealed the terrible shock his nervous system must have received; then the alien faded and Joseph Avneri spoke once more with the Kunivar's lips, begging forgiveness, asking for release.

Turning to Gyaymar, Shlomo Feig said, "Have such things happened on this world before?"

"Oh, yes, yes," the chief replied. "Many times. When one of us dies having a guilty soul, repose is denied, and the spirit may undergo strange migrations before forgiveness comes. What was the nature of this man's sin?"

"It would be difficult to explain to one who is not Jewish," said the rabbi hastily, glancing away. "The important question is whether you have a means of undoing what has befallen the unfortunate Seul, whose sufferings we all lament."

"We have a means, yes," said Gyaymar, the chief.

The six Kunivaru hoisted Seul to their shoulders and carried him from the kibbutz; we were told that we might accompany them if we cared to do so. I went along, and Moshe Shiloah, and Shmarya Asch, and Yakov Ben-Zion, and the rabbi, and perhaps some others. The Kunivaru took their comrade not to their village but to a meadow several kilometers to the east, down in the direction of the place where the Hasidim lived. Not long after the Landing, the Kunivaru had let us know that the meadow was sacred to them, and none of us had ever entered it.

It was a lovely place, green and moist, a gently sloping basin crisscrossed by a dozen cool little streams. Depositing Seul beside one of the streams, the Kunivaru went off into the woods bordering the meadow to gather firewood and herbs. We remained close by Seul. "This will do no good," Joseph Avneri muttered more than once. "A waste of time, a foolish expense of energy." Three of the Kunivaru started to build a bonfire. Two sat nearby, shredding the herbs, making heaps of leaves, stems, roots. Gradually more of their kind appeared until the meadow was filled with them; it seemed that the whole village, some four hundred Kunivaru, was turning out to watch or to participate in the rite. Many of them carried musical instruments, trumpets and drums, rattles and clappers, lyres, lutes, small harps, percussive boards, wooden flutes, everything intricate and fanciful of design; we had not suspected such cultural complexity. The priests—I assume they were priests, Kunivaru of stature and dignity—wore ornate ceremonial helmets and heavy golden mantles of sea-beast fur. The ordinary townsfolk carried ribbons and streamers, bits of bright fabric, polished mirrors of stone, and other ornamental devices. When he saw how elaborate a function it was going to be, Moshe

Shiloah, an amateur anthropologist at heart, ran back to the kibbutz
to fetch camera and recorder. He returned, breathless, just as the rite
commenced.

And a glorious rite it was: incense, a grandly blazing bonfire,
the pungent fragrance of freshly picked herbs, some heavy-footed
quasi-orgiastic dancing, and a choir punching out harsh, sharp-
edged arrhythmic melodies. Gyaymar and the high priest of the
village performed an elegant antiphonal chant, uttering long curling
intertwining melismas and sprinkling Seul with a sweet- smelling
pink fluid out of a baroquely carved wooden censer. Never have I
beheld such stirring pageantry. But Joseph's gloomy prediction was
correct; it was all entirely useless. Two hours of intensive exorcism
had no effect. When the ceremony ended—the ultimate punctuation
marks were five terrible shouts from the high priest—the dybbuk
remained firmly in possession of Seul. "You have not conquered me,"
Joseph declared in a bleak tone.

Gyaymar said, "It seems we have no power to command an
earthborn soul."

"What will we do now?" demanded Yakov Ben-Zion of no one in
particular. "Our science and their witchcraft both fail."

Joseph Avneri pointed toward the east, toward the village of the
Hasidim, and murmured something indistinct.

"No!" cried Rabbi Shlomo Feig, who stood closest to the dybbuk
at that moment.

"What did he say?" I asked.

"It was nothing," the rabbi said. "It was foolishness. The long
ceremony has left him fatigued, and his mind wanders. Pay no
attention."

I moved nearer to my old friend. "Tell me, Joseph."

"I said," the dybbuk replied slowly, "that perhaps we should send
for the Baal Shem."

"Foolishness!" said Shlomo Feig, and spat.

"Why this anger?" Shmarya Asch wanted to know. "You, Rabbi
Shlomo, you were one of the first to advocate employing Kunivaru
sorcerers in this business. You gladly bring in alien witch doctors,
Rabbi, and grow angry when someone suggests that your fellow Jew
be given a chance to drive out the demon? Be consistent, Shlomo!"

Rabbi Shlomo's strong face grew mottled with rage. It was
strange to see this calm, even-tempered man becoming so excited. "I

will have nothing to do with Hasidim!" he exclaimed.

"I think this is a matter of professional rivalries," Moshe Shiloah commented.

The rabbi said, "To give recognition to all that is most superstitious in Judaism, to all that is most irrational and grotesque and outmoded and medieval? No! No!"

"But dybbuks *are* irrational and grotesque and outmoded and medieval," said Joseph Avneri. "Who better to exorcise one than a rabbi whose soul is still rooted in ancient beliefs?"

"I forbid this!" Shlomo Feig sputtered. "If the Baal Shem is summoned I will—I will—"

"Rabbi," Joseph said, shouting now, "this is a matter of my tortured soul against your offended spiritual pride. Give way! Give way! Get me the Baal Shem!"

"I refuse!"

"Look!" called Yakov Ben-Zion. The dispute had suddenly become academic. Uninvited, our Hasidic cousins were arriving at the sacred meadow, a long procession of them, eerie prehistoric- looking figures clad in their traditional long black robes, wide- brimmed hats, heavy beards, dangling side-locks; and at the head of the group marched their tzaddik, their holy man, their prophet, their leader, Reb Shmuel the Baal Shem.

It was certainly never our idea to bring Hasidim with us when we fled out of the smoldering ruins of the Land of Israel. Our intention was to leave Earth and all its sorrows far behind, to start anew on another world where we could at last build an enduring Jewish homeland, free for once of our eternal gentile enemies and free, also, of the religious fanatics among our own kind whose presence had long been a drain on our vitality. We needed no mystics, no ecstatics, no weepers, no moaners, no leapers, no chanters; we needed only workers, farmers, machinists, engineers, builders. But how could we refuse them a place on the Ark? It was their good fortune to come upon us just as we were making the final preparations for our flight. The nightmare that had darkened our sleep for three centuries had been made real: the Homeland lay in flames, our armies had been shattered out of ambush, Philistines wielding long knives strode through our devastated cities. Our ship was ready to leap to the stars. We were not cowards but simply realists, for it was folly to think we could do battle any longer, and if some fragment of our ancient nation were to survive, it could only survive far from the bitter world Earth. So we were going to go; and here were suppliants asking us for succor, Reb Shmuel and his thirty followers. How could we turn them away, knowing they would certainly perish? They were human beings, they were Jews. For all our misgivings, we let them come on board.

And then we wandered across the heavens year after year, and then we came to a star that had no name, only a number, and then we found its fourth planet to be sweet and fertile, a happier world than Earth, and we thanked the God in whom we did not believe for the good luck that He had granted us, and we cried out to each other in congratulation, Mazel tov! Mazel tov! Good luck, good luck, good luck! And someone looked in an old book and saw that mazel once had had an astrological connotation, that in the days of the Bible it had meant not only "luck" but a lucky star, and so we named our lucky star Mazel Tov, and we made our landfall on Mazel Tov IV, which was to be the New Israel. Here we found no enemies, no Egyptians, no Assyrians, no Romans, no Cossacks, no Nazis, no Arabs, only the Kunivaru, kindly people of a simple nature, who solemnly studied our pantomimed explanations and replied to us in gestures, saying, Be welcome, there is more land here than we will ever need. And we built our kibbutz.

But we had no desire to live close to those people of the past, the Hasidim, and they had scant love for us, for they saw us as pagans, godless Jews who were worse than gentiles, and they went off to build a muddy little village of their own. Sometimes on clear nights we heard their lusty singing, but otherwise there was scarcely any contact between us and them.

I could understand Rabbi Shlomo's hostility to the idea of intervention by the Baal Shem. These Hasidim represented the mystic side of Judaism, the dark uncontrollable Dionysiac side, the skeleton in the tribal closet; Shlomo Feig might be amused or charmed by a rite of exorcism performed by furry centaurs, but when Jews took part in the same sort of supernaturalism, it was distressing to him. Then, too, there was the ugly fact that the sane, sensible Rabbi Shlomo had virtually no followers at all among the sane, sensible secularized Jews of our kibbutz, whereas Reb Shmuel's Hasidim looked upon him with awe, regarding him as a miracle worker, a seer, a saint.

Still, Rabbi Shlomo's understandable jealousies and prejudices aside, Joseph Avneri was right: dybbuks were vapors out of the realm of the fantastic, and the fantastic was the Baal Shem's kingdom.

He was an improbably tall, angular figure, almost skeletal, with gaunt cheekbones, a soft, thickly curling beard, and gentle dreamy eyes. I suppose he was about fifty years old, though I would have believed it if they said he was thirty or seventy or ninety. His sense of the dramatic was unfailing; now—it was late afternoon—he took up a position with the setting sun at his back, so that his long shadow engulfed us all, and spread forth his arms and said, "We have heard reports of a dybbuk among you."

"There is no dybbuk!" Rabbi Shlomo retorted fiercely.

The Baal Shem smiled. "But there is a Kunivar who speaks with an Israeli voice?"

"There has been an odd transformation, yes," Rabbi Shlomo conceded. "But in this age, on this planet, no one can take dybbuks seriously."

"That is, *you* cannot take dybbuks seriously," said the Baal Shem.

"I do!" cried Joseph Avneri in exasperation. "I! I! I am the dybbuk! I, Joseph Avneri, dead a year ago last Elul, doomed for my sins to inhabit this Kunivar carcass. A Jew, Reb Shmuel, a dead Jew, a pitiful sinful miserable Yid. Who'll let me out? Who'll set me free?"

"There is no dybbuk?" the Baal Shem said amiably.

"This Kunivar has gone insane," said Shlomo Feig.

We coughed and shifted our feet. If anyone had gone insane it was our rabbi, denying in this fashion the phenomenon that he himself had acknowledged as genuine, however reluctantly, only a few hours before. Envy, wounded pride, and stubbornness had unbalanced his judgment. Joseph Avneri, enraged, began to bellow the Aleph Beth Gimel, the Shma Yisroel, anything that might prove his dybbukhood. The Baal Shem waited patiently, arms outspread, saying nothing. Rabbi Shlomo, confronting him, his powerful stocky figure dwarfed by the long-legged Hasid, maintained energetically that there had to be some rational explanation for the metamorphosis of Seul the Kunivar.

When Shlomo Feig at length fell silent, the Baal Shem said, "There is a dybbuk in this Kunivar. Do you think, Rabbi Shlomo, that dybbuks ceased their wanderings when the shtetls of Poland were destroyed? Nothing is lost in the sight of God, Rabbi. Jews go to the stars; the Torah and the Talmud and the Zohar have gone also to the stars; dybbuks too may be found in these strange worlds. Rabbi, may I bring peace to this troubled spirit and to this weary Kunivar?"

"Do whatever you want," Shlomo Feig muttered in disgust, and strode away, scowling.

Reb Shmuel at once commenced the exorcism. He called first for a minyan. Eight of his Hasidim stepped forward. I exchanged a glance with Shmarya Asch, and we shrugged and came forward too, but the Baal Shem, smiling, waved us away and beckoned two more of his followers into the circle. They began to sing; to my everlasting shame I have no idea what the singing was about, for the words were Yiddish of a Galitzianer sort, nearly as alien to me as the Kunivaru tongue. They sang for ten or fifteen minutes; the Hasidim grew more animated, clapping their hands, dancing about their Baal Shem; suddenly Reb Shmuel lowered his arms to his sides, silencing them, and quietly began to recite Hebrew phrases, which after a moment I recognized as those of the Ninety-first Psalm: The Lord is my refuge and my fortress, in him will I trust. The psalm rolled melodiously to its comforting conclusion, its promise of deliverance and salvation. For a long moment all was still. Then in a terrifying voice, not loud but immensely commanding, the Baal Shem ordered the spirit of Joseph Avneri to quit the body of Seul the Kunivar. "Out! Out! God's name out, and off to your eternal rest!" One of the Hasidim handed Reb Shmuel a shofar. The Baal Shem put the ram's horn to his lips and blew a single titanic blast.

Joseph Avneri whimpered. The Kunivar that housed him took three awkward, toppling steps. "Oy, mama, mama," Joseph cried. The Kunivar's head snapped back; his arms shot straight out at his sides; he tumbled clumsily to his four knees. An eon went by. Then Seul rose—smoothly, this time, with natural Kunivaru grace—and went to the Baal Shem, and knelt, and touched the tzaddik's black robe. So we knew the thing was done.

Instants later the tension broke. Two of the Kunivaru priests rushed toward the Baal Shem, and then Gyaymar, and then some of the musicians, and then it seemed the whole tribe was pressing close upon him, trying to touch the holy man. The Hasidim, looking worried, murmured their concern, but the Baal Shem, towering over the surging mob, calmly blessed the Kunivaru, stroking the dense fur of their backs. After some minutes of this the Kunivaru set up a rhythmic chant, and it was a while before I realized what they were saying. Moshe Shiloah and Yakov Ben- Zion caught the sense of it about the same time I did, and we began to laugh, and then our laughter died away.

"What do their words mean?" the Baal Shem called out.

"They are saying," I told him, "that they are convinced of the power of your god. They wish to become Jews."

For the first time, Reb Shmuel's poise and serenity shattered. His eyes flashed ferociously and he pushed at the crowding Kunivaru, opening an avenue between them. Coming up to me, he snapped, "Such a thing is an absurdity!"

"Nevertheless, look at them. They worship you, Reb Shmuel."

"I refuse their worship."

"You worked a miracle. Can you blame them for adoring you and hungering after your faith?"

"Let them adore," said the Baal Shem. "But how can they become Jews? It would be a mockery."

I shook my head. "What was it you told Rabbi Shlomo? Nothing is lost in the sight of God. There have always been converts to Judaism—we never invite them, but we never turn them away if they're sincere, eh, Reb Shmuel? Even here in the stars, there is continuity of tradition, and tradition says we harden not our hearts to those who seek the truth of God. These are a good people—let them be received into Israel."

"No," the Baal Shem said. "A Jew must first of all be human."

"Show me that in the Torah."

"The Torah! You joke with me. A Jew must first of all be human. Were cats allowed to become Jews? Were horses?"

"These people are neither cats nor horses, Reb Shmuel. They are as human as we are."

"No! No!"

"If there can be a dybbuk on Mazel Tov IV," I said, "then there can also be Jews with six limbs and green fur."

"No. No. No. *No!*"

The Baal Shem had had enough of this debate. Shoving aside the clutching hands of the Kunivaru in a most unsaintly way, he gathered his followers and stalked off, a tower of offended dignity, bidding us no farewells.

*

But how can true faith be denied? The Hasidim offered no encouragement, so the Kunivaru came to us; they learned Hebrew, and we loaned them books, and Rabbi Shlomo gave them religious instruction, and in their own time and in their own way, they entered into Judaism. All this was years ago, in the first generation after the Landing. Most of those who lived in those days are dead now—Rabbi Shlomo, Reb Shmuel the Baal Shem, Moshe Shiloah, Shmarya Asch. I was a young man then. I know a good deal more now, and if I am no closer to God than I ever was, perhaps He has grown closer to me. I eat meat and butter at the same meal, and I plow my land on the Sabbath, but those are old habits that have little to do with belief or the absence of belief.

We are much closer to the Kunivaru, too, than we were in those early days; they no longer seem like alien beings to us, but merely neighbors whose bodies have a different form. The younger ones of our kibbutz are especially drawn to them. The year before last Rabbi Lhaoyir the Kunivar suggested to some of our boys that they come for lessons to the Talmud Torah, the religious school, that he runs in the Kunivaru village; since the death of Shlomo Feig there has been no one in the kibbutz to give such instruction. When Reb Yossele, the son and successor of Reb Shmuel the Baal Shem heard this, he raised strong objections. If your boys will take instruction, he said, at least send them to us, and not to green monsters. My son Yigal threw him out of the kibbutz. We would rather let our boys learn the Torah from green monsters, Yigal told Reb Yossele, than have them raised to be Hasidim.

And so my son's son has had his lessons at the Talmud Torah of Rabbi Lhaoyir the Kunivar, and next spring, he will have his bar mitzvah. Once I would have been appalled by such goings-on, but now I say only, How strange, how unexpected, how interesting! Truly the Lord, if He exists, must have a keen sense of humor. I like a god who can smile and wink, who doesn't take himself too seriously. The Kunivaru are Jews! Yes! They are preparing David for his bar mitzvah! Yes! Today is Yom Kippur, and I hear the sound of the shofar coming from their village! Yes! Yes. So be it. So be it, yes, and all praise be to Him.

We end our journey with a fun, comedic story from multi-award winner Mike Resnick, who posits how the Earth and its inhabitants might appear to aliens scouting our planet in preparation to colonize it, when they come across some interesting pop culture images and confusion ensues. . .

OBSERVATION POST

MIKE RESNICK

Diary entry #17:

It has been a long, hard struggle, but of course, if the conquest and subsequent colonization of the galaxy is your goal, you don't expect it to come easily. There was a time, in the Antares skirmish, when I thought for a few days that we might actually lose, and I suppose most historians would say that we *did* lose the initial battle of Betelgeuse, though of course, we later recaptured the system and settled all its worlds.

Many of us have died for the greater glory of the Empire, and space is littered with the debris of ships, both the conquerors and the conquered. But each planetary system we capture brings us that much closer to our ultimate goal of total galactic colonization, and it was with pride and honor that I accepted the task of being the advance scout in the galaxy's Spiral Arm. My job is to appraise the situation, determine which systems will surrender and welcome us immediately, and which, if any, can put up meaningful resistance—and when I find the latter, I am to study them as closely as necessary to determine their weak spots, to see how and where to launch our attacks. This is essential, because if we attack with the full firepower we have at our disposal, we can turn a world to dust and ashes in nanoseconds, and it's not our objective to colonize dust and ashes.

—Kragash

From Commander Braque:
    I cannot wait any longer, Kragash. Trocyon III and Benedetti V surrendered without a single shot being fired. As far as I can tell, the planet called Earth is next in our line of expansion. Can we land our citizens there, or will there be resistance? I need your evaluation before I commit my troops and my ships.

From Kragash:
    I understand and appreciate your eagerness, Commander, and I will be issuing regular reports as soon as I set up my observation post, either on Earth's moon or on one of its abandoned space platforms.
    Thus far things look encouraging: there is comparatively little neutrino activity, the orbiting space stations are incredibly primitive, and I see nothing to imply that they have more than a rudimentary knowledge of 4th dimensional quantum mechanics.

From Commander Braque:
    I simply cannot sit here twiddling my digits while you evaluate every aspect of life on Earth. Just tell me if they will welcome our colonists with open tentacles, or if not, are they are capable of putting up a vigorous defense?

From Kragash:
    Sir, I am a highly-trained observer—but I must have time to observe and appraise. Remember: until this year we did not even know the planet was inhabited.

From Commander Braque:
All right, if you need more time, you need more time. But while we're waiting, I'm ordering one of the asteroids located between the fourth and fifth planets of Sol's system to be moved out of orbit and directed toward Earth. It will take approximately one hundred revolutions of Earth upon its axis for the asteroid to hit. If you feel that the citizenry would make good workers in our mines, we can always divert the asteroid. If, on the other hand, you find nothing, either in terms of life forms or raw materials, that is worth salvaging, this will at least save us the bother of obliterating all life on the planet with our XQ bombs before moving our people in. Those damned things are expensive; I'd much prefer just hurling the asteroid into the planet and eradicating all life there.
Remember: you have 100 revolutions ("days", I think you called them) to find some reason to salvage all or part of the planet before we destroy it and we have to build all new structures for our colonists.

From Kragash:
Here are my preliminary findings:
Literally half the world's land mass is ideal for farming organic crops. Unfortunately, given our metabolism, that will prove useless to us (but it *is* lovely and productive land).
Hidden beneath the surface are oceans of oil, which powers much of their machinery, but of course, we abandoned fossil fuels centuries ago.
Almost three-quarters of the planet's surface is covered by a vast saltwater ocean, and this ocean is home to literally hundreds of millions of fish. Again, our metabolism would prevent us from partaking of the fish, and saltwater would be poison to our systems.
I will continue searching the planet and evaluating my findings; there must be *some* reason not to obliterate this tranquil world by smashing the asteroid into it.

From the New York Times, *January 28, 2012:*

Astronomers today were able to confirm that an asteroid almost twice the size of the one that killed the dinosaurs some 65 million years ago is on a collision course with the Earth. "There is less than a five percent chance that it will miss us," states Nobel laureate Dr. Edmond Khalinov of the Mt. Wilson Observatory. When asked if the military was capable of knocking it off course, he was noncommittal. NASA is working on a probe that will hopefully explode on contact, but, to quote Dr. Irene McDevitt, "First we have to be able to hit it, and second, we have to be able to destroy it. It happens in movies all the time, but you have to understand that we're talking about totally obliterating an asteroid that's the size of a small country. It is conceivable that far from demolishing it, we could break it into half a dozen large pieces that will all come hurtling at the Earth."

There have been no official statements from the White House, the Kremlin, Number Ten Downing Street, or Beijing.

Diary entry #18:

The Commander is pressuring me to gather information about the beings on the world known as Earth. I think he's still very sensitive about the problem on Gibal VII, where we mistook the strangely-shaped population for a mutated form of corn, and harvested and ate them before realizing our mistake.

The easiest way to learn about a civilization is to monitor its video transmissions, and starting tomorrow I shall be doing just that. If they have the ability to divert the asteroid and withstand a military attack, the sooner we find out the better. Also, I need to analyze their physical capabilities, as we are always in need of slave labor and cannon fodder, and the more of them we take for that purpose, the more of our own people we can move into their deserted dwellings . . .

As I look at it now, through my ship's computer, it seems a placid, tranquil, blue and green world. I wonder whether we really needed to push the asteroid out of its orbit. It's hard to imagine a little nondescript world like this presenting any threat to the most powerful military machine in the galaxy.

Ah, well, it's not for me to worry about the inhabitants, or to mourn their almost-certain passing. My job is to observe and appraise, and I shall do so as soon as I have my lunch.

—Kragash

Diary entry #19:

We were badly misinformed. Earth *does* have faster-than-light drives. Worse still, they are installed in a huge fleet of military ships. One in particular, named the *Enterprise*, seems more than a match for even Commander Braque's flagship.

It is commanded by something called Kirk, a fair-skinned biped, with two opthalmic lenses, two auditory appendages, opposable thumbs at the ends of its upper-body tentacles, and something that looks like brown grass covering its cranium. This Kirk is subject to emotional outbursts, but is clearly competent at his job, and his job, from the brief transmission I have seen thus far, seems to be threatening and attacking any ship that is not of Terran origin.

Worse, he has a non-human officer with misshapen ears who hails from the planet Vulcan. I have checked and re-checked my star maps, I have run every variation of the word through my computer's enormous data banks, and I cannot find any planet named Vulcan, nor any name of any known planet that translates as Vulcan in any Terran language or dialect. So not only are we dealing with a world possessed of a starfaring military, but one with allies whose existence was totally unknown to us until this morning.

I am still calculating how fast these ships can go, as I am hampered by the terminology. I am aware that they can exceed the speed of light, but until I learn just how fast a "warp" is, I cannot estimate their top speeds . . .

It has been some time since I wrote the above paragraph. During that interval I observed more of the transmission, and it is most disheartening. This *Enterprise*, and doubtless all other ships in the interstellar navy, has some invisible force field known as a shield or shields, and this field gives every indication of being able to resist our pulse and laser cannons.

Not only that, but it seems almost a certainty that Earth itself has colonized worlds up and down the Spiral Arm, and possibly into the main body of the galaxy. Clearly its military was not created solely for defense, just as ours was not. In fact, I am struck by the similarity of our goals, though of course our colonization will be beneficial to the galaxy at large, while theirs is a clear and present danger to all intelligent life and must be halted.

This is been an enlightening and upsetting experience. It also presents a major question: there are obviously hundreds, possibly thousands, of ships in Earth's military, and the strong implication is that all or almost all have the same or even greater capabilities than the *Enterprise*. Hence the question: why have we never observed even a single one of them. Does every ship in this vast fleet have some heretofore-unknown cloaking device?

And if so, can they fire their weapons while the cloak of invisibility is operative? If they don't have to drop it during a pitched battle, how are we to defend ourselves and fight back?

A most disturbing conundrum. I must observe more before I make my preliminary report to Commander Braque. I know he wants me to hurry, but I must be thorough and methodical, for I have the distinct feeling that the fate of our invasion, indeed of our empire, depends on what I can learn of this previously-unknown superpower.

—Kragash

Diary entry #20:

The situation is worse than I thought.

This afternoon I observed the *Enterprise* again, but it had an entirely new crew. The Kirk thing seems to have been replaced by a Picard thing, physically similar except for the lack of grass atop its cranium, but clearly less emotional and more competent.

So why is it worse? Because there are multiple transmissions to be studied, and when I'd finished my preliminary examination of the *Enterprise* commanded by the Picard thing, I captured another transmission, *and it displayed the Kirk thing commanding the same ship*!

How is this possible? How many dimensions does this race control? How many thousands of heavily-armored multi-weaponed faster-than-light *Enterprises* can co-exist? Do the Kirk and Picard things communicate through some telepathic or extra-dimensional bond? If we get into a shooting war with them, as now seems certain, will they exchange messages that our sensors and computers can capture, or will they give and receive orders on a mental or spiritual plane that is forever denied to us?

—Kragash

Diary entry #20A:

I almost forgot to mention the android.

We have awkward, clunky robots doing menial jobs on our farms and in our factories, and of course we ship them to all our colonies— but not one of them, not even the most advanced model, can be trusted with even the most menial duties aboard a military ship.

But third in command to the Picard thing is an android named Data, human to all appearances, fully capable of interacting physically and mentally as an equal with the living crew members.

There is only one conclusion to be drawn: their science, based on their cloaking mechanisms, their multi-dimensional mastery, and their creation of the highly intelligent and physically graceful Data thing, is far in advance of our own.

How could such a superpower remain hidden from the rest of the galaxy?

And how are we ever to defeat it?

—Kragash

From the Washington Post, February 7, 2012:
    The rogue asteroid that appears to be on a collision course with Earth is just now passing the orbit of Mars. The military is still considering its few remaining options for obliterating or diverting it, but thus far has not come up with a viable option. For up-to-the-minute details please check our website at . . .

From Commander Braque:
    This is most disconcerting news, Kragash. Still, I have the utmost confidence in our fighting forces. If we could win the Battle of Maratino V and effect that remarkable escape

when we were surrounded and far outnumbered in
the Djambi system, I believe we can hold our own
against any military force in the galaxy.

You have forwarded the transmission of the
Enterprise in action, and our best scientific and
military minds are analyzing it, searching for
weak spots (which I assume will exist throughout
the fleet, even if it contains ships other
than the many clones/versions/whatever of the
Enterprise.)

My advice to you is that you leave that aspect
of the war to us, and see what other potential
trouble spots we need to be made aware of.

From Kragash:

Am I to understand that we still plan to attack?

From Commander Braque:
The asteroid is hurtling toward the Earth.
Why in the world would I make any effort to stop
it? You've discovered their starfaring fleet. Our
experts will study it, find its weaknesses, and
exploit them. Your job now is to determine if
there are any more unforeseen obstacles awaiting
us, or indeed, if there is any good reason not to
destroy all life on the planet.

From Kragash:

I will do so as long as they permit me to. I can't believe that
with their advanced technology they are not aware of my presence.
Has it occurred to you, sir, that they could be studying *me* while I
am studying *them*?

From Commander Braque:
Just do it, Kragash.

Diary entry #21:

I have been observing what the inhabitants do for pleasure, and I am appalled. Their games are violent beyond belief. There is a game known as "football", in which two sides line up opposite each other and, at a given signal, leap forward and meet in battle. Rarely does the battle last for more than a few seconds, but they hold more than one hundred such battles in barely half of an afternoon.

Then there is another game, also called "football," and, alternatively, "soccer," in which men race around the floor of an amphitheater kicking a small, round, totally defenseless animal, and at some point thousands of people who have been watching from the most uncomfortable benches imaginable race onto the stadium floor and indulge in a brutal bloodletting.

Then there is "wrestling," also called "rasslin'," where small numbers of incredibly muscular beings throw each other around a small enclosure, bite and gouge and kick each other, throw chairs and other objects at each other—and yet such are the recuperative powers of this race that at the end of the demonstration none of the parties seems any the worse for wear.

Should I report this to Commander Braque? I have a feeling that he won't believe me; I can barely believe what I saw myself. I expect that his response will be that whatever their physical abilities, if we meet them in battle they will be enclosed in their *Enterprises* and thus we have no need to worry about their physical attributes.

And yet, if I do not report it, and we should ever come face-to-face with these creatures while plundering their planet and preparing it for our colonists, we *must* be ready.

I think I must tell him what to expect.

—Kragash

From Commander Braque:
All right, they're a remarkable race, no question about it. But you overestimate their ability to do damage. Every last one of them will perish when the asteroid hits their world. Show me that they are invulnerable to our laser and sonic weapons, and then I'll start to worry about them.

Diary entry #22:

I am so glad I remained at my post and continued my observations. The *Enterprises* are *nothing*. They are merely starships, fast and deadly to be sure, capable of cruising at many times the speed of light, armed and armored, with truly awesome captains, but when all is said and done, they are just ships, and our military has defeated every type of ship we have faced.

But what I have learned from today's transmission puts a whole new light on things.

We are not the first to attempt to conquer this race. It turns out that before we even considered conquering and colonizing the worlds of the Spiral Arm, there was already an Emperor. He claimed to be a galactic emperor, but our historians could not have missed such a thing on a galactic scale, so I must assume that he operated solely within the Arm.

I have been watching what I assume is historical footage of the downfall of this civilization. The Emperor's top general was a human or humanoid whose name seemed to translate as Dark Invader, though my universal translating mechanism is a bit unsure of the accuracy of its conclusion.

It makes no difference, because I am not concerned with names. This empire was brought down not by weaponry, not by a superior military, but by something intangible, something known only as The Force. It seems to be a unique mental weapon, possessed by only a handful of warriors, and it wields a power so great that I do not believe there is any known way of measuring it. In the bluntest possible terms, one Skywalker—the generic name for those possessing this Force— can conceivably wish or think our entire fleet into non-existence.

We can fight the *Enterprises*. We can possibly grapple hand-to-hand with footballers and rasslers. But how does one go to war against a thought so powerful that it can blink you out of existence in a fraction of a nanosecond?

I must report this to the Commander immediately!

—Kragash

From Commander Braque:
    Are you quite sure? I mean, we have conquered
more than one hundred races — bipeds, quadrupeds,
oxygen breathers, chlorine breathers, methane
breathers; you name it, we've pacified it— but
I have never heard of a race with the mental/
telepathic powers you claim this race possesses.

From Kragash:
    You are misunderstanding me, sir. I did not say that the entire
race has these powers. Only a very small percentage does—but that
very small percentage was quite enough to overthrow the military
machine of the galactic emperor in the historical footage I just
finished studying.
    Nor, I must point out, is this power limited to the inhabitants of
Earth. Just as the Kirk thing had an ally from Vulcan, the Skywalker
has partnered with some creature of a race known as the Yodas.
Earth has so many alliances, I don't know how it could have
escaped our notice, unless they used the Force to blind us to their
presence.

From Commander Braque:
    Do you think this Force is powerful enough
to deflect the asteroid that we have set on a
collision course with Earth?

From Kragash:
    I truly do not know, sir.

From Commander Braque:
    I guess we—and they—will find out, won't we?

From the Paris Match, *February 10, 2012*
    *The military is remaining tight-lipped and noncommittal, but
inside sources have stated (off the record, of course) that we probably*

*do not have the capability to either destroy the asteroid or divert it.
It is now up to the Americans, the Russians and the Chinese. If they
cannot come up with a solution to the problem, then all life on Earth
—in fact, Earth itself—will be destroyed in a matter of 53 days.*
      Also: 6 new ways to prepare snails: see Page 17.

Diary entry #25:

I have spent two full days watching the Skywalkers and their
lackeys, the Solos, apply the Force, and I still can find no flaws or
weakness in this startling weapon. Therefore, this evening I have
moved on to other things, and will study an historical documentary
confined to the Earth itself.

—Kragash

Diary entry #26:

The more I learn about this race, the more I wonder why we are
not all their vassals, speaking Terran and looking to them for orders.
      Last night's historical was about . . . well, it is difficult to define
exactly what it was about. It had something to do with a Matrix,
which seems to be vaguely related to The Force.
      But my latest discovery has nothing to do with that. We already
knew about The Force, and the Matrix is just another version of it.
      I remember the shock and surprise I experienced when I found
out that the Picard thing had a fully-functioning incredibly competent
android working in a position of authority on its *Enterprise*. Well, that
android is nothing compared to what I learned last night.
      This race, these Earthlings whom no one has ever even heard of
before, has somehow discovered the secret to creating living computer
programs (or Agent Smiths, as they are known). Physically identical
to the planetary inhabitants, these Smiths are immune to pain and
are virtually indestructible. Their cerebral functions are as fast and
accurate as one of our Class X34 plasma computers. They are, in
short, super beings (if one can call them beings at all). Between the
Smiths and the Datas, I am becoming convinced that when we finally

clash head-on with the military of Earth in the final confrontation, as now seems inevitable, what our soldiers will be facing will be not warriors of flesh and blood, but incredibly sophisticated androids and computer programs in human form.

Now that I think of it, even the Skywalker had robot vassals, primitive compared to the Datas and Smiths, but indicative of the fact that all inhabitants of Earth have humanoid creations to fight their wars and do their menial chores.

Dare I report this latest discovery to the Commander?

On the other hand, dare I not?

— Kragash

From Commander Braque:
Computer programs in bipedal form, indistinguishable from the native inhabitants? Have you been taking your medications on schedule, Kragash? I find this all but impossible to believe.

From Kragash:
I can capture and forward the operative transmissions to you, sir.

From Commander Braque:
I think you'd better.

From Kragash:
Sending . . .

From Commander Braque:
I'm sorry to have taken so long studying the transmissions, and I apologize for ever doubting you, Kragash. How did this race and its scientific achievements remain unknown and undiscovered for so long?

We need more information, and we need it now. You've sent me enough about the military and on

scientific creations. Now I need to know what the
average, everyday inhabitant is like.
     Always assuming that somewhere on this world
there *is* an average inhabitant . . .

Diary entry #28:

     Well, at least the inhabitants in the documentary I have captured
seem normal. I might even call them harmless. They plant their fields,
they care for their animals, they gather in small villages, they show
no sign of the awesome powers I have been studying in recent days.
     In fact, if I were to use a single word to describe their society, I
would call it *primitive*. This is a society protected by *Enterprises* and
androids and this indefinable Force, yet these people use quadrupeds
and buggies for transportation, and although we know they have
armed their ships with laser cannons and pulse torpedoes, the citizenry
seems to prefer swords, difficult as that may be to believe.
     So tranquil is their daily life, so simple, that I find myself
wondering if a number of humanoid races actually share the planet—
the Skywalkers and Picards and Kirks on the one hand, and these
gentle beings on the other. It is quite a dichotomy, to say the least.

                                                           —Kragash

Diary entry #28A:

     I spoke too soon. These people are nothing but livestock, kept alive
solely to provide food for a far more powerful race. I kept thinking of
them as humans, but I was mistaken. Closer study of the transmission
informs me that, far from being humans, they are something called
Transylvanians. The absolute master of this extensive farm, and of
these animals, is the Drag-You-La. He is physically unimpressive, he
clearly has need of a dental hygenicist, and he wears no weapon at all.
Why do the animals—the Transylvanians—not revolt?

                                                           —Kragash

Diary entry #28B:

What kind of world is this???
Not ten minutes ago I asked why the animals did not revolt. Now I know.
The Drag-You-La has the ability to morph into a small, black, winged creature, and in this form he can fly, climb the smooth vertical walls of buildings, and change back into his original shape at will.
Not only that, but in either form—the humanoid or the winged creature—his sole diet is the blood of the Transylvanians that he clearly breeds and keeps for that purpose and no other.
If this is what is waiting for us if we actually conquer the *Enterprises*—excuse me: I meant *when* we conquer them, of course—I wonder if we'll be able to resist the Drag-You-Las any more than the poor Transylvanians can.

—Kragash

Diary entry #29:

Immediately after the transmission I previously described there was another, similar in all meaningful ways, except that this time the owner of the humanoid livestock was Nosferatu. My comprehension of the various Terran dialects is still lacking, but I get the distinct impression that Nosferatu is a race rather than an individual. This world possesses the most unnerving food chain I have ever encountered.

—Kragash

From Commander Braque:
    I think you're looking at this all
wrong, Kragash. If this humanoid race, these
Transylvanians, are food animals, our colonists
won't have to bring their own supplies but can
live off the land — well, off the Transylvanians -
once we have conquered the planet.
    Clearly you haven't thought this through.

From Kragash:
You're missing the point, Commander. You are concentrating on the Transylvanians, whereas I am warning you that two entire species—the Drag-You-Las and the Nosferatus—have the ability to transform themselves from large bipeds to very small flying animals. You couldn't ask for a better spy than a humanoid who can morph into a small flying creature on no more than a second's notice and fly to safety.

From Commander Braque:
Ah! I see what you mean, Kragash. This will take further thought and planning. Can you transmit an image of this Drag-You-La?

From Kragash:
Here it is, sir. Note the misshapen teeth, which seems to be one of the two ways to determine if the biped *is* a Drag-You-La. (The other, of course, is the black cape.)

From Commander Braque:
Amazing! Just what are we up against here, I wonder? First the Kirk things, then the Vulcans and androids, then the Force, then the living computer programs, and now a race of shape-changers. Why have they not attacked and conquered *us*, I wonder?

Diary entry #32:

There have been no surprises for the last three revolutions of the planet on its axis, for which I am incredibly grateful. I have been studying the flora and fauna, and am starting to feel comfortable identifying the various members of each.
One thing troubles me. This morning there was a transmission,

clearly meant to indoctrinate the very young. Men wore very bizarre make-up, and everybody seemed to be in a hurry but their destination was never defined, and then I saw one more disconcerting thing. A small member of the quadruped species known as Elephant had abnormally long auditory appendages (known as "ears"). At one point it began flapping them, and suddenly it actually began flying! It used its ears as a power source, and also as external gyroscopes. It is known as the Dumbo, and while it seems harmless enough, I estimate that the average adult Dumbo can weigh well over 10,000 pounds.

One more thing to worry about.

—Kragash

From the London Times, *February 18, 2012:*

NASA reported this evening that mankind's first attempt to divert or destroy the rogue asteroid that is bearing down upon the Earth was a failure when the ship's second stage failed to ignite. Another attempt will take place on February 23.

From Commander Braque:
   I don't care how it appeared to you, Kragash, our experts state categorically that a beast of the type you have described simply cannot fly by flapping its auditory appendages, even if its bones are hollow.
   I don't think it's worth your time to study the creature any further. Since it has no natural or artificial armaments, it's difficult to see it doing us any harm, even if it can fly.
   My suggestion is that you go back to studying their transmissions, and continue reporting any unusual talents or behavior that you observe.

Diary entry #34:

I have spent the day watching ancient records, captured even before this race knew how to instill color into their visual files.

Thus far I have been concentrating on two humanoids who possess no extraordinary powers, but seem to emerge triumphant against overwhelming odds. I suspect they are the precursors to the Kirk and Picard things, and since they are not aboard any *Enterprises* I must assume they have elected (or perhaps been ordered) to remain on Earth to protect it should any of us get past their defenses.

Their titles are Flash Gordon and Buck Rogers, and while their weapons are primitive compared to those I have been observing all along, they seem to be every bit as efficient. I would not be surprised to learn that one or both were progenitors of the Solo thing; they have much in common.

—Kragash

Diary entry #35:

I was about to stop studying the transmission and ingest some food. I am so glad I decided to watch one last one.

The Flash Gordon and the Buck Rogers were formidable, to be sure, but they had nothing unusual in their arsenal except for luck.

But then I was introduced—via the transmission; I still have not set foot outside my ship—to Lamont Cranston. He resides in a city populated by literally millions, and from what I could tell about 80% of them belong to the criminal class. And it is Cranston who is single-handedly bringing thousands of these criminals to justice, filling the jails with them—not as Cranston, but as a creature known as The Shadow, a sobriquet which makes no sense since he is quite substantial and clearly exists in three dimensions.

How does one lone biped go to war with the criminal element that pervades his municipality and emerge triumphant? The answer may shock you. He does it by clouding their minds.

I personally have no idea *how* he clouds their minds, or what the ultimate effect will be, but it is clearly related to The Force, and may even be a variation of it. If I can study The Shadow and learn the methodology by which he "clouds" men's minds (by which I mean the means by which he applies The Force), perhaps we will be able to negate the Skywalker and the Yoda when we launch our all-out final attack.

It is absolutely essential that we learn more about this, because thus far I have not seen a single biped who has been able to retain an unclouded mind.

—Kragash

From Commander Braque:
    Curse it, Kragash - don't you ever have any *good* news?
    Does the Shadow ever leave his municipality?

From Kragash:
    Not that I am aware of, but you must understand that thus far I have only seen a single transmission about him.

From Commander Braque:
    I half-suspect that he is clouding your mind.
    The asteroid hits in 22 more days. In most cases, the mere anticipation of being hit by such a body causes the inhabitants to call off their warships and surrender. I hope that will be the case with Earth, though if there is any truth at all to your observations we will probably just let the asteroid do its damage while we prepare to fight all the Enterprises.

    Diary entry #43:

    Still nothing untoward or unusual since I last observed The Shadow. There are only a few days left for Commander Braque to divert the asteroid or claim what very little will remain of Earth after it hits. What I cannot understand is why, given the awesome power I have observed, the Earthlings have done nothing to destroy the asteroid.

—Kragash

From Sub-Commander Bloor:
  Kragash, quick - what is a Texas Chainsaw?

From Kragash:
  I have no idea. Why?

From Sub-Commander Bloor:
  Another observation post mentioned that due to audience demand they will be transmitting the Texas Chainsaw Massacre this afternoon. What kind of perverted creatures consider a massacre to be entertainment? Who are the Texas Chainsaws? If we come to their aid, do you think they might be willing to come over to our side and act as our agents?
  These are diabolically-twisted beings, these Earthlings. Take care of yourself, Kragash. If you spend enough time watching these psychopaths, you might start thinking like they do. The day you don't find them both horrifying and disgusting is the day you should request an immediate transfer back to the flagship, or perhaps the mental hospital back on Chezona VII.

From L'Osservatore Romano, *March 2, 2012:*
  The asteroid is due to collide with the Earth in just a matter of days. The most optimistic estimates are that three percent of the population will survive. If you have not confessed and made your peace with the Lord, this would be a good time to do so.

From Kragash:
  I believe I have finally found a serious flaw in the Earthlings.

Do you remember our concern over Data, the totally competent android in the Picard thing's *Enterprise*?

Well, I couldn't help wondering why they used living beings at all in the military. I mean, why risk a single life if you can create an army of artificial beings, identical in almost every way, to take all the risks for you?

I believe I have found the answer.

There is a physically perfect android called Terminator, and far from serving Earthlings, its sole function seems to be to kill as many of them as possible. Clearly this was not its intended purpose—after all, why would you create a perfect killing machine and then turn it loose upon your own populace? I think it is obvious that this Terminator was meant to fight against Earth's enemies—it is conceivable that it is an upgraded model of the Data android—and yet something went wrong with its programming, and it turned into a deadly killer of the humanoids it was created to defend.

From Commander Braque:
    Interesting. Where is this Terminator now?

From Kragash:
    Oh, didn't I mention that? A young female biped destroyed it.

From Commander Braque:
    The greatest killing machine you've yet seen, and a single female destroyed it? You are not making my job any easier, Kragash.

Diary entry #46:

I have delved further into the Data/Terminator situation, and my conclusions are discouraging. Terminator was not the first such construct to turn upon its creator. It seems that a scientist named

Frankenstein had the same experience long ago: he created an artificial biped, which immediately upon activation ignored all of its directives and began killing humanoids wherever it encountered them. I suspect there have been other experiments that have gone equally wrong, but somehow, despite their overwhelming strength and the fact that they seem impervious to pain, these experimental creatures, be they android, robot, or humanoid, never survive. They are killers, but eventually they are overwhelmed by even greater killers—the race we have chosen to face in combat.

I must report this to Commander Braque. He has to be made aware of what we're up against.

—Kragash

From Commander Braque:
They make their own warriors in laboratories???

From Kragash:
It would seem so, Commander. I suspect the reason so few are in the military is because the humanoids are simply more efficient killers than their artificial constructs.

From Commander Braque:
Kragash, you are giving me a terrible headache.

Diary entry #47:

I am shocked and depressed to learn that the Drag-You-La wasn't unique. He is what the humanoids term a vampire, a creature that can appear to be one of them (except for the canines, that is) or can morph into a bat. I already knew that, of course.

What I *didn't* know is that there are thousands of them, almost all of them males, and that humanoid females find them irresistible.

This can cause us serious problems should we attempt to occupy and then colonize the planet. These Drag-You-La creatures are far stronger and more formidable than the normal humanoid, they can blend right in with any crowd, and once we figure out how to identify them, half the populace—the female half—will hide them, tend to their wounds (if any), and feed them for as long as the food supply, which is to say the female, lasts.

As nearly as I can ascertain, garlic and objects shaped like a plus will hold the Drag-You-Las at bay, but I have yet to find anything that will kill them. There was some mention of running a steak through the creature's heart, but that is a very vaguely-worded suggestion. Does one use a tenderloin, a sirloin, a rib-eye, or some other cut of meat? I must delve further into this.

—Kragash

From Commander Braque:
Forget about the Drag-You-La creatures, Kragash. We have much more important things to worry about.

For example: the asteroid is only five days away from smashing into the planet. Why aren't the humanoids reacting? Are their weapons so powerful that they can vaporize the asteroid at the last second? And if so, an asteroid is a lot bigger than even my flagship; what can their weaponry do to *us*?

And while I'm thinking about it, what is the origin of the asteroid belt? It has been suggested by some of our crew that the asteroids are the remains of a planet that either went to war with Earth, or (more likely) did something in all innocence that annoyed the humanoids and brought forth a cataclysmic retaliation.

I am starting to understand why Fleet Admiral Vreem elected to remain in the Crab Nebula and chose to send us instead. I suspect he is still bitter about that innocent little incident between myself and his thirteen wives while he was busy winning the Battle of Orion.

Diary entry #48:

The more I learn, the more I find cause for alarm. I had thought, or at least hoped, that the androids and the Drag-You-Las were the only aberrant humanoids to be found on this planet, but further captured transmissions have proven me wrong.

For one thing, there is an entire sub-species known as werewolves, humanoids capable of morphing into carnivorous quadrupeds as easily as the Drag-You-Las can morph into flying creatures.

This so unnerved me that I found a new transmission source, one aimed at the humanoids' young, one that I was sure would prove restful and allow me to regain my composure.

I was wrong again.

Every time I think I know the limit of the horrifying aberrations we will find on this world, I discover still more. For example—and for reasons unknown, these transmissions do not frighten the young, but delight them (which may explain why they become such fearsome warriors in adulthood)—there are rodents and rabbits and birds that actually *talk*! Some of them even wear clothes, similar in all ways to humanoid clothing.

Worse still, these creatures are virtually indestructible. Let one of them get pushed off a cliff and fall thousands of feet to land with a deafening *splat!*—and he immediately gets up and brushes himself off as if nothing out of the ordinary has transpired. Another holds a bomb in his hand, watches the burning fuse with an expression of horror, and flies into a hundred pieces when the bomb explodes . . . and seconds later the pieces all join together and the creature is none the worse for his experience.

I must report this latest finding to Commander Braque.

—Kragash

From Sub-Commander Bloor:

I regret to inform you that our beloved Commander Braque suffered a nervous breakdown (right in the middle of reading your latest message, in fact), and has been confined to the Violent Ward of the Infirmary.

You will address all future communications to me.

From Pravda, March 8, 2012:

The asteroid is due to strike the planet sometime tomorrow afternoon. The best estimate has it crashing down in central Europe. It is entirely conceivable that the only living humans 48 hours from now will be those few men and women who are currently in the orbiting space station. The government's last official act will be to move Lenin's tomb to a deep underground chamber, where it will hopefully survive the initial shock when the asteroid hits.

From Sub-Commander Bloor:

They have less than a day and they still haven't vaporized the asteroid. What are they waiting for? I get the distinct impression that they are toying with us.

It seems that we will shortly find ourselves in a life-and-death conflict with a race that seems to provide a new distressing surprise every time you monitor it. You must stay at your post, Kragash, and search for any weak spots we have overlooked. The entire invasion, possibly the entire war, may depend on what you can find in the next day.

Contact me at any time. There will be no sleep for anyone in our armada until Earth is either conquered or destroyed.

Diary entry #49:

I can hardly believe the testimony of my own eyes. I have been monitoring transmissions non-stop, and I think I have uncovered the most disconcerting data of all, which is that there is a super-race living all-but-unnoticed among the bipeds. No two are alike, but all are able to easily pass as ordinary humanoids until circumstances require them to display their true persona and abilities. There is a creature that looks as if it is made entirely of stone, called The Thing. Another has the strength of a starship in its green, oversized body, and is known only as The Hulk. There is a false Drag-You-La, clad as a blood-sucking creature of the night, called The Batman. Yet another has the proportional strength of a spider (an eight-legged Earth insect), the ability to climb up vertical walls, and a weapon that immobilizes his enemies with a spray that is fired from one of his appendages.

I must do more research in the brief time remaining. Could there be something even more dangerous lying in wait for us?

—Kragash

Diary entry #49A:

I cannot find any data on him, but at least one member of the humanoid's race seems to be immortal. It is something called an Elvis, and every report of its death has been disputed and discredited. I wonder how many other zombies are walking the Earth, and how can we fight something that cannot be killed?

—Kragash

From Kragash:

Sub-Commander, it is my unhappy duty to present the following transmission to you. As troubling as all my previous messages have been, they are nothing compared to this. I am so sure you would think I was exaggerating if I merely described what I have seen, that I have captured the operative sections of the transmission.

Briefly, you will be watching something called a clarkent, who seems normal in every respect. But watch what happens when the orderly life of the planet is threatened. He sheds his identity and becomes an invulnerable warrior, faster than a speeding missile and able to leap enormous mountains with a single bound.

It is my conclusion that the humanoids didn't bother to blow the asteroid off course or vaporize it because they knew that the clarkent, which is known as Superman in his warrior incarnation, could push it out of the system, and even the galaxy, on a few seconds' notice. Which is to say, Earth was *never* in danger—but they have had almost 80 days in which to study us, probe for weaknesses, and prepare for the coming conflict.

From Sub-Commander Bloor:

You are to be commended for your diligence, Kragash. You may well have saved the entire fleet. I have just ordered the asteroid to be diverted and aimed into the sun as a gesture of good will.

I must charge you with one final task, unquestionably the most important in the history of our race. You must contact the highest authority on the planet, present it with our unconditional surrender, and sue for peace.

Prague Daily Monitor, *March 9, 2012:*
　　Asteroid Misses Earth!

Melbourne Leader, *March 9, 2012:*
　　Aliens Surrender!

Los Angeles Times, *March 9, 2012:*
　　Elvis seen in Hollywood Nightclub!!!
　　Earth Saved (story on Page 27, Section B)

COPYRIGHT NOTICES

ACKNOWLEDGEMENTS

Editing anthologies has quickly become one of my favorite things to do. All the more so, when four of my writing heroes headline for me. To be among the first to read stories from Mike Resnick, Kristine Kathryn Rusch and Nancy Kress is thrilling. To bring back a fantastic Robert Silverberg tale from faded memory is also an honor. So thanks to Bob, Mike, Kris and Nancy for trusting me with their stories and for working with me to create a special experience for all of us.

Thanks to the other writers as well: Maurice, Jennifer, Anthony, Jaleta, Autumn, Erin, Nancy, Jean, Simon, Cat, Jamie, Jason, Alex and Brad. One of the reasons I love doing this is that it allows me to pay writers and create opportunities for them as well as myself. I hope this will remain an opportunity you treasure well into the future.

Thanks to Patrick Swenson for coming aboard to take this project to the next level, even though his Fairwood Press slate for 2013 was already full. I've wanted to work with Patrick for a long time. I'm thrilled it's finally happening.

Thanks to all of our Kickstarter supporters, especially Matt Forbeck and Aex Shvartsman, who were ready with advice for this neophyte and helped walk me through the process. Even when it took a miracle to fund, their cheerleading and support kept me encouraged and on track.

Thanks to fellow editors Jennifer Brozek, David Lee Summers, Paula Guran, Rich Horton, Cat Rambo and Ellen Datlow for free advice and encouragement at the touch of an email. I respect and admire so much what they do and to be able to call them friends is a treasure.

Thanks to Mitch Bentley for yet another great cover. To have your trust before I had the funds to pay you and also to give you a chance to reach new audiences is a privilege. Our working relationship has been a blessing as has your friendship.

Thanks to Sarah Chorn for helpful notes and feedback on stories. You underrate your gifts of analysis. Your thoughtful comments have made these stories and this anthology better. I'm pleased to help you reach a new dream, even as your old one book blogging at Bookworm Blues, continues to garner respect and be a success.

To the writers who submitted but didn't make the final TOC, your friendship and trust is also a treasure. You're a part of this regardless of inclusion or not because the creative energy you brought is part of the whole that made *Beyond The Sun* a reality. Thanks Dana, Matt, Anna, Gene, Sarah, Grace, and Jessica. May your words find many happy homes in days to come!

Thanks to my family—Ramon, Glenda, Lara, Kyle, Amelie, Louie—for accepting that sometimes the dream can become the real job and allowing me to succeed even if it took longer financially than any of us would have liked. Patience is truly a virtue, but from family it's also a gift and an act of love.

I also thank the Great I Am for the gift of talent in His image, opening amazing doors and blessing me with endurance and passion to keep going despite many obstacles.

Last but not least, thanks to you, the readers. Whether you were a part of the Kickstarter or not, your passion for stories and authors like these make such opportunities possible. I hope these stories allow you live the dream for a little while and inspire dreams of your own.

Bryan Thomas Schmidt
Ottawa, KS
February 2013

ABOUT THE EDITOR

Bryan Thomas Schmidt is the editor of *Blue Shift Magazine* and an author and editor of adult and children's speculative fiction. His debut novel, *The Worker Prince* (2011) received Honorable Mention on Barnes & Noble Book Club's Year's Best Science Fiction Releases for 2011. A sequel, *The Returning*, followed in 2012 and *The Exodus* will appear in 2014, completing the space opera Saga Of Davi Rhii. His first children's books, *102 More Hilarious Dinosaur Jokes For Kids* and *Abraham Lincoln: Dinosaur Hunter—Land Of Legends* released in 2012 and 2013 from Delabarre Publishing. His short stories have appeared in magazines, anthologies and online.

In addition to *Beyond The Sun*, he edited the anthology *Space Battles: Full Throttle Space Tales #6* (2012) and is working on *Raygun Chronicles: Space Opera For a New Age* for Every Day Publishing (November 2013), *Shattered Shields*, a military fantasy anthology with co-editor Jennifer Brozek for Baen Books in 2014, and *Choices*, a YA reprint anthology, among others. He hosts #sffwrtcht (Science Fiction & Fantasy Writer's Chat) Wednesdays at 9 pm ET on Twitter and is an affiliate member of the SFWA.

ABOUT THE ARTIST

Mitchell Davidson Bentley spent the last 20 years moving physically from place to place and artistically from traditional oils to cyber compositions. Trained in the traditional medium of oil by his mother, and inspired by his grandfather's love of science fiction, Bentley began his career as a full-time science fiction artist in 1989 from his home base in Tulsa. While actively involved in the science fiction art world, Bentley also moved from Tulsa to Austin to Central Pennsylvania where his search for knowledge earned him bachelor's and master's degrees from Penn State University. Over the same period of time, Bentley shifted from the more traditional oil painting to airbrushed acrylics, and since 2004 has been working exclusively in electronic media.

As the Creative Consultant of Atomic Fly Studios, Bentley produces cover art, marketing materials and Web sites while he continues to produce quality 2D artwork marketed through the AFS Web site and at science fiction conventions across the United States. Bentley has lectured at universities, worked in film, edited publications and served as Artist Guest of Honor at more than a dozen science fiction conventions. He has also earned 35 awards, is a lifetime member of the Association of Science Fiction and Fantasy Artists and is currently serving as President.

He currently resides in Harrisburg, PA with his partner Cathie McCormick and their spoiled cats, Mr. Spike, Zöe and Drucilla. Bentley's Web address is: *www.atomicflystudios.com.*

ABOUT THE AUTHORS

Maurice Broaddus has written hundreds of short stories, essays, novellas, and articles. His dark fiction has been published in numerous magazines, anthologies, and web sites, including *Cemetery Dance, Apex Magazine, Black Static,* and *Weird Tales Magazine.* He is the co-editor of the *Dark Faith* anthology series (Apex Books) and the author of the urban fantasy trilogy, *Knights of Breton Court* (Angry Robot Books). He has been a teaching artist for over five years, teaching creative writing to elementary, middle, and high school students, as well as adults. Visit his site at *www.MauriceBroaddus. com.*

Jennifer Brozek is an award winning editor, game designer, and author. She has been writing role-playing games and professionally publishing fiction since 2004. With the number of edited anthologies, fiction sales, RPG books, and non-fiction books under her belt, Jennifer is often considered a Renaissance woman, but she prefers to be known as a wordslinger and optimist. She is coediting *Shattered Shields,* a military fantasy anthology for Baen Books (2014) with *Beyond The Sun* editor, Bryan Thomas Schmidt. Read more about her at *www. jenniferbrozek.com* or follow her on Twitter at @JenniferBrozek.

Anthony R. Cardno's first published work was a "hero history" of *Marvel Comics' The Invaders* for the late, lamented *Amazing Heroes* magazine back in 1986. His short stories have been published in *Willard & Maple, Sybil,* and *Space Battles: Full Throttle Space Tales Volume 6.* In addition to a full time job as a corporate trainer, Anthony is a proofreader for *Lightspeed* magazine, writes book reviews for *Icarus* magazine, and interviews authors, singers, and other creative types on *www.anthonycardno.com,* where you can also find some of his other short stories. In his spare time, Anthony enjoys being tuckerized into other authors' work, and a collection of those stories is forth-coming in late 2013. Besides his website, he can be found on Twitter as @talekyn.

Jaleta Clegg enjoys exploring space. Since she can't do it for real, she writes about it. She also loves living in worlds that don't exist anywhere except in her imagination. She has published the first three books in a space opera series, *The Fall of the Altairan Empire*. More information can be found at *www.altairanempire.com* She has numerous short stories published in a variety of venues in every genre from silly horror to high fantasy to science fiction. You can find links at *www.jaletac.com*. Her day job involves starship simulators, an inflatable planetarium, and lots of school kids.

Autumn Rachel Dryden is a Colorado native, but spent her childhood bouncing around the country before settling in Denver as a teen. In addition to writing, she spends most of her time working as a massage therapist and wrangling her three young children. "Respite" was based on a nightmare (many of her stories come to her while sleeping), but launched her writing career, becoming a dream come true. She currently spends most of her writing time focused on short stories, but has a novel or two in the works. She enjoys inventing and populating science fiction worlds, and re-writing fairy tales in the fantasy genre.

Nancy Fulda is a Hugo and Nebula Nominee, a Phobos Award winner and a Vera Hinckley Mayhew Award recipient. She is the first (and so far only) female recipient of the Jim Baen Memorial Award. She has been a featured writer at *Apex Online*, a guest on the *Writing Excuses* podcast, and is a regular attendee of the Villa Diodati Writers' Workshop. Visit her web site at *nancyfulda.com*.

Erin Hoffman is the author of the *Chaos Knight* trilogy from Pyr Books, whose concluding volume, *Shield of Sea and Space* is forthcoming in May 2013. Her work has appeared in *Beneath Ceaseless Skies, Bull Spec, Electric Velocipede,* and elsewhere. She is a professional video game designer who lives in northern California with dogs, parrots, a husband, and no cats. You can read more at *erinhoffman.com* or follow her on twitter @gryphoness.

Jean Johnson is a multiple bestselling author in military science fiction, including a nomination for the Philip K. Dick Award for the first in her *Theirs Not To Reason Why* military scifi series, the same setting as her story in *Beyond The Sun*, and in fantasy/paranormal romance, including several reader's choice nominations. Regardless of the genre, she strives her best to write entertaining stories. She also hopes you're enjoying all of the other tales in this anthology as well.

Nancy Kress is the author of 29 books of science fiction and fantasy, plus three about writing. Her work has won four Nebulas, two Hugos, a Sturgeon, and the John W. Campbell Memorial Award (for *Probability Space*). She frequently writes about genetic engineering. Nancy lives in Seattle with her husband, writer Jack Skillingstead, and Cosette, the world's most spoiled toy poodle.

Simon C. Larter's stories have appeared in *Per Contra, Short Story America, LitNImage, Space Battles: Full Throttle Space Tales #6,* and elsewhere. By day, he works in the construction industry. By night, he attempts to emulate his literary heroes by drinking vodka and writing until well past his bedtime. He's convinced, however, that Hemingway wouldn't have written nearly as much as he did if he'd had Facebook and Twitter accounts.

Cat Rambo lives, writes, and reads omnivorously in a candy-colored condo beside eagle-haunted Lake Sammamish in Redmond, Washington. Her short stories have appeared in such places as *Asimov's, Tor.com,* and *Clarkesworld* as well as in three collections. Her most recent book is *Near + Far*, from Hydra House Books. Among the awards she's been shortlisted for are the Endeavour, World Fantasy, Locus, and Nebula. You can find more of her fiction and information about her online classes at *http://www.kittywumpus. net.*

Mike Resnick is, according to *Locus*, the all-time leading award winner, living or dead, for short science fiction. He is the winner of five Hugos, a Nebula, and other major awards in the United States, France, Spain, Japan, Croatia and Poland. and has been short-listed for major awards in England, Italy and Australia. He is the author of 68 novels, over 250 stories, and 2 screenplays, and is the editor of 41 anthologies. His work has been translated into 25 languages. He was the Guest of Honor at the 2012 Worldcon and can be found online as @ResnickMike on Twitter or at *www.mikeresnick.com.*

Jamie Todd Rubin is a science fiction writer, blogger, and *Evernote Ambassador* for paperless living. His stories and articles have appeared in *Analog, Daily Science Fiction, Lightspeed, InterGalactic Medicine Show, Apex Magazine*, and *40K Books*. Jamie lives in Falls Church, Virginia with his wife and two children. Find him on Twitter at @jamietr.

Kristine Kathryn Rusch has won awards in every genre for her work. She has several pen names, including Kris Nelscott for mystery and Kristine Grayson for romance. She's writing two different science fiction series, *The Retrieval Artist* and the space opera *Diving* series. Her next novel, the standalone *Snipers*, a time-travel thriller, will appear in July, followed by *Skirmishes*, the next *Diving* novel, in August. WMG Publishing is releasing her entire backlist. She's also editing the anthology series *Fiction River*. For more on her work, go to *kristinekathrynrusch.com*.

Jason Sanford, born and raised in the American South, currently lives in the Midwestern U.S. with his wife and sons. Among his life's adventures includes work as an archeologist and a Peace Corps Volunteer. A dozen of Jason's story have been published in the British magazine *Interzone*, which has devoted a special issue to his fiction. He's also been published in *Year's Best SF, Asimov's Science Fiction, Analog: Science Fiction and Fact, Orson Scott Card's InterGalactic Medicine Show, Tales of the Unanticipated, The Mississippi Review, Diagram, Pindeldyboz*, and other places. Among his awards includes being a finalist for the 2009 Nebula Award for Best Novella and winning three *Interzone* Readers' Polls. His first short story collection *Never Never Stories* is now available. More details are available at *www.jasonsanford.com*.

Alex Shvartsman is a writer and game designer from Brooklyn, NY. He has traveled to over 30 countries, played cards for a living, and built a successful business from scratch. His short stories appeared in *Nature, Daily Science Fiction, Galaxy's Edge* and many other magazines and anthologies. To read more of his work, visit *www.alexshvartsman.com*.

Robert Silverberg is rightly considered by many as one of the greatest living Science Fiction Writers. His career stretches back to the pulps and his output is amazing by any standards. He's authored numerous novels, short stories and nonfiction books in various genres and categories. He's also a frequent guest at Cons and a regularly columnist for Asimov's. His major works include *Dying Inside, The Book of Skulls, The Alien Years, The World Inside, Nightfall* with Isaac Asimov, *Son of Man, A Time of Changes* and the 7 Majipoor Cycle books. His first Majipoor trilogy, *Lord Valentine's Castle, Majipoor Chronicles* and *Valentine Pontifex*, were reissued by ROC Books in May 2012, September 2012 and January 2013. *Tales Of Majipoor*, a new collection bringing together all the short Majipoor tales, followed in May 2013.

Brad R. Torgersen was a 2012 nominee for the Campbell, Hugo, and Nebula awards, and is a past winner of both the Writers of the Future award, and *Analog* magazine's AnLab readers' choice award. A frequent contributor to *Analog*, Brad has collaborated with Hugo and Nebula award winner Mike Resnick, is currently collaborating with Hugo winner and bestseller Larry Niven, and has several works pending publication in 2013. His web site is *www.bradrtorgersen. com.*

Tremendous thanks to our backers who funded this project on Kickstarter!

CADETS:

Sabrina Vourvoulais
Matt Adams
Samuel Montgomery-Blinn
Gary Vandegrift
Andrew House
Mike Schaer
Nicole Manasco
Michael Scholl
David Annandale
Keith West
James Bartlemay
Jerry Gaiser
Paul McMullen
Madison Woods
Greg Baerg
Janine A. Southard
Travis J I Corcoran
Frances Wu
Alex Shvartsman
Hugh Blair
Michael Wallace
Leah Petersen
Dayton Ward
Michael Cummings
Benjamin Liska
Janet Oblinger
Andrew Mayer
Lori Eppright

Johan Ljungman
Dafydd Nicklin
Jamie Todd Rubin
Shervyn von Hoerl
Erin M. Klitzke
Flavio Mortarino
Brenda Cooper
Sandra Ulbrich Almazan
Jen Warren
Guy Anthony DeMarco
Adam Hill
Jeffrey Allan Boman
Steve Mashburn
Rebecca M. Senese
Evaristo Ramos, Jr.
Dave Gross
Jon Freestone

EXPLORERS:

Sue Lewis
Lisa Deutsch Harrigan
Infinity Ltd.
Emiliano Marchetti
John Devenny
G. Mark Cole
Bear Weiter
Nathan Burgoine
Gordon Duke
Austin Williams
Jason Sanford

PLANETARY ROVERS:
Christopher Kastensmidt
Jean Allison Namaste Stuntz
Cat McDude
Rosemary Foley
Jimmy Plamondon
Brian White
Mark Zimmerman
Karl-Erik Sonvisen
Rich Laux
Victoria Adams
Darrell Long

COLONIAL MERCHANT:
David Chamberlain

COLONISTS:
Danielle Gembala
Gary Olson
Simo Muinonen

COLONIAL DIPLOMATS:
John Osuna
David Bridges

JUNIOR OFFICERS:
Christian Berntsen
Johne Cook
Gregory S. Close
Ken Kenyon
Lydia Ondrusek

OFFICERS::
Grace Bridges
Evan Ladouceur
Teresa Spencer
Anthony Cardno
Greg Cueto